Kirsten

Kirsten McKenzie was born i
with her husband and two chil   *Chapel*
at the Edge of the World, is also published by John Murray.

Praise for *The Captain's Wife* and *The Chapel at the Edge of the World*

'What McKenzie excels at is using period detail in the right
way: just enough to give a feeling of authenticity but never
so much that the history outweighs the story.
McKenzie has a natural, fluid writing style' *Scotsman*

'Warm, humane and finely written' *The Times*

'Unusual, fluently written . . . [an] unshowy,
absorbing read' *Guardian*

'McKenzie's book grows impressively and movingly into its
author's distinct vision' *Daily Mail*

'Delightful . . . the two stories are brought together with
marvellous skill' *The Times*

Also by Kirsten McKenzie

The Chapel at the Edge of the World

The Captain's Wife

Kirsten McKenzie

JOHN MURRAY

First published in Great Britain in 2010 by John Murray (Publishers)
An Hachette UK Company

First published in paperback in 2011

1

A CIP catalogue record for this title is available from the British Library

ISBN 978-1-84854-153-5

Typeset in Sabon MT by Palimpsest Book Production Limited,
Falkirk, Stirlingshire

Printed and bound by Clays Ltd, St Ives plc

John Murray policy is to use papers that are natural, renewable and recyclable
products and made from wood grown in sustainable forests. The logging and
manufacturing processes are expected to conform to the environmental regulations
of the country of origin.

John Murray (Publishers)
338 Euston Road
London NW1 3BH

www.johnmurray.co.uk

For Derek

Part One

I

On a cold clear morning in January a little girl called Mary sat in her mother's arms. In front of her stood the man, the crowd and the executioner. Behind her was the rest of the world.

To the south she could see the narrow spine of Edinburgh, the jagged teeth of the castle curling down to the great volcanic cleft of Arthur's Seat, and a patchwork of land below, laid out in small nursery gardens. To the north there was the strip of salt water swept in from the sea.

At length she saw the man's long grey hair brush in the light wind as he stepped up on to the platform. The murmuring crowd paused, as if everyone had stopped to draw breath at the same time. A moment ago she'd watched him pray, his hands thrust together and his head upturned. It was a long prayer, and the man's face held an expression of what was described by the women around her as *exultation*. It was a long word that Mary tried to repeat, but when she did it came out as *excelentantion*, which made the women laugh and Mary bury her head in her mother's shawl. She knew it had something to do with nearness to God. It was unfair, she thought, that a man so wicked as to be executed for his sins could be so much nearer to God than she was. But things seemed often unfair to her. Her mother had told her that she would understand these things when she was older. She was waiting to be older, but time passed slowly. She guessed that was partly why her mother had brought her here, to help her grow.

The executioner was busy strapping the man's hand to a piece of wood, and he was taking so much time about it, that before long the impatient bustle of conversation started up again. The man had fallen into a kind of fit, but he was soon revived, and made another kind of piteous, pleading confession to the crowd. The words were unclear; she made out only 'penitence', and 'forgive'. Some of the women took out their handkerchiefs and began to sniff, but then he started to cry, and the crowd turned against him, baying and jeering at what they called his hypocrisy, another word that Mary wasn't sure she could pronounce. This time she didn't try.

So near to God did the man seem now that it was as if Mary could already smell the breath of the Lord in the crisp air. She sucked it in, trying to savour its icy sweetness. But the taste was bitter and disappointing, not like she would imagine God to taste at all. It only made her cough. She craned her neck to see, and her mother held her higher, though her arms began to shake with the strain.

'You're too heavy for this,' her mother said.

The executioner struck down with his blade on the man's wrist. It was blunt, and bounced away as though made of leather. Mary watched as the mouth opened, a luminous pink gash in the ghost-white face. The man was screaming, but she couldn't hear it, because of the shouts of the thousands of people around her. The executioner's axe struck down again, and the hand must have come off clean at last, because a great roar went through the crowd.

'Why does he not keep his blade sharper?' asked Mary, looking down at her mother. She was irritated, because a constant stream of people was filtering forward, and every moment of delay placed another head between her and the man. As a result she had missed the actual release of the hand.

Some heads in front of them turned around, and even through the powder that flaked from her mother's face in the sunlight, she could see the soft lined skin turn red.

'How am I to know?' she asked.

'Why waste a good blade on a bad one,' said a woman standing nearby, and a ripple of laughter went through the nearest of the crowd. Mary felt a slight swelling of pride that she had been the instigator, if not the inventor, of this wit.

One of the women turned to smile at her. 'You're a curious soul, aren't you,' she said, and smoothed her hand on the curls of hair that had sneaked from Mary's bonnet.

'Too curious for her own good,' said her mother.

'Look at the ringlets,' said another. 'Adorable.'

Mary smiled sweetly, as she had learned to do following comments like this.

'I can't hold you any longer,' her mother said then, her breath uneven. 'I have to let you down.'

'No, Mama, no,' Mary protested. 'I want to see.'

Her mother sighed and lifted her once more, moving Mary to her other hip. Mary curled her thin arms around her mother's neck and nuzzled her cheek. Then she turned to watch the execution.

But as the chimney sweeps prepared to tighten the rope, Mary felt a familiar nausea. It was different from the sort that had accompanied the cutting of the man's hand. That had been a natural animal revulsion. This nausea was the result of hunger. She remembered that it was now after midday. Suddenly she became bored, and began to fidget and squirm in her mother's arms.

Just as the rope was about to be pulled, her mother lowered her to the ground.

'You've seen enough,' she said. 'I'll not have you see him hang.'

Despite her gnawing hunger, Mary was disappointed. She had wanted to see if his spirit would rise upwards, if the Lord would take him. But her mother turned her small body in towards her skirts. Mary craned her neck away from them, looking into the blue of the sky, but there was no ethereal glimmer. She tried to turn her head and see through the slits of light that occasionally shone through the wall of petticoats. They stood for what seemed like hours, but in fact it was only half an hour, until the frantic kicking of the man's legs began to slow. By then the balls of Mary's feet ached and her stomach felt hollowed out, with little sharp needles of pain shooting upwards. She no longer hoped to see a rising spirit. She only prayed for it to end, so that they could go home for dinner. And she knew when her prayers had been answered, when the moment of death was approaching, because a peculiar lull went through the crowd, a new solemnity.

When finally the man was pronounced dead there were

a few jeers at the front. Towards the back, where the more delicate constitutions stood, people's shoulders seemed communally to relax, and a mutter of conversation began. These were the people who told themselves they had come not out of morbid fascination, but out of moral and religious duty. Now that duty had been performed, some stood and chatted, but most started to disperse, so that Mary had a good view of the limp body being cut down and tied into what looked like a round metal cage. The hand was secured above his head, with the knife stuck through it.

She turned to see her mother looking intently at the side of her face. Mary could tell by the tight lips and the red-tinged eyes that she was close to tears.

'Don't pity him,' she said to Mary. 'This is his just punishment.'

'I wasn't,' said Mary, truthfully. She didn't feel pity, but she didn't feel whatever it was that her mother felt either. She could see that the man in the white robes had gone, and had been replaced by the dead body in the cage. Her only thought was what a strange and wonderful shell he had left behind, and how she was able to examine this shell much more carefully than she would have felt able to had he been alive.

'What are they doing with him?' she asked her mother.

'Getting him ready for the gibbet.'

'The gibbet?' asked Mary.

'It's what happens to murderers. He'll hang there,' said her mother, 'as a warning to others of the penalty for what he's done.' As she said this her teeth were set close together and her chin projected from her face. She watched Mary, again, it seemed, for some kind of reaction, but

Mary didn't know what she was supposed to do, so she smiled and took hold of her mother's hand. This wasn't the right reaction at all, apparently, for her mother took hold of her roughly and pulled her down the dirt road towards home.

The day was bright, like a smile without warmth. The frost turned the black fields white around them and the cattle stood close together in groups, steam rising from their bodies. Mother and daughter followed the procession that teemed down the wide bridleway. The air was filled with the shuffling of hundreds of old and young women, a few men, the scuff of carts, a private chaise and Paxton's Edinburgh coach, which bounced over the hard and uneven road. Mary's feet crunched in the frozen dirt. A stiff wind blew in from the north, over the blue of the Forth, and from their position high on the hill that came down into Leith Mary could see the masts of the ships huddled together in the harbour. There were all kinds of ships, square-, fore- and aft-rigged smacks, brigs, snows and schooners. There were more, it seemed, every time she looked, even though her uncle was always protesting about the lack of markets, the problem of tariffs and the ridiculous cost of marine insurance due to strange wars over places she had never heard of. But the ships in the harbour held a deep fascination for Mary, because she knew that a long time ago, her father had sailed away in one of them. Mary had never met her father, but she thought of him often. Thinking of him now, she began to sing a nursery song that she had heard some other children sing:

The man in the wilderness asked me
How many strawberries grow in the sea?
I answered him as I thought good
As many red herrings as grow in the wood.

'What is that nonsense?' asked her mother, suspicious. Children were able to veil their insolence in so many ways.

Mary read her mother's signs and was quiet. She thought of the man now hanging in his iron cage further up the hill.

'How long will he stay there?' she asked.

'Oh, weeks, months, however long they see fit,' answered her mother. She said it as if she herself were angry with the man, although she hadn't known him. Mary had noticed that her mother was often angry with people she didn't know. Indeed, she had noticed that her mother was often angry.

'Can we go to see him?' asked Mary.

'No, we can't,' said her mother, pulling her into the Wester Leith Road. She stooped to tighten Mary's coat and wrap her shawl so that it came high around her neck. 'You look pale,' she told her. Then she looked up for a moment as another coach rattled past.

Mary saw that it was her mother's colour that had drained away, and she pulled on her sleeve to attract her attention. 'What is it, Mama?' she asked. She looked to where her mother's head was inclined, and saw that the coach had come to a halt a little further up the road. A man's face peered out from it. It was covered with a thick growth of beard; but his eyes were black, gleaming, and there was a kind of terror in them. They watched her mother, but the crowds thickened in front of them and for a moment he was lost. Then he appeared again, and his eyes found Mary's. She felt frightened and pulled her mother's arm again.

Her mother shook her off, and tried to wind through the crowd, but as she did so there came a shout from the coach and the horses started up, the splintered sound of their hooves kicking the hard ground.

'Did you know that man, Mama?' Mary asked, finding her again.

Her mother seemed to come to a little and shook her head. 'No, I don't think so. He only looked like somebody.' And she turned around briskly. 'Let's walk quickly to keep warm,' she said, attempting to smile brightly but only grimacing. 'You know I heard that the cook is making a sweet junket. Your favourite.'

It wasn't Mary's favourite at all. She thought that it must have been her mother's, once. That was another strange thing she had noticed about her mother, that she often got confused between her own desires and Mary's.

They had come to the head of the Kirkgate, the tall old buildings with their tower tops bending into the streets like peering ministers. It was the old part of the town, not as smart as the grand new mansions being built on the outskirts. Her mother complained that it was not as prosperous as it once was, because of the scum that lived in the new wynds. These were being built in increasing numbers for the people coming in to work in the factories, the glassworks and the ropery. These people kept their geese, ducks and pigs out in the street and the effluence of the animals mingled with the effluence that was emptied out of the houses not at the allotted hour but at all times of the day. The streets were so poorly lit that the constable could not catch them. Mary and her mother had to walk through the area to get to her uncle's house, where they lived.

Mary's uncle had a lot of money. Mary knew this, because her mother was always telling her how lucky she was, and how kind her uncle was to let them live in his house, and to feed and clothe them as he did. Mary had never lived anywhere else, so she wasn't sure why she should be thankful for being allowed to live in her own house. After all, where else would she go? But she was a good girl, able to be appreciative when it was called for, since she had learned that failure to act this way was usually followed by a swift skelp when she and her mother were alone.

Her uncle's house was relatively new, built from his father's profits in trading wine and wood. It had big windows, and a large doorway tall enough, it seemed to Mary, for a giant to pass through, should they care to invite one in. There was a small garden, with a kailyard to one side, surrounded by a high stone wall. There they grew not only kail but parsnips, carrots and savoy, and the year before had experimented with the potato, which Mary had eaten and thought a dry, tasteless thing. Her mother said it was only because they had grown them at Pilrig House, and had said her sister-in-law would eat a plate of thistles if she thought it was the latest fashion.

The table was not yet set for dinner, and because of the cold Mary was told to sit on a small chair near to the fire and given some sweet milk with grated nutmeg. It had been well whipped and a frothy foam tipped over into the saucer, a smooth skin forming on its surface. Mary scooped the cup thankfully into her hands. She dipped in her fingers and wrinkled the skin, licking off the sugar spice cream from the top. After it was finished she set the cup down on the tiles, and sat for what seemed like a long time. The chair was hard and uncomfortable and she twisted her feet as her mother turned to glare at her. Then Mary's aunt, Isobel, came in and lifted Mary's foot to examine her silk shoe, which was covered in pale clay, now defrosted and dusty.

'A little cold for walking, surely,' she said, frowning and looking at Mary's shoes.

Mary saw her glance behind her to see if she had left a trail of dirt on walking into the room. 'I wasn't cold,' said Mary, noticing her mother's expression.

'Nonsense. Your toes are little blocks of ice. I doubt these shoes will ever come clean, you know,' said Isobel, looking at Mary's mother with an air of disapproval.

'They'll do for their purpose,' said her mother stiffly.

But Isobel rang for the maid. 'Well, we'll see if Janet can't burn them up a little,' she said, removing them from Mary's feet and handing them to the small girl who stood quietly behind her.

Mary could tell by the way her mother's lip had thinned that she was angry again. But she said nothing.

'Where have you been?' asked Isobel.

'Up at the Gallowlee!' began Mary excitedly, then saw her mother's frown and stopped.

Isobel swung round. 'You took Mary?' she said.

'What of it?' said Mary's mother, looking straight at Isobel. 'Mary's tough.'

'Not as tough as you think,' said Isobel. 'The poor child will have nightmares.'

'At least she'll know the difference between right and wrong,' said Mary's mother. 'Anyway, she didn't see it all.'

'Mama wouldn't let me,' said Mary sulkily.

'In any case, she was quite untouched by it all,' said her mother, taking off her cloak. 'As she is by everything.' She looked at Mary with a mixed expression of concern and scorn that only her mother seemed capable of. 'Perhaps we'll wring some humanity out of her one of these days.'

Mary knew that her mother was not pleased with her, but what it was she had done, or had not done, she couldn't tell. In response, she wore her habitual blank expression, which she had found the safest way to deal with all her mother's varying humours. Isobel shook her head, but she said nothing, as they were summoned to dinner at that moment.

The table was spread with a large lunch of giblet broth, salmon, some mutton, moorfowl, at least twelve small birds and small plates of roasted parsnips and buttered kail. The small birds were all about the size of a sparrow, arranged in a circle on a plate around the moorfowl. Their little stick feet stuck up out of the dish, as if they had died there and then and fallen on their backs. But Mary had tasted small birds roasted this way before, and she knew that, torn apart, the flesh of the smaller birds would be the stickiest and the sweetest of them all. Beside the fowls there was a plate of light junket, decorated with a posy of lemon verbena. She wondered if it would be bad manners to put some on her plate along with her meat.

'Would you believe,' began Isobel, as soon as they were

seated, 'Margaret has had the child at an execution. That Ross fellow.'

'Ah, is that so,' said her uncle, looking at Mary. 'I heard he was for the gibbet.'

'He was,' said Mary, excited again. 'He's going to be there for days and days!' But she stopped short when she saw her mother glaring at her.

Her uncle bit into a large slice of meat and began to chew slowly, as though thinking it over. They waited for his judgement. 'I can't see much wrong with it,' he said. 'What's the use in waiting until a child is an adult before showing them what befalls those who turn out bad? By that time their habits are formed, their fate is set. She'll not be the worse for knowing now.' And he gave a short, hard nod to put the stamp on his verdict.

Isobel cut her meat into ever smaller morsels, but no matter how much she cut, thought Mary, there always seemed to be the same amount on her plate. She looked at her husband. 'Of course you're right,' she said, a little irritably, and Mary marvelled at how quickly she had changed her mind.

'Yes, I believe in telling children the truth at *all* times,' said her uncle, and Mary saw him looking directly at her mother.

Isobel looked from her husband to Margaret and gave a small smile, and her mother stopped eating. They sat in silence. Isobel continued to rattle her fork but after a while pushed her full plate aside. Her uncle gulped down the last of the bottle of claret, and picked up another small bird. Mary looked at them all, and stared at her empty plate. She knew that something had happened, but she had no idea what it was. She tried a trick that had always worked in the past. With a deft movement, she flicked the edge of her fork so that it flew into the air and landed with a clatter on the floor. Everyone looked at her.

'Mary, you are so clumsy!' exclaimed her mother.

Isobel bent to pick it up. 'There you are, dear,' she said. She was always kinder to Mary when her mother was cross with her.

'Let's go for a stroll,' said her uncle, and Mary congratulated herself on having broken the spell.

They stood at the doorway for some time, putting on cloaks and hoods, mittens and muffettees, muffs and shawls. Isobel wrapped Mary in a smart blue cloak and hood that had once been her own, in order to demonstrate how poorly her mother had dressed her. Then they left the house and walked through the narrow wynd that led to a gate in the old wall of the town. On the other side of the gate the ground opened out into a wide piece of land, well grazed, all patchy scruff and rough meadow. Beyond that lay the dunes, the sand, and the enormous blue of the sea, dotted with cream-coloured sail.

A row of fine carriages was lined up along the edge of the grassy area. Despite the cold weather the sands were crowded with people rich and poor, as well as cattle, sheep, pigs and poultry. Some people, like themselves, were walking. Irritable men chipped at the hard ground with long bats, trying to drive small leathern balls into holes they had dug out of the grass. They shouted at walkers to get out of their road, but since it seemed impossible not to be in their way, other than by leaving the common altogether, their shouts were ignored. Some ragged small children were fighting in the dunes, and a couple of horses were being exercised on the sand. Beyond them, the water was tranquil and arctic blue.

'Look,' said Isobel, pointing to the water, 'it's frozen.' Platelets of ice floated at the edges of the firth, near the rocks.

Mary sat down on the hard sand and listened while the grown-ups talked. A memory came to her, of two years before, when she had walked with her mother by the frothy edge of the sea. Her mother had taken off both their shoes and stockings and they had held hands while they dipped their toes in the freezing water. The chill had made the bones of her ankles ache, but she had waded in still deeper until they became numb and all she could feel was the stab of the occasional sharp stone beneath her toes. Her mother had laughed, and she had looked young.

That was before Isobel had come to marry her uncle. Now Mary had to keep her shoes tightly fastened wherever she went.

Mary looked out to the water, and the Kingdom of Fife, where she knew there was a place called Kinghorn, to where a ferry ran from Leith. Mary had often thought that one day she would buy her own boat, and sail out to find her father, who was himself on a boat, somewhere out on the ocean. She was sure he would paddle in the water with her. And then a thought came to her, and she turned to her mother.

'Mama,' she said loudly.

Her mother glared at her, because she had interrupted some tedious sentence of her uncle's. 'What is it?' she said irritably.

'Perhaps that's where he is?'

Her mother's eyes widened. 'What?'

'That place. Fife. Is that where my papa is?'

There was a silence. Her uncle coughed. Isobel appeared to give a thin smile. But her mother wrenched her away by the arm, turned her almost upside down, and whacked her so hard that the water came out of the corners of her eyes. She sat down again on the sand and cried tears of pure, bitter, seven-year-old hatred. Her mother and her uncle then walked a little distance away, and talked. Mary entertained herself by drawing images of her mother in the sand and then scoring lines through them with her fingernails.

'Margaret,' she heard her uncle say, 'don't you think it's time?'

~

Later, in the room they shared in her uncle's house, her mother brought her warmed milk with a touch of real chocolate, brought back by her uncle from his last trip to Rotterdam. She was trying to make amends. Mary drank it slowly in the light of the fire, building an Edinburgh Castle of blocks.

'Mary,' her mother said, 'could you stop that for a moment?'

'Why do I have to!' said Mary. She was always being told to stop playing.

'I just want to talk to you,' her mother said, and her voice was unusually soft.

Mary looked up, and she saw again the intensity of her mother's eyes that she had seen earlier that day. Her mother breathed out and Mary could smell the syrup sweetness of brandy.

'Mother, what is it?' she asked, feeling nervous.

'Your uncle says I should tell you the truth. Do you want me to tell you the truth, Mary?'

Mary shrugged. She didn't know what the truth was, so was unsure how she could answer. 'I don't mind,' she said.

'Mary, we can't ever go to see your father,' said her mother.

'Why not?' Mary cried out, indignant. It wasn't fair. Her mother never let her do anything she wanted to do.

'Because your father . . .' She hesitated. 'Mary, do you know what it means to be pressed?'

Mary sat for a moment. She wasn't altogether sure what being pressed meant. She had an idea of being squashed, like the raspberries for the jam, pressed beneath the hooves of a horse or an overturned carriage.

'Does that mean he's dead?' she asked.

Her mother shook her head. 'Not exactly. But it means we have no way of knowing when, or whether, we will ever see him again. It means that one day, a few years ago, some men came and took him away. He was put on a ship, and taken away to fight for his country.'

'Oh,' said Mary. At least he hadn't been crushed. It didn't sound that bad after all. She wondered what her mother expected her to do. She didn't feel like crying. Perhaps her mother would think her heartless. But then perhaps she might want her to be brave. It wasn't as though a real person had been taken away from her, after all, but rather an idea of a person. She felt as though a weight of sadness was being lowered upon her very gently, so that it was only just perceptible, then growing.

At last she spoke in a small voice that she hoped was both brave and sad. 'Mama,' she said.

'Yes.'

'I'm sorry that my father has been pressed.'

'I'm sorry too, Mary,' said her mother. Then her words were lost as her voice turned into a soft wail. Her breath came quicker and her chest began to expand.

Mary watched her, confused. 'Shh,' she said, approaching her mother and placing a hand tentatively on her knee. 'Someone might hear you.'

This made her mother sob even louder. Mary removed her hand from her mother's knee, since her mother did not seem to be aware of her presence.

'It can't be that bad, Mama,' she said. 'Don't cry, Mama, please. I hate it when you cry.' It was another thing that Mary had noted. After the sweet brandy breath, there often came tears.

'You don't know what it's like,' came her mother's voice, 'to be alone.'

'You're not alone,' said Mary. 'I'm here.'

But it seemed that wasn't enough. Mary noticed that her mother had run her hands over her hair and it had come undone, and she reached out her hand as if to fix it, then stopped, wondering if her mother would be angry. But this only made her mother's crying louder and deeper, and then it was Mary who began to feel alone. The dark walls of the room behind the candles seemed to flicker faster, at first because of the force of her mother's crying but soon, she realized, simply because they were burning down to their wicks. Her mother usually replaced them before then. She wondered if there were more in the cupboard.

After sitting in the darkness for a time she saw that her mother was probably not going to stop crying, so she climbed into the little bed built into the corner of the room. The sound her mother was making was turning her stomach, already delicate thanks to the sight of the man's severed hand and the richness of the food she had eaten, so she put her fingers in her ears and her head under the blankets, and curled up tight so that her knees touched her elbows. She stayed like this into the deep of the night, until she was aware of the warmth of her mother's body lying next to her. She curled into it, but the body turned away and began to snore.

After that, Mary lay awake, listening to the sound of her mother's breath and the crying of one solitary sleepless gull.

2

I

John Fullarton had put on his coat, and his mother was looking at him.

'Where are you going?' she asked.

'To see my father.' He waited for her expression to change.

'Why don't you just flit there then?' she said bitterly. She banged the yetlin down on the stove. From a corner of the room, his grandmother watched them, her face like stone, wrapped in her heavy vadmell cloak. Her lip curled slightly in a smile that seemed to pity and despise them both.

John spat on the earth floor. 'Aye, maybe I will,' he said. Then he walked past them. He moved aside the cloth door, soaked in seal oil and dried to make a waterproof lining, now hardened and thick like hide. The cold air blasted into the room and sent splinters of red stone dust flying up into his eyes. He blinked and looked out. The sea was a dark, soupy grey. The recent storms had stirred the water and created whirlpools of opposing tides all over the bay. It was weather for staying indoors. But there was no going back, not with them in that mood. He left the house with his mother still muttering and his grandmother watching him with her cool, hard eyes, and walked the mile-long path through the tounmal. He was followed by the rain, a sudden cold lash of a shower, forming black pools where the peats had been cut away. John watched his feet carefully, stepping along the ridges of soil. Now and then he stopped, and looked up. From where he stood he could see right over to the bay of Stromness, the masts of the ships anchored in the harbour, so many lines of rope, yards and sail.

John's father lived in a smart new house, with a good-sized living area and a separate bedroom. John had helped him to build it a few years before. It had a gable-end chimney instead of a central hearth with plenty of room for a good blaze, far better than their own smouldering heap. His father worked the nulla rig at the end of the township, not only the largest, but the most productive piece of land. His grandmother claimed he had got it by bullying the Honymans into granting it, or more likely, she said slyly, in return for the many favours he was known for providing them with. John knew that his father ran errands for the Honymans, bringing the contraband luxuries they loved most in from the shore, and that the largest share of his wealth came from these errands, rather than from the land. He also knew that the greater part of his grandmother's scorn was directed upon John, for not benefiting enough from his father's enterprise. It was only recently she had persuaded his father to let him come out in his smack, after the leaky little boat his grandfather had left him had finally broken up on the rocks in bad weather.

Today he found his father and his brothers about to put out. He walked with them across the rain-lashed brekka to the little harbour, where around twenty other boats like his father's were moored. John walked a little apart from his brothers. It wasn't that he didn't like them, or they him. They had always accepted him, the strange brother who lived in a different household. It was more that he knew himself to be different, and they knew it too. Because of this, they were never entirely sure of him. The youngest of them all, John was the only one who had captured his Ayrshire father's looks, his dark hair and eyes, his olive skin. His brothers were pale, with the wide-set eyes and broad frame of their Orkney mother. His grandmother had said that it was the only reason his father had ever acknowledged him. As soon as he saw the resemblance, it couldn't be denied. His mother said that it wasn't true, that his father had gone willingly with her own father and brothers to baptize him. But John knew that his father examined him, even now, as if his existence were a mystery, as though he were still sizing him up, judging him, and might at any moment disown him as an impostor.

They climbed into the small smack, laying their rods along the length of it, and made their way round the islands, sticking close to the shelter of the land. They rounded the Houton Head, past the skerries of Clestron, and beyond it the Grand Hall of the same name. There, some twenty years before, the pirate John Gow had robbed the lady of the house and carried off two of her servant maids. Apparently they had let them off on the island of Cava, which they now passed, with plenty of gold, though nobody seemed to know the women, and nobody had seen the gold. John knew this, and he knew that Gow had been hanged, but somehow the story still fascinated him.

John watched his father as he picked up a bucket of half-boiled limpets. He pulled each one from its shell and chewed it to soften it further, an almost thoughtful expression on his face. Then he threw a handful of the chewed boiled limpets from the boat. Immediately the fish were up at the surface and biting.

They caught a good number, but finally the catch began to dwindle and they rowed further out to see if they could find another shoal. They passed the bay of Stromness full of numerous smacks, some little merchant snows and a few larger brigs anchored further out. Then they rounded the lump of black rock known as the Breck Ness, and hit the force of the Atlantic waves breaking in from the north. The wind had changed direction. At the same time it had died a little, and the swell had lowered, but there was now an arctic chill in the wind, and the metallic sky threatened sleet or snow. The other fishing boats had all turned back and were well into the bay, and John's brothers started to follow them. But suddenly John spotted a large, dark shape in the distance. It was far away from the harbour, out in the Atlantic side of the islands, and even from this distance he could see it bouncing in the waves.

'What's that?' he asked, pointing.

His father turned sharply, and they watched the shape for some time as it emerged from the fog. Soon they could see the tall masts and rigging of a large ship. She seemed to be moving sideways, and wrestling the wind. She drove towards them faster than they expected, blown in by the stiffening gale.

'Whatever she is,' said John's father, 'she's in trouble,' and he reached for his oar. 'Row against the tide while I take a glinder at her,' he ordered. He took out his prized ebony eyeglass that had been given to him by the Honymans, and watched the ship carefully for a few moments. Her bow was sunk deep in the waves, and it was clear that she was taking on more water than she could handle.

'She's hit the skerries,' said John. 'She's going down.'

A light came across his father's face. 'She'll be wrecked!' he said.

The boys immediately started to pull furiously at the oars. John watched his father's face, clenched against the wind. He tried to clench his own in the same way. By the time they reached the ship, the sea had got so rough that it was difficult to see what was hidden in the waves. The ship seemed to be half under already, but as they grew closer boxes and bits of wood began to appear in the water around them. Soon they were surrounded by floating pieces of the ship. John's father leaned over to haul in a large box.

'What are ye gawkin' at, boy?' he said to John. 'Get over here and lend a hand.'

Together they reached over and heaved the box into the boat. They let the smack drift with the waves as John's father cracked the box open with his knife and pulled out a bottle of treacle-coloured liquid. He pulled off the top and smelled, then took a drink.

Immediately he spat it out into the sea. 'Oil,' he said. 'Let's see what else we can find.' Their smack was showered with the spray of a wave and John's father turned quickly.

'That's a coarse wind,' he said, shouting to be heard above the fuss of the waves. 'We'll take what we can and make for the Flow.'

Then John spotted something attached to a large section

25

of ship. The water broke around it and he saw a man's head pulling above the froth, sinking, then rising again. The skin was pale and greenish but the dark eyes were open. Even from this distance John was sure he could see them fix upon him.

'Father,' he called out. 'It's a man.'

James Fullarton looked round briefly from where he was heaving in another box. 'Dead,' he said.

'Na,' said John, 'there's breath in him, look!'

His father half turned again, impatiently. 'Lend a hand with this and then we'll see,' he said. He pulled in his box, then turned around fully.

'Na,' he said, shaking his head. 'He's too far off. We canna get close enough.' He went back to hauling in the boxes.

John thought he saw the man's head again before it sank below the waves.

'Can we not try?' asked John. He looked around at his brothers for support, but they looked away. He felt his face burn.

'It's too dangerous,' said his father, shaking his head.

John turned to the youngest brother, Sandy, who was always the kindest to John.

'He's going to die, Sandy,' said John, appealing to him. His brother's eyes wavered, and he looked for a moment as though he might speak in John's favour.

His father whirled around. 'Listen, boy,' he said. 'You canna risk all our lives for the sake of one. What God in his providence has decided will be his fate of these men is not something we can change.'

John was quiet for a moment. 'What about the fate of the cargo?' he asked.

James examined John closely. 'Well,' he said at last, with a smile that John couldn't read, 'what the Lord in his bounty has seen fit to provide for us is not something we can refuse.'

John looked towards where he had seen the floating man. But he had gone, and in his place was a large wooden box.

'Well!' said his father. 'Pull it in.'

John hauled it into the boat. His father leaned across him and wrenched it open with a metal bar he had brought with him. He pulled out a dusty-looking glass bottle and smiled.

'This looks more like it . . .' he said. He dashed the neck of it on the side of the boat so that the glass broke, brushed off the shattered glass, then poured some of the liquid into his hand and dipped his tongue in it to taste. He looked up, smacking his lips. Then he broke into a grin and punched a hole in the air. 'That's it,' he said. 'Liquid gold.' He passed the broken bottle around.

John put his lips cautiously to the jagged edge and swallowed the liquid which made fire in his throat. His core, which had become frozen, began to thaw.

His father placed his hand on his shoulder. 'You've a good pair of glouriks there, boy,' he said. 'Well spotted.'

John felt the warmth come into his face again, and for a moment forgot the greenish tinge of the drowning man. Then other boxes started to appear; one after another they bobbed to the surface, each one filled with its own liquid treasure.

'Out with the pitlocks,' said his father. 'In with the brandy!'

They threw the half-dead fish into the water around them, save for a few bags. They filled the boat with as many boxes as they could haul in, their smack dipping lower in the water. Then they set off for home. They passed a bottle around and sang loudly with the wind. It felt good to sing together like that. The more John drank, the warmer he became, and his fingers, which had lost most of their feeling with the cold, tingled with a pleasant smirr.

II

When John returned to his mother's house he found her filling the lamps with sillock oil. The room was filled with the smell of strong fish and peat.

'Catch anything?' she asked.

'Na,' answered John, still standing at the door.

'Not even a seal?'

John shook his head.

'That's a great pity. We could have done with the oil. This stuff's near out.'

His grandmother came in from the oot-by with a pot of water and set it on the stove. 'In the name o' . . .' she said, turning to look at him. 'You're sirpan. Stop standing there like a loon and get dry by the fire.'

John lowered his head slowly and looked down at his wet clothes. She was right enough, he was soaked through. He laughed, quietly at first, but then he began to bellow, and his grandmother eyed him suspiciously.

'What's up with you?' she asked.

'I'll comn whenm goodn raddy,' John murmured. He took a step into the room and swayed to the side. Then he lurched to the other side and the floor came at him unexpectedly. He found his head next to the patie neuk where the day's peats were stored. He smelled the dust of the floor. It was earthily pleasant. He picked up what looked like a piece of chicken shit, and squashed it between his fingers. Then he began to chuckle.

Somewhere in the distance, he heard his father's voice. James had come to the door behind him.

'I should have kent this was something to do with you,' he heard his mother's voice say. From the corner of his eye he saw the figure of his grandmother leaving the room.

'Wheesht, lass. He's been out in the smack today, on the coarsest day of the year. He just needs a good meal. It's thanks to him we're set for the year.'

'You've got him fu',' said his mother, looking at the body in the dust. 'He's just a boy.'

'Aye, and you'd have him one for ever,' said his father. 'Or worse, a lass, brought up in a house full of women.'

John's mother gave a sardonic laugh. 'He's not the cause of that.'

His father ignored her. 'Sooner or later he has to do something, other than feed the hens that is. He's got a family to support.'

'Let's hope he does a better job of it than you.'

From where he lay on the floor, John saw his father come close behind his mother. He saw him kiss her neck.

'Come on, Christina,' he said. 'You ken how hard it's been this year. But today we've had a bit of luck. A wrecked Dutchman, off the coast. Cargo worth a fortune.' He reached his arm down and into the folds of her skirts. 'And you ken I'll make sure you get some.'

'That's good of you, James,' said his mother quietly, her breath uneven. 'But please, go away now. I could smell you standing at the door, and at this distance you'll get me under the influence too.'

John lay half conscious, with the taste of dust in his mouth and the sting of smoke in his eyes. He blinked them until finally they closed. When they opened again, his father was gone, and he heard his grandmother talking.

'You need to get away from that man,' she was saying. 'He'll never do anything for us.'

'But he says he'll support the boy,' his mother said. 'He's just never had the money.'

'How long's he been saying that?' said his grandmother, and her jaws were set tight.

'I'm not the fool you think I am, Mother. You ken that Katherine's aye ill,' said his mother, looking sideways at his grandmother.

'No surprise, with that man for a husband. If it was you, you'd be ill too. You see how he mistreats her.'

'Well, he's never mistreated me. And he says that if anything ever happens to her, he'll marry me.'

'And you're waiting to see if he keeps his promise? If he ever does, and that's not likely, you'll end up dead, same way she will. You are a fool. You aye were,' said his grandmother harshly. He could see that she was angry now. 'You need to find yourself a real husband, an old man who works hard and isna fussy.'

'Like my father?' he heard his mother say, and John saw her cringe and shudder as the blow from his grandmother's hand fell down upon her.

'Dinna speak ill of the dead,' said his grandmother.

John sat up quickly, and the room spun around him. 'Leave her alone,' he said.

His mother's eyes were full of water. His grandmother's were like ice.

'So you're with us now,' said his grandmother, turning.

John put his hands up to his face and tried to shrink away, but it was too late, she caught him hard across the head with the back of her large hand.

'That's for succumbing to the folly of men,' she said. Then she shuffled to the stove. She lifted a ladle and spooned out a little beremeal broth into a dish, handing it to him. 'And this is for behaving like a bairn. Bairn's food,' she said.

John sipped the milk-thick, grainy mixture and felt it coat the scorched lining of his stomach. At first he only felt his sickness, but then he remembered the cargo. He smiled to himself.

'Look at him,' said his grandmother, 'grimacing like an idiot.'

'He said he'd take me out in the smack again,' he said to his mother, feeling like a man, but unable to conceal his small boy's excitement.

'He'll end seeing you to an early grave,' said his mother. 'You ken there was a French privateer spotted out in the Flow yesterday, just afore you returned. They've already taken two Stromness ships. And they'll not be the last.'

John shrugged. As he ate he felt the swimming of his head settle a little. He was remembering the way his father had looked at him, his hand on his shoulder, after he had seen the ship. Then he was juggling numbers, price per hogshead, firkin, puncheons, pipes and barrels. His mother watched him, and her eyes seemed to dim. Suddenly she turned and grabbed him, holding him tight in her arms.

31

He shook her off with violence, but she gripped him all the tighter.

'Mother,' he said, shaking her off a second time, but laughing.

He was aware of his grandmother watching them.

'He's too old for that coddling,' she said. 'No wonder he acts the big bairn when you wilna let him grow.'

His mother released him, and turned to his grandmother. Her voice was tight in her throat as she spoke. 'It's my right,' she said. 'It's what I deserve, and I'll take it if I like.' Then she stepped up to the meal girnel and began to crush the beremeal with violence.

His grandmother looked at John and, seeing his expression, let out a soft, low laugh, almost a growl, deep in her throat.

III

His mother was feeding the hens. His grandmother sat back in the great hooded chair that had been his grandfather's, and picked up her spinning. John sat opposite her, on a little hassos stool. He made patterns with his feet in the dust of the floor and watched her hands work. Though many of the women had fashionable new spinning wheels, his grandmother would not have purchased one even if she could have afforded it. She still spun in the old-fashioned way, with card, comb and rowar. At length she put down her spinning and leaned forward.

'John,' she said, 'that ship was a rich find.'

'I ken that, Gran,' said John.

'But your father's due you more than what he's given you. I want you to ask for it.'

'He'll only say no,' said John sulkily.

'John,' said his grandmother, with undisguised contempt, 'you're near a full-grown man now, or at least the closest to one we have in this house. Your mother won't say it to you, but it's about time you were earnin' your keep.'

John shrugged. 'Maybe I'll marry a rich lass,' he said.

His grandmother let out a spit of a laugh as she extended her arm and removed a small seed from the thread. 'Maybe, but you'll not find one in these parts,' she said. She stopped, as though a thought had occurred to her. Then she let out a rattling cough. It had been a cold June and the damp of late voar had crept into the house and infected the peats; the room was clouded with peat smoke. She waited for John to move, but he was staring into the clouds of smoke, thinking of the rich girl he might marry. At last she got up clumsily herself and turned the skylin' board this way and that in an attempt to drive it out.

'Your mother's been letting you off with idleness for too long,' she said, sitting down again. 'If you had been mine, things would be different.'

John stared at his shoes and said nothing. When he looked up she was still watching him with her sharp, hawk-like eyes, and he shrank back a little, almost expecting a blow. He stood up and walked away. His grandmother only tutted and went on with her work.

But he would do as she asked. Though he would not admit it, he was frightened of his grandmother. This in itself would not have been enough, however, had it not been that her words had implanted a seed in him, one that would feed off his greed. She knew this, and she only had to wait for it to grow.

He waited until they were next in the smack, about to put out, so that there was still time for him to jump off if he had to. There was a good wind up, and a few of the boats were getting ready to put out, so that John struggled to be heard above the noise of the wind and the clanking of wood and metal.

'Father, I need to speak to you!' he shouted, hating the high pitch of his voice in the wind.

'What?' shouted his father, screwing up his face with impatience.

'About my share,' John shouted back.

'What share?' his father said. His brothers had turned around at their father's voice. Peter laughed at first, but Sandy put his hand on his shoulder and looked at him, and he stopped.

'Exactly,' said John. 'What share?'

'What do you mean, boy? Explain yourself.' His father stopped his work and came closer to John so that he could hear better.

John swallowed and his dry lips clicked so that he was sure his father could hear it. 'It was me that saw the ship, and did as much work as you to bring in the goods,' said John.

'Five bottles of brandy, that's what we agreed.'

'That's what you decided.'

His father stopped and looked at him. He seemed hesitant. Then he laughed, a little forced. 'I see,' he said. 'I see what's happening. You're making a peedie rebellion, eh?'

'I just want what's fair,' said John.

'Well,' said his father, still smiling, almost affectionate, 'I suppose I might have done the same when I was a lad. But I'm sorry, son, five bottles is the deal.' And then he turned away from John, back to his work. His brothers too turned away, relieved that the small drama was over.

John felt suddenly desperate. A burning wetness stung the corners of his eyes. 'It's not good enough,' he burst out.

'John!' he heard Sandy warn.

His father wasn't laughing any more. 'Na!' He swung around and brought his face close to John's. He shook his head. 'Na, na,' he said again.

John felt his presence and the width of his father's body in comparison to his own tall but narrow frame. He took a step back, and shrank into himself. But then he breathed a gust of wind, and it seemed to knock some courage into him.

'It's about time you kept some of your promises to her,' John said. 'That's all. It's food she needs, not liquor. Right now she's still cooking crappened livers.' He almost spat the last words, a rage rising in him that he himself had not predicted.

His father began to smile. It spread across his face and into his eyes.

'I just think,' said John, gaining courage, but lowering his voice, 'that we might as well start as we mean to go on.'

'I agree,' said his father, his voice quiet. 'Come on,' he said, 'let's row.'

John was surprised at his father's compliance, but turned around to where he was to sit. As he did he met Sandy's eye. He saw a momentary expression of panic on his brother's face, before the world fell away around him.

He remained conscious for a moment longer. He heard the roar of the sea in his ears, as though he had been placed in a gigantic seashell. He smelled the mushroom smell of wet wood. He turned his head slightly and saw the grey sky above. Then he saw the base of his father's boot come down upon the side of his head and the sky turned black.

~

He woke some time later with the sudden chill of ice at his neck, believing a wave had washed over him. He felt his hair wet and the taste of salt on his lips, and opened his eyes. Sandy was standing over him, holding a bucket of water.

'What did you do that for?' he said, hearing the squeaking pitch of his own voice and hating it again, as much as he knew that his father already did. He sat up and saw that the boat was back in the harbour at Orphir. He was lying in a sea of squirming fish.

'He told me to,' said Sandy, pointing to his father. 'We couldn't wake you up.'

His father turned around. 'You think he's learned his lesson now?' he shouted to the others.

John put his hands on the side of the boat and pulled himself up, dazed. His brothers laughed, all except Sandy. John looked at him and he looked away.

'When you're old enough to stand up to a man, you can get paid like a man,' said his father. 'Now at least you can shake hands like one.' His father held out his hand, but John couldn't keep his still. His body shuddered with the cold, and he didn't have the strength to grip. His

36

father took hold of his limp hand, and instead of shaking it, raised it to his lips and kissed it. Then he handed him a bag of fish.

'Here,' he said. 'Your mother can have a feast tonight.'

He heard the laughter of his half-brothers around him and saw that even Sandy was smirking slightly, shaking his head. John took the bag of fish and turned from them all.

IV

That evening when John walked through the door his mother rushed towards him.

His grandmother looked up from her spinning.

She saw the bruising, and tutted with disdain. 'You asked him then,' she said. His mother looked from one to the other, her mouth a little open.

'If it wasn't for you, you greedy auld bitch,' shouted John, suddenly close to tears, 'I'd not be in this condition.' His throat contracted until he thought he might choke. Then he threw the bag of fish at the old woman, knocking the work out of her hands and causing it to unravel. His grandmother stood up, her lips tightly pursed, and seconds later a jar came hurtling across the room in his direction. He ducked to avoid it and it clattered against the clay wall. But John was already on his way out.

'That's it, coward, run awa,' shouted his grandmother after him. 'Like father like son.'

It had begun to rain, and he kicked the dirt outside. Throwing the fish had helped him, he was beginning to feel calm already. It wasn't as though they'd never had scenes like that before. They happened every six months or so. He had expected his grandmother to shout, to call him names; he was almost glad she had, because it justified his own behaviour. He would go for a walk in the rain and return a bit later, and his mother would take pity on him, as she always did, and give him a bannock or some hot broth. At least they wouldn't beg his father to give him work any more. But then from outside the door he heard the slightly raised voices of his mother and grandmother, and stopped to listen, peering through the crack in the seal-oil flap.

'He's overdue for it,' his grandmother said. 'Most of the other lads are away before now, if not to sea then full-time at the labouring. John just flits about doing this and that, looking for some way to get by that doesn't involve any work. There's no land for him here. And you ken, Christina,' he heard her say in a lower voice, 'you can start again better without that burden on you. God knows some healthy widower must have you.'

John saw his mother look at his grandmother, and he saw her head move in one silent and treacherous nod.

He started to walk away from the house, away from the village. He didn't turn back. As he walked his vision clouded with tears, mingling with the rain that lashed his cheeks. He could hardly see, but stumbled on. Gradually the rain cleared and as he walked his own face dried. At first he saw his mother's nod, repeated over and over again, but then he pushed all thoughts of his mother and father, and his grandmother, from his mind. It was growing cold, but it was still light. His clothes were sodden and the water in them was beginning to freeze. To make up for it, he started to jog, and his skin began to feel warm, almost feverishly so. But even at this fast pace it was a good hour before he reached the bridge at Stenness. He stood there for a moment, looking over the loch, blue and smoky in the fading light. He knew the town of Stromness was near from the lamps that glowed in the distance, from the windows of houses, and the ships preparing for morning voyages.

As soon as he found the harbour front he sank to the ground with exhaustion. His breath was tight and wheezing. It was some time before the world around seemed to stop spinning and he became aware of his surroundings. Despite the creeping darkness, the harbour was still busy with a few fishermen unloading their catches. Some women in coloured clothing were walking up and down, and two of them saw him and fussed around him, stroking his smooth chin and hair. He stood up shakily and tried to wind his way around them but they only followed. Finally he pushed one of them away, as gently as he could, and immediately a well-built man stepped out of nowhere.

'I hope you're not mistreating one of my lasses?' he said, his face close to John's.

John turned and started to run along the dark street, but as he did so he ran straight into two men walking along the promenade. The burly man came up right behind.

'What's all this?' said one of the gentlemen.

'This young boy's been striking one of the poor defence-less lasses.'

'Is that right?' said the gentleman. He looked down at John. 'He doesn't look like he could hurt a fly. Are those the offended ladies?' he asked, glancing over to where the two women now stood, whispering together. 'They don't look to me like the kind of ladies to become easily offended,' he added, smiling at his friend.

'Come here, Cathie,' said the man. 'Show these gentlemen your bruise.'

'Aw, Mansie,' she said softly, 'leave the boy alone, it's nothing.'

'Aren't you a bit young to be wandering the shore alone at night?' said one of the gentlemen, in a tone that sounded kind to John.

He felt almost delirious with tiredness, and looked up at the man.

'Just what I thought,' said the burly man. 'I thought we could take him in, that's all. Take good care of him till he remembers where he's come from.'

'I can imagine the kind of good care he'd get with you,' said one of the men.

'I ken where I'm from,' said John.

'But do you know where you're going, my lad?' said the kind man.

'I've come to sign up to a trader,' said John firmly. He hadn't. As he walked away from his mother's house, he had felt only anger, fury that they did not recognize his worth. His mother knew it, she had always called him her treasure, but she had been poisoned by that witch. Now he saw that if he stayed on these islands, he would never be anything but a poor onca, a labourer. He would never have the luxury of a real chimney. But standing here, looking up at the man with his gold watch glimmering in the fading light, the row of ships with prows raised, the silhouette of their figureheads, serpents and long-haired girls with breasts bared, he saw that he could have more than a real chimney. He could have the kind of wealth his father had only imagined.

'A Hudson's Bay trader?' said one of the men.

John hesitated. He had heard of these ships that had started to visit the islands in recent years, and had already taken away several of the young men from his township. As yet, not one had returned. This made John uneasy.

'I don't know,' he said.

The gentleman examined him. 'Have you been at sea before?' he asked.

'Every other day on my father's boat. And I'm strong,' he said, holding up his skinny arm.

'That's the ship I've come from, there,' said the man, pointing to a dark hulk lit here and there by lanterns on the deck. 'We're not a Hudson's Bay trader, but a rich one nevertheless.'

John looked up at the ship, which seemed enormous in the half dark. He swallowed, and hesitated. But then he remembered his mother's nod. One day she would wake up and realize that her treasure was gone for ever. He pictured her silent agony with some satisfaction.

'Will you have me, sir?' he asked the gentleman.

The man looked at him for a moment. He turned to his friend. 'I could do with a boy,' he said. 'I'm the only officer who hasn't got one already,' he added peevishly.

'There's your chance,' said the other man. 'If the captain will agree to it.'

The man narrowed his eyes. 'Perhaps if we're far enough out to sea he'll have no choice.'

'But the boy will be noticed.'

'The captain said himself we need extra hands.'

The first man turned back to John. 'Well,' he said, 'there'll be no wages, mind, not till you're sixteen, but you'll have better accommodation than the common sailors, if you'll work hard. You'll sleep in the officers' cabins, and you'll be well clothed and fed.'

John nodded solemnly. A tingling of excitement started to come over him. When they reached their first port, he would write to his mother, and tell her she would never see him again. He imagined her opening the letter.

A short time later, he was rowed out to the ship, the *Catherine*. There were no spare hammocks, but the man who had spoken to him found him a corner in the part of the ship he called the fo'c'sle, and he lay down on his coat. It was cold and slightly damp, and the air was full of strange and unpleasant smells. But John was exhausted from his long walk, and fell asleep almost immediately.

He was woken abruptly the next morning by a rough shake from a boy about the same age as him. He was small and wiry, with brown skin and black eyes. He spoke with an odd, foreign-sounding accent.

'Wake up, boy, don't you hear the bell? What watch are you on?'

John rubbed the corners of his eyes, which were gritty and sore. He stood up unsteadily, and then, being near the door, was swept along by a sudden surge of men emerging from the fo'c'sle on to the decks. When he reached the top he felt himself lifted off the ground, and awkwardly turned his head to see a man holding him by the scruff of the neck.

'Aha,' said a voice. 'What's this, some vagrant? Come to beg a passage?'

'Na, sir,' said John, shaking his head vigorously. 'I was brought on board by a gentleman, says he wants me as his servant. He went awa to speak to the captain.'

'And what's wrong with one of the ship's own crew, that's what I'd like to know,' said the man, scowling at him. 'Like Jeremiah here,' he continued, pointing to the brown boy. 'A better worker you never saw there. That's it, Jeremiah, slush her up.'

John looked up to see that several of the crew had climbed on to the masts and along the yards, and were busy unfurling sails and tying ropes. Jeremiah had climbed halfway up the mainmast and was holding on with his feet and one hand, a bucket of grease slung over his arm, smearing it on to the surface of the wood.

'Let's see how well these peasant hands take to some seaman's work,' said the man, now releasing John. 'Awa up there and help Peter reeve the studding sail gear.'

John looked at him blankly.

'Well, what are you waiting for?' said the man.

Jeremiah had jumped down, and hissed in his ear, 'Better do as the bos'n says, else he'll start you good.'

John walked towards the mast a little, and the man who Jeremiah called the bos'n was called over to the other side of the ship.

'I dinna ken what he means,' John whispered.

Jeremiah looked at him for a moment, as though he didn't understand what John meant, but then he pointed to one of the men high up at the top of the mast. 'Just climb up there, and Peter'll show you what to do.'

Then Jeremiah disappeared, and John began, warily, to climb the mast. The height was dizzying, especially as they had got under weigh at last and the pitching of the ship in the swell was even more violent the further up the mast he climbed. But he was small and agile, and managed to keep a firm grip on the ropes. The man called Peter showed him how to fix them. At last the sails were bent and, with a stiff breeze filling them up, the ship moved rapidly out to sea.

When he had finished, John jumped down. The bos'n had disappeared. The rest of the crew seemed to know what they were doing, but John had no idea, and nobody had given him any orders. He needed to pee, but couldn't see where he was supposed to go, there being no private place that he could see anywhere on the ship. At last the urge became too much, and he stood urinating through the rail, into the sea, trying to avoid the yellow spray that flew back towards him. He looked across to the smooth flat land, fringed with red rock, and remembered for the first time that day his grandmother's words, his mother's silent nod. Two small salt tears emerged on his face, and were immediately blown dry by the wind.

He was startled by a voice from behind him.

'Easy seein' you're new to sailin',' said the voice. 'You'll soon learn to piss on the leeward side.'

John Fullarton coloured and put away his penis. He watched the dots of his home as they faded into the distance, and then disappeared altogether.

3

For five days John was unable to speak to the man who had promised to hire him. He only knew that his name was Hampton, and that he was the second mate. He had tried to tell the bos'n he wanted to see him but the bos'n's only reply was a blow over the shoulders with a short rope which he had knotted in several places and carried with him at all times. He had little time to think of it, in any case, because after only one watch of scrubbing decks, greasing masts and hauling rope, they came out into the Pentland Firth, where the strength of the opposing tides made the ship lurch and heave. The men were ordered down into the fo'c'sle, and the hatches were boarded up and sealed with oilskin covers. John had found a hammock at last, and curled on it, the motion of the hammock to some extent correcting the shifting of gravity caused by the ship's movement. As a boy, the sailors who came into Stromness had told stories of great earthquakes in foreign lands where the land opened up beneath people and swallowed them whole. John thought that this must be what it would be like to be swallowed by the earth.

'This is the worst stretch,' said a man who lay beside him. 'Once we're out of the firth it'll settle down.'

John had been going to sea since the age of six, but the slow, heaving movement of such a large ship was quite different from the regular rocking of small boats. On the fishing boats, they would turn for home when the weather got too rough. It was only on the whaling trips, or the few wrecker expeditions he had been on, that he had experienced very rough seas, and then there was the excitement of the haul, and the cooling effect of the rain and spray to ward off sickness. Here, shut up in the hold, there were the smells: the bilge water that leaked through the gaps in the rotten wood of their ship, the clogged-up stench of the men, the smells of their bodies and of their food intermingled. They were supposed to relieve themselves over the sides of the ship, or in the little round cut-outs in the heads, but when they were shut in like this they were forced to use pots, and some men didn't even bother with those. More than once John was woken by someone relieving himself in the corner of the hold. The offence was so bad it was supposed to be punishable by flogging, but it was always too dark to see who it was. Some of the men lay with their noses up against the slots, as if by smelling the sea water they could relieve their nostrils. But most were unperturbed. They lay on their bunks, chewing tobacco and numbing their senses by drinking the greater part of their allowances. John was sick at first, but when he recovered he was able to eat some of the dry salt beef and biscuit brought to him by Jeremiah. It was tough, but he had eaten nothing for two days, and the very touch of the salt to his tongue brought the juices into his mouth. He washed it down with hot molasses-sweetened tea, and then sat back in his hammock, trying to lick the memory of flavour from the inside of his mouth before it disappeared.

At length the weather improved a little, and the hatches

were opened. They worked in four-hour shifts, with at least ten men required on deck during day and night. Sometimes they talked and told jokes, or slept on and off. One or two read, those who could. John leaned over towards one. He was lying down, reading an old broadside. John could read a little, having received a short education in the parish school, before the minister ran out of money to keep it going. But in the dim light he could make out only the picture on the front, depicting a man hanging from the gallows.

'What's that?' he asked.

'This?' The man turned. 'The only reading material I got, picked it up in Stromness, but I know it word for word now. It's about one of your lot, a Captain Gow.'

'I ken him,' said John, with a slight swelling of pride.

'You know him?' said the man, suddenly interested.

'Well, my father kent him.'

The man sat up, as much as it was possible to without being thrown backwards again.

'Here,' he called, 'this boy says his pa knew the pirate Gow.'

Some others gathered round, and John saw that he would have no choice. So before a group of thirty eager eyes he told a story he had heard his father tell, of how he had met John Gow, the kind of boy he was, the kind of man he had become. They found his accent difficult, and kept stopping him, so he told the story slowly. But that suited him fine, because it gave him time to think about the details. The story he told was not the same as his father's. He had never enjoyed his father's account, where Gow was a shoeless beggar who had never been competent enough to be a good pirate and even had to be hanged twice, since the rope broke on the first attempt. His father's stories were always full of misery and failure. Instead, John told his own version, the story of the strong and hardworking lad Gow, who had been a good and faithful son to his loving mother and father. They had turned against him and cast him out, but he had found wealth and adventure at sea, and had died with dignity after being betrayed by those jealous of his success.

The man who had first asked appeared to listen carefully to everything that John said, but he was clearly having thoughts of his own. 'It's a fine life on a pirate ship, they say, as much as you can eat, drink, and enough money to be prince of your own small kingdom.'

An older man spoke. 'But what about the hundreds more that've ended up on the gallows, or been tossed into the ocean?'

Nobody paid him any attention. They sat huddled in the darkness and their eyes gleamed like opals, with grinning teeth of gold and pearl.

~

When Hampton finally received approval from the captain and came for John the next day he was almost sorry. He had grown fond of the company. It was the first time he had felt as though he were among men who viewed him as their equal, even if it was in their mutual misery. As Hampton's cabin boy, he would tidy his things, fetch his morning draught and replenish his stock of brandy. John would be no powder monkey, Hampton told him, and while he wouldn't receive a formal wage, he would have the clothes Hampton had finished with, and he would be a kind of apprentice, someone who could learn a little of the trade.

'You can read?' he asked.

John nodded hesitantly, though it had been some time since he had been called upon to read anything more than a broadside, and that often took him several minutes, his finger running stiltingly over the words.

'And to arithmetic, can you count?'

John's agreement was more certain this time. He had been totalling up quantities and figures since he was a small boy.

'Excellent, I think you'll be just to my purpose,' said Hampton. He showed John into the small cabin that he was to share with his master, and the little galley kitchen where he could prepare the light meals Hampton said were necessary to his constitution.

'Now fetch me some brandy, and some bread and cheese,' Hampton said, as if to test him.

John disappeared along the quiet corridor of the quarterdeck, so different from the noise and bilge-water stench of the fo'c'sle. He could still hear the rest of the men in the distance. It gave him a peculiar, homesick kind of feeling, but he shook it off. Not only was he better off where he was, but this man was offering to give him something it would take years to achieve elsewhere: the possibility of a future as an officer, and the wealth he had dreamed of in Stromness. Hampton himself had clearly reaped the benefits. John had noted the neatness of his laces, the bright glint of his silver buckles, the whiteness of his frills. He had admired the gleam of his fine gold pocket watch, and a large gold ring with an emerald inset. Hampton was loosening at the middle, perhaps, but nonetheless made a fine figure for his age, which must have been more than fifty years. He tried to imagine living the life of such a man, with private quarters and fine clothes, and roast beef at the captain's table, instead of salt herring and dry, weevil-riddled biscuits below deck.

When he reached the little galley kitchen a small boy was standing there, stoking the fire. He turned suddenly and glared at John.

'Who are you?' he asked.

'John Fullarton. Mr Hampton's steward. Who are you?'

'Oh, you're Mr Hampton's new boy,' the stranger said casually, and he smiled. 'Heard about you. He picked you up in Stromness, did he not? Thought you'd a funny accent.'

'Your accent sounds pretty funny to me,' said John defensively. He picked up the bread and cheese his master had asked for and turned to leave. But when he reached the door the boy called after him.

'No need to take offence now,' he said. 'I'm David, the captain's boy. You'll find things quite different here. But by and large,' he added with a strange, thoughtful smile, 'I think you'll find we've the better of the bargain.'

There was something about the boy's smile that filled John with a sense of unease. He only nodded, and left.

~

His sleeping quarters were a bunk that lay opposite Hampton's own bunk, since the ship was too small to accommodate servants in separate cabins. The room itself was little more than a cupboard, without air or windows, and a door that opened into the gunroom where he was to help serve the officers at their meals, but it was his own small space, bigger than a hammock. At least now he didn't have to share his sleeping space with coils of rigging and old torn canvas. There was even a shelf along the wall that was his and his alone. On it he was able to arrange the few possessions he had had in his pockets when he left: his pocket knife, which he spent much time sharpening, an old handkerchief and a stone he had picked up on the beach, many years before, because it was wound through with little bright threads that looked like gold or silver. Worthless, his mother had said, but he had kept it anyway. One day, he thought, he might prove her wrong.

Each evening, Hampton asked John to read to him. It was a means of improving his reading skills, Hampton said, for John still picked out the words slowly. Hampton sat on his chair sipping from a large jug of port, then left to take a brandy with the other officers in the gunroom. He would arrive back late at night, and often Fullarton would have to help him into bed. On the fifth night, however, after John had finished reading, Hampton began to talk with him. He had taken more brandy than usual, and the drink had loosed his tongue. He talked about himself, his life, and how he had come to be at sea. He was married, he said, had a wife and son in Portsmouth. He returned as often as he could. His wife was not a retiring creature, and happy enough in society without him. But his son was a degenerate boy; it was all he could do to keep him from the gambling and debauchery that would be his ruin.

'Now if he could only learn to work for a living, like you do, John. My boy could learn a thing or two from you . . .' and then he would look at John in a way that John found both flattering and discomforting. 'You know I admire boys like you, John, who'll do anything for a living.'

John wanted to tell him that this wasn't true. That he had chosen to be here, that he could just as easily have stayed at home. But he said nothing. His silence seemed to annoy Hampton.

'And what about you, John?' he said. 'What can you tell me about yourself?'

John shrugged. 'Not much to tell, sir.'

Hampton shifted in his seat. 'You must have a mother, or a father, or brothers and sisters to tell of, surely.'

'I've all of those,' said John, 'except sisters. But I don't remember much about them.' He had forced the images of his mother, father and brothers from his mind. He had started a new life, one that they would have no part of.

'What happens tomorrow,' said Hampton, looking at him closely, 'depends on what happened yesterday.' He crossed his legs, looking pleased with himself. 'You can't escape your past, eh, John?'

'I'm not sure I understand, sir,' said John, though he understood perfectly.

'Ah, well, that's philosophy,' said Hampton, sucking on his pipe. 'A great art, and when you've mastered the art of reading, well, maybe we'll move you on to it. What do you say?'

'I'm sure that would be fine, sir,' John replied.

'Do you have to agree with everything I say?' Hampton snapped.

52

'No, sir,' said John.

But Hampton seemed to have forgotten his anger already. He bent forward and poured John out a large port.

'Well, here's to us,' he said, and they both drank. Hampton emptied his glass.

John thought the taste a little sour, but had watched Hampton, and downed his as well. He screwed up his face at the acrid flavour.

'It's not the finest I've had,' said Hampton, 'but you'll get used to it.'

Then he began to tell the story again, in different variations, about his wife and her desires for money, silk and tea, his son's depravity, and the insincerity of those who called themselves friends. John was hardly listening. It was late. He had slept poorly the previous night and had been up since five to help with the breakfasts for the officers. The port had gone to his head and he felt dizzy, but Hampton leaned forward and refilled his glass.

'You see, John—' Hampton began.

'I'm sorry, sir,' said John, interrupting. 'But I'll have to retire.' He attempted to stand up, but lost his balance and sat down again in the same position.

He saw Hampton's face above him. It was laughing gently. 'Of course,' he heard him say. 'I'm forgetting you're still only a boy.'

John felt himself lifted by Hampton and placed on his own bunk.

He tried to speak, but it was as though his jaws were locked together. He could feel Hampton's breath on his face, and tried to lift his hand to push it away, but his arm wouldn't move. It lay by his side like a piece of lead. Hampton's body drifted away.

When John awakened some time later, it was still night. His head pounded and his tongue was like leather.

'Oh, God, I am sick,' he said to the darkness. Then he felt a presence beside him. He put his arm out to one side, and his tongue seemed to freeze in his mouth as he felt another hand grab hold of it. Then he heard Hampton's voice, smelled the sweet tang of stale port in the air beside him.

'My dear boy,' it said.

He tried to release his hand, and in doing so came into contact with the plump, pink flesh of Hampton's body, lying next to him.

He pushed it away and sat up.

'In God's name, sir,' he said, 'what are you doing?'

There was no reply, but he could hear scuffling movements in the darkness and felt a shift in weight. He put his hand out again. But Hampton was gone. He heard movement in the darkness of the room, and, after a while, steady breathing. Hampton had climbed back into his own bunk. John lay awake for some time, until eventually the effect of his own liquor overtook his fear, and he fell asleep.

He barely knew where he was in the morning. He turned over, away from the light that streamed through the half-open door. His arms and legs felt like lead, and his lips and tongue were on fire. He heard himself ask for water.

Hampton was already up and appeared with a small mug. 'There's only washing water,' he said roughly, raising it to John's lips. He looked away as John drank.

The water tasted of coal, but John gulped it thirstily. His head pounded, but the room began to settle into the motion of the ship. It creaked and heaved around them as he propped himself up a little, looking at Hampton.

'What happened?' asked John.

'You had a little too much to drink,' said Hampton.

'No,' John said. 'That's not what I mean.' He hesitated a moment. There was only the sound of their breath. 'I mean last night.'

'I don't know what you mean,' said Hampton, still looking away.

'You were beside me. You were unclothed.'

'I don't care for wearing garments in bed.'

'You lay beside me,' John repeated.

Hampton's face became dark. 'You are mistaken, boy. You have dreamed something that did not happen. What do you accuse me of?'

John's senses were returning. He began to make calculations in his head. He knew that his future depended on being able to stay here in Hampton's cabin, and, after all, nothing had really happened. 'I'm sorry, sir,' he said. 'But then, what were you doing?'

There was a silence now, as though Hampton were considering. And he turned a little, inclining his head towards John. 'Can you blame a man for wanting to feel the closeness of another human body, in the absence of his good lady wife?'

John said nothing, just held on to his pounding head.

'Surely that makes me no unnatural,' Hampton went on, 'just a man, that's all. But if it makes you feel uncomfortable, here is the proof. I will kiss you,' he said, as he leaned forward, 'as a father might kiss his son.' He brought his lips to John's, lingering just a second longer than required.

4

The following day the ship anchored in Leith Roads. John felt he had been away for months, though it had been little more than a week, and that largely because of the storm. Once they had been piloted in, they were allowed shore leave, although they were supposed to come back to the ship to sleep. John and David left together. They were rowed past the ships unloading boxes of kelp, the same kelp that he had watched his mother cut and dry for the first time last year. She had said it would be boiled into cakes of rainbow-coloured tar, to be sent south to keep rich folk clean. And now he had seen the rich folk in question, he wondered that they seemed no cleaner than he did himself.

He didn't know what he would do with himself. The other men had proper wages, and so had disappeared into inns and whorehouses, but Hampton had only given him a little money, probably to make sure he came back. He thought about what had happened the previous night and his stomach lurched. He could run away, find his fortune in this town. But as he walked through the streets and saw the beggars, prostitutes and shoeless peasants that seemed to make up the greater part of the population, he had a clear and desperate picture of what would happen to him should he choose to make a living on his own. He could take a commission on another ship, but with no letter of recommendation he would be nothing better than a deckhand or a powder monkey on a navy vessel, and from the tales he had heard other sailors tell about their time in the navy he knew that would put him in a worse situation than he was in now. The only other alternative would be to beg or work a voyage home. He imagined his mother's face if he returned. She would cry tears of joy at first, but then things would return to normal, with his grandmother's scornful looks and poisonous remarks infecting his mother. And the thought of his father's mocking expression decided it. There was no way he could return.

David talked incessantly about various trivial matters, and it irritated John to see how content he seemed to be. For him shore leave was simply a holiday. They passed a shop full of sugar-encrusted fruits, cakes and other confections. David drooled over the window like an excited child, and then disappeared inside. John left him there and walked on, through the dark little street that appeared to be the main thoroughfare of the town. At the end of it he came to a lane that suddenly opened out into a much wider, brighter street, with some grand houses of pale stone with windows the size of his mother's entire house. They looked like they had only just been built. He stood for some time looking at these houses, their gardens newly planted with little trees in blossom that peeked over their high walls, and the smell of young honeysuckle reaching around the windows. He looked down at his clothing. He was wearing a silk shirt and waistcoat of Hampton's, along with a velvet frock coat, silk stockings and breeches and shoes with silver buckles. The clothes were ill-fitting and sagged around his small body, but he knew they were rich, and he was proud of them. He had as yet no beard, and so did not look like a sailor. He could almost be taken for a resident of this place, and he strutted along the wide streets, imagining that one of these grand houses was his, and that he could just turn and go inside whenever he wanted.

He came to a small churchyard, lined with mature trees. The day was bright and mild, and he was glad to get away from the noise of the animals and dusty wheels of the street, and into the cool green of the graveyard. The lime green of the leaves concealed it from the streets all around. John had rarely seen trees – there were only a few low-growing ones where he lived – and it was pleasant to stand in the hollow dark space below them, listening to the choir of birdsong above.

He saw a small blackbird pulling a fat, glossy worm from the soil of a newly dug grave. Then he watched as an enormous seagull swooped down from the roof of the church and grabbed the worm from the blackbird's mouth. It flew off in the direction of the sea. John had never noticed the difference in size between the two birds before, and it struck him as odd that the seagull should want to return to the sea, when it would clearly be in such a position of dominance on land.

Then he heard a rustle in the grass behind him and turned to see a young girl enter the graveyard. She looked no older than himself, with hair the same reddish brown as his mother's, the colour of the sandstone cliffs of Hoy. Her movements were slow and somehow unsteady. In her hands she carried a bundle of flowers, which she placed at the foot of one of the graves. The soil there was still soft and brown. Then she kneeled down. At first he thought she was crying, but she made no sound, and he thought she must be saying some kind of prayer.

Immediately he realized he should not have been there, watching her, and he stepped towards the gate, but as he did so she saw him, and called him back.

'Please,' she said, 'don't leave on my account. I was just going.'

'I'm sorry,' he said, 'I was just enjoying the trees.'

She looked at him strangely. 'Yes,' she said, 'it is pretty here,' as though she had only just noticed.

'Someone close?' asked John, nodding to the grave.

'My father.'

'I'm sorry.'

'Don't be. His time had come. He'd been very ill, and unpleasant with it,' she added. 'But still, he was a father, and the only parent I had left. My mother died two years ago.'

'My parents are also dead,' said John, deciding that from that moment, they would be.

The girl regarded him with interest. 'I'm sorry for you,' she said. John noticed her milky-white complexion. Although she was young, her hazel eyes were bound with dark red rings from crying and sleeplessness, and this gave her the appearance of someone older. Despite this, she had a kind of resilience, and a familiarity, that attracted him. The sound of the birdsong rang like thousands of tiny bells in his head.

'Well,' she said, 'I must walk home.'

John nodded, and stood back to let her past.

She hesitated. 'Will you walk with me?' she asked. 'Just as far as my house? It might help me to forget.'

'Of course,' he said, both flattered and terrified at the prospect of having to converse with her.

As it turned out, however, she talked for both of them. 'My brother is on his way home,' she said as she walked. 'But he is at sea, halfway across the Atlantic Ocean, and so he'll return to find his father already buried.'

They seemed to pass out of the village itself. The houses became fewer, and the road open, lined with small fields and plots. Then they arrived at a large house surrounded by high walls, constructed of the same white stone as the others John had seen.

'A fine house,' he said.

'My father built it not ten years ago,' the girl said. 'It never felt like home. But it is for now. At least until my brother returns, and my father's estate is settled.'

'Are you all alone?' asked Fullarton.

She turned her sharp eye on him. 'More or less,' she said. 'Except for the servants. And Mr Coull, my father's lawyer, calls from time to time.' She made a face, and then laughed for the first time. 'He seems to want to court me, but he is over forty at least! He is a friend of my brother's.' She looked at him and the smile vanished, leaving only her hollow, melancholy eyes. 'What an unusual accent you have,' she said, thoughtful, 'I can't place it at all.'

'I am from Orkney,' he said. 'My name is John Fullarton.'

'Well, Mr Fullarton from Orkney, thank you for keeping me company,' and she turned to open her gate. 'It was nice to meet you,' she added.

'Wait!' said John. 'I'm on shore leave again tomorrow. Perhaps you would walk with me then?'

'Perhaps,' she said, smiling. 'And what is it that you do, Mr Fullarton?' she asked.

John straightened a little. 'I am second mate,' he said, 'of the trader the *Catherine*, now in Leith Roads.'

She nodded, looking him up and down. Either she believed him or she didn't care. 'I see. Well, I lay flowers at the grave at the same time every day. My name is Margaret,' she said shyly. Then she gazed beyond him, towards the road that led to the churchyard. 'I nursed him, you see, for this past year. It was hard work. But it's harder to stop.' Then her face seemed wild for a moment and John wondered if she might cry, but instead she turned away and opened the gate.

'Goodbye,' she said quickly as she went, without a backward glance.

As he walked back to the ship he realized that he had not thought about Hampton for the past two hours. There was something fascinating about the girl. He couldn't place it, but it was almost as though he had known her before. She was not forward, yet she had none of the shyness associated with girls of her age, or the frivolity. When he had walked with her, he had felt a complete absence of any kind of care or concern. He had lost all sense of time. Now he was aware that the road back to the ship was much longer than he had thought, that it was growing dark, and that he might miss the curfew for returning on board. His stomach clenched with nerves as he hurried on.

He made it with only minutes to spare, and was the last sailor to be rowed over. When he arrived, Hampton was in a foul temper because he had been made to wait for his meal. Fullarton served it quickly, and then returned to the cabin. He lay on his bunk, thinking of the birdsong in the overgrown churchyard.

He must have drifted off to sleep, because when he woke the candle had petered out. A noise had woken him, and when he heard it again he knew that Hampton was in the cabin. He froze, so as not to make the slightest sound that would betray his wakefulness. Hampton was somewhere in the middle of the room, and by his fumbling movements John guessed that he was trying to undress. He heard a couple of muffled curses, and buckles thrown down. Then came a scuffle, and a loud thump followed by the tinkle of glass, and he realized Hampton had fallen on to the floor.

He was drunk, and for a moment John was tempted to leave him where he was, but knew that if Hampton woke there he would blame John. He climbed quietly out of bed, pulled on his shirt, and picked his way tentatively across the dark space, aware that there would be broken glass on the floor somewhere. Then he found the warm cushion of Hampton's body. He was naked, and seemed to be fast asleep. John knew there was no possibility of his lifting him alone, but if he called for help he would expose him to the indignity of being seen in this condition, which would put him in an even fouler mood. So instead he began to shake the body.

'Sir, sir!' he called in his ear. 'You must wake up.'

Hampton stirred a little and began to moan, but he woke enough to help John as he tried to lift him. John dragged him to his own bunk and laid him down, fumbling to find the blanket to draw over him. As he did so he felt

Hampton grab hold of his hand, and pressed it down on his own body. John cried out as he felt the spongy texture of Hampton's skin, rising and hardening under his touch.

'Sir, stop!' he said, pulling his hand away. He retreated at once to his own bunk, stepping on a piece of broken glass on the way. He lay on the bed, grimacing, trying to pull it out.

'If you will,' came Hampton's drowsy, laughing voice in the dark, 'or if you won't. You are my boy, and sooner or later I'll have you.'

It crossed John's mind, as he lay alone with Hampton in the darkness, that it would be easy, now, to take his pocket knife and drive it into Hampton's soft flesh. He could cut his throat with broken glass, or smother him with his own bedclothes. Nonetheless, he had no intention of actually murdering him. It was perfectly clear to him that killing Hampton would simply lose him his position and earn him the gallows. The truth was that he had never been capable of true acts of passion, or violence. Even the tantrums he had as a boy only occurred when his grandmother was out. He knew his mother would tolerate them. Walking away from his mother's house had been, in a way, an act of passion, but getting on this ship had not. He had been thinking about himself, his own personal gain. The thoughts of the various ways in which he could end Hampton's life were no more than a kind of pleasant imagining, a childish indulgence that somehow helped to soothe him to sleep.

~

Margaret was standing with her back to the grave, looking at the dog roses that lined the railings of the churchyard.

'You know that where my mother was from, they say that if the dog rose and birch grow together on the graves of lovers, then their love will endure for ever.'

'There are no birches in Orkney,' said John. 'They wouldn't grow there.'

'There aren't too many here, either,' said Margaret. 'Funny how only the dog rose seems to survive. Or maybe it's just that the men come and cut all the birches down. Perhaps it should be two dog roses. You couldn't have a churchyard full of tree roots, after all,' she added, laughing. 'Quite a job for the gravediggers.'

'You are beautiful,' John said quite suddenly, looking at her, and meaning it. She turned to face him, and he saw that she wasn't beautiful, exactly, but that there was something in her, a strange combination of dark and light, that made her seem so to him at that moment.

She smiled and moved her head a little in a gesture that told him she knew it already, but was pleased he was of like mind. 'Why don't you come back,' she said, 'and take tea with me?'

'Won't the servants think it odd?' asked John.

'Let them,' she said, with a smile. 'Why shouldn't I ask a friend for tea? After all, that lawyer asks himself often enough, and they seem to think it's a great honour for me to have him there, even though I haven't requested his presence.'

John only nodded, holding her arm, wondering how he could hold on to her for longer. He had that same sense he'd had with her before, of being protected.

As they walked under the cool shade of the trees, looking out on the memorials of the spirits, a plan suddenly came to him. It was spontaneous and unreasoned, and it ran just up to their marriage, but all at once it seemed like the only plausible solution. What would happen afterwards, if her brother discovered he was not who he said he was, didn't concern him. All that mattered was that she agreed to marry him, and to marry him within two days. Then they could both be free, he of his indenture to Hampton, she of her unwanted suitor. She had means enough. And though he hardly knew her, there was some connection between them that told him they could survive together. It seemed an absurd idea, but also as natural as the wild dog roses that grew in the rich soil of the graves.

In the house a maid with a sour expression served them, and John sat sipping tea from a china cup with a lid, poured from a silver teapot. Margaret sat back on her chair and appeared to relax for the first time; as she did so he saw the greyish pallor of her face, the dark rings around her sleepless eyes. The quick, anxious movements that had fascinated him in the graveyard now became slow and languid. It was John, now, who felt anxious, glancing around him at the walls clothed in small portraits and cameos of well-dressed merchants and their wives. There didn't seem to be a space in the room that was not hung with a picture or decorated with a vase. The furniture was new, probably bought in with the house, highly polished and unmarked. But he felt as though the walls were closing in around him. His throat seemed to contract, and he looked through the large window to the cherry blossom of the garden outside. He saw a lane there that had been planted with mature, fast-growing hedges, screening that part from the house. He remembered his plan, and his purpose.

He was about to ask her to show him the garden, but she saw him gazing out of the window. 'It's such a lovely day,' she said. 'What a shame to be shut up in this dark house.'

She took his hand, and he smiled at her, though fear had struck deep in his gut.

It was easier than he imagined. She didn't flinch when he put his hand on her shoulder. She didn't complain when he kissed her, or when he slipped his hand beneath her cloak, her camblet, and up and into the skirts of her gown. Instead she took a short, gasping breath, and grabbed the back of his head, bringing it towards her. He had not expected this from her, this fervent need. He hadn't expected that it would be he who would be hesitant, only knowing vaguely what to do, and not understanding the nature of a woman's anatomy, especially when hidden beneath folds of skirt and underskirt, so that it was almost impossible to get close enough to find anything at all. His anxiety overwhelmed any desire he once had, and she seemed to perceive his desperation.

'Over there,' she whispered. 'They might see here,' and they moved to an area of bushes just behind the trees. It was there, on the cushioning of her net skirts, and against the prickle of hawthorn and gorse, and with the smells of fresh spring growth and decomposing kail stumps intermingled, that she too finally began to seem a little unsure.

'What about . . .' she breathed, but it was too late then, he was already inside her. At least he thought he was. Some part of him was. She gasped a little when he tried to push further, and clutched the back of his neck again. He slipped about her for a while. But somehow he couldn't quite get things right. He found himself too conscious of the world around him. The trees whispered and watched them from above, the birdsong became an orchestra, a fanfare telling the streets all around about their union. Every crack of an animal in the trees was a footstep coming towards them. He felt himself begin to shrivel with fear. He was sure she felt it too. She did her best to take hold of him and guide him, until finally they managed to come together. And he felt it then, closed his eyes and tried to forget everything else around him, not only Hampton and his mother and grandmother, but Margaret too, even the girl he was making love to. In his mind's eye he saw only himself, the shape of his own body, taut and curved, strung tight like a bow. Only then was he able, with a final movement, a gasp, and a groan, to make a real finish to his pretended passion. Then they pulled themselves apart and sat quietly, a little breathless, spending some time tidying skirts, buttoning breeches, folding and patting back into place.

He couldn't look at her for some time. When at last he did, she was staring away from him.

'Of course,' she said, 'we shouldn't have done that.'

'No,' said John, glancing down.

'I just wanted, for a moment, not to think. Do you understand that?'

John nodded. 'Yes,' he said drowsily.

'But now the thoughts come flooding back. Like waking up in the morning,' she said, 'after a death. For a second you are in blissful ignorance. Then it hits you, the reality of it all. Sometimes I think a memory is no more than a curse.'

John didn't reply. In truth he hadn't heard. He had lain

back on the grass, listening not to her words but to the sound of her voice, the familiar anxious music of her. It reminded him of something soothing, something that had happened before he became aware of the people around him, or the passing of time.

As they were about to go in, he stopped her.

'Margaret,' he said, holding on to her hands. 'We should get married.'

She laughed, throwing her head back a little so that he could see the vibration of her throat. 'My brother would love that, coming home to find me already married. He thinks he'll make his fortune by marrying me well, since he squanders all of his own on claret.' But her eyes had grown wild, and they flicked around, considering.

'That would be a fine surprise for him, wouldn't it?' she said quietly.

'I love you,' John lied, after waiting long enough for her to doubt it. He took hold of her hands and drew close to her.

She looked up at him, so that he felt her breath tickle the base of his nostril as she spoke. 'I know,' she lied back. 'I love you too. But how can it be done?'

John brushed his lips against the back of her hand. 'Tomorrow is my last day of shore leave,' he said. 'Meet me at the churchyard, at one o'clock, and by then I'll have made some arrangement. Your brother will return, and he'll not be able to marry you off to some old man, because you'll be married already.'

She smiled then, and her expression was both uncertain and excited. They embraced then the way they felt young lovers should, both passionate and delicate, and the surroundings of the garden, the birds and the cherry blossom overpowered their senses so that their arrangement felt perfectly real and natural, and not in any way ill-conceived.

Margaret reached into her cloak and pulled out a finely engraved ladies' pocket watch, in solid gold. 'Take this,' she said. 'It will help you to keep time.'

John took hold of it, and looked at it. It reminded him of the watch that Hampton carried. The sickness of reality returned to him, the sickness that Margaret had mentioned, and he turned to leave before he could change his mind.

~

That evening, John told David about his plan. He didn't have to. He could have grabbed any two witnesses from a nearby bar. But something niggled at him, and he felt he couldn't leave the ship without offering some explanation.

'But why should you want to escape, when you have such a favourable position here?' David asked.

John was quiet for a moment. 'You know,' he said, 'that Hampton is not all he seems.'

'What do you mean?'

'He harbours unnatural desires.'

David laughed heartily at this. 'Don't we all!'

'I mean,' said John, scowling and colouring at the same time, 'for me.'

'Ah,' said David, nodding slowly. 'I see.' He shook his head. 'What a strange peasant boy you are.'

'What do you mean?' asked John.

David turned at a noise in the corner. John looked up too. His fingers clenched into his palms. Then a small mouse ran across the room, and they both relaxed.

'I'll do what I can to help you,' said David, turning to John again.

'Thank you,' said John, feeling somehow that David had not quite understood what he was trying to say. He looked at David and felt a sudden melancholy. In a short time he had become fond of the boy, and David, too, seemed sorry to see John go. He sat quietly, making a steeple with his fingers and watching them as they were upturned, revealing the people inside. It was something John remembered his brother Sandy had taught him to do.

'Where did you grow up, David?' he asked, trying to expel the thought of home from his mind.

'On the road between Newcastle and York. Me and my brothers. Well, they were like brothers. We all grew up orphans, stuck together, and made our living by robbing the stages. We looked after each other, fed each other. We loved each other,' said David, suddenly intense, looking at John. 'We loved each other like brothers, like kin. We were everything to each other.'

'Then why did you leave them?' asked John. He thought that he would have liked to be one of David's brothers. He began to pick at the brocade of his waistcoat, some of which was coming loose.

'Don't know. To avoid ending up hanged, like most of them. To show I could make it myself, I suppose, to make some money, see a bit of the world. That's why I left. Made my way to Hull, got on a boat, never saw my brothers again.'

'Were you sad to leave them?'

'No,' said David definitely. 'My family is here now. And in the end, we're all on our own, aren't we?'

John nodded. He stopped unravelling his waistcoat.

'When I leave,' he said to David, 'I'll miss you as I would my own brother.'

David laughed a little, but quietly, looking into the fire. 'Well,' he said, 'that depends on how much you miss your own brothers.'

~

When John arrived at the churchyard the next day she was already there, by the grave as usual. She still wore her black mourning dress, but when she saw them she dug into a bag she carried and brought out a white ribbon. She tied it around her arm.

'Can't marry in mourning!' she laughed. John was surprised at how ordinary she seemed today, and how much more self-assured. The day was overcast, and a light drizzle forced its way through the canopy of trees, frizzling the little curls of hair that escaped from her cap.

As he took her hand she seemed to shudder a little.

'I just can't stop thinking about him,' she said, looking at the grave of her father. 'If he was here, he'd know what to do.'

'Don't worry,' said John, not as convincingly as he would have liked. She looked up at him and he saw a hint of fear in her eyes.

'Do you think we ought to do this?' she asked.

'Don't be afraid,' he said, because he couldn't answer her question.

'Will you go back to sea, afterwards?' she asked.

John shook his head, but he realized it hadn't occurred to him that she would expect him to. It had not occurred to him how he would explain his lack of income, or even possessions. Lots of things had not occurred to him that were beginning to occur to him now.

Then David arrived with the man he had found to be the minister. It was one of the sailors from the ship. He had found him in a local inn, and he walked unevenly across the grass. John almost laughed when he saw him. He had combed his hair straight and neat and had somehow managed to get hold of black clothing, but his full sailor's beard was still apparent, and the smell of brandy came off him as soon as he was nearby. He wondered now whether employing a mock minister was a ridiculous notion. He knew that the marriage would be legal even if only declared before two lay witnesses, but somehow he thought Margaret would not believe it to be so. If she noticed anything, however, then she was too polite, or too desperate, to remark on it.

'I've brought the ring,' said David, and he pulled out a ladies' fine gold band.

John almost asked David where he had got it, but he was sure the answer would shock Margaret, so he kept quiet.

As he turned to place the ring on her finger the branches of the bushes behind them snapped in two. He heard quick footsteps on the stone path, and as he looked round he only saw from the shoes, and the gait of the walk, that it was Hampton, because before he had time to raise his eyes Hampton whacked him so hard with his cane that he blacked out on the mossy carpet of the graveyard.

~

When he woke in his locked cabin, they were already at sea. David brought him food, and told him what had happened. After he had fallen, Hampton had hit Margaret too, and they took her home crying, with some story that she had fallen and knocked her head on the gravestone. Hampton said he had saved her from being abducted by John, who was a cowardly deserter, having absconded from his naval vessel. Some friend of the family had been there, a lawyer, and he gave Hampton money for his kindness. She had not contradicted their story. Perhaps she believed it, in part, or was still dazed from the blow.

John was still sullen when Hampton came into the cabin that evening.

'You still sulking,' Hampton said. 'Don't be such a baby!'

'I am a legally married man,' said John.

Hampton laughed. 'How many legal marriages do you think half this crew have to whores they met in port, and "fell in love with",' he said disparagingly.

'She wasn't a whore,' said John.

'No,' said Hampton, 'you were the whore.' He sat down beside him and put his arm round John, stroking his cheek tenderly.

From then on, John did as Hampton asked. He was a good cabin boy, and an excellent apprentice. Hampton shared the luxuries of his life with him, his clothes, his wine, his food, and occasionally his bed. All this John accepted. But he gave nothing other than what he was contracted, or forced, to give.

5

Mary's uncle tried to make enquiries after her father. He wrote to the Admiralty, but they had no records of any such person having been in the service of the navy. Mary's mother never believed he was a deserter, but was convinced he had been press-ganged. At length she had to accept that he was probably dead. She had believed, for a while, that she might see him again, but she had known that would never be the night she had finally told Mary. She had cried then, not for a love she had lost, but for the love she would never know.

It wasn't that her case was hopeless. Mary's Aunt Isobel tried to persuade Margaret to remarry. Her brother would provide her with a reasonable allowance, and with a little investigation he could no doubt find a respectably endowed husband for her. But she was not prepared to give herself up for less than she thought she was worth. To fritter away her sense of tragedy on a gentleman's powdered wig would be to give away one of her most valuable assets. This was a powerful quality, more powerful than the wealth of her brother or the efficiency of her brother's wife. She held on to it, nursed it, ready for the day when it would help to secure both her daughter's future and by consequence her own status in the world. In doing so she gave herself up to Mary and put all her energies into shaping her daughter, dressing her in silks and laces as others might dress a doll.

'My mother used to make me wear homespun,' her mother said, as she laced up her stays in the morning. 'But my daughter will have finer things.'

At other times, Mary's lustre seemed to fade. Then, her mother said, 'If it wasn't for your extravagant tastes perhaps we'd be richer than we are now,' and pulled tight on the cords until Mary coughed for breath.

Mary listened to both comments without making any of her own. She wore her habitual blank expression, especially as she knew it frustrated her mother. And she grew to despise every present her mother gave her, because she knew they would only become a source of guilt. She understood her mother's feelings perfectly, largely because her mother made no secret of them. Every advantage that Margaret gave her daughter was a reminder of what she herself had missed out on. Mary felt her mother's interest in her not as flattery, not as a desire to improve her for her own sake, but as a need to see her succeed where Margaret had failed, because Mary's success, now, was also her mother's success.

Her uncle, too, saw the jewel in Mary. He knew that finding her a good marriage was the only way to lift his burden of care, which had become ever more burdensome with the increasing pressures on trade that were affecting his financial situation, and which he was not reticent about mentioning. Feeding a large family was getting harder, what with the price of good claret these days. But he knew that even the dustiest stones could be made to sparkle if they were burned and polished well. At the age of ten, Mary was introduced to a Mrs Inglis, who was to be her tutor. She was taught all the necessary skills, and some of the unnecessary ones. By the age of fifteen she was almost ready. She could read and write, sew in white and coloured seam, wash gauze and lace, make tassels, cords and loops, paint flowers on to the backs of shells. She was given some lessons in mathematics and French, morals and posture, with the help of a special steel stay to ensure she stayed upright throughout all her lessons. All this Mary bore with pride for her mother's sake. But the more she achieved, the more her mother wanted. She exalted her, telling her that there was nothing she couldn't do, and every success was a failure to do something more.

'There's something missing in Mary,' she had once heard her mother say. 'I can't place it. She doesn't . . . seem real.'

'She's too quiet, that's all,' said her uncle. 'Wants bringing out of her shell.'

'Wants getting out of this house,' said her Aunt Isobel, 'out to see a bit of the world. It's not good for a young one, cooped up in the house with us all day. Why don't you see about a husband for her?' she suggested to Mary's uncle.

'But she's only sixteen!' Mary's mother cried out.

'She'll never be old enough for you to give her away,' said her uncle. 'I can't afford to raise another spinster, Margaret.'

And so it was that Mary was sewing in her small room one day when her mother called her into the sitting room to tell her that all her efforts had been rewarded. Her uncle had found her a husband, a wealthy ship owner, captain of his own vessel.

'One of the best,' said her uncle. 'His accounts are immaculate.'

'Of course he is a little older than you,' said her mother. 'A widower. He lost his first wife, Elizabeth, in a terrible tragedy. She drowned after taking some kind of fit during the night. But he is determined that life must go on, and that a new wife is just what he needs to bring him out of it.'

'And I've been told, confidentially,' said her uncle, with a glint in his eye, 'that he has a great fortune coming to him some day, by way of his uncle, who raised him.'

'It's a good offer, Mary, especially in your . . . circumstances.'

Mary knew what that meant, that her uncle would not bring much to the match on her behalf, despite not having any children of his own.

'I've worked hard to find a good arrangement for you, Mary, and if I'm being honest, this exceeds my best expectations,' he said.

'I don't know,' she heard herself say.

'There is one thing, Mary,' her uncle said. 'He does expect you to go to sea with him.'

There was a silence and Mary held her breath. The idea of going to sea was terrifying. But the idea of escaping from this house, with its judgements, criticisms and conflicts, which were never openly expressed, but never quite concealed, was fascinating. She turned to her mother.

'Mother, do you think I will like him?' she said, half bewildered.

'Of course you will,' said her mother sharply. 'You're like me, and I like him, so you'll like him.'

Mary nodded slowly, and her mother softened.

'So you'll meet him?' she said, with hope in her voice.

'Yes,' she said, 'if you advise it, then I will.'

Now it was her mother's turn to look bewildered, but she nodded, and the meeting was arranged.

Captain Jones was invited to a supper party at her uncle's house, and Mary watched the door each time it opened. It opened many times, with gentlemen of all shapes, sizes and ages entering, but each time she looked to her aunt, she shook her head slowly. Finally her uncle came in with a fairly small, round man, and they both looked at Mary with meaning. Her aunt nodded. The man bowed his head slightly. Mary felt an immediate surge of disappointment, but forced it away, then glanced at her mother's eager face, and stood up with a smile. She regarded the man more closely and relaxed a little, seeing that he was at least neat and well turned out, with a modest, if old-fashioned, black wig and clean leather shoes with silver buckles.

Over their meal, he sought out her eye and smiled often. Mary gave a flicker of a smile in return and quickly lowered her gaze to the untouched food on her plate. She was hungry, but her mother had pulled her stays in so tight that it hurt to think of eating. Her Aunt Isobel considered her approvingly, though whether because of her lack of appetite or her seemingly modest behaviour Mary wasn't sure.

Later, Mary gambled at cards with her mother and Isobel. She sipped her sweet brandy punch and tried to listen to the talk of the men, her uncle's business acquaintances and some of Captain Jones's crew. They drank port, and a platter of oysters was brought out. Her uncle talked of the necessity of a good squeeze of lemon juice in an egg sauce. Captain Jones spoke in his peculiar southern accent of his experiences of Edinburgh, of the way people stood in the open streets in the middle of the day, just to hear the tune played by the church bells of St Giles, and of how he had seen a macaroni in a wig fall most ungracefully out of his sedan chair, just the other day, when it was blown over by a strong gust of wind. This last story entertained all the gentlemen so well that Mary's uncle spat out the oyster he was about to swallow, and the half-chewed mucous blob landed on the newly carpeted floor, which made Aunt Isobel throw up her hands and the men laugh all the more heartily. Captain Jones, however, did not laugh. He looked away and called to the maid standing in the corner.

'Well,' he said, 'can't you see this mess needs tidying?'

But then he started to describe the foreign places he had travelled to – the ports and the markets with goods nobody had ever seen before, not only silks and rugs and the most beautiful porcelain but also strange animals in cages and colourful birds. 'All the wealth of the world,' he said, 'there for the taking.' Mary found herself listening more carefully.

'Well,' said her mother, leaning forward nervously when the men were out of earshot. 'What do you think, my dear?' Her voice was high, sharp and impatient.

Mary said nothing. She bit her lip.

'Of course perhaps there is another you have your eye on,' said her mother impatiently. 'A lord, or a viscount, perhaps.'

'Mother!' said Mary, rolling her eyes. But still she said nothing.

'For God's sake,' Mary's mother exclaimed, a little too loudly. 'Why do you always make things so difficult? Why won't you just say what you feel?'

Mary didn't know how to say that she was always trying to work out what she should feel, and that this took some time. She wasn't used to being allowed to have feelings, and she certainly wasn't used to being asked to express them openly.

'What do you think I should do?' she asked her mother.

Margaret looked at her daughter hopefully and Mary could see the fear in her eyes. 'Your uncle has worked hard for you. You must make the right decision. For you,' she said, 'and for all of us.'

Mary understood. She glanced at Captain Jones and nodded slowly.

It was as if, Mary thought afterwards, a cook had been preparing a grand feast for more than a week, only for it to be devoured in less than an hour. Mary and Captain Jones were married in a short ceremony at South Leith Parish Church the following week, since Captain Jones's ship was due to leave in a fortnight. Then he took her back to his house in Jamaica Street, where he undressed her gently and made short, slightly painful love to her between the oak posts of his small Dutch bed. Afterwards he fell asleep quickly, and Mary lay awake in the darkness. But it wasn't her own darkness, the one she had known in the little room she shared with her mother. She wished for that darkness now, and for the unsettled, discontented breath of her mother beside her, not the wet, heavy sound of this unknown man.

6

The carriage rattled down the frozen road from Edinburgh to Leith. Hampton sat back in his chair, almost asleep from the quantity of port and oysters he had taken. Fullarton felt groggy too, but it had been a long time since they had stopped in Leith, having traded from the west coast these past years. He looked over at the patches of field and grass, the hills behind. The street was busy, and they passed a large assembly of people. He saw in the distance a figure in a wire frame behind the construction of the gallows. He stroked the soft hair of the beard that now covered most of his face.

'Who are they hanging today?' he shouted to the driver.

'Some man murdered his old mistress for her money,' he said. 'They said he'd got some servant girl pregnant and needed the money to keep the child.'

Fullarton nodded. 'Seems a great length to go to for a child,' he said, smiling a little.

The driver said something in reply, but Fullarton wasn't listening. He had seen a face in the crowd, and it had sparked something in him.

'Stop the carriage!' he called.

The driver stopped, and he looked for the face again, but it was lost among the sea of bonnets. Only a little girl stood watching him now. Her eyes were wide with terror.

'It was nothing. Drive on,' he said.

'I'd say the lass drove him to it,' said the driver. 'Crazy for money, they all are.'

'That's true enough,' grunted Hampton, who had woken slightly.

~

Their lodgings were in one of the old houses in the town, and were dark and gloomy. Fullarton lit a candle. Hampton sat down on a big chair and was quiet. Fullarton sat on the bed and watched him. He was waiting, he had been waiting these past seven years, for Hampton to fulfil a promise he had made to him.

Hampton had become Captain five years previously, and had made Fullarton his first mate. Fullarton was young for the promotion, and though he could have taken a commission on another ship, Hampton had said that if he stuck with him then he would find him a ship of his own to command. Now, at the age of two and twenty, he felt sure his time had come. Hampton had aged. His face had become red and ruddy, as if rubbed raw by the wind, and the fat skin around his lips and eyes stuck out like jelly. There had been a time when Fullarton had almost admired him. He had had a vigour, and a sharpness in his understanding of the business, the ways to turn profit. But now he wore a habitual look of defeat, especially when he spoke to Fullarton. This was natural, Fullarton thought, the inevitable surrender of an aged man to the superiority of youth. It pleased him, but also revolted him, as though it were a disease that might be transmitted to him if he grew too close.

'John,' Hampton said at last, 'I have something to tell you.'

Fullarton couldn't help a slow smile spreading over his face.

Hampton swallowed. 'I was waiting until we got into port, because I had to confirm some business arrangements with an old acquaintance. I think you know what it concerns.'

Fullarton shook his head, letting off a fine spray of fragranced powder from his new black wig, pretending to be surprised. 'What do you mean?' he asked.

'You're a good worker,' said Hampton, and his voice seemed to shake a little. 'And an ambitious man. But more than that . . . Well, the point is, John, we couldn't go on like that for ever.'

Fullarton looked at him for a moment and then nodded. It was true. They couldn't.

'You need to move on,' said Hampton. 'I need to . . . think about going home.' He gulped his drink. 'By God, John,' he went on, 'there's nothing like a wife and a wayward son to drain the old pot dry. The wives, they will have the latest cloth from London, to make dresses all done up with ribbands and lace and petticoats of silk and muslin. And the boys, they will have their card games, their cockfights, where they run up debts for you to pay.' He stopped as his face began to swell and redden.

'You have to go home?' said Fullarton. It was both a question and a statement. He realized that the delay in finding him a position had been nothing to do with markets or practical difficulties or any of the other complex reasons that Hampton had spouted over the years, or even to do with his supposed affection for Fullarton himself, but only to do with his fear of going home. He could see Hampton wince at the suggestion, made plainly before him, and it gave him a twinge of pleasure.

'Yes,' he admitted. 'But in any case,' he said, with a hint of impatience, 'I have made my decision, and I have spoken to some people. I have obtained a commission for you as master of a small trading sloop.'

Fullarton coughed to hide the elation that was building inside him, and Hampton gave a wry smile. 'A small one, mind, but I think the position will be very suitable for you,' he said. 'You're a good apprentice. You've earned it.'

Fullarton nodded, in thanks.

Hampton looked down into his drink and the smile fell from his face. 'You know, John, as you get older, change becomes difficult.'

'I don't plan on growing old,' said John lightly.

'Ah,' said Hampton, 'but time takes us nevertheless.'

Fullarton said nothing. He looked at the gold watch in his pocket. 'Time for bed,' he said. He stripped off his shirt and turned back the scarlet damask of Hampton's bedcover, looking at Hampton with the quiet signal they had both learned to understand.

Hampton shook his head.

'Suit yourself,' said Fullarton. He climbed into bed and lay in the half dark. He lay awake for a time, watching Hampton slowly drink himself unconscious in his chair. Then he closed his eyes, and his dreams were filled with the ghosts of the past and the future.

Part Two

7

Mary watched the merchants' big white houses and grey magazines slip away, as the ship drifted into the Forth, under the weight of a light wind pushing on the canvas with a gentle pat-pat-pat. The wind wove and sang between the ropes and the rigging, and the wooden frame creaked beneath her feet. The day was calm, the water a viscous spirit, oozing softly and wavelessly away from the sides of the ship as she edged along the coast. Mary watched the sands of Leith that she had stepped on so often, the grassy dunes beyond peppered with small dark spots that moved like insects on the lawn. She could see the hulks of the new houses being built behind them. Then they passed a long strip of golden sand overlooked by a grand house that she had seen in a picture. It was called Puerto Bello, after a battle in a place of that name, part of that war over somebody's ear that people said had won its owner a great deal of silver. She wondered if she would ever see the original Puerto Bello, and she felt a tinge of excitement, as if someone had brushed the edge of a knife along her spine.

Despite the stillness of the day, or perhaps because of it, the ship buzzed with activity behind her. Men climbed ladders, wound coils and pulled on ropes. William strode up and down the decks, bellowing commands that were repeated, parrot-like, by the people they were directed to. But Mary hardly heard them. She only looked out on the shoreline, amazed by the number of places she had never seen, had never known existed, only miles from her home: inlets with white specks of gulls emerging from frothy caves; tiny islands; ancient, ruined castles on promontories; small villages huddled on the sea. On the other side lay the patchwork fields of Fife that she had dreamed of sailing to as a child, dotted with little villages and more sands, less yellow and more bleached than those of the southern side.

She turned briefly to see William brush by her, giving her a slight nod as he went. A wisp of feathery grey hair had come loose from beneath his wig and fluttered in the wind. She could feel his anxiety as he passed. The wind was too light, and he was keen to be out of the firth. His commands had an urgency to them, and the volume of them seemed to increase, as if by ordering them in a louder voice he could increase the volume of the wind. Mary turned away from him, tried to block them out, to dull the restlessness inside her. She put her hands over the rail, to feel the slight breeze. William might think their progress slow, but she was moving faster and further than she'd ever moved before. She stood watching these unknown places slide away from her, wishing she could command the ship and order her to stop at one of the sandy inlets. She felt a sudden need to lift her skirts and paddle in the clear water, or turn her toes in the sand as she had as a child, the sheer pleasure of that gritty abrasion hardening the soft skin. She looked down at her own feet, tightly fastened into the short riding boots picked out for the voyage by Isobel.

Finally the wind picked up and the land became no more than a smudge of grey. The activity of the men, too, seemed to settle for a time. It had clouded over, and the air was raw, the ocean the colour of ash. Mary heard William come up behind her. He put his hands around her shoulders and picked up the cloth of her shawl. His fingernails scratched through the fabric.

'Thin stuff,' he said. 'You must be cold.'

'No,' said Mary, stopping a shiver, reaching up for his hand, 'I'm fine.' She turned around to face him, and smiled into his round, reddish face. Since the night of their wedding she had barely seen him. They had been short of crew members, and good men were even harder to find than usual, because of Spain's entry to the war, so William had spent most of his time at the harbour, returning only late at night and sleeping on the day bed in the room where he conducted his business. Now, as she examined his face in the strained light, he looked away from her, and appeared almost awkward.

'You must be careful,' he said, stuttering slightly over the words. 'You'll catch a dreadful chill, some fatal palsy. We'll need to make you some proper seafaring clothes if you want to be on deck so often. Have you seen the apartments?'

Mary shook her head. The steward had carried her sea chest down, but she had wanted to stay on deck.

'Come,' said William, attempting a smile. He had a strange, formal manner, almost military, that she had thought at first was due to awkwardness with her, but now she saw was simply his way. He led her down the narrow wooden steps as though he were conducting her to a ballroom.

The apartments would have been better described as compartments, they were so tiny, but Mary was grateful that she had, unusually, been given her own cabin. William said that he was so often up and on watch during the night that he would only wake her, but it connected to his own cabin through an internal door. Mary was to sleep in a small square room with a narrow bed at each side of it, and a desk. Every wall, every surface, seemed to have had shelves or drawers cut into it. There were drawers beneath the beds, a cabinet built into a wall, and a bookcase lined with books. The remaining floor space was taken up by Mary's sea chest, and she saw at once that there would be no other place for it.

'How do you find your accommodation, madam?' William asked. It was a sign of his age, calling her madam. She had only ever heard her uncle using the term to address her aunt, and even he had given up the habit in recent years.

'I'm sure it will be very comfortable,' said Mary. They stood in silence for a moment as she looked at the bare walls, creaking around them. She noticed that there were no pictures. She felt a sudden stab of some emotion that she could not recognize. Not sadness exactly, because there was an excitement with it too. It was more of a sense of things passing, of the movement of one stage of life to another. But it overwhelmed her all the same.

'May I have a drink of water?' she said, suddenly sitting down. The strength seemed to have gone from her legs.

William poured out some water from a small tumbler. 'It'll take you a while to find your sea legs,' he said.

Mary finished the glass, gulping it down in exactly the way her mother had always told her not to. Then she stood up and approached the bookcase. She looked at the spines. 'May I?' she asked, stretching out her hand.

'By all means, pick out anything you like,' said William. 'They're there for your pleasure.'

Mary pulled out a volume, and William leaned in to look at it. He seemed to start back.

'Oh!' he said. 'I wouldn't recommend that.'

'Why not?'

'Strange, I thought I'd removed them all,' he said.

'What is it?'

'Oh, just some atheist nonsense,' said William.

Mary looked down at the book in her hand and wondered if she should drop it. 'The cover is pretty,' she said, hating the stupidity of her words but unable to find anything else to say.

'Yes,' said William, a little more quietly. 'That's probably why she read it.'

'Oh, I see,' said Mary, immediately replacing it on the shelves. It must have belonged to Elizabeth.

'She slept here?' she asked. Her mother had warned her not to mention his late wife, but she couldn't help herself. Suddenly she knew that this was the reason the walls were bare. Except for one handsome gold clock, there was no decoration of any kind, because they would be her pictures, her decoration, her taste. She looked at William, touched at his thoughtfulness in removing all trace of a woman he had formerly loved, for her sake.

William spoke, as though he had read her mind. 'When we reach Amsterdam,' he said, 'you may choose some books of your own, an ornament or two. The room is a little empty.'

Mary nodded and thanked him. William didn't leave straight away. He stayed for a moment or two, and they sat together in silence, listening to the creaking of the walls, until a shout from on deck gave William the excuse he needed, and he got up to leave.

'There are many other instructive texts here,' he said before he left. 'I think there's a poetry book or two. Some old copies of the *Ladies' Diary*.'

Mary smiled at him politely. But she wanted to do more than that. What was the use in being on a ship if she was only to sit in a cabin and read? She could have done that in her uncle's house.

'Isn't there something else I can do?' she asked. 'Can't I be of some use?'

William appeared to think. 'You can keep the cabins neat and tidy,' he said.

This wasn't what Mary had imagined, but she had never been much of a reader. She preferred to be active, so she nodded her head.

Then William looked unsure. 'I'll have to show you where everything goes,' he said.

'That's all right.'

William hesitated, then led her through the narrow door into his own small room, and opened up a panel of the wall to reveal a closet. 'Lay me out a shirt and waistcoat for the morning, would you,' he said. 'I always wear a clean one every day.'

When he had left Mary opened the closet and saw that William did indeed have seven shirts lined up there, and four waistcoats, ready to be exchanged each day. They were carefully stacked and pressed. She looked around the cabin and noticed how neatly placed everything was. Even the books and papers on the desk were at right angles to one another. Even though Mary was a naturally tidy person herself, the sight of the wardrobe terrified her.

Leaving the adjoining door open, she drifted back to her own room, which she found less frightening. She looked at the bookcase again. Her fingers ran over Elizabeth's book. Perhaps it would give her a clue as to what his previous wife had been like. She had not been young, Mary knew, thirty-five when she died. But before she had time to look at it the door to the next room opened and a gust of wind blew in with William on its tail. Mary dropped the book and stood up, feeling immediately that she had done something wrong. She opened the door to his room and saw him standing, looking around in wild panic.

'My hat,' he said, his voice more impatient than before. He waved his hand in front of her. 'My hat. Come on. Come on.'

She looked towards the closet. 'Which one?' she asked, looking at an array of military-style hats, all trimmed in gold braid.

'The Kevenhuller Cock!' he said, gesturing towards it. 'Quickly now.'

She had no idea what a Kevenhuller Cock was, but saw the one he was pointing out, the most ridiculously large one with three turned-up points, and picked it up. He grabbed it from her and tucked it under his arm. Once he had it, he seemed calmer. But then his eye drifted to the closet door, which she had left open. She saw the change in his expression.

'What is it?' she asked, wondering if she had given him the wrong hat.

'The door,' he said, 'you've left it open.'

She turned and pushed it shut.

Once he had gone, Mary looked at the room around her. She began to tidy it a little. She emptied the wash-bowl and wiped it out, and folded a clean dry towel beside it. She put all his clothes into the closet. But there was nothing more to do, except return to her own room and pick up her sewing, a decorative piece that suddenly seemed entirely without purpose. She looked at Elizabeth's book again. She wondered if Elizabeth had understood her husband, or if she had been as perplexed by him, at first, as Mary felt now. The conversation they had had seemed the longest since they'd married. But she found it impossible to judge his mood. His facial expression was continually changing, as though thousands of tiny clouds were being blown across his face by a hard and persistent wind, and she had just got prepared for one type of weather when another one blew in. He was different, somehow, from the man she thought she was going to marry. The man she had seen at her uncle's house seemed more self-assured, more humorous. His age had perhaps given him a fatherly appearance, and he wore an air of authority that she imagined fathers had. But sometimes, she saw now, he was as petulant as a child.

Mary filled her afternoon with unpacking her belong-ings and putting them in the closet, trying to set them out as neatly as William's. She seemed to have far too much space when she had finished, despite the fact that her wardrobe was much smaller than William's. Then she looked out her best clothes and began to dress for supper. There she would meet the other officers formally for the first time. She wanted to give a good impression of herself, for William's sake. No doubt he wanted them to think he had made a good choice in his young wife, and perhaps that was the cause of his nerves. She looked in the mirror, and tugged at her hair with a tough comb. Her hair had become frizzed and tangled in the wind and there was no taming it. She gave up and powdered it instead, then coated her face, neck and chest. She rouged her cheeks a little, and thought of applying the rouge to her lips, but decided that would be too much. She rubbed them instead with lip-salve that Isobel had given her, fragranced with rose-water and sweetened with sugar, so that she could taste it in the wax when she licked her lips. She looked again in the glass. Her hair would not do. She opened the drawers of the cabinet in front of her, hoping to find some piece of gauze or lace with which to tie it, but when she reached for what looked like a piece of ribbon she pulled out instead a fine linen and lace mob cap.

It must have been Elizabeth's. There seemed something chilling about wearing a dead woman's cap, but somehow she felt drawn to it. It was quite beautiful. She fingered the thick linen and stiff lace, with a silk ribbon to be drawn around it. She guessed now that captains' wives, that is, those who went to sea, being always blown about by the wind, must never wear anything except bonnets like this, but she had only brought one plain old cotton one. She tried it on, running her fingers over the fine silk ribbon.

She turned her head to the side and looked into the glass. She made a good picture in it, she thought. Then the door opened and William came in.

Her hand went to her head when she saw him in the mirror, and her mouth opened. William stopped, and looked pale. But he recovered himself quickly.

'Oh,' he said. 'Are you wearing that?'

'I'm sorry,' said Mary. 'I found it in the drawer, and since I don't have one of my own, or such a fine one, and my hair is in such a mess, with no time to dress it, really . . . I thought . . .'

'Yes, yes,' he said, waving his hand impatiently, 'it looks fine on you.'

'But if it was hers,' began Mary, 'if you'd rather I didn't . . .'

'Nonsense,' he said, looking away. 'It reminded me of her for a moment, that's true, but if you wear it long enough, it'll remind me of you. Just keep it. Else I'd only have to buy you a new one, and that ribbon didn't come cheap, I can tell you.' He turned to face her and gave a strained smile, and she tried her best to return it.

They went together to William's cabin, where Mary straightened her gown and tied a scarlet handkerchief around her neck.

William put on his scratch bob wig. Then he reached into a drawer and pulled out a tub full of a waxy substance. It had once been scented with orange flower water but now the smell of stale oil overpowered it. Mary turned her head away. She had been hungry, but felt a rising sickness again. She couldn't stop thinking about how they would compare her to Elizabeth. She imagined that Elizabeth would have had no problems conversing at the captain's table. But Mary was less sure of herself. She wondered whether she should talk freely or only when spoken to. To speak would be to betray her ignorance, but if she remained silent they would think she had nothing to say.

Finally William was ready, and they turned to leave. As he passed the washstand, he reached forward and straightened the two towels hanging there.

'The edges must match,' he said. 'See here, like this.'

Mary bent forward. 'Oh,' she said. 'I thought they were matching.' She could see little difference.

'Well,' William said abruptly, 'you'll remember for next time.' He tucked his Kevenhuller under one arm, and reached out his hand for hers. He looked at her once more and a new expression came into his eyes. His firmness dissolved and he appeared to tremble.

'Oh,' he said. 'I am sorry, but I can't see you wearing that cap after all.'

'I understand,' said Mary, taking it off. She found a piece of old cotton ribbon and tied back her hair. When she came out and reached for William's hand she noticed they were both shaking. She gave him a wavering smile, and thought how they seemed to clutch each other for support as they made their way to the gunroom for supper. William, she could see, was as nervous as she was.

She nodded and curtseyed to each of them in turn, knowing she would never remember either their names or their positions. There was the first mate, Mr Russell, who seemed remarkably young, not much more than seventeen. There was the gunner, Mr Peterson, whose name she tried unsuccessfully to forget, as it was only a reminder that they were sailing during wartime and of the small cannon and barrels of powder that had taken so long to lift on board. The first mate had his own servant, a ragged boy whom he seemed very proud of and who seemed equally proud of him, standing behind him at dinner. There were others including the Second Mate, the carpenter, the cook and his boy, whose names she immediately forgot, and a couple of other young boys who seemed to have no distinct role but spent most of their time swarming at the feet of the crew looking for one.

Then there was the surgeon, Mr Cole. She recognized him, and remembered that she had seen him at her uncle's house. She had noticed him because he had spoken often with William, and because he was quite different in appearance from the rest of the crew. His frame was narrow, almost boyish, his wig was short, and he was clean-shaven. He had the look of a younger man, though William explained that they were in fact the same age, and had gone to school together near Plymouth. The first thing Mary noticed was the blackness of his eyes, like the chaldrons of coal they carried in the hold. They were framed by long black lashes that were almost feminine, and as Mary looked into them she saw, as well as her own image reflected there, a kind of impatient sadness. They reminded her of eyes she had seen before, that she still remembered well, staring at her from a carriage on the long Wester Road to Leith.

'Mr Cole is also new to the sea,' said William abruptly, looking between both their faces. 'He has been sailing for only a few years.'

'I am a doctor first and foremost,' said Mr Cole, taking

her hand. 'But I am learning the ropes, as they say, and am happy to climb one with any common seaman.'

'Ah, but we would never ask that of you, sir,' said William, looking serious. 'We value your skills too much to have you break your neck.'

William's nervousness had not abated, Mary noticed, but seemed to have got worse. He danced from one foot to another. Mr Cole was still holding on to her hand, and she wondered if this was what was affecting him. She pulled it away gently and found her seat, but cradled the hand the surgeon had released in her other.

Mary sat quietly throughout the meal. She had decided silence was the better of two bad options. At the other end of the table, some of the men were deep in conversation, bursting every so often into hard, shouting laughter. It unsettled her somehow. It seemed forced, and she could never understand the joke. They talked in a language she could not understand, about yardarms, runners, marline-spikes and futtock-shrouds, and what seemed like at least a hundred different types of sail. She watched William as he drank his claret and ignored his meal, now engaged in animated conversation with Mr Cole. Mr Cole spoke now and then, and often he glanced up at Mary. As he did, she blushed and lowered her gaze, but when she raised her eyes his were still directed towards her.

She looked at her food. She was starving, but she became suddenly conscious of how she ate. Everything she put to her lips seemed to go wrong. It would fall out again on to her plate or stain the side of her cheek so that she had to wipe it with her napkin. Grease would run down on to her chin, or she would try to take a delicate bite of something and it would squirt out over the table. She dabbed at her mouth, she dabbed at the tablecloth. After a while she stopped eating altogether. She had been taking such tiny morsels that it seemed to fill her up all at once. She sipped her glass of claret and felt it burn. It was poor-quality stuff, compared to that she had tasted at her uncle's table. She looked up to see that Mr Cole was still watching her.

She caught William's eye now, and saw that he was watching her as well. She smiled at him, and he nodded solemnly.

After they had eaten, Mary returned to her room. William stayed longer to drink brandy with the officers. She picked up Elizabeth's book; she could see what William objected to, but she could not make head or tail of it either. Her eyes scanned the pages wildly, but each letter seemed to form the image of the surgeon's eyes in her mind. Her own eyes closed over them, as the candle flickered and died.

She woke in blackness to the smell of sour breath and the touch of William's hand.

'You're still dressed,' he said, trying to slide his hands into her stomacher.

Mary got up and began to undress in the dark. She left her chemise on, unable to find her nightgown, and slipped back beneath the bedcovers. She felt William's hands on her, a stilted, mechanical movement, and her stomach tightened. She had learned on the few occasions it had happened that there was to be no pleasure in their lovemaking. But at least now it was dark, and she could pretend that she was anywhere, anywhere but here, and that he was anyone, anyone but her husband.

Afterwards, William placed a hand on her abdomen. He felt sure she would soon swell with child, he said, as though he were giving her a gift. Mary rested her hands on his body and attempted to touch it with some tenderness. Perhaps, she thought, she could grow to desire it. She listened to the thump of hard rain on the deck above her, as William's breath began to deepen. She ran her hands over the wisps of wiry hair that gathered in the dip below his neck, his Adam's apple jagged with the stubble of this growth. She wondered if his first wife had done this, if she had run her hands over his round, taut, satisfied body, and loved it in a way that Mary had yet to understand.

William was asleep. Mary climbed out of the narrow bed, as there was no room for her to lie comfortably beside him. She shivered and stumbled as the ship lurched. She found her mantua at last and attempted to step into it. Then she climbed into the narrow, cold bunk at the other side of the room and curled into herself until she felt warm again, a warmth that must have come from within her, since there was none to be gained from either the bedcovers or the damp little cabin.

8

St Peter Port, Guernsey

Ten years after he last laid eyes on Charles Hampton, Captain John Fullarton stood on deck, watching as the little port of St Pierre pulled towards him. A mild wind breathed in from the Channel. The harbour was a mass of masts and rigging, an elaborate tapestry of tiny threads, holding together the collection of sloops, snows and brigs anchored there, their launches tied up to the stone walls. Behind them the little town leaned forward, beckoning, and at the base of each house was a flight of steps leading from a cellar down to the water's edge. Many of the cellar doors were open, like greedy little gaping mouths, and men loaded and unloaded their goods from the doorways. Fullarton felt the mild salt breeze of the Channel Islands slap the side of his cheek gently, teasingly, and he smiled.

He had already changed out of his ship's dress, the baggy linen trousers and woollen waistcoat, and into a smart frock coat, white stockings and shoes with silver buckles. He looked like a man of wealth, but in truth he was as poor as the sailors who pulled the ropes behind him. It wasn't that he hadn't made enough money. Since Hampton had found him his new position he had made a good profit smuggling wine, tea and tobacco between the coasts of Britain and northern Europe. But he had spent most of his profits, not at the brothels – he prided himself on the fact that he was not bound by his own flesh – but in the inns, in card games and cockfights, or on the brandy that went with them. As a result, all he had as he approached St Pierre was his ship, a good collection of fine clothes and a purse stocked with some guineas and a few shillings.

This was the main reason he had come. Fullarton knew that St Pierre was a haven for those engaged in free trade, and that a man could earn a good living bringing goods through the port. It would provide him with an opportunity to replenish his funds. But there was another attraction: the idea of some different human company. He had hardly spoken to a soul since they had left the last port. He knew the crew considered him a loner, but he found conversation difficult. He had discovered that he could not remain an equal with the common sailors while still commanding them, and he had never learned the skill some officers have for a kind of superior camaraderie. But neither did he feel comfortable speaking to the men whose class he was supposed, now, to be part of. They had a starched ease about them that he had never quite been able to master. He always imagined that they must see him as he truly was, as he couldn't help remembering, a poor peasant boy gifted his position by a sad, dependent old man.

In port things were different, connections were glancing, the past unimportant. Looking through his glass he saw fashionable ladies with silk-ribboned hats and fat, well-dressed gentlemen, their gold pocket watches glinting in the sun. It wasn't like the strict uniform of seamen, where every detail made the difference between ranks. It was the elaborate dress of merchants and their wives, that had nothing to do with rank and everything to do with wealth. They seemed as though dressed for a play, and he saw no reason why he should not be one of the players.

A little later he sat in the bar of the King's Arms inn. French was being spoken all around him, though it was a variety he could not understand. It was hard to believe that less than a mile away out on the rock sat an English garrison ready for an attack by France. Most of the men around him regarded him with indifference. He was just another one of the strange foreign men who crossed their paths many times each day. When he listened carefully he could hear the rough edges of other languages: some Dutch – he recognized this tongue now from his time in Amsterdam – another northern tongue he had encountered before, Danish perhaps, and some Spanish too, and through it all suddenly a voice in English, polite, but with the distinctively pronounced consonants of a Scotsman.

Fullarton felt an unexpected twinge, like a distant memory. He turned around to find the source of the voice.

'And there he was,' the voice was saying to two other men who sat near him and listened intently, 'about to board her – his warrant in his hand, and us all watching. I had stored the cargo deep down beneath the salt, but you know that he had a reputation for a thorough job. When along comes one of the local lads, in his boat, slides up behind him sleek as a kitten, and before you know it he's hooked the exciseman's warrant and dropped it in the sea.'

'What did he do?' asked one of the men with a laugh.

'Well, he drew his pistol, of course, made a big show of that, turned it on the poor fisher lad, but the lad's put up his hands, saying, sorry, sir, 'twas a pure accident, sir, and meanwhile every man on the ship's drawn their pistols and aimed it at the exciseman, for threatening a local lad. Then we told it to him directly, that if he was to run telling any stories about what he thought his version of events was, we'd see to it that every man in the bailiwick would know to set him straight. That put him in a sweet pickle, all right. He was fair backed into it. For what could he do but promise us his silence, for fear of his life? There's many who would dispose of him soon enough, that don't care much about the consequences, and of that he's but too well acquainted.' He laughed heartily at this and was joined by the others at the table.

During the course of the conversation Fullarton had walked up and sat himself down at the speaker's table. This had attracted the attention of the other men, who looked at him, perhaps taking him for a drunk, but the Scotsman, facing away and intent on his story, had not noticed. Now he turned and, seeing Fullarton, made a start away.

'Who in God's name are you, sir, to appear from nowhere like that?' He took a deep breath and then narrowed his eyes. 'You'll be one of his agents,' he said.

Fullarton saw the other two put their hands to their waists, where they carried handsome swordsticks.

'No,' said Fullarton casually. 'Just an honest trader, home-sick for the voice of a fellow countryman.'

'By God, it's a Scotsman,' the man cried. Immediately he stood up, laughed, and shook Fullarton's hand. 'The name's Bell,' he said. 'Thomas Bell. How do you do, sir. Let me buy you a drink. By God, that accent's like music to my ears.'

'Captain John Fullarton,' said Fullarton, bowing.

'Excellent, a fine name,' said Bell. 'A fine name indeed. And what kind of trade are you in?'

'Fish, mainly,' said Fullarton. 'And a little wine.'

'Claret, of course,' said Bell, a gleam in his eye.

'And Burgundy.'

'Ah, I like a good Burgundy, too,' said Bell. 'But both go down easily enough with a good supper of roasted collops.' He licked his fat lips to demonstrate.

'Indeed,' said Fullarton, admiring the gold brocade on Bell's frock coat.

Bell was looking Fullarton up and down, sizing him up. 'But you're not an ordinary Scotsman are you? A Highlander of some sort, are you not?' he said.

'Orcadian,' said Fullarton.

'I knew it was some northern tongue. Been in Stromness myself,' said Bell. 'A dark, treacherous piece of water that, and cold. There was no getting warm, I remember. But a busy little place, for one so far north, full of the Hudson Bay folk with their furs and suchlike. Almost joined one, once, but that's another story.' He paused, looking away, lost in reminiscence.

'I'm not from Stromness,' said Fullarton.

Bell turned and looked at him strangely. It was a look that seemed for a moment to remind Fullarton of his father. 'No, it seems not,' Bell said. 'Well, as it so happens, we do have something in common, for I'm in the wine business myself.'

Fullarton said nothing, but raised his glass.

'Well,' said Bell, who had finished his. 'There's not much room in these glasses, is there? What about a bottle?'

'Let me,' said Fullarton, opening his purse. What he had would not last long, but for some reason he felt it was worth taking the gamble on this man.

They sat, and drank a bottle between them, and soon the other men left. Bell told Fullarton his life history. He was from Leith, had gone to sea as a boy, and hated it, which was why he had almost deserted at Stromness and signed away his life to the Hudson's Bay ships. But then he had found a way to make a little extra money, the one we all know about, he said, winking at Fullarton, and had finally earned enough to run his own voyages, trading in claret from Leith. Before too long, however, the port got all clogged up with traders, the duties were high, and the excisemen grew a little more active; then he heard about this place, these islands where the burden of government did not yet restrict the bounty of free trade and a hard-working man could go about his business and be rewarded for it, without being robbed of the proceeds by those who had taken no part in the gaining of them. As he said this Fullarton observed that his face grew redder and redder until the end of his nose was almost purple with rage, and Fullarton felt obliged to interrupt lest the man should explode right there in the tavern.

'You told a good story there,' he said, trying to appease him, 'of how you managed to outwit them.'

Immediately Bell's face changed, and spread into a broad

smile. 'Indeed we did,' he said, beginning to laugh, 'indeed we did.' He leaned forward until his face was within an inch of Fullarton's and even through his own claret fog the smell of alcohol seemed to singe the hairs of his nose. 'Now listen, Fullarton,' said Bell, 'I can tell you're a man of taste, and a Scotsman too, so it's no wonder.'

Fullarton nodded, smiling. He wasn't sure if he was even an Orcadian any more, let alone a Scotsman. But Bell seemed to want him to be, so he said nothing.

'Come,' said Bell, 'let me show you a rare secret. Come with me, and I'll show you what a good Burgundy really tastes like.'

'That sounds like a proposition I can't refuse,' said Fullarton, 'from such a gentleman.'

It was flattery, but Fullarton was also impressed by this man Bell. He was rich. By his dress, that much was clear. He seemed to be well known, respected and popular. But more than that, he had a kind of warm confidence in himself that was infectious. To stick with him a while, thought Fullarton, may be no bad move.

They left the bar with Fullarton already slightly dizzy from the speed at which he had necked his wine. Bell, however, seemed unaffected, and Fullarton struggled to keep up with him. The streets were narrow, a little dirty and packed with men, women, children and animals. The houses were tall, like those of Edinburgh, giving the passageways a darkish appearance. There were only a few main thoroughfares, and they seemed to walk along them all, but each street was lined with little open-windowed shops selling beautiful silverware, confectionery, shoes, cloaks and fashionable hats displayed directly alongside oranges and lemons, ivory-tipped canes and snuffboxes. There were tobacconists and tanners, seamstresses and carpenters. Fullarton counted no fewer than four butchers, with carcasses hung near shaded windows to dry and ripen, the sweet vinegar smell of them mingling with the harbour smells of rotting fish, brine and oil. He felt his mouth water. The ship's supply of fresh meat had run dry some weeks ago and he had been surviving on the last of the salt fish. They passed a large square signed Le Grand Carrefour where the houses seemed handsome and well maintained. Merchants strolled past, both respectably and expensively dressed, leading elegant ladies in elaborate sacque robes. Everything he saw improved his opinion of the town, and of the man leading him through it.

Where the tall buildings ended they came upon some lower, magazine-type buildings. Bell pointed to a large, newly built warehouse. The water came up to its edge and Fullarton could see men working, unloading hogsheads from small launches and transporting them into the building.

Once away from the sea breeze it was quite hot, and Fullarton began to pull at his thick velvet waistcoat. He wouldn't take it off, however, because the shirt beneath was not of the same quality, and he was glad when they stepped inside the cool vaults of the cellars. There he could see row upon row of hogsheads stacked up against the stone walls.

'The finest Burgundy,' said Bell, 'that you'll taste anywhere. And over there' – he waved his hand towards the adjoining cellars – 'French brandy, some Dutch gin, and a little Caribbean rum.'

Fullarton looked around and let out a little whistle of breath. 'This must be worth a fortune,' he said.

'Oh, it is,' said Bell, smiling. 'I am worth a fortune, in fact.'

He pulled out three bottles, one of Burgundy, one of claret, and another of brandy.

'Here,' he said, 'a sample. Follow me.'

They walked back a little, along the narrow street, until they reached the door of a large dwelling house. It seemed grand, Fullarton thought, for a lower-storey dwelling, so close to the animal filth of the street, but he had noticed that the people of the south seemed to prefer it that way.

'My current lodgings,' said Bell. 'Not ideal, but they're only temporary. We're having a new house built outside the town.'

Fullarton looked around as they went in; a housemaid met them and took their coats. They were in a large hall with several doors leading off it, and they entered a small parlour, expensively furnished with gilding, painted walls and chairs of fine silk chinoiserie. Fullarton had never been in such grand surroundings, but said nothing, not wanting to appear awed. He sat down in the largest of the gilded chairs.

'I admire your taste,' he said to Bell.

Bell was busy opening a bottle of black liquid.

'My wife takes care of all that,' he said. 'She says I'm colour blind.'

'Your good taste was then in choosing her,' said Fullarton, in what he thought was a gracious tone, but then wondered if it was a little crawling. He watched as Bell poured a little of the black liquid into two small glasses and tilted it to observe as it slid down the inside, leaving a clear glutinous film behind it.

'Yes, yes,' said Bell impatiently. 'Now taste that, and tell me you've tasted better.'

Fullarton took a sip. It tasted much the same as any other wine to him. But he smacked his lips, smiled and nodded. 'That's good stuff,' he said.

The maid had lit a fire, but the two men were already glowing as they finished the Burgundy and started on the claret. Fullarton looked around again at the sumptuous fabrics, the tapestries, Dutch paintings and gilded French chairs, and he seemed to grow even warmer.

'It seems there's money to be made in these parts,' said Fullarton, stroking the arm of his chair.

'Indeed there is, for those who know how to make it,' said Bell. 'Keeping your eyes open, and never closing them again. That's the key.' And as he said this he sat forward and stared intently at Fullarton. 'You looking to make some?' he asked.

Fullarton tilted up his head. 'Always.'

'I have some work for an able seaman,' Bell said. 'An accomplished captain, and a gentleman, such as yourself.'

Fullarton nodded, and couldn't restrain the small smile that crept over his face at being called a gentleman. And why shouldn't he be? he thought. He was certainly dressed like one. 'Go on,' he said.

'But it must be said that there are risks,' said Bell.

'There are always risks,' said Fullarton. 'Are the rewards worth it?'

'In this case,' said Bell, 'most definitely.'

Fullarton nodded for him to continue, and Bell assumed a confidential air.

'You are to transport a ship of my cargo to England. On arriving somewhere near the bay of Looe, or Cawsand, or some nearby port' – he waved his hand vaguely – 'you are to hover, and look out for a signal. When you see it, some small fishing smacks will come out to you on the pretext of selling you some local wares. If they are my own men, they'll give you a watchword, so that you can know them. They'll then give you a weight of gold. They always pay before the cargo is sold. That's important, mind, else I couldn't be sure they would not run away with it. They will come back at night, and under cover of darkness you will give them the cargo, save for a couple of hogsheads, which you will then take into the town, and sell legitimately. When you return, you shall see your share.'

Fullarton listened carefully, and looked thoughtful. 'And what would that share be?' he asked.

Bell laughed approvingly. 'A quarter share of the profits. A good deal, I think you'll agree.'

Fullarton hesitated, nodding slightly. It was a good deal, what he expected, but something told him he could push for more. 'Seems to me,' he said at last, 'that I'm the one taking the risks, yet you make the most part of the profit.'

Bell stopped smiling and looked hard at him. 'That's what I'm offering. Do you want this work or no?'

Fullarton didn't falter. 'I'm willing to do it in principle,' he said, and he saw Bell's face lighten. It was the sign he had been looking for. 'But it has to be worth more than what I can make alone. A third share,' he said, returning

Bell's gaze, 'and I'd be happy to take it on.' He saw Bell thinking. He looked disgruntled, but Fullarton had calculated he would have no choice. He would not have asked a stranger to do this work if he had not found it hard to recruit of late.

'Done,' said Bell.

'But why,' asked Fullarton, now that the deal was settled, 'have you asked me, someone you've just met, when there must be many men in this port who would jump at an opportunity of ready cash?'

'Ah,' said Bell, beginning to slur. 'It's hard to get the men engaged in a little free trade now that the war is on. They prefer to operate privateers.'

This caught Fullarton's attention. He had noticed the number of posters in the town advertising sales of French prizes. 'They do well out of it?'

'Some make nothing, some do tolerably well,' said Bell. 'Men will always chase greater and greater riches. The greater the prize, the more they'll risk. But some things are not worth risking, like life, for instance.'

Fullarton blinked. He wasn't sure he understood. 'It depends on the prize, I suppose.'

Bell waved his hand away, to signal that he was getting tired of this conversation. 'You're young,' he said. 'I'm old, I know what it means to die. Stick with me, and you'll find the easiest way to riches. Now,' he went on, 'if you are approached by customs officers, you must say that all the wine is of Portuguese origin, and be careful to hide the tobacco among the salt, and the good French wine among the poorer stuff.'

Fullarton nodded again. 'I can do that,' he said coolly.

Bell was pulling out the cork from another bottle. He looked up and grinned. 'Wine is for men in the first flush of youth. Port is for the English, but brandy,' he said, with an uneven smile on his face, 'brandy is the drink of Scotsmen, and of real men everywhere.'

Fullarton laughed in return and held out his glass, as Bell tipped out the contents, half in the glass, half on the oriental carpet.

~

Some time later Fullarton awoke, aware that his head was next to the toe of a woman's small silk boot. The toe of the boot edged towards his chin and he raised his head.

'Fancy,' said a woman's voice, 'it moves.'

Fullarton sat up, rubbing the top of his head. 'I beg your pardon, madam,' he said. 'I must have fallen asleep.'

'Clearly,' she said. 'But you do know that we have beds for that kind of thing?'

Fullarton looked around the room. The fire had burned down to an ember, and Bell was nowhere to be seen.

'Where's Bell?' he asked.

'Nursing his sore head in bed,' said the woman, 'where he should stay, since he can cause less trouble there.' She held out her hand as Fullarton stood up unsteadily and her eyes closed a little, cat-like, in a kind of sly smile. 'I'm Mrs Bell,' she said. 'Margot.'

'What time is it?' asked Fullarton.

'Late,' said Mrs Bell.

'I've no idea what happened,' said Fullarton. 'We were just sitting here sharing a drink and talking . . .' He looked around and saw his coat over a chair. He picked it up and walked unsteadily towards the door.

'Where are you going at this hour?' asked Mrs Bell. She seemed alarmed.

'Back to my lodgings,' said Fullarton. 'I won't impose on you any further.'

'Goodness, no, it's two o'clock in the morning,' said Mrs Bell. 'There's nobody on the streets except robbers and murderers. I won't hear of it. You must sleep here.'

She took his arm firmly and led him into a small chamber. It was no more than a cupboard really, but it had been fitted out with a little bed.

'This is where our housemaid sleeps, normally,' said Mrs Bell, 'but she left this evening. Her mother is ill, and she's on her way to the country to visit her, so we are having to make do ourselves. It's not much, but more comfortable than the floor, I would have thought.'

'No doubt,' said Fullarton. 'Thank you.'

'Do let me know if there's anything you need,' she said.

'Thank you,' he said again.

But still she stood. 'Anything at all,' she said.

'Thank you, again,' said Fullarton.

At last she smiled and left him alone.

Fullarton lay in the dark, listening to the noises of the strange house. He had always been able to sleep anywhere, but suddenly the comfort of the bed and the warmth of the room overwhelmed him, and he fell into a deeper sleep than he had had in many years.

~

When he woke he heard voices from the next room. Opening the door slowly, he saw that Bell, looking red-faced and fresh, and his wife were already seated at the table taking breakfast, both fully dressed.

'At last,' said Bell. 'I wondered if you'd been poisoned, there was so little movement in you.'

'Did I oversleep?' said Fullarton.

'Just a little. Come and take some tea,' said Mrs Bell. 'But how rude of me, perhaps you'd like to wash. There's a basin and jug in that room,' she said, pointing through to a little antechamber. 'Go on in.'

Fullarton went into the little room. He took off his shirt and stood splashing the ice-cold water over his face and neck. He turned around and saw Mrs Bell standing at the open door.

'I'll just close this,' she said, with her sly smile. 'Give you some privacy.'

As he dried himself with the linen cloth he heard voices in the next room. He strained to hear them as he buttoned his shirt.

'You like him?' Bell's wife was saying.

'A little rough around the edges perhaps, but I think he's a fine young man for the job,' said Bell. 'Reminds me of myself, somehow, when I started out.'

'And he is unmarried?' said Mrs Bell. 'Fancy, such a well-made young man.'

'Well made,' said Bell, 'but without means, as far as I know.'

'You can fix that, my dear.'

'Now don't be starting one of your schemes, Margot,' said Bell, his voice tired.

There was a tinkle of laughter. 'Benevolent schemes, that's all.'

They fell into the silent clatter of their forks as Fullarton entered the room again.

9

For days the sea was the colour of plaster, dirty white and formless, and creeping arms of fog seemed to strangle the ship. There was little difference between being indoors and being outdoors, since the damp was everywhere, so Mary chose to stay on deck. She could see nothing except the white void of sky and sea, but at least she could fill her lungs with real air, and savour the salt taste on her tongue.

Finally, on the fourth day, she felt a lift in the air around her. A few breaths of warm sunlight were beginning to burn through the haar. She looked into the water, and caught a sudden flash of colour; something was moving in the depths, something glossy, like oil. Then the creature leapt into the air, and she saw several more behind it.

'What are they?' she asked the sailor nearest to her, as she watched the strange multicoloured fishes, flipping and casting little rainbows into the air.

The man took his arms out of a pot of grease, and turned to look at her quizzically. 'Dolphins,' he said, tying in the cord. He spat on his rope-reddened hands and rubbed them together with the grease. He moved closer, leering a little, and Mary caught a stiff breath of fish-scented oil and salt beef.

'They're quite beautiful,' said Mary. She had never seen

anything like them before, and though she had edged unconsciously away from the sailor, she saw that his face had softened. He leaned on the rail, watching the creatures with a childlike expression of wonder and interest that he could not conceal.

'There's good eating on them,' he said.

'You're not going to kill them?' said Mary, horrified, not least because they didn't look at all appetizing.

The man shook his head, laughing. 'Not while we've got a couple of barrels of beef and pork left, anyway! You've not been at sea much, have you, ma'am?'

Mary shook her head, a little shyly.

'You'll get used to it,' he said. 'Master's last wife loved it. A fearless creature she was. And handsome, too,' he said.

'William must have loved her very much,' Mary said.

'Aye,' he said, looking sideways at her, curious. 'I suppose he must've, not that he'd've shown it to us. She seemed fond enough of him. And he was distraught all right, when she was gone. Never spoke for days. A tragedy, all right, and a mystery too.'

Mary looked up. 'Why a mystery? She was drowned, wasn't she?'

'So they say. She'd taken to night wanderings, you see. We all saw her, when we were up on our watch. We'd call out to her but she never answered. It was like she was in some kind of daze. Nobody dared to wake her, because they said she was sleepwalking. You never wake a sleep-walker, and she always found her way back to bed all right. I used to look out for her, keep her in sight. I didn't think any of the lads would dare touch her, the captain would have had them hanged, but you can never be sure. There was something in her eyes, I thought. Something more than sleep. They were all watery and empty, like she'd ta'en a drink.'

'She was in liquor?' Mary asked, shocked.

'Maybe,' said the man. 'But I don't think so. You'd have smelled it. Maybe it was something in her mind, some demon or other. Or some fever. She'd been seeing a lot of the surgeon, for one malady and another. He said it was only the effect of some balance of humours gone wrong. He tried her on all kinds of tinctures of this and that, as well as odd diets and whatnot. None o' them ever did her any good, though. When she came out of her cabin she was wrapped in so many cloaks you could hardly see her.'

'How did they know she'd been drowned?' asked Mary.

'Nobody could find her. Her cabin door was open and no sign of her. A whole day they spent, searching every corner of the ship. Then the next day somebody spotted her body, floating in the water. The master had all the men out that'd been on watch that night. There had been mutterings, and the captain knew it. There were some who thought she wasn't good enough for him. And some who didn't like her on account of her foreign accent.'

'Where was she from?' asked Mary.

'Nobody knew. Anywhere and everywhere. She had a strange way of speaking, a whole mixture of places in one. But none of them had a bad word to say about her then, they were all terrified of being accused of murder, I'd guess. So the master ordered the crew to be flogged, all except the cook. Nobody likes to offend the cook.' He gave a short, bitter laugh. 'Perhaps they're afraid he'll poison them. I wouldn't put it past the old buzzard.' He laughed again, and then appeared anxious.

'Not that the cook would do anything like that, you understand. He'd taken a liking to her anyway. But eventually one of the boys cried out in his agony that he'd seen a figure, trying to climb on to the bowsprit, and that was it. Never heard no more about it.'

Mary wondered why William had never spoken about any of this. She looked at the sailor and then out to the sea that was widening around them. She felt a sudden unease. Her earlier sense of excitement at entering the unknown was fading. Perhaps it was the cold. A thin film of mist had drawn over the sun, and the dolphins had turned grey in the water.

'How long before we reach land?' she asked, suddenly longing for the security of solid ground.

'Oh, it'll be at least a week yet, the wind's against us,' said the man. 'Funny,' he went on, watching the dolphins again, 'they've got the whole run of the sea, yet they'll follow the ship for hours.'

There was a shout from the bos'n behind them, and she looked round, seeing the man she had spoken to leaping on to the rope ladder beside them and climbing on to the foremast to furl a sail. She watched the tattooed soles of his feet as they disappeared into the rigging.

But she had discovered that it was not the bos'n, who commanded them on a daily basis, who was the most important among the crew, but the cook, who controlled that essential aspect of their lives, their sustenance, and whose galley was the only means of drying clothes or keeping warm. When Mary had told William she wanted to help in the kitchen, he had hesitated.

'You'll have some difficulty with the cook,' he had said.

'Surely he'll be glad of the help,' she had replied. 'I can't bear to be idle.'

'By all means then, do as you like,' he had said, with his usual impatience.

But William had been right. The cook relished his position, and was not pleased to have Mary taking any part of it. When she came into the galley he refused to meet her eye. On the first night she was to help serve the meal, she asked which food was to be put out, but he only pointed vaguely to the cooking pots and then at the crockery. She arranged the plates as she thought best, and even added a few decorative flourishes of her own, taught to her by Mrs Inglis. When the cook saw them, he took them off, before carrying the plates out to the table. She had watched, furious, but she had bit her lip. She did not want any dispute between herself and the cook to upset William.

Today she remembered that William had told her to serve the beef that evening. He said the pork they had the night before was foul. So she left the dolphins and the deck and made her way to the little galley. When she reached the galley door she saw that the room was empty, though the fire was lit and she could smell the round, sharp smell of melted pigfat. She looked around, checking that nothing had been left unattended. Neither the cook nor his boy could be seen. But as she turned to leave she heard an odd noise, a kind of strangled squeal, coming from somewhere in the room.

She stopped and listened carefully. It might have been the cat, she thought, after a mouse. She listened again, and heard nothing. Then, just as she was about to go, there was a slow rustling.

She decided that it must be mice, but as she reached the door, something made her turn back. Standing beside the table, his eyes darkened and bloodshot, was the cook's boy.

Mary was shaken by his sudden appearance, and concealed her fear with anger. 'Where did you come from?' she demanded. 'I was here a moment ago, and there was nobody here.' The boy had been up to something, she was sure. Perhaps he was stealing food.

The cook's boy had a bad stutter and looked at her with his pale quivering eyes. 'Nnnnn . . .' he said.

'Try a different word,' she said, trying to be kind, but unable to conceal her impatience. She ought to feel some pity towards the boy, she thought. He was young, only a few years younger than herself. He was an orphan, like most of the young boys on ships, but there was something about him that she recoiled from, despite her good intentions. His long hair lay lank around his shoulders and his face had the jaundiced colour and dry, flaked texture of the sick. It was something more than his ill health, however, or his poverty, that repulsed her. It was the way his desperate state was mingled with an expression of leering arrogance. Who was he to be so proud of what he was, to feel himself superior to her?

'I . . . I was in the pantry, ma'am,' he murmured. 'J . . . just checking on supplies.'

She took a step forward into the room and looked at

him more carefully. A greasy black line had formed on his cheek.

'Have you been crying?' she asked, trying to make her voice sound soft.

'Oh, don't mind him, ma'am,' said the cook, suddenly appearing from behind her. 'He's always snivelling.'

She jumped and turned around.

'Didn't mean to frighten you,' he said. He walked to the fire and started stirring something in a pot.

'Please don't creep up on me like that,' she snapped. She looked back at the boy. It was true enough, she thought, he was always snivelling. Most times she saw him he had a greasy trail running down his face, and he regularly wiped the greenish slime from his nose with his dirty sleeves. She swallowed. The room smelled bad, of cooking fat, guilt and fear. Then the boy turned his head, and she saw the blue-tinged balloon of skin bulging on the side of his head.

Sickened, she moved towards him. 'What's that?' she said, reaching out her hand.

'I'm fine,' he said, backing away.

'He's always bumping into one thing or another,' said the cook. 'Clumsy boy, he is.'

She looked again at the boy. He was clumsy, it was true. He frequently knocked into her when passing, as if he had no awareness of other objects in the room. Even now he kneeled on a chair, balanced precariously as he swung the chair on to two legs.

'Did you beat him?' she asked the cook.

'Not that he doesn't deserve it,' said the cook, 'but no, I did not.'

She stared into the cook's face, and he scowled back at her. She didn't believe him, but suddenly she lost the energy to do anything about it.

'Well, get some kind of dressing on it, anyway. It's not clean, near the food. He's your boy, after all. Oh, and William will have the beef tonight.'

'I've boiled up the pork.'

Mary looked at him. 'But my husband wants the beef.'

'Pork's got to be eaten,' said the cook. 'Can't waste the food. The master understands that.'

'Not if the meat is rotten,' said Mary.

'Ma'am,' said the cook, his voice now low and scored through with an edge that made her step towards the door, 'I don't serve rotten meat.'

'I'm only telling you what the captain wants,' said Mary. 'And I want to go back and tell him what he wants to hear. Perhaps you'd like me to recount, instead, how the cook mistreats the boy entrusted to his care.'

The cook held her stare. 'Do it if you like, miss. I told you the truth. The master trusts me.'

Mary coloured. 'Don't address me as miss,' she said.

The cook disappeared to the pantry, and the boy continued to stare at her sulkily, while she fought to contain the pressure building behind her eyes. Even when the cook reappeared with the beef in his arms she felt close to tears, and was forced to leave without another word. As she walked away she bit down hard on her lip. She couldn't understand what was happening to her. Before she had come on board the ship it had been years since she had cried, not since she was a child. Now at least once, every day, she felt that pressure in her head, the tightening of her throat.

She knew that she would have to try to find a way to get along with the cook, but she didn't see how she could do it without showing her weakness, and she refused to give him that satisfaction.

She decided she would find William, tell him how she felt, how hard she was finding it all. Perhaps he would understand, would speak to the cook, or find her some other occupation. There was no sign of him on deck. She looked into the gunroom, but there was nobody there except the gunner, sleeping on a bench, with the charts and maps spread out upon the table. It was only as she was making her way back to her cabin that she heard a faint voice that sounded distinctly like William's. Then she heard another, low and urgent, and recognized it as Mr Cole the surgeon's.

Backing along the corridor, she came to Mr Cole's cabin. The door was closed, but it was badly weathered and cracked, so that it was possible to kneel down and see through the cracks into part of the room. She could only see the legs of her husband, who seemed to be lying down, but she had a clear view of the surgeon's head as he sat on the bunk beside him.

'I do understand,' the surgeon was saying, 'but you must remember this stuff costs money, and we have to make the supplies last. What will happen if we are attacked and I must perform surgery on men with nothing more than a bottle of brandy for support?'

'It's the only thing that takes it away,' William was saying.

'Takes what away?' came the surgeon's voice, and his tone was impatient.

'The memory,' said William.

Then Mary shrank back as she caught a movement, and a pale patch of skin appeared to cover the hole in the door for a moment. As soundlessly as she could, she brought her eye to the hole again. The surgeon had moved, so that he sat at the foot of the bed, next to William's legs.

'You mustn't blame yourself,' she heard him say.

'I can't control it,' William said.

'I'll give you a little, just enough to quell the nerves,' the surgeon said. 'But you must remain strong.' Then he leaned forward and lowered his voice. 'Remember,' he whispered, 'only one more voyage.'

'Only one more,' repeated William drowsily. His legs twitched.

'You don't know how fortunate you are,' said the surgeon. 'She will make a fine wife, and a fine mother.'

Mary realized they were talking about her, and then she sprang back in fright as the ship's bell sounded. There was a scuffling movement from the room, and she somehow found her feet and scurried away as quietly as she could. She sat in her cabin, thinking over all she had heard. She wondered about the guilt that William had mentioned. She wondered about what the surgeon had said, that this would be their last voyage. If that was true, then was he planning to return home? But they had barely left Leith. She had not yet seen any of the places she thought she might see.

The gold clock on the wall continued to tick loudly. But there was a change, as though the pressure of the air had grown heavy; the candle began to dance, and then dimmed.

The hairs on her arms appeared to stand up, and she wrapped an extra coat around herself as she became suddenly cold.

At that moment the ship made a strong lurching motion to the larboard side. Mary was almost knocked off the bed. She heard noises from the deck above, and went to the door. There were the usual shouts, the usual unintelligible commands and scattering of feet running for stations. But something was different. Their rhythm was uneven, disorganized.

She made her way along the corridor, holding on to the sides of the walls as the ship was now beginning to roll. She climbed the wooden ladder to the deck, the surface of it already made slippery by the rain.

The wind hit her first, throwing a grapeshot of hail at her face, and she turned away. When she looked back she saw that all hands were on deck. Men were running back and forward, climbing ropes, hanging from yardarms, furling sail. One was tying down the scuttlebutt that held the fresh water, others were tying down the few chests and barrels that had been stored on deck. The wind snapped at the remaining sail. The hens and ducks were shut into their pens and these were attached with long straps to iron rings on the deck.

Now she saw a wave come over the stern of the ship, and a deeper lurch than before. She turned to go back down to the cabin, and was hit by a sudden squall of wind that seemed to have circled round the wall of the upper cabins and come in search of her.

'What are you doing up here?'

She jumped a little as she heard William's voice sharp

behind her head. He was still some distance away, the wind having carried his cry to her ear, already sealed into his tarred watch coat and hat.

'I came to see what the noise was about. I'm just going down now,' she said.

'You'll get soaked. Go down below at once. It's nothing to worry about,' he added, but his eyes told a different story. 'Just shut the cabin door, and make sure everything is secured and lashed in tight to the moorings.'

~

The air in the cabin was as cold as on deck. It gave a high-pitched whistle. As the ship moved her frame cracked, heaved and moaned. Metal clanged and ropes were plucked, guitar-like, by the wind. She heard more shouts above her head, the thuds of running footsteps. Mary picked up one book after another, but replaced them all on the shelves, unable to focus on the text. Each time a great wave hit the flanks of the ship, it was like thundering hooves, while the rain and waves washing the deck were like the crack of rifles. The door of the cabin resembled a little stable door that opened in two halves, and she had left the top half open so that she could hear what was happening above. It was better to know the danger they were in than to sit in antici-pation. But as the beating of the waves grew louder and the lurch of the ship more violent, she decided to shut the door properly. Just as she was swinging it to and reaching for the iron latch, she felt a spray of water at her head, followed by a large wave that crashed into the cabin through the open door, extinguishing the candle, knocking over the little stool and soaking the scarlet bedspread.

Mary was drenched from head to toe, and had the wind knocked from her chest. She coughed out salt water. She closed the door at once and secured it, and the water began to drain away through the floorboards. She searched in the darkness for another candle. By the time she managed to light one she could hear the men climbing into the hold and the officers coming down to the cabins. She heard banging and rattling and then one of the men shouting, 'Put the deadlights up.' She knew what this meant. The weather was as bad as it could be and there was nothing they could do but shut themselves in and hope for the best.

She picked up all the clothing and possessions that were near the door and moved them to the furthest corner of the tiny room. The light was now flickering wildly as the candle, which was already made fast to the table with cord, swayed in its moorings. She lay down on the damp bed, listening to the creaking and heaving of the great vessel, and thought of her mother, her aunt and uncle, her own little room, the house she had been so desperate to leave. She waited for William to come and comfort her, to tell her all was as it should be, or that the storm would not grow worse, but she saw and heard no one. Had it not been for the whalebone stuck between her ribs, she would have curled into herself like a whelk.

Days passed like this, sleepless, slow and uneven. The cook's fire had to stay out until the deadlights were put down, but the cook brought her cold ham and biscuit, and he was the only soul she saw. He was still unsmiling, but didn't leer as he had before. Away from the galley, he seemed more humbled.

'The swell seems a little reduced,' she said to him one day, when he brought her meal, but he only shook his head.

'You've only got used to it,' he said, and he must have seen her face fall, because he added, in a kinder voice, 'No storm ever lasted for ever. It'll end, one way or the other.' But Mary did not feel comforted by these words.

Still William didn't come. Mary felt as though she were balancing on the tip of a wave, and the slightest motion would be enough to send her plunging into the depths of the swell.

~

One morning she became aware of noises next door. William must be in his cabin. At first she felt relief; perhaps this meant the storm was nearing an end. She got up and opened the door that led to his room, but when she saw him she stopped. He was kneeling on the ground, facing away from her, and appeared to be shaking. At first she thought he was crying, and almost stepped forward to comfort him, but as he raised up his body a little she saw that he was speaking. He was not crying at all, but praying. He spoke fast, but his words were jumbled, and she could make little sense of them, except that he was praying to God to save them, and praying for forgiveness, and somewhere within it all, she heard the word Elizabeth.

Mary quietly shut the door that connected their small rooms. She felt as though she had seen something she should not have seen, intruded on something almost indecent, a kind of desperate, private grief.

It seemed like weeks, but in fact it was only two days later when the uneven lurch of the vessel grew more regular. Then, very suddenly, it ended. The ship stilled, the hatches and shutters were opened. Mary opened the door tentatively, came up on deck, and saw the damage that had been done. The sails were badly torn. They no longer made a gentle pat-pat-pat but a fierce put-put-put in the remaining stiff breeze. Feathers and treacle and broken glass were strewn all over the deck, and a few hens wandered loose, pecking among them. The men worked on hands and knees to clear up the mess, their own clothes filthy and sodden.

But the most damaged of all, it seemed, was William. He was fidgeting and anxious, and even more irritable than before. He found fault with everything she did, the food she served, the way she laid out his clothes, the neatness of the cabin. Mary knew that she would never find the moment to speak to him about the cook, or about the conversation she had heard, so she got on as best she could, smiling at the cook even when he scowled at her, dealing with William's comments largely by ignoring them entirely. He responded by ignoring her in return, save for the occasional evening visit to her cabin to make unpassionate love in the dark.

The only thing that calmed him, she noticed, was the presence of the surgeon, and she saw them together more and more. Sometimes Mr Cole would visit his cabin, and she would bring drinks to both men. She would offer to leave them alone, but Mr Cole always insisted that she stayed, and William did not object. This was almost the only time she spent with her husband. She would bring through some of the men's mending, which she preferred to her fancy work, since it made her feel of use, and quietly sew in the corner of the room while they drank brandy and talked. Most of what they said was about trade, and sailing, and sometimes medicine, and most of it was unintelligible. They talked as though she wasn't there, but she heard every word. One conversation in particular caught her interest.

'You know my father has married that woman,' said Mr Cole. 'I knew she'd get her claws into him at last, and she'll no doubt find many ways to spend what little money he has left.'

William shook his head. 'Your father is more comfortable than you think,' he said.

'Perhaps he just won't let me see any of it,' said Mr Cole, with a coarse laugh. 'You were lucky you never had any of that to worry about.'

'I'm not sure one's parents dying when one is only five years old can be described as luck,' said William.

'But you were well provided for. Although your uncle was strict.'

'Oh, yes, he was strict,' said William. His eyes had glassed over and Mary knew that he was likely soon to turn angry or sentimental. 'But he knew the way to do things. He taught me well, about discipline and organization. And regardless of his money, I've come to where I am through my own efforts. I'm proud of that.'

'I suppose the security of wealth makes it easier to be confident of success,' said Mr Cole, so softly that William did not appear to hear. But there was a bitterness in his tone that Mary caught. She looked up, and met his eye.

William shook his head. 'I don't need my uncle's money. I never did.'

Mary thought he looked on the edge of tears, and Mr Cole seemed uncomfortable.

'Well, that's very honourable of you,' said Mr Cole. He held up his glass. 'But finest French brandy doesn't get washed up on the beaches, now, does it?'

William only shrugged and filled his glass again.

The surgeon sighed, and looked down at his feet, smiling a little, with an air of resignation. 'What do you think, Mrs Jones?' he said. 'Is money necessary to happiness?'

Mary put down her sewing. 'I suppose some money is,' she said. 'Not great wealth, but security, yes.'

Mr Cole nodded, smiling.

'But I dare say it's possible to be unhappy even with wealth,' she said.

'Very wisely put,' said Mr Cole. 'And may I say, William, how beautiful your wife looks tonight.'

Mary coloured and looked down at her mending.

'Yes,' said William sarcastically. 'In her linsey-woolsey dress and working boots, she is positively radiant.'

Mary glared at him with a flush of anger. It was true that she was still dressed in her working clothes, but she had kept her best things for mealtimes and social occasions, and Mr Cole's visits were never announced.

'I dress as respectably as my wardrobe, and the occasion, allows,' she said quietly, but her voice simmered.

'Now, Mrs Jones, Mr Jones is only teasing,' said Mr Cole. 'Remember, William and I have been friends for many years.

He may seem a little brusque at times, but inside he is soft as butter. Is that not so, my friend?' And he leaned forward and placed his hand on William's knee, patting it gently.

William looked up, and gave a reluctant smile, first to the surgeon, and then to Mary. 'I'm only tired,' he said. 'It's been a long fortnight, and the storm didn't allow us much sleep.'

'Then I'll leave you alone,' said Mr Cole. 'With your wife.'

But when the door was closed William was silent. After sitting for a few moments Mary gathered up her sewing, said goodnight, and retired to her cabin. William was still sitting on his chair, in a kind of daze, and he barely raised his head, except to murmur a goodnight. In her cabin she let the mending fall into a heap and sat down on the cot. For the first time she found herself wishing that William would visit her, that she would feel his rough, fumbling hands in the darkness. For all that they brought her little pleasure, they were warm, they were human, and in some sense they belonged to her. But there was no sound, and when at last she crept to the connecting door and opened it, even considering a whispered invitation, the candle had been extinguished, and she heard only the deep laboured sounds of his breath.

10

She knew it was a boy by the size of his hands. They were small and pale, and tied to the rigging by the mainmast.

She felt an immediate flush of anger at William for punishing a child in this barbaric way. She almost ran towards him to stop it happening, but when the boy turned his head and she saw his face she recoiled a little. It was the cook's boy, and instead of looking frightened, or penitent, he leered at her, as if despising the weakness that caused her to pity him.

Behind him, she saw William. He had removed his coat and waistcoat so that he wore only his shirt, but his prized Kevenhuller was still under his arm. In his other hand he held a rope, knotted at the end, and he strode up and down the deck with it, as though frightened to touch the boy.

When almost at the other side of the deck, he suddenly turned round and ran at him. Mary saw a kind of seething venom in his expression, there for one moment only, just before he struck the blow. At once his face tightened and he turned his back on the boy, then revolved to strike again.

'What's he being punished for?' she asked a sailor who had appeared beside her.

'Cook says he's been stealing food.'

The boy flinched, but did not cry out at first. On the third blow, though, he let out a high-pitched whimper, and Mary stepped forward.

'William!' she cried out. 'Stop!'

William turned. He appeared shocked at first, but then he spoke calmly. 'Go below deck, madam,' he said. 'You shouldn't be here.'

'But, William,' she said, 'I think there's been a mistake.'

There was a low titter from some of the men behind him and William spun around.

'Who wants to be at the end of this next?' he growled at them, and they were quiet.

Mary thought quickly. She knew that an appeal to William because of the boy's youth would carry no weight. And in any case, it wasn't concern for the boy that made her intervene on his behalf. He had been flogged before. He probably welcomed it, since it gave him more reason to detest the world as he did. But she felt sure that the cook had orchestrated this somehow, to show her he had more influence over William than she did. The boy was always stealing food, and the cook and William both knew it. So why punish him now?

She took hold of William's arm gently.

'It's not the boy's fault. The cook blames him for everything, and he beats him too often,' she said in a low voice. 'He mistreats him. Even if he is stealing food, perhaps—'

'Mary, this is not the time. The boy is a thief.'

'But what if it's not true? How do you know the cook is telling the truth? Things are not always as clear as they appear to be, William.'

William looked at her for a moment and she saw the

flicker of uncertainty. But then his face became tight again and he gripped her arm. He hissed a spit breath of brandy in her face.

'Don't question my authority in front of the men,' he said, 'or you will feel the weight of my cord.' He said this second part loud enough for the crew to hear.

Mary looked at him, and then at the faces of the crew, focused on the couple, waiting for signs of weakness in either one of them. She shook off his arm and turned away as her eyes swelled. William tried to catch hold of her again but missed and only clutched the fabric of her dress. She tore it from his grasp and walked away.

In the cabin she waited. She had almost hoped that William would follow her down. She heard a few screams from the cook's boy, who had relented at last and given everyone the cruel entertainment they demanded, and then all was quiet. She could tell by the regularity of the noises above deck that things had returned to normal. She could feel the tension building in her head, accompanied by a sharp, stabbing pain. She closed her eyes.

When William walked into the cabin twenty minutes later, his waistcoat was still off, and the pressure of his elbow had dented the felt top of the Kevenhuller under his arm. He stood looking at her wildly, and as he did so he reached for his hat and tried to straighten it out. His hands were fumbling and his fingers shook.

'Can I . . . ?' she said, stretching out her arm for it.

'Damn it,' he said, throwing the hat on to the bed. 'Damn it, and damn you!'

'William,' she began, 'I'm sorry, it was only that . . .' She picked up the hat and nervously began to restore its shape. 'I had spoken to the cook before about his treatment of the boy,' she said. 'I didn't tell you because . . . because I thought you had enough to think of.'

'What kind of wife,' said William, starting to seethe again, 'questions her husband's authority in front of his men?'

'I only wanted you to be fair. I don't trust that cook.'

'I've known the cook a lot longer than I've known you, my dear, and I dare say I trust him better, too.'

Mary gave no reply. She had fixed the hat, and she put it down on the bed. Inside, she felt desperate. It had all come upon her at once: William's irritability, the cook's disdain, the boy's leering face, the distance from home. William said nothing more. After a while he picked up his hat, and Mary looked at him. She wanted to tell him how she really felt. The essence of it, that she was lonely, far from home, and all she really needed was for him to sit down for an hour or so and talk to her, let her ask questions, let her find out who he was, this man she had contracted to spend the rest of her life with. She wanted to break down and let him see the turmoil within her, but she couldn't. Her face remained immobile, unmoved.

'He doesn't like me,' she said at last. 'He doesn't want me in the kitchen.'

'Why don't you find something else to do?' said William quietly.

'Because I'd only be treading on somebody else's toes. You can't go anywhere on this ship without treading on someone's toes.'

'But you don't have to go anywhere,' said William. He sounded tired. 'You have everything you need right here.'

'How do you know what I need?' asked Mary fervently, her eyes wild and challenging.

William looked at the hat, and took a breath. He seemed to calm a little. 'Well then, why don't you tell me?'

'I need you to get rid of that cook. I can't be on this ship with him a moment longer.' She didn't really care so much whether the cook stayed or left. But she wanted to see William make some kind of sacrifice.

William sighed. He sat down beside her and spoke more quietly, taking a strand of her hair and letting it slide through his fingers.

'I can't do that,' he said. 'The cook has been with me from the beginning.'

'And I am supposed to be with you until the end,' said Mary. 'Yet you won't do this thing for me.' Her eyes filled at last, and William stroked the hair on the side of her head.

'You're no more than a child,' he said. 'I expect too much of you. I expect you to be like . . . like . . .'

'Like Elizabeth,' said Mary softly and deliberately.

She heard the noise before she felt the blow, a sharp clap on her temple, but strong enough to knock her over. It was only when she realized she had fallen on to the floor, and put her hand to her brow, that the stinging began.

'Don't,' said William, and his voice trembled as it came from deep in his throat. 'Don't ever mention her name again!'

She looked up at him, more confused than hurt. He looked as though he might hit her again, but instead he threw his hat at her and left the room. His aim was poor, and the hat caught a current of air and sailed upwards, landing on the floor at her feet. But the door had already slammed and William was gone.

A few tears ran down Mary's face, and then stopped. She wished they would start again, but they wouldn't. She could only look at herself in the glass, wondering what had happened, how she could repair things, what she would say to William when she saw him again, and how she could make her face look acceptable for supper. She powdered around her eyes to hide their redness. Then she tried powder on the swelling, but she couldn't hide it entirely. She attempted to make up for it with more rouge on her cheeks and lips, but it only made her look like a clown. In the end she rubbed it off. She tied a ribbon round her head, which looked ridiculous, and then an idea occurred to her. She knew that William would be furious, but nonetheless it seemed to satisfy some deep-rooted anger. She opened the drawer and pulled out Elizabeth's fine lace mob cap. She put it on her head.

When she entered the galley the cook refused to catch her eye. She carried the dishes into the gunroom and set them down. She noticed Mr Cole looking at her, and put her hand to her head to feel if the bruising was visible, but no, it was completely covered by the cap.

She smiled brightly at the small group as she worked, and then she turned and smiled at William too, meeting his eye. She saw him staring at her, his eye raised, looking at her cap. She leaned forward to put the plate down in front of him, and the lace of it brushed the side of his wig.

'You're wearing her cap,' he hissed.

'Yes,' she said. 'I can take it off if you like,' and she faced away from the rest of the group, lifting the cap a little so that he could see the bluish skin beneath.

William said nothing. He picked up his glass, and, seeing it was empty, became agitated.

'Get me some wine, won't you,' he said. Then he looked down at his plate, and stared at the food as though it were something alive. 'What in the name of God is that?' he bellowed.

Mary was on her way to the kitchen for the sauce and turned around slowly. 'It's a dumpling,' she said. 'The sauce is just coming.'

'No, I mean what is this!' he said more quietly, picking up a small green pea in his fingers.

The officers looked from Mary to William and back to Mary again. She could feel the heat in her face and knew that her colour was high. A slow, burning anger began to simmer beneath her skin, prickling it all over like tiny pins.

'It's a pea, sir,' she said softly, waiting for his reaction. The others around the table had stopped eating and watched them both.

'It all looks delicious, Mrs Jones,' said the first mate, in his high-pitched child's voice. William glared at him and he lowered his gaze.

'Delicious!' said William, looking at Mary. She noticed that his eyes were swollen and puffy. He threw the pea across the room, aimed at Mary, but missing her by several inches. 'I don't know how many times I've told you not to put greenery on my plate.'

It was such a ridiculous gesture that she couldn't help

letting out a short laugh. William's face turned violet, and Mary wished she had remained quiet. But then Mr Cole put his hand on William's arm.

'It's not her fault, William,' he said softly. 'The cook should have told her.'

William looked at Mr Cole and nodded slightly. His colour retreated a little. He seemed confused, and then sad.

Mr Cole lifted the plate. 'Perhaps you could just take the peas off, Mary,' he said.

Mary coloured again. He smiled as she took it from him, and raised his eyes a little, as though they shared a common understanding. She thought how strange it was that the surgeon always seemed to know just what to do to calm William down.

In the kitchen the cook leered at her. 'The other missus soon learned never to put greens on the master's plate,' he said.

Mary glared at the man. 'Why didn't you tell me?'

'You never asked me, miss.'

'What is it,' said Mary, her eyes fierce, 'that you have against me? Is it only that I'm not her?'

The cook was quiet for a moment. 'No, ma'am,' he said. 'It isn't that. You're different from her, that's true. It's only that I know just the way the master likes things to be done.'

'Well,' said Mary, with a wild, bitter tone, 'perhaps he should have married you instead of me.'

The cook said nothing, but muttered under his breath and left for the bread room.

Between the resentment of the cook and the unfathomable behaviour of her husband, Mary felt the familiar contraction of her throat. She bit her lip, and fought back a surge of her previous anger. Then she picked up a spoonful of peas and crushed them into the sauce. William would have peas, she thought, whether he chose them or not.

When she returned to the table she saw that he was engaged in conversation with the man next to him, and smiled at something he said. She wondered at how quickly his mood had changed. She handed him his plate, placed the sauce near him and watched as he scooped some over his dumpling and began to eat. She sat down at the table and curled her toes in childish delight, knowing that he was eating the crushed pea purée. He didn't seem to notice at all, even raising his glass to her with a smile.

After she had finished her meal she made her excuses and returned to her cabin. She was restless all evening, wondering if William would appear. Somehow she had thought, or hoped, that he would return to her, not to apologize perhaps, but to smooth things over. As the clock ticked on she grew resentful. She told herself she didn't care. The time would come when he would want her, and she would make it as difficult as she could for him. When she heard his heavy footsteps in the corridor she would snuff out the candle and pretend to be asleep.

She picked up Elizabeth's book and tried to read. She took a little of the brandy beside her bed, but she had not eaten well at supper, and immediately the words began to swim on the pages of her book. The air inside the little wooden room grew hot and clammy. After she had thrown her cover on and off for the fourth time, she got out of bed, lit another small lamp, and put on her mantua. She must get some air. Opening the door to her cabin, she crept out of the small room and along to where the steps led up to the deck.

As she did so she passed the gunroom, where the men were engaged in heated conversation, with the occasional burst of laughter. She saw William, sitting opposite the surgeon, playing cards. His back was turned to her, and he dealt the cards. She saw him throw back his head, heard his laughter, deep and loud. He said something to Mr Cole and then called for one of the boys to pour him a drink. She watched him deal the cards again with a steady hand. Then the surgeon looked up, and saw her standing at the open door.

Without knowing why, she immediately ducked behind the doorframe. Then she became angry. Why should she feel as though she were the one doing something wrong? The men in the gunroom were drinking and laughing and entertaining themselves, while she was supposed to sit and cry in her cabin. So much for William's grief. He could always obliterate it in strong liquor. A frustration began to seethe in her. Then it ignited, like petrol, and blazed.

She walked quickly back to her own little cabin, dark and empty. She picked up her glass of brandy and drank it down. Then she entered William's cabin, and picked up the decanter of brandy that he kept beside the bed, hiding it inside the folds of her mantua. She left the room and climbed on to the deck.

It was a cold, clear night with a hint of frost in the air. Even the sea seemed almost frozen, washing lightly around the ship. There were only a few lights on deck, from the men at the helm and some others scattered around the ship. Two or three men stared at her as she passed over the quarterdeck, but her mantua made a good substitute for a cloak, so after a while they paid her little notice. She made her way to the back of the ship, where the animals were quartered. They seemed to have been lulled by the cold and she only heard the occasional bleat of a goat or the scuffling of hens' claws. From the other side of the ship she heard the faint whine of a fiddle and the occasional shout from the fo'c'sle. Otherwise all was silent. The black sky was littered with stars that merged in places to form lacy veils. The moon was out in full and cast pale silk ribbons of light across the dark water. For the first time, she was overcome by the sense of space around her, the quiet boom of the sea, the vastness of the distance between the little patches of land on which people built their short lives. It was a strangely comforting thought.

She found a spot in between some barrels of water that had been lashed to the deck, behind a box of pigeons. Sitting there, balancing the decanter between her legs, she looked up at the stars, with the gentle cooing of the birds in front of her. She took a sip of the brandy. The vapours stung her eyes and nose and danced on her lips even after the liquor had passed to her throat. At first it made her cough. But then a numbness spread over her skin that gave her a pleasant floating sensation. She took another sip, and another. She began to examine the stars, looking for the constellations she had read about in books as a child. But it seemed to her that she could make each constellation into any shape she chose, it was only a matter of how she joined them together. At last she closed her eyes and for the first time since they had left Leith an unimaginable happiness came over her. But it wasn't a real happiness, it was an almost happiness. A promise of what might be. For a moment the prison walls fell away. In her half dream William shook off his grief, became kind and attentive, and her mind began to race with plans and dreams, things they could do, she and William, a different, imagined, happy William.

But then she saw William's face before her, as it was, as she knew it would always be. She knew, as she had known with her mother, that unhappiness like William's did not suddenly disappear. It was as though a switch had been flicked, and the walls came up around her again. She laughed in the darkness, but her laugh sounded older, more bitter.

Without really knowing what had prompted it, she put her hand to her cheek and felt that it was wet. But it didn't feel as though she were crying. It was an extra-ordinary, noiseless, blissful kind of grief, and though she could feel her own desperation she also felt a sense of release. She rested her head against the iron frame of the barrel beside her, and fell asleep with the decanter in her hand.

She was awoken some time later by an arm gripping her shoulder. She let out a small cry.

'Be quiet, Mrs Jones,' said a voice that had the hint of a smile in it. 'Do you want the world to know you prefer this place to your husband's bed?'

She looked up and saw the lemonish light of the moon reflected in a pair of black eyes.

'Oh, it's you, is it,' she said. Then she laughed suddenly. 'How strange, I thought you would be here.' She knew she was slurring her words, and laughed again. 'Can't speak,' she said.

'You're intoxicated, madam,' said Mr Cole, seeming shocked. Then she thought she heard him laugh.

'Am I?' said Mary, looking at her hands, as if they would provide the answer. 'Oh, dear, I seem to be.' She put her arm out to her side and tried to push herself up, but she lost her balance and toppled over. The glass decanter fell to her side and smashed. She started to giggle.

She felt an arm come round her shoulders, and another around the back of her knees.

'Put me down,' she said groggily.

'I'm only carrying you out, my dear, because it seems to me you're in no condition to be doing it yourself.'

'How dare you take such liberties, Mr Cole,' she said, but she was giggling again. She put her arms loosely around his neck.

They walked over the decks, and men must have stared, because she heard the surgeon talking to them. 'She's feeling unwell,' he explained.

Somehow he managed to bring her down the ladder, though later Mary couldn't remember that part. What she did remember was coming into her own cabin. They got stuck in the door, because of the width of Mary's mantua, and this made her giggle all the more. Then she was throwing her head back into the crook of his arm, laughing, and him whispering urgently to her.

'Madam, please stop moving, I can't hold you.'

She was aware of being laid in her bed. Mr Cole was holding on to her hand, wrapping it in something.

'What are you doing, Mr Cole?'

'Please call me Robert. I'm bandaging your hand.'

'There's nothing wrong with my hand.'

'It's bleeding. You laid it in broken glass.'

Mary looked at her hand, and at once saw the blood, little flecks of it running in narrow trickles across her palm.

'Oh,' she said. She tried to sit up.

'Please, madam, don't move.'

'I think I will be sick.'

'Here,' he said, holding the chamberpot beneath her head. She looked at the pisspot, and at Mr Cole, and suddenly the sickness was gone, and the whole thing had become unbearably funny.

'Whatever is the matter, Mrs Jones? You're quite hysterical.'

'Oh, don't be so serious, Mr Cole,' she said. He still held on to her hand, then with his other hand he smoothed away a strand of her hair that had come loose. Mary stopped laughing and winced as he came to the swollen mark on her brow.

'What is this?' he asked, getting on to his knees to look more closely at it.

'Oh, a mark of love, I suppose,' she said, hating the bitter edge to her voice. 'Only not for me,' she said more quietly.

'I see,' he said, and she flinched again as he brushed his thumb across the raw powdered skin.

~

Mary woke some time later in her own bed, with a vague feeling of contentment. Her mouth filled with saliva and her stomach churned. She sat up in panic. She leaned over the side of the bed and at once the chamberpot was thrust beneath her face. She coughed a trickle of pink water into it.

'You are not well, madam,' said William's voice.

She looked up to see him, fully dressed, standing beside her bed. 'What time is it?' she asked groggily, wiping her mouth.

'Late,' said William. 'Almost eleven o'clock. I could see that you were feverish, so I left you to sleep. Here.' He held out a small glass of brandy, but as soon as her nose caught the vapours she vomited again, this time not quite managing to reach the pot.

He must know, she thought. He must know why I feel like this.

'This is worse than I thought,' said William. His voice was calm, and almost satisfied. 'You must see Robert at once.'

'No!' Mary almost shouted. 'No,' she said, a little more quietly. 'Just bring me some water.'

'I have to go,' he said, picking up his hat. 'I'll have some sent down to you with Robert.'

'But, William, I really don't need to see Mr Cole, I am not ill. It's just a . . . something I have eaten, I'm sure.'

'We can't be too careful,' said William firmly. 'Robert

will look after you. Just do as he says.' He picked up her bandaged hand. 'You've hurt yourself.'

'I broke a piece of glass and cut myself on it.'

'You've bandaged it well.'

Mary only nodded, her eyes filling with tears. William's eyes were on her all the time. He brushed his lips against the fabric of the bandage and then left the room.

11

A short time later, there was a knock on the door. Mary turned over a little, but her head still clattered and she couldn't sit up. She pulled the covers up to her chest. The surgeon peered around the door.

'May I come in?' he asked.

She nodded briefly, her head still on the pillow. 'But I don't need anything,' she said, refusing to look at him. 'I told him not to send you.'

'You look pale,' said Robert. He put his hand to her brow. 'And you are hot. You may be running a fever.'

Mary looked at him at last, and met his eye. She thought for a moment that she saw a glimmer of uncertainty in them, and she felt her shoulders relax.

The surgeon smiled. 'It was a cold night last night,' he said. 'You may have caught a chill.'

'Thank you,' she began hesitantly. Though her memory was hazy, she could remember enough of the night before to know that she should be more ashamed than she felt. 'I know you brought me back here, and I am grateful to you. I don't know quite what happened. I suppose I'm just feeling a little strange, here. Everything is so different.'

'It's all right, Mary,' he said. Despite his closeness of the night before, she was surprised at his familiarity. 'I understand perfectly,' he went on. 'Remember, I've known William for many years.'

Could he really know how William was with her? she wondered. He opened the small leather case that he had brought with him and propped it up in front of Mary. She studied its contents. It was filled with rows of bottles, small jars and blocks of substances wrapped in paper. She read the labels, and was fascinated by the unusual words: anodyne balsam, locatelli's balsam, Jesuit drops, rhubarb, and chalybeate wine. There were jars of rosewater, vitriol, and liquid laudanum, and powders wrapped in paper labelled: mercury, alum, gum kino, Peruvian bark, gum ammoniac, white lily root, mustard, anise seeds, filings of iron, mace, asafoetida. It smelled both familiar and strange, like her uncle's breath, her aunt's painting room, the foetid harbour in late summer and the most exotic fragrant gardens all mixed into one.

'You won't tell him, will you?' she said suddenly.

'I don't see what you have to hide,' said Robert, staring into his case. 'After all, you only fell asleep on the deck. Odd place to sleep, I'd say, but each to their own.'

A small smile played on the edges of his lips, and she looked at the back of his arms, bony, sinewy and long, covered with fine black hairs.

'You're teasing me,' she said.

Robert smiled again. He picked out a small blue bottle and held it up to the light. 'Don't worry,' he said. 'I just need to be able to tell William that I've been, and given you a dose of something or other.'

Mary felt a little more relaxed, and sat up a bit, leaning

on her elbows. 'He trusts you?' she asked, and instantly regretted it.

Robert looked at her. The smile had left his lips but played around the creases at the corners of his eyes instead. 'Why wouldn't he?'

She shifted her gaze towards the window. 'Where is he now?' she asked.

'I believe he is taking some dinner. He supposed you wouldn't want any.'

Mary shook her head.

'So what was it,' he asked, 'that caused you to risk freezing to death?'

'I don't know,' said Mary. 'I was looking at the stars. I'd never seen them like that before, so many of them. I used to look out of my window at home, sometimes, but I could only see into the gap between the buildings, and then there might be one or two very bright ones, not such a crowd of them.'

'Didn't you notice your hand in the broken glass?' he asked, picking up her bandaged arm.

Mary shook her head. 'I've always been like that. Sometimes I don't seem to feel things that other people feel. Not at the time, at least. It's painful now.'

Robert carefully unwrapped the bandage. The blood had dried in rivulets across her palm, turning her hand into a finely drawn map of lines and crosses.

'It's healing up well already,' he said. 'But keep the bandage on for a few days.' His fingers curled around her hand for a moment, and then he let it go.

'This should do it,' he said, squinting at the label. 'Just keep it beside you, so he thinks I've given you something.'

'What is it?' she asked.

He looked closely at the label again. 'Jesuit drops. Don't drink them, for heaven's sake, they'll do you no good at all.'

'What are they supposed to be for?' she asked.

'Eliminating parasites from the digestion,' Robert said, after a short pause. 'I'm sure you don't have any of those!' He put the jar on the table beside her bed, then shut his case and stood up.

Mary saw that he was about to leave, and felt a sudden panic. 'Please,' she said quickly, 'could you bring me some fresh water? I did ask William, but he must have forgotten. My lips are parched.'

Then Robert put out his hand to Mary's lips and touched them. She opened them slightly in surprise and took in a quick breath. He ran his fingers over the dry crust of her lip. She closed her mouth, and her gums were sticky with thirst.

'You're right,' he said softly. 'I'll get you some at once.'

When he had left the room, Mary breathed out. She put her finger to her lips. Had he really touched them? But then surgeons were different, freer, than ordinary men. They had to be. People were merely machines to them, vehicles for various manoeuvres and secretions, to be measured, investigated and treated. She liked that idea, the examination of living things as though they were objects, free from emotion. She had been doing it, in one sense or another, since she was a child, examining her mother in her various emotional states. She had learned to control her own desires and fears. She knew that since her mother was often out of control, it would do no good for her to be as well. So that often she could barely feel her own emotions, much less display them. Until recently she had remained this way. Even as they had waited to leave the harbour at Leith, she had leaned over the rail, examining the jellyfish. She loved the way their transparent skin exposed their organs, the little luminous threads that carried the life through their bodies. Now, since she had wept on the deck, and been carried back by Robert, she felt as though she herself had become like one of those jellyfish, transparent and exposed, and it both thrilled and frightened her.

He appeared again with a tin cup full of fresh water. She reached out for it, but he held it back.

'No,' he said. 'Only one drop at a time, to start with, or you'll be sick. But first, moisten your lips.' He dipped his finger in the water and ran it along her lips.

She looked up and caught his eye. He took his fingers away.

'Now,' he said, 'a small sip,' and he held the glass to her mouth.

She took a few eager gulps, before he removed it. Usually the water on board tasted of wood, with the sharp metallic tinge of tin, but today it was like the purest mineral spring.

'No more,' he said. 'Let that sit for a while, until you know your stomach will take it.'

Mary sat up a little straighter. She was feeling better, only a little dizzy, but she said nothing. From the corner of her eye she could see where the lace edge of her *manteau de lit* had fallen open, exposing the white skin beneath. She leaned forward. 'I don't know how he does it,' she said. 'William, I mean, how he drinks what he does. If this is what it does to you.'

'You get used to it,' said Robert. 'And he is a man, his stomach is not as delicate as yours, as fragile.' He met her eyes again. 'And if he carries on, one day it will kill him.'

'It will?' said Mary, her eyes wide. And then she felt ashamed, almost before the feeling came to her. She was scared to recognize it, because it was a kind of relief. She started to cry again. The tears came more easily than they ever had before.

'Mary, I didn't mean to upset you.'

Mary realized that, without knowing it, she had taken hold of his hand, and he was staring down at the small white fingers that had clasped themselves over his own. He leaned forward. He put his hand on her head and stroked her hair, and she took a quick, shallow breath.

'Please,' she said, though she didn't know what she was asking him to do.

Robert made as if to pull away, but then hesitated. Mary looked at him, waiting for him to speak.

'I'm going to leave you now,' he said.

But Mary held on to his hand. 'No. Please stay,' she said, a note of desperation in her voice. 'It's good to have someone to talk to.'

She saw the hesitation in him, and let go of his hand. She sat up a little more and her eyes brightened.

'Tell me about Elizabeth,' she said at last.

'Why do you want to know about her?' he asked.

'Because it might help me understand William,' said Mary. 'That's why I have this, you see,' she said, pointing to her head. 'It seems that her name must never be mentioned.'

Robert sat back and appeared to think for a moment. Then he sighed and opened his mouth. 'Elizabeth was troubled,' he said. 'William couldn't understand why. He wasn't able to save her, and that's why he won't talk about her.'

'Did you help her?' she asked. She remembered what the sailor had said, about the surgeon spending time with her, giving her various treatments, and she felt a pang of jealousy.

'I only gave her something to ease the symptoms,' he said. 'But it was too late, by then. William blamed himself. He badly wants things to be different this time. After she died, William never forgave himself. He said he would never marry again. And nobody believed that he would.' He paused. 'I certainly didn't think he would.'

'Was he always like this?'

Robert waited for an instant, and Mary could see that he was remembering.

'He was almost the opposite, in many ways,' he said. 'He was so disciplined as to be almost unnatural. His uncle insisted on every aspect of his behaviour being perfect. My upbringing was quite different; my father couldn't care less what I did or where I went. William wanted what I had, and I wanted what he had. It's always been that way. I think that's why we were friends.'

As Mary listened to him she thought that his shoulders seemed to tremble a little. When he smiled at her, his smile was fixed.

'You didn't get on with your father?' she asked.

'Oh, no,' he said quickly. 'We weren't close, that's all.'

She looked down at where his fingers had crept towards

hers. As she tapped them in their little dance over the linen they touched momentarily. He took hold of her hand, but she withdrew it, retreating.

'I'm sure, in time, things will work themselves out,' Robert said.

Mary shook her head, tears in her eyes again. 'But how much time?' she asked pleadingly.

Robert looked grave. 'I don't know. He's trying hard, but these last months he's got worse, rather than better. I fear,' he added, 'that he may never be the husband you deserve.'

Mary sat quite still, but her mind was on the narrow map lines of skin around Robert's eyes. He reached out for her hand again, and this time she let him take it. Then he leaned forward and kissed her, and she put her bandaged hand at the back of his neck, felt the short, firm hairs of his wig. She breathed his strange smell, of rosemary, cinnamon, opium and alcohol. She pressed herself towards him and he slid his hands beneath the bedclothes, under the *manteau de lit*, and into the folds of her chemise. In comparison to William's clumsy fumbling in the darkness his touch was delicate, gentle and soft.

'He might be back,' she whispered, as he slid his hands between her legs, parting them slightly. She closed her eyes and felt the trickle of moisture against her thigh. Then the warmth of his body beside her, the touch of his skin. She pressed her lips against it, tasted his perspiration of salt and cinnamon.

'He won't,' he breathed. 'He's on his watch for the next two hours.'

Mary was never aware of William's watch times herself,

he was so rarely with her. It occurred to her for a moment that Robert must have checked, that he must have wanted to make sure William was gone, and so in a sense must have planned this, but then it hardly mattered, because she had already melted into him. She pulled him closer, trying to find something she desperately needed from him. But however close she pulled him to her, however smoothly their skins slid together and melded to one another like molten wax, the need was still there. And after he had come into her and shuddered and cried out his last forced breath, she found that she only needed him more.

Afterwards she fell into a drowsy sleep, and woke to find Robert on the bed beside her, dressed, watching her. He looked concerned.

'What is it?' she asked, sitting up quickly.

'Nothing,' he said. 'I was just thinking how different you are.'

'From what?'

'From Elizabeth.'

Mary sat back. 'So everybody says,' she said desolately.

'I mean in a good way. You're more delicate than she was,' Robert said. He picked up her hand. 'It's so tiny.'

'My uncle says my bones never formed properly.'

'Look,' Robert said, picking up the empty tin cup from the side of the bed. 'I bet it fits in here. Try!'

'Don't be ridiculous.'

'Please, I'm sure it would fit.'

'No.'

'For me,' he said.

Mary looked at him and shook her head, smiling. 'I've never done anything so ridiculous in my life.' She curled up her unbandaged fist and put it inside the cup. It fitted perfectly.

Robert watched her and laughed. He took her hand and uncurled it. 'How ridiculous,' he said. He kissed it and folded it inside his, so that not an inch of her white skin could be seen beneath his own. She felt the pressure of his bones, prominent against her own, and he gripped tighter, seeming deep in thought. Then he looked at her and released his hold, bringing her fingers to his lips and kissing along the red indentation his own had made.

~

Before he left he gave her a tincture of something. She fell into a warm, drowsy sleep, like lying in a warm bath, full of dreams where she lay with Robert and he squeezed her hand and nobody called William ever existed or appeared. Some time later a shout made her sit up, and she heard thuds of activity above her head. A sliver of early dawn light oozed through the spaces in the door. She heard men's voices outside and the feet of more men climbing up on to the deck. She pulled on a thick cloak and climbed up herself, and immediately saw how close to land they were. They had entered the inlet known as the Tye Stroom, with strips of flat land on either side, and a stiff westerly wind was driving them further into it. The men worked hard with ropes and sail around her as she stood at the bow, watching the miniature town draw nearer. Soon she could see the walls of a city, lined with the little windmills she had heard about but had only seen in paintings. As they sailed further into the port she could make out the red brick of the buildings, tall and narrow with little peaked caps. There were some churches with tall spires, and the masts of at least a thousand boats anchored there. There was a whole dock full of East Indiamen, huge ships with gilded, sculpted figureheads of mermaids and serpents. She felt as though she were sailing into a painting, something she had always imagined doing as a child, where the people and the events had been imagined and created by her. This time, however, she could not only see it, but she could also feel it, smell it. All her senses were heightened and she felt a sudden rush of joy.

Her eyes opened a little wider, and she felt a catch in her breath. This was what she was here for. 'Isn't it beautiful?' she said to a sailor standing beside her.

He had seen it many times before. 'Aye,' he said, unsmiling. 'It's handsome enough.' Then he turned away, leaving her standing alone at the rail, as they pulled in alongside the *timmerwerf*.

12

Perhaps it was because she was called Nancy, the name of the first ship he had commanded. Perhaps it was because she was the most beautiful woman in the town, with dark curls framing her pale face and eyes the colour of warm chocolate. Perhaps it was because she was the younger sister of Thomas Bell, the wealthy merchant, and there was more recommendation in that simple fact than in all the charm and beauty in the world. In fact it was all of those things. But mostly it was the way his engagement had made people, especially Bell, look at him with a kind of new, curious respect.

Margot had introduced them not long after that first night at Thomas's house. She had organized a picnic at the new, neatly laid-out gardens of L'Hyvreuse, looking down into the bay, and invited Fullarton. After they had eaten, Margot took his arm and asked him to walk with her. Fullarton looked at Bell, as if for approval, but Bell was drinking from a hip flask, deep in conversation with another merchant, and Margot had already taken his arm and squeezed it tight. He could feel her breath close on his neck as she spoke, and he turned his head away from her. She had large bulging eyes that he suddenly saw were almost reptilian, especially when fixed on him, as they so often were.

'You know,' she said when they were out of earshot from the rest of the group, 'you've turned out to be a little goldmine for my husband, haven't you? You've swelled that head of his, as though it needed swelling, for he says he knew your strength when he picked you out.'

'Thank you, madam,' Fullarton said, unable to conceal his pleasure.

'I think he likes you very much,' she went on. 'He sees in you something of the vigour of his youth, and he likes the fact you're willing to take risks.'

'Calculated risks,' corrected Fullarton.

'And I, for one,' said Margot, ignoring him, 'have come to think of you as a sort of surrogate son.' Here she squeezed his arm, and Fullarton realized that he had never heard of the couple having any children.

'Thank you,' said Fullarton again, looking out to sea.

'My husband has some grand plans for you,' said Margot.

'Does he?' said Fullarton, turning to her. 'Plans of what nature?'

She raised her small pale face up to his and her eyes appeared to fizz with excitement. 'Ah,' she said, 'that got your interest, didn't it? He wants to make you a rich man, Captain Fullarton.'

'And why would he want to make me rich?' asked Fullarton. He glanced over to Bell, who raised his flask in his direction.

'Well, for his own benefit, of course. Only a fool would invest without prospect of return. But everyone needs a protégé, and my husband more than most. I've made a suggestion to Thomas, Captain, that would be even further to his advantage, and, I believe, to yours.' She squeezed his arm tighter as she said it, as though encouraging a small child to sing.

'Well madam,' he said, smiling, 'I'm always open to suggestions of that nature.'

'You've met Nancy Bell, Thomas's sister.' She pointed back to the group, where a young woman in a straw bonnet sat in the shade of a tree.

'I believe we were introduced.'

'You believe!' said Margot. 'Surely you can't have forgotten such a pretty creature so quickly. Your heart must be hard to capture, Captain Fullarton.'

'I don't know,' said Fullarton. 'Nobody has yet tried.' He looked at her from the corner of his eyes and smiled. He knew she adored him, and sensed that it would be to his advantage, at that moment, to reciprocate.

'Well, I'm sure I don't believe that,' she said. 'But perhaps your eyes will see a little better when I tell you what is secured on her.'

Fullarton tried hard not to vary his expression, and continued to face forward. 'She has an income?' he asked.

'No,' said Margot. 'She is supported by Thomas, but as you may have noticed, Captain Fullarton, Thomas and I have unfortunately not been blessed with offspring.'

'I am sorry to hear that, madam,' he said, but she waved him away.

'Nonsense, we're better off as we are,' she said. 'I have enough to be doing, but in any case, Thomas has for some time been looking for someone suitable to take on his business when he retires. Thomas adores his sister,' she went on. 'She's so much younger than he is, and with her own parents dead, he's raised her as though she were his daughter. He's hardly let a man near her for fear he might steal her away, but I think he would be willing to relent, for you. You know, Captain Fullarton, I think he admires you very much, almost as he might his own son.'

Fullarton turned to her and bowed a little. 'And Thomas has been like a father to me,' he said. 'I am eternally grateful to both of you for your kindness to me.'

He said it out of politeness, as he had developed a great sense of what needed to be said when. But since he had arrived in St Pierre he had become so convincing that he even believed himself, and felt a strange warmth coming over him. Perhaps he really could become part of a family like this. It was never something he had considered before. When Hampton had dragged him away from Leith he had left any connections of that nature behind. He had never written to his mother, not even to tell her he would never return. What Margot said next, however, swept any doubts aside.

'You know that Thomas intends to settle his business and estate on the man who marries Nancy,' she said.

They walked on in silence, with Margot still holding on to Fullarton's arm, and looking intently at the side of his face. Fullarton was careful to show no expression, but his mind was turning.

'Clearly,' he said, 'I should speak to her.'

Margot squeezed his arm again. 'I know you'll love her as I do,' she said.

~

A little later, Fullarton took the girl's white hand and kissed it. He noticed her face, which was what they called beautiful. He noticed her manners: she was reserved and quiet, but sensible enough when she was called upon to speak. He noticed her dress, which was elegant and not overstated, and he also noted the rich lace of her cuffs and the gold rings on her fingers.

She was silent as they walked through the gardens together, and he began to wonder if she was afraid of him. But after a long five minutes she suddenly looked at him and said, 'Tell me about yourself. Where are you from?'

'I'm from Orkney,' he said.

'Orknee,' she said, her French accent feeling out the word. 'And what is that like?'

A pressure began to build in his head. He turned to face her, looked at her eyes. They were questioning eyes, and he could not hold her gaze.

'It's a poor place, in the main,' he said at last.

'Are your family poor?' she asked.

'No. They are dead,' said Fullarton.

'Oh,' said Nancy. 'I'm sorry.'

Fullarton suddenly remembered the last time he had told that lie to a woman. So much time had passed now, that it might no longer be a lie. Where the first time he had almost wished it to be true, this time he didn't care. They could be alive or dead, it meant nothing to him. He thought of his mother's squalid little hut, his father's slightly less squalid one, which he had admired as a child. He had not known the wealth that was just a little further than his own doorstep, there for the taking, the treasure that was before him now, watching him cautiously. He coloured to think of it, and then laughed out loud. Nancy looked at him strangely. He recalled their previous conversation, and saw how odd his laughter must appear.

'I'm sorry,' he said, 'I was thinking of a happy time, when my parents were alive.'

'I'm sure I would have liked to have known them,' said Nancy.

She appeared contented again, and they walked on. Fullarton saw Bell and his wife now, sitting on the grass, with all the tea things laid out by the servants on a silk counterpane. The sun was gentle and warm, and before them the brilliant sea frothed and fizzed like the champagne he had tasted when in France. He pulled Nancy towards him and kissed her on the lips. When he stood away from her again he bowed a little and smiled over her shoulder to where, through the trees, he could see Margot's pale little face watching them.

'Oh,' Nancy said again.

'Is that all you can say?' he said, almost irritated. She lacked Bell's warmth, his buoyancy. He thought that she regarded him as she might consider a hat in a shop, examining colour and fabric, calculating worth. He looked into her dark brown eyes. It was like looking at a painting; her image was beautiful, but flat and lifeless. Still, she would look fine when placed in a mansion of his own.

'I should say a good deal more!' she said with comic anger, walking on a little.

Fullarton laughed and followed her. 'Wait, Nancy, I'm sorry, I didn't mean to be so forward.'

She turned, softened a little. 'It's just that . . . if my brother sees . . .'

'He'll see enough of it, when we're married,' said Fullarton, and he took hold of her hand.

She looked at him, her face a pretence of astonishment, and then nodded slowly. They walked on in silence. Then after a while she cleared her throat and spoke.

'My brother likes you, and my brother is always right,' she said. 'But I will have to know a little more about you, if we are to be married,' and she squeezed his arm in the same way that Margot had done.

Fullarton felt a stab of pain just below his breastbone, and swallowed. His fingers tightened on the hard stone of Nancy's emerald ring.

'Of course,' he said, clearing his throat. 'In good time, you shall know all there is to know.'

13

I

The fug of drugged sleep still hung over Mary as she walked with William through the streets of Amsterdam. It gave her a strange, surreal sense of wellbeing, so much so that she held tight to William's arm, more for support than anything else. They wandered along the water-lined streets, past merchants, hawkers and pedlars, bumping into acquaintances, it seemed to Mary, every few steps. She listened with interest to the singsong, sometimes harsh accents of the passers-by, many Dutch, but also Scots, French and German. She felt as though she were walking in a dream, but every so often she remembered the stranger, surreal dream of herself and Robert and a kind of warm sickness trickled up and burned at the bottom of her ribcage. She stood up straighter, walked with more purpose, and held on more firmly to William's arm, but the memory of Robert was everywhere. It was in the newness of things, the warmth of the spring air around her, the constant sound of the water that ran in the little canals they passed, the scratch of the housemaids' besom brooms as they swept the dirt from the houses into the water. Even the peculiarity of the street names reminded her, somehow, of Robert. They passed the Onde Kerk, the Damrak leading to Nieuwe Kerk. There were so many dams and dykes she was sure she would never find her way around if she were left alone. But then she almost wished that she would be. She would wander the streets, happy to be lost in this world that had been reborn around her.

When they passed St Antonis Markt, with a new collection of street sellers, she insisted on visiting each one. She spent some time at the spice sellers, sniffing the nutmeg, saffron and cardamom. And there were others that she had never seen before, seeds and pods and powders, in the most beautiful, rich shades of red and gold. Other stalls held great piles of oranges and lemons, and there was a stall devoted entirely to stiff lace, where Mary flicked through the various widths and weights. They seemed to come alive beneath her fingers. She remembered choosing fabric and lace with her mother as a child, hours spent standing at market stall after market stall while her mother argued about the weight and price of lace that, to Mary's touch, all felt exactly the same. But now she felt quite different. Each piece of lace, each scented spice, each face, every breath of wind brought a new sensation, and she knew she would be able to tell the different weights of fabric with her eyes closed.

She turned to see William standing by her side patiently, and he even smiled at her, as though he took pleasure in her happiness. She felt a flicker of guilt then, and moved to the next stall, only to find it stocked with different kinds of medicines, philtres and tinctures.

William picked up a bundle of Peruvian bark. 'I must

tell Robert about this one,' he said, and Mary turned swiftly, but his expression was benign.

'Hadn't we better find some lodgings?' she asked.

'Oh, I always stay at the same place when I'm here,' said William. 'With Anneke. I've known her for years. She married a French merchant that I used to trade with.'

'But we've walked a long way. How long will it take to get back?' Mary's silk-encased feet ached.

'We'll hire a schuit,' he said, raising a hand.

Mary looked at him, too scared to ask what a schuit was. She soon found it to be the strangest kind of carriage she had ever been in, a small boat drawn by horses that walked along the side of the canal. She sat back to watch the town drift by as they glided through the water. The streets were quieter now; there was only the clip of the horses' feet and the light clap of the water against the sides of the boat. It was a warm day, and Mary adjusted the parasol of the boat to shade her face. She dipped her fingers into the cool water beside her, making little whirlpools and watching the circles dissolve into one another. Through the most unusual glass gates she caught glimpses of ladies in cool courtyards pouring jugs of water over the bright flowers that seemed to grow out of every crevice of the town. She was enchanted by these little squares of domestic life, so far from the wind-sharpened bitterness of her mother or the damp, drab routine of life on the ship. She wondered if she would ever know that kind of gentle, domestic happiness.

The thought seemed to snap her awake, as a sober reality came to her. She looked at William, and he must have seen the terror on her face, because he sat up a little.

'My dear, are you quite all right?' he asked.

She nodded, unable to speak. William brought his arm around her shoulders. She thought that it was the first time he had touched her so tenderly, but instead of being flattered, she felt a desperate urge to jump into the water of the canal and swim off. She shifted in her seat, turning her head away.

~

They reached their lodgings at last, and Mary walked into a bright, marble-tiled hall where they were met by Anneke and her French husband. Mary warmed to her at once. She was not dressed like the other Dutchwomen she had met. Instead of the usual black and white she wore bright colours, although she must have been over fifty, and her hair was not tied back in the simple style but dressed and raised a little, almost casually, as if she wore it like that every day. Her husband was round, red-faced and jolly. They greeted William warmly, especially the Frenchman, who gave Mary barely a glance before he led William into the drawing room for a glass of claret. Anneke looked kindly at Mary, and showed her to her room.

'I hope you like it,' she said. 'We have many people from Scotland staying here.'

Mary looked around in wonder at the spacious suite decorated with flowers and large paintings and tapestries on the walls. 'It's quite beautiful,' she said.

'Thank you,' the Dutchwoman said, looking genuinely pleased. 'I love making things look pretty. I think beauty matters, don't you? It eases the mind. Now,' she went on, 'why don't you rest a little, and then I'll have the maid call you for tea directly.'

~

After tea, and after William had taken several clarets and a few brandies with his old friend, he announced that they had been invited to supper.

'But I haven't got anything ready,' said Mary. 'My clothes are still in my portmanteau. They need standing time. And my hair.'

'Don't worry about all that – these people don't stand too much on ceremony,' he said. 'Get the maid to do something with the dress, and I've already spoken to Anneke about a tire-woman to do something with your hair. God knows,' he said, seeming irritable at merely being forced to look at her, 'you look like you've been dragged through a hedge backwards.'

Anneke had ordered the tire-woman to dress Mary's hair in the latest style, which she said was very *à la mode* in France, so that when she had finished Mary emerged almost as tall as William, and so frizzled and decorated with coloured beads and little silver boats that she was almost afraid to turn her head to talk to anybody. When she arrived at the hosts' house she found that she was by far the most elaborately dressed of all the women there, many of whom looked quite dowdy in comparison.

William immediately went to drink with the host, who was an old friend, and Mary was left trying to fend off the young men of the party who either didn't know or took no notice of the fact that she was a married woman, and at the same time trying to ignore the jealous glances of the ladies, who were all a good bit older than her.

One man followed her the whole evening, bringing her glasses of punch which she kept leaving on tables and mantelpieces and behind jugs and silverware. She did not want to speak to him, but she could not find a way to tell him, and so kept making excuses, and disappearing, only for him to find her again minutes later. He had come via Leith, and had taken this as proof of an unshakeable bond between them. Finally Mary announced abruptly that she would have to take some air.

'I'll accompany you,' said the man.

'No!' she said firmly. 'I'd rather go alone.'

'You'll want some company,' he said.

'I have to find my husband,' she said, a small, shrill edge to her voice.

'I think your husband is otherwise engaged,' said the man, smiling slyly.

She broke away from him and walked to the door, though she could hear him follow. She opened the door and came out on to a short terrace that led into a courtyard at the back of the house, lit up by tiny lanterns hanging from a terrace above. Standing at the entrance to the courtyard she saw two dark figures. She stopped at once. They stood close together, and were speaking in hushed tones. Their voices were unmistakable.

'I can't keep doing this,' Robert was saying.

'You know how grateful I am,' said William.

'And you know how much I want to help you,' said Robert, 'but gratitude won't pay the bills for ever.'

'Only you can change that,' said William. 'I don't know if I can go on with this. It's killing me!'

'But be patient. It will be worth it for all of us,' said Robert.

She saw him pass something to William. She was so intent on watching them that she barely heard the footsteps as they came up behind her in the dark, and the man's arms circled her waist.

'I knew you'd wait for me here,' he whispered, and Mary screamed.

'Who's there?' called Robert's voice, alarmed.

Mary cried out in the dark. 'Robert!'

'Mary, is that you?'

'Mary, what the hell are you doing out here?' said William.

Mary had shaken the man off, and now turned, pointing to where he had vanished.

'That man,' she said, breathless, 'he followed me out here, and . . . I was trying to get away from him.' She turned to William. 'Where were you?' she demanded. 'I was looking for you.'

'Well, if he was bothering you, why in God's name did you think coming into a dark terrace was a good idea? Why did you not go to our hostess?'

'I had to get some air,' said Mary, 'I didn't want to bother her.'

It felt as though she were making excuses. She had expected William to be angry with the man who had followed her, rather than with her. 'Aren't you going to speak to him?' she asked.

'Of course he is,' said Robert quickly. 'William, go and

tell him that your wife is not available for any rake who wishes to accost her. Go, now, and I'll look after Mary.'

William looked at Robert, and then at Mary, and then disappeared back into the house.

At once Robert was beside her. 'I'm so glad to see you here,' he said. 'I haven't been able to think about anything else.'

'What are you doing here?' asked Mary, with panic in her voice. 'He didn't say you would be here.'

'A last-minute decision,' said Robert. 'I had some papers to give William, to do with the trade, you know. They had to be signed right away.'

Mary nodded. 'You don't normally concern yourself with that side of the business,' she said. 'I wish I had known.' She felt unprepared to meet him like this, especially in William's presence, and was almost angry with him for appearing.

'Well,' said Robert, putting his arm around her waist, 'I had other reasons.'

He pulled her into a darker part of the terrace and kissed her, and she began to forget her anxiety.

'We must go in,' she said, 'or they'll wonder why. My hair seems to have got me enough of a reputation tonight already.'

'It's quite extraordinary,' said Robert, as they stepped into the light, making for the house. 'Who did it?'

'Our landlady, Anneke, hired a tire-woman,' said Mary.

'I see,' said Robert. 'You're staying with Anneke.'

'Do you know her?'

She heard Robert laugh, a blown sniff under his breath as he guided her back downstairs. 'Yes, I know her a little,' he said. 'And that explains the hair.'

They went inside and Robert went off to talk to some of the other ladies who were present. Mary followed him with her eyes, watching the women flutter and demean themselves before him. Then she turned to see that William was also watching Robert, and that his expression was dark.

She sat there for what seemed like hours, until it was only she, William, Robert and the host and hostess left. Anneke had said that she locked the door at midnight and Mary began to grow anxious. She tried several times to signal to William with her eyes that they needed to leave, but he only ignored her.

She felt sick and so full of oysters that she could barely keep her back straight against her chair. Robert sat quietly, watching them with a small smile.

'No doubt you'll be very tired,' said the hostess finally.

'Oh, yes, I'm afraid I am,' said Mary, jumping on the opportunity. 'We've had a terribly long journey.'

'Of course you have,' said the hostess delicately. 'I believe my husband is keeping you back.' At that she got up and whispered into her husband's ear, shaking him gently.

He stood up and took William's arm, and Mary breathed a sigh of relief. But as William tottered towards her he leaned on her so heavily that she toppled over, lost her footing, and fell into the hostess, who managed to push them back up again.

'Oh!' said Mary, attempting to hold him up with one hand. 'I'm so sorry.'

At once Robert was beside them, grasping hold of William. 'I'm afraid we've had a rather difficult voyage,' he said. 'And Captain Jones is quite exhausted. I'll make sure that he and Mrs Jones get home safely.'

'That's most kind of you, Mr Cole,' said the hostess. 'I fear it's my husband's fault for giving him a little too much to drink.' She looked reproachfully at her husband.

'Come along then, William,' Robert said.

'Thank you so much,' said Mary after they had walked a little way in silence. 'I don't know how I'd have managed on my own.'

But Robert was quiet. She could hear only his footsteps, and the sound of William's heavy breathing. The town, which had appeared so gentle and welcoming in daylight, was in darkness a cold and uncertain place. She felt as though she was walking with two strangers, and she tried to ignore the stumbling black figures she passed every now and then. Some were silent, but some called out to her in languages she couldn't understand. They seemed to walk for a long time.

'Are you sure this is the right way?' said Mary, after a while.

'It might be a bit of a long way round,' said Robert. 'So hard to tell in the dark.'

Mary could hear the water on one side of her, but she couldn't see the edge, which frightened her. Another corner, however, and the house came into sight, and she began to relax. It must have been the effect of the liquor she had taken, and the darkness.

As they approached the house she felt Robert's hand on her arm, and he whispered in her ear.

'I need to see you again. Soon.'

'I know, but I can't,' she hissed, sure that William would hear.

'You must find a way.'

'How can I?'

'Elizabeth?' said William. 'Is that you?'

'Come on, William,' said Robert, raising his voice, 'it's not Elizabeth, it's Mary.'

'Robert,' said William, his words running into one another, 'this has gone too far. Too far.'

'What does he mean?' asked Mary.

'He means we took the long route home after all,' said Robert. 'Don't worry, old boy. We're back now.'

Then he was at her ear again. 'Find some reason to send for me,' he said. 'Anneke knows where I lodge.'

'I can't promise.'

'You must try,' he said, pressing her hand tightly in his. 'You must. Promise you'll try.'

'All right, I promise I'll try.'

~

When Anneke opened the door Mary almost fell in. She pushed William gently into a chair where he sat, muttering to himself. She heard Anneke talking to Robert for a moment. She could not make out what they said, but their voices seemed raised for a moment, and then she heard the sharp click of the door.

'Are you all right, my dear?' Anneke said, coming into the room. She looked flushed.

'I feel a little unwell,' said Mary.

Anneke looked at her with an expression of real concern. 'You are very pale. Here, come with me,' and she led her into a little side closet and sat her down on a chair.

'I'll see to William,' said Anneke quickly, 'and then I'll come back to make sure you're fine.'

Mary heard a few stumbling steps above her head, and the sound of low voices. One of them was William's. He must have revived a little. Then she heard light footsteps on the stair and Anneke was back.

'Is he all right?' asked Mary.

'He came to a little on the way up the stairs. Said he could get himself to bed. But what about you, my dear? How are you?'

'I think it was the oysters,' said Mary defensively. 'I really didn't take much punch at all. Robert had to help me find the way, and help me with William, and I thought we were lost.'

'You couldn't get lost, my dear,' said Anneke. 'You were only a few streets away. But never mind. He often does this on the first night.'

'Has my husband been coming to you for many years?' Mary asked, starting to feel a little better. There was something soothing about this woman's presence.

'Many,' said Anneke, and there was a sadness in her smile. 'I remember him when he was just a young man. Ambitious and full of life.'

'And did you know Elizabeth?' Mary asked.

The smile fell from Anneke's face. 'Why don't you come into the parlour, and take some chocolate. The milk will settle your stomach.'

Mary sat in a large upholstered chair, warming her nose in the chocolate steam. Anneke sat opposite her holding a piece of brightly coloured silk thread work, and seemed thoughtful. Mary wondered if she had offended her. But after sitting for a moment Anneke spoke.

'I did know Elizabeth,' she said. 'I knew her well, because it was through myself that William was first introduced to her. I was greatly saddened by her death. Somehow that pairing was never destined to be. But you, my dear, are very different. Perhaps you may be the tonic he needs.'

'Sometimes he acts as though I am more of a poison than a tonic.'

Anneke looked at her, and the expression of concern returned. 'He's not himself, is he?'

'I don't know. I'm not sure if I really know what himself is.'

'He feels it badly. But nobody could have predicted what would happen.' Anneke looked distant for a moment. 'Nobody should be blamed.'

'Was somebody blamed?' asked Mary.

Anneke looked at her again, as if she had just noticed her presence. 'People often blame themselves, when someone dies. Especially the way it happened.'

'One of the sailors said it was a mystery. They said the weather wasn't rough.'

'It wouldn't need to be, my dear, she couldn't swim. But then she would have known that. That's why she did it at night, when there was nobody to save her.'

Mary sat up in her chair. '*She* did it?'

Anneke had her needle halfway through the fabric. She stopped and put it on her lap. 'You didn't know?'

Mary shook her head. She felt numb. 'Why wouldn't he tell me?' she asked.

Anneke looked bewildered.

'I know he didn't want it to be widely known,' she said. 'For the scandal, that was to be expected. But I thought at the very least he would have told his wife. Oh dear.' She put her hand over her mouth. 'I've made a most dreadful mistake. You must forgive me.'

'You've only told me the truth.'

Anneke paused for a moment, deliberating. She shook her head. 'I don't know what's happened to William. Of course, it was a great shock for him, not only losing her, but the way that it happened, straight after losing the child.'

Mary sat up again and her eyes widened. 'There was a child?' she said.

Anneke put her work down and looked at Mary. 'It seems there's quite a lot he hasn't told you.'

'He doesn't like to talk about it,' said Mary quietly. Then, without meaning to, she began to cry. 'He won't even have her name mentioned.'

Anneke came over to her and put her hand on her lap. 'Don't cry,' she said. 'That's not unusual. He just wants to make a new start. It'll get better.'

Mary wished she could tell the truth. That not only did she not know her husband at all, but she thought she was in love with another man. That given the opportunity, she would leave him at the drop of a hat, grieving or not. That she was not the good, concerned wife Anneke believed her to be.

'It's nothing,' she said, 'I'm just a little homesick, that's all.'

'I can understand that,' said Anneke. 'I was at sea myself, with my husband, and it can be a lonely life at times, but at least you're together. There are thousands of women in this port, whose husbands have gone to sea, who wait for years on end for a sign and, more importantly, a living to take care of sailors' children. Some of them wait for ever.'

'You seem content now,' said Mary. She wished she could be as relaxed as Anneke, sitting in her bright parlour, her needlework neat and straight. Mary had no concentration for needlework now. Her hands shook and she grew impatient with it, making mistakes every few stitches and having to unpick all she had done.

'Well,' said Anneke, 'I've known darker days, and so now . . .' She paused and smiled, looking up at one of the floral paintings on the wall. 'I make a point of always looking to the light.'

'Tell me about the baby,' said Mary, drying her eyes.

'She only lived a few days,' she said. 'William said she was poorly from the moment she was born.'

'A little girl?'

'Alice, she called her,' said Anneke. 'Elizabeth was devastated, of course.'

'And that was why she killed herself?'

'I'm sure it's what triggered it,' said Anneke. 'But there was always something tragic about her. Even before she met William. She was more troubled than usual, though. I saw it the last time they came. She was expecting then, had a kind of fit in her room, and the surgeon was called. William was up there too, and there was a dreadful fuss. She screamed and flew at the surgeon. She had to be restrained. It was odd; she had always been unpredictable, but never violent. The next morning she was perfectly calm, as though nothing had happened. She didn't seem sad any more, though; I don't know how to describe it, expressionless. She hardly even took leave of me . . .'

She hesitated, and took a sip of her chocolate. 'She had been, at times, like a daughter to me.' She paused, and took another sip. But the liquid seemed to stick in her throat and she coughed.

'They set sail the following day,' she said, once the coughing had subsided. She looked down towards her work again. 'She was such a beautiful young woman. There were some who said she only wanted his money. There was a time when I almost thought it myself, even though I cared for her. We can all be misled, at times. But now I believe that she loved William deeply. He should have been more grateful for that.' Mary thought there was an edge to her voice, as she leaned forward and continued: 'She confided in me that when they set sail he never paid her any attention, as if she were hardly his wife but some kind of officer of the ship.' She sat back again and shook her head. 'She couldn't understand it. No man in the world could resist her, until William.'

'Really,' said Mary. She didn't say he had done the same with her. 'There's so much I don't know about him.'

'Same in any marriage, my dear,' said the old woman. 'You think I know him up there? He gets stranger every year.'

II

When she awoke the next morning William was gone. Anneke told her he had had to go to Rotterdam on business, and would be two days at least. With William gone, her thoughts returned to Robert. He must have known about Elizabeth, and about the baby. And though he had not actually lied about their deaths, he had concealed the facts from her in a way. She would have to find out why. She would have to see him.

She dressed, but deliberately made herself a little dishevelled. She went downstairs.

'How are you this morning, my dear?' enquired Anneke.

'Oh, Anneke,' she said, 'I have the most dreadful headache.'

'I suffer from headaches often,' said Anneke. 'I can give you some of my own special balm. It's scented with peppermint. You rub it on your temples, like this.'

'That's too kind,' said Mary. 'But these headaches are something I've had before. It's a condition, and there is a medicine that the ship's surgeon, Mr Cole, gives me for it. But I have no idea where he is, or how to find him.' She clutched her head with both hands, and sat on a chair.

Anneke looked at her for a moment, then smoothed back her hair. 'My dear, you can't go looking for him, not in this state.' She raised Mary's chin and examined her face closely. 'You are pale. I think you should go back to your room.'

Mary stood up, and then stumbled a little. 'I think I will,' she said. 'Oh, Anneke, can't you call for Mr Cole?'

'Well, I can probably find out where he lodges,' said Anneke. 'But won't you let my own doctor examine you? Are you sure it absolutely has to be him?'

Mary tried not to show the panic in her voice. 'It has to be Robert . . . Mr Cole. William wouldn't want me to see any other surgeon but his own.'

Anneke seemed concerned. But then she looked resigned. 'Well,' she said, hesitating, 'perhaps there's nothing I can do for you. If you go upstairs, I'll try to find out where he's staying.'

A little later, as Mary sat up in bed, the door opened, and Anneke peered in.

'Here is your doctor,' she said. 'I'll bring you some tea directly, Mr Cole.'

'Thank you, Anneke,' said Robert, smiling at her. 'But there's no need . . .'

'Of course there is,' said Anneke, and Mary thought her voice sounded sharp. 'I remember how you like it.'

Robert turned to face her. 'I forgot to say, Anneke, how well you are looking.'

Anneke curtsied. 'Thank you. I live a simple life nowadays, not too much of anything, and I surround myself with beautiful things.'

'I can see that,' said Robert, now turning to face Mary and smiling warmly.

As soon as Anneke had gone Robert locked the door.

'When she comes she will want to know why it's locked,' said Mary.

'And I'll explain that my patients always prefer privacy during an examination.' He sat down on the bed beside her, and slid his hands into her robe. 'I knew you would call for me,' he said.

She felt her skin bristle, and she raised her head to kiss him. Then she stopped for a moment, and pulled away, remembering what she had to ask.

'What is it?' he whispered, as his fingers played with the lace around her throat.

She tried to say it, but when she looked at his eyes, that seemed so absorbed in her, she knew that to mention it now would be almost to pollute the pure air around them with her own mistrust of him. Now that he was with her, these details of the past seemed practically insignificant. She shook her head, and said nothing, and let him kiss her again.

~

At first she thought that Anneke would reappear at any moment with the tea, but soon she forgot about it, and in fact Anneke did not return, not for at least an hour.

'Your colour has come back,' she said when she appeared at last, smiling warmly at Mary, as the maid brought in the tea behind her. She sat on the bottom of the bed while Robert pretended to close his medicine chest.

'No doubt you've given her a tincture of something or other from that magic chest of yours,' she said. 'Surgeons always did seem a little like magicians to me. At least they are as full of quackery and hocus pocus.'

'Now, Anneke,' said Robert. 'You know that I am a professional.'

'Are you enjoying your stay here, Mr Cole?' Anneke asked, changing the subject.

Robert nodded. 'As always.'

'And your lodgings are comfortable?'

Robert smiled, looking at her. 'Very, thank you.'

'Of course you could have stayed here,' said Anneke. 'But perhaps this district of the town doesn't provide the same distractions as the livelier area you favour?'

'Oh, I wouldn't say that,' said Robert, his eyes on Mary.

'Of course I would have stayed at your beautiful lodgings,' he went on, now turning to Anneke, 'but I understood you had no space.'

'Well, that's true,' said Anneke.

'Your lodgings always were popular,' said Robert. He put down his teacup then picked up his case as he got to his feet. 'Goodbye Mary, I hope you'll feel better soon.'

After he was gone, Anneke turned to Mary. The perpetual smile had vanished from her face.

'I don't trust that gentleman,' Anneke said. 'I don't care how long he's known William.'

'But why not?' asked Mary.

'That place where he lodges. It is not a respectable place to stay.'

'Perhaps he can't afford better,' said Mary.

'Perhaps,' said Anneke, looking towards the window. 'But I wonder. I knew him, you see, in a former life.'

'Did you?' said Mary, interested.

'Yes. He is from a good family, I understand, but they lost all their money gambling. I don't believe he has anything other than what he earns on board the ship.'

'I see,' said Mary. She wondered why Anneke was telling her this. Surely Robert could not be held responsible for the errors of his family.

'Mary,' said Anneke, sitting on the bed for a moment. 'I have something to ask you, about Mr Cole.'

Mary felt her whole body tighten, and her teeth clenched together. She was sure that Anneke had guessed, and was going to ask her about the nature of their relationship.

'What is it?' she said quietly.

'That tincture that Mr Cole gave you. Does he treat you with it often?'

Mary's expression must have betrayed her confusion. 'Well, no,' she said. 'That's only the second time.'

'Well,' said Anneke, sitting back and looking more satisfied. 'That's good. Be sure that you don't take it often. Medicine is like love, poisonous in large doses.'

III

Mary's mysterious headache returned again and again during the following days. This became even easier to achieve, since Robert had apparently told Anneke that Mary's condition had worsened, and that he would have to treat her more often.

But perhaps some of the poison was starting to linger around her liver, to infect her blood. Her sensations were beginning to dull. Her pretended headaches were becoming real, and they didn't disappear after Robert's visits. They were joined by an almost constant nausea, worse in the mornings, and then the date of her menstruation came and went with no sign of bleeding. For the first time a small sense of panic crept over her. She put her hand on her abdomen. It was hard to believe that a new life could grow within it, but it was possible, perfectly possible, and if it was, then she also knew that it was more probable it would be Robert's than William's. The thought burrowed deeper, and was joined by thoughts of Elizabeth and her baby, and the doubt crept in again.

On the day before William was due back, she had Anneke call Robert once more. This time her headache was real and blinding. She was sitting on her bed with her head drawn down to her knees when Robert came in.

'You're turning into quite an actress,' he said approvingly when the door was shut.

'No, Robert, this is real. Please give me something for it,' she said.

'I see,' he replied, and she thought his voice sounded a little cooler. He opened his case and pulled out a small book. He seemed to consult it for some time.

'Oh, please hurry up, Robert,' she said. 'The pain is unbearable.'

When at last he had found the right bottle, she turned over her pillow and lay back on the bed with her head resting on the cool surface.

'I have something to ask you, Robert,' she said. 'It's about Elizabeth.'

Robert looked up sharply. 'What do you mean?'

'Something Anneke mentioned, and I can't understand why William wouldn't have told me.' By focusing on William she hoped that he would not take the question as a slight upon himself.

'Wait,' Robert interjected, and he looked troubled for a moment. 'I know what you're going to say.'

He hesitated, and Mary waited.

'It's about the fact that she took her own life, isn't it?' Mary nodded.

'You know he was only trying to protect her reputation.'

Mary nodded. 'That's what Anneke said. But what about the child?' she went on. 'The little girl, Alice.'

Robert tilted his head to one side and frowned slightly. 'How do you know about that?' he asked sharply.

Mary was taken aback. 'Anneke,' she said, her voice beginning to tremble. 'Like I told you.'

Robert shook his head. 'Strange. I didn't think that William would have told another soul, but perhaps in a weaker moment. God knows he has enough of those these days.'

'Why wouldn't he tell?' asked Mary, feeling perplexed, and suddenly very lonely.

Robert was quiet for a moment. He stood at the window with his back to her, looking out. Then he gave a deep sigh, and turned around.

'Do you really want to know the truth?' he said.

Like so many years ago, with her mother, she didn't quite know how to respond to this. But she nodded her head.

'It's a sad story,' he said. 'And no doubt one he didn't want to burden you with. Elizabeth wanted it kept a secret,' he said. 'You see, she hid her pregnancy for so long, under folds of clothing that she was always adjusting and adding to. And at the end she hardly came out of her cabin. She didn't want the child, you see. I know that must be alien to you, such a beautiful and innocent young creature. I shouldn't imagine you could understand so unnatural a feeling in a female as not to want her own child, but then she was not herself. Her malady, it brought out unnatural behaviours in her. So that when it was born, the poor thing, she couldn't care for it. She only wanted it gone.'

Mary watched him, shocked. 'You're not saying that she got rid of the child?'

'Not exactly,' said Robert. 'Only that she refused to care for it. She wouldn't feed it. She put it away from her, so she couldn't hear its cries, and then she bound her breasts tight with cloth, to stop the milk, and though we tried to feed the creature with the ship's supplies, a little water and grain, it wasn't enough. It caught a fever and died.'

Mary looked away. It was more than she could comprehend, either wanting the child or not wanting it, and she felt lost.

'Of course afterwards she was tortured by what had happened, and so she took her own life as well. You can see now, I think, why William didn't want the story told.'

'Yes,' said Mary, though she was shaking her head. She felt as if she should cry, but she didn't. She only stared at the detail of the tapestry on the wall.

'Poor Mary,' said Robert, coming close to her. But then there was a knock at the door. It was Anneke to say that William had returned, and Robert pulled away.

Later that day, when Mary went to the little closet off their room to use the pot, and lifted her skirts, she saw the trickle of black blood on her leg.

There was no child growing in her womb.

But instead of feeling relief, she felt terrified. It was not only how close she had been to ruin, but simply the thought of bearing a child at all that frightened her. Sometimes she wondered if she had ever been a child herself, they were so alien to her. They had always seemed no more than small, senseless creatures, full of needs but with little to give. Robert had said how unnatural Elizabeth was for not wanting her child, but Mary felt for a moment that she could understand the terror there must be in trying to protect such a fragile creature from the world around it. Men talked of the importance of bringing new life into the world, she thought. But they placed scant importance on preserving it once it was there.

William appeared, but barely spoke, and then left for another party. Mary pleaded successfully to avoid it, on account of her headache, and William seemed almost glad to have her stay at home. When he was gone she went downstairs and found Anneke in the parlour.

'Are you all right, my dear?' she said. 'You look paler than ever. I wish you had let my own surgeon see you.'

'I've been thinking,' Mary said. 'About Elizabeth.'

Anneke looked at her. She opened her mouth, as if about to say something, and then closed it again. A moment later, she spoke.

'You must try to forget,' she said decidedly. 'As I have. It's all dead, in the past.'

'Maybe she didn't want a child at all,' Mary said to Anneke, wondering if she would understand.

Anneke looked at her strangely. 'Why would you think that?'

'Maybe she was scared.'

'Who told you that?' said Anneke.

'Nobody,' Mary lied. 'I just wondered.'

'Don't let anybody tell you that!' said Anneke, seeming almost angry. Mary wished she hadn't spoken. 'I knew Elizabeth better than that. She wanted a child more than anything else in the world. That's why she was so distraught.'

Mary must have looked as desolate and confused as she felt, because Anneke came closer and took hold of her tiny hand, squeezing it tight in her own. Mary noticed her long fingernails were painted with jagged patterns.

'I don't think this is about Elizabeth at all,' Anneke said. 'This is about you. And I don't blame you. Don't think I don't know what you are thinking, my dear. We've all thought it, especially as young married women. We've all been in your place. Children are frightening, at first, it's true. But soon they're your reason for being. It's why we're put into this world, after all.'

'To create more of ourselves.'

'Well, yes.'

'But why?'

Anneke took a breath. Her voice was reassuring, but her expression was confused. 'You'll understand,' she said. 'When you have your own.'

'How many do you have?' said Mary.

'Oh, just the two boys,' said Anneke, looking away. 'We've a French-style family.'

'Why no more?' asked Mary.

'Two is enough for me,' said Anneke.

'But how . . .' Mary hesitated, stumbling over the words. 'Could you not . . . have more?'

'I made sure not to,' said Anneke, smiling, understanding her at once.

Mary looked at her. She was desperate to ask what she meant, but it felt indelicate. She bit her lip.

Anneke laughed lightly. 'I see. Two pieces of advice I can give you, in that department. First, don't admit him to your bed any more than is necessary. But that's often harder than it might seem, especially when you live in close quarters on a ship.'

Mary wished she could tell her how easy it would be, for her. She could resist William and he, it seemed, could resist her. But with Robert it was a different matter.

'Yes,' she said, 'it can be.'

'So then you resort to the second method.'

'And what's that?' asked Mary, her curiosity overcoming her reticence.

Anneke looked at her for a while. 'Come with me,' she said, and she got up, leading Mary to a small room just off the main parlour. It was Anneke's own bedroom, decorated with an elaborate and colourful arabesque-style wallpaper, covered with yet more paintings of flowers and plants.

'It's beautiful.'

'A house is a kind of cage,' said Anneke. 'And if one must live in a cage, then it may as well be beautiful. I sleep down here,' she went on, 'so I can let in any guests during the night, and for night wanderers like me, it's easier.'

She went to the side of her bed and opened a drawer, and took out a small enamel box. When she opened it Mary saw it was lined with velvet, and inside was a velvet bag, from which Anneke drew out a small sponge.

'You soak it in vinegar, or oil,' she said, 'and put it . . .' – she hesitated, as if wondering how to phrase it – 'inside yourself. It stops the seed from taking root,' she explained with a little smile.

'Does Monsieur Alberts know you use it?' asked Mary.

'Of course he does,' she said. 'It was him who told me

of it. He doesn't like too much noise around the house. And you'll find that however polite society tries to pretend otherwise, the only way to avoid listening to the noise of children is not to be with them at all. Some people choose that option,' she went on, smiling, 'but I liked to be with my children, where possible.'

Mary reddened, but she knew she had to ask. 'And where would you find such a thing?'

'Any old piece of sponge will do,' Anneke said.

Mary was quiet, trying to think of where she could get hold of a piece of sponge.

Anneke looked at her sympathetically. 'You don't have my advantages, of course,' she said, 'in living here. And you need help in that regard more than I do, I think. Come, I'm sure I have another somewhere.' He buys them for me, you see. He gets them from the kind of place a lady like yourself would not want to visit.' She pulled out another small velvet bag and handed it to Mary.

'Are you sure?' said Mary, putting out her hand tentatively.

'Of course. I don't need it. He doesn't show much interest now anyway; he has . . . other distractions. I'm reaching the end of the line,' she said sadly. 'I'm too old now. But I've often thought I would have liked a daughter, to keep me company in the evenings.' As she closed the drawer Mary saw a hint of sadness on her face again, but then she looked up and smiled brightly. 'One thing,' she said. 'You mustn't tell William.'

'I wasn't going to,' said Mary. 'But why?'

'He badly wants a child. He . . . well, perhaps he thinks it will undo some of the wrongs, make things somehow simpler. But of course it won't. A child is only another person, and as you'll find out, my dear, people are anything but simple.'

They returned to the parlour and took up their seats. Mary's stomach had begun to ache and beads of sweat were forming on her face. She was hot and flushed.

'Try to have a boy,' said Anneke. 'Boys are little worry, and they go out into the world. You have no hold on them. But a girl,' she said, 'a girl is bound to you, she is closer to your own flesh.'

Mary thought of her own mother. When she was a child, her mother wanted her near all the time. She would have liked Mary to be bound to her flesh for ever. But when the time came, she'd had no more control of her than if she'd been a son. 'Until they marry,' she said.

'Yes,' said Anneke sadly. 'Isn't it strange? You think you own them, but in the end you only have them to lose them.'

~

Some time during the night she felt the weight of a body beside her. She stirred a little and realized that William had come to bed. She turned to face the body and a small noise came from it, like the squeak of a mouse. She put out her hands, as though to reassure herself that it was him, and she felt a greasy wetness. It was his tears.

'William, what is it?' she said.

But the body gave no answer.

'William!' she said again.

The body snorted, turned over, and began to snore.

He was crying in his sleep.

Mary brought the bedspread up around him, and wiped the tears from his face. She watched him and wondered who this man was that she had married.

14

Fullarton walked along the promenade of St Pierre. He wore a new suit of dark blue velvet, breeches and waist-coat, the proceeds of his third voyage for Bell in as many months. His braided military hat set off his new shortish black wig, his silk stockings and the brass buttons of his coat. Some plain ruffles, fresh in from Paris, the man had said, enriched his sleeves and the neck of his shirt. The women watched him as he passed and whispered among themselves, and this gave him some satisfaction, until he remembered the reason why they were whispering, because they were telling each other that he was already betrothed.

For a nobody from Orkney who had turned up only four months earlier, there was no doubt that Fullarton had won himself a significant prize. He was aware of how these small changes to his appearance and fortune had raised him in their opinion. It was part of the attraction of this port, where, as strangers passed by every day, there was no way of telling who were the real gentlemen, and who were merely dressed for the part. Fullarton had relished buying these new clothes, had looked forward to showing them off in St Pierre. But now he felt as though he were in costume, for the benefit of an audience.

He sat on a wall and looked out over the water. It was a dull day, and it no longer looked like sparkling champagne, but more like weak ale. He thought how the sea was always moving, always changing, just a great collection of tides being pulled back and forward between different ports. He watched the coast of golden rock, imagined how it stretched around the island, thousands of inlets of yellow sand. How easy it would be, he thought, to take the wages he had earned and disappear into one of these narrow channels, carry on with his old life of smuggling and spending. But he knew it wasn't enough for him, not now that he had a sense of something better. It was a pebble of a desire for something he knew, like memories of home, and it was swept away again as small pebbles are when they linger too close to the shore.

He closed his eyes. But when he opened them again, the world looked the same. He was still the same, and he was still to be married the following week. Bell would be his brother and Margot his sister. He would be a new man, with a new family, and put the past behind him altogether.

'Hello,' said Nancy. They had arranged to meet, but somehow her appearance gave him a start nonetheless.

'I've just seen the plate for our wedding,' she said, a little breathless. 'It's quite beautiful. Thomas is sparing no expense for us, you know,' and her eyes gleamed like polished silver.

Fullarton only nodded.

'Are you all right, my dear?' said Nancy, sitting down beside him, with what seemed to him mock concern. She put her hand on his arm. He took it away and used it to pull out his gold pocket watch, pretending to check the time.

'What a beautiful watch,' exclaimed Nancy. 'But isn't it a lady's?'

Fullarton looked down at it, and a flash of memory – sunlight through lime-green leaves – came to him. He raised his eyes to Nancy. 'It fits more neatly in my pocket,' he said.

'We shall get you a man's one, once we are married. I rather like that one myself. My dear, you do look pale,' she said, squeezing his arm again in that way that had begun to irritate him, as though she were testing fruit for ripeness at a market stall. Or worse, as though she actually cared about his welfare, and was not only waiting to get hold of her brother's money. That was why they were both there, after all, he thought, and he was tired of keeping up the pretence.

'I'm only tired. The weather was poor at sea and we didn't get much sleep. Perhaps I'll go back to the lodgings and sleep it off, and meet you later.'

'Of course,' said Nancy, skipping up. 'I have plenty to do anyway. Margot has picked out some lace and ribbons she wants me to look at. I do hope you like them.'

'I'm sure you'll look beautiful whatever you wear,' he said wearily. You could turn up dressed as a hen, he thought, and I would still marry you.

'Meet me at the Jardin de L'Hyvreuse,' she said. 'At three o'clock.' And then she gave him a sly look. 'I'll be without a chaperone. So I'll be relying on you to take good care of me.'

He watched her as she walked along the promenade in the direction of her brother's house. Could it be that she really was attracted to him? She was fond of her brother, that much was clear, and her brother had taken a liking to him, for a reason he still couldn't understand. He couldn't shake off a growing suspicion that this whole engagement was part of some elaborate trick to rob him. Though of what, he couldn't tell.

He got up, made his way along the promenade, and entered the front door of the King's Arms. He could hear the shouts and voices inside of men playing cards, and checked his watch again. There were some hours to go until three. Sleep could wait. He sat down at the bar and the *cabaretier* poured him a rum.

He was taking his first sip when he heard a shout from the door at the back of the tavern and turned his head to see Bell standing there.

'Fullarton, my boy,' he called. 'Won't you try your luck? We're just starting.'

'Starting what?' asked Fullarton.

'*Combat de coqs*,' said the *cabaretier*, overhearing.

Fullarton knew the phrase well from his time in France. As he picked up his glass and followed the increasing numbers of men filing through the small door at the back of the room, he could already hear the frenzied, high-pitched crowing of the birds. The yard at the back of the tavern had been partially covered and a ring created in the middle, so that it formed a small *gallodrome*. Men stood around it, and Fullarton noticed that one of them was particularly well dressed, with immaculate white stockings and a velveteen jacket of a deep red check. In his arms he held what looked at first to be a thin, scrawny bird, but on closer inspection Fullarton could see the muscle that pulsed from its shoulder blade, and the powerful thighs that showed beneath its shorn belly, which had already been plucked, as if for the pot. Then he saw a flash of steel, and watched the man strapping the spurs on to the bird's legs. The spurs were inscribed with a floral pattern; they had been specially made, and from their white-hot gleam he could tell that they were pure silver.

The man strode into the ring and held the bird high above his head. The bird held out its claws, complete with their razor-sharp spurs, and crowed proudly. It received a complimentary caress from its owner for its effort.

Then to his surprise Bell appeared holding a bird of his own.

'I didn't know you kept cocks,' said Fullarton.

'I keep some at a place outside the town, but now we've moved I'll have room to rear them myself,' said Bell. He showed Fullarton his bird. Then another man pinched its throat until its beak opened wide, and poured a silver cupful of some kind of liquid down its throat.

'What's that you're giving it?' Fullarton asked, leaning forward.

'It's the cock-ale,' said Bell. 'A potent brew – Margot makes it herself. Taste it,' he offered, holding it out.

Fullarton accepted the vessel and took a cautious sip. If it was ale, it had been made with something very high, because it nipped his eyes before it touched his throat. He handed it back to Bell.

'Good stuff,' he said.

'Really gets 'em going, this does,' said Bell, and he opened up the top fully and drank the rest down himself, burping loudly. 'Stirs the blood,' he added over a splutter.

Fullarton watched him and for the first time felt a distaste for his fat self-assuredness.

A bell rang. Immediately there arose a great din from the assembled audience as they began to wager furiously with one another. Fullarton felt the blood pulse in his neck and fingered the bulge of his purse. He walked quickly around the men, giving himself time to eye up each bird before he made his final decision.

Bell's bird was excited. It held its wings in the air and arched its neck, squawking and dancing from toe to toe. Looking over, Fullarton saw that the other seemed calmer. Its owner held it back and it emitted a low growl from the back of its gullet. Fullarton watched them closely for a few minutes. Then he pulled out his purse and drew out one guinea, looking around for someone with whom to place a bet. He didn't have to look far. Nearly every other man seemed to be counting money and the little court-yard echoed with the music of coins changing hands, and the rustling of promissory notes. He gave it to a tall man with a thin nose and small, bright eyes.

'One guinea on the bird with the silver spurs,' he said.

The man looked down at the gold coin and beamed at Fullarton.

Fullarton found a comfortable perch on the opposite side from Bell, on one of the steps that led to the kitchen, where he had a good view of the ring. The stable boys were dampening the sawdust, and the birds were getting frustrated. They were held to each other for ten seconds, beak to beak, until they screeched and held up their claws, struggling to break free from their keepers' hands. As they did so the roar of the surrounding audience grew to a high-pitched, feverish buzz and this seemed to fluff up the birds even more, so that by the time they were let loose they flew at one another like geese, wings flapping and necks outstretched.

'Which one you got?' asked a voice beside him.

Fullarton turned to see a roughly dressed French boy. He recognized him as one of the boys who worked in the tavern. He was not used to being spoken to so forwardly by a person like this, and at first frowned, but the boy grinned at him with such childish openness that he forgot to be offended.

'I've got that one,' he said. 'I think it's called Thunder.'

'A classy old cock, that one,' said the boy, 'but no match for the Black Bull.'

That was Bell's bird. Fullarton looked over to where Bell stood, and noticed that the tall man who had taken his money was standing beside him.

'Look at him, built like one too,' said the boy.

'He's a burly one, all right,' said Fullarton, smiling back now, still watching Bell. The tall man had disappeared and Bell looked directly at him. He seemed a little lost, and suddenly Fullarton regretted not having backed his bird.

'It's only a game,' he said to himself quietly, and the boy turned round.

'Don't let the trainers hear you say that,' he said. 'It's life and death to them.'

The birds had been taken back, and fed more of the cock-ale, and then they were released again. They flew at each other with fervour. Immediately the men began to shout. Thunder leapt into the air and down upon Black

Bull, his silver spurs gleaming, and dug Black Bull a good blow in the thigh, so that the sawdust around them began to turn pink. Then he made a grab for the neck with his beak. Black Bull let out a screech and pulled away, limping and dragging his leg to the other side of the ring, to the jeers of the assembled crowd. Bell was mad, and shouted at the bird, and the bird turned, slowly, as though obeying, and began to run at his opponent. This time both birds leapt together, and fell upon each other in such a way that both their spurs dug deep into the other and they could not extract them. The owners had to step into the ring and pull the birds apart, and the referee, a small, fat man with a single, thin strip of hair and a great air of importance, allowed them a little resting time before the fight began again.

'Get on with it,' shouted Fullarton, becoming impatient. He had left his drink somewhere along the way and wanted to get back to the bar, but the crowd was tight. There was no leaving the fight until it was over.

'No,' said the boy beside him, 'it's better this way, makes the fight longer. Might as well get your money's worth out of them.'

Then they were on each other again, this time more hesitant, as if they had learned the folly of their previous enthusiasm. Instead of leaping at one another they pecked at each other's necks and eyes. Fullarton saw that a lot of blood was leaching out on to the sawdust and realized that one of their wounds must be weeping badly, but he couldn't see which one. Meanwhile the men were hopping around from foot to foot, calling and jeering, a little like cockerels themselves, or even old hens, or leaning over the ring with their drinks in their hands, open lips like beaks, slavering into the sawdust.

Suddenly one of the birds lost his footing, and fell on to his breast. Fullarton saw with dismay that it was Thunder, and at once Black Bull was on him, leaping from a great height and digging his spurs into the soft, shaved flesh.

'That's the way, Bull, roast me a good cock,' shouted Bell.

The boy beside him grinned, and Fullarton wished he wore his own spurs. The boy turned to Fullarton. 'Nothing like a good cockfight,' he said.

Thunder managed to rise again, and reached out to peck Black Bull. It was a weak, hopeless movement. He began to retreat, leaving a trail of blood, and Black Bull followed him, his chest inflated, crowing with what seemed to Fullarton to be an edge of mocking triumph. Thunder must have felt it too, because he turned and took one last, feeble jump at Black Bull. But his eyes were dull, and he bled badly, and it was clear that his heart was no longer in it. He fell again, and his beak opened, the small tongue protruding, palpitating quickly at first, then more slowly, and finally, after a few more pecks from Black Bull, slowing to a stop.

Several of the men who had salivated into the ring now fell to their knees in despair. They must have lost a great deal, thought Fullarton, and he looked at them in disgust. They were promptly picked up by some of the larger men who surrounded the outside of the ring, and forced to pay up. One man, who clearly couldn't, was taken by the neck and slung into the street outside.

Fullarton approached the well-dressed man, the owner of Thunder.

'Bad luck,' he said. 'Thought you were in with a chance.' He looked at the bloody carcass of the bird.

The man stepped into the ring and stooped to untie the silver spurs. He shrugged. 'That's the game. You lose some on him?' he asked.

'A little.'

Then Bell came up beside him and put his arm on his shoulder. 'What a fight, eh! Come on, I'll buy you a drink.'

They sat down at a table and Bell finished most of the contents of a bottle of wine. Fullarton said little. He was thinking of the wedding plans, and what Nancy would want from him once they were married.

Bell was also quiet. As he drank he tapped his fingers on the table in a way that began to irritate Fullarton. Eventually Bell sat forward in his seat.

'You didn't bet on my bird, did you?' he asked Fullarton.

Fullarton looked up, surprised. He coloured deeply, suddenly ashamed. 'No,' he said.

Bell nodded. 'You should have been more loyal,' he said.

'I'm sorry,' said Fullarton. 'Truly, I am.' There was a catch in his voice.

Bell suddenly threw his head back and roared with laughter. 'Don't take it so seriously,' he said. 'It's your money, though I could have told you you were throwing it away. You did exactly what I expected you to do. What everyone does. You chose the fancier-looking bird, the one dressed for the part.'

Fullarton felt Bell was mocking him now. 'He seemed a better-trained bird,' he said defensively.

'Ah,' said Bell, and then he leaned forward, lowering his voice. 'That's the trick, you see. What you didn't know, and nobody else here either, is that both of those birds are mine. So I gain regardless, the prize money for one, and the bets on the other. Remember what I said before: stick with me, son, and I'll show you the easy ways to make money.'

Fullarton looked at him for a moment, and he coloured again. He felt embarrassed, and angry, at being laughed at so conspicuously. People at the bar had turned round and were looking at them both. But he also felt cheated.

'Aren't you going to pay me my money back, then?' he said.

'I'm paying for your damned wedding,' said Bell, roaring with laughter again. 'And a lot more besides. What more do you want from me? See it as a lesson in life, boy. Didn't I tell you you're like a son to me? And what are fathers for if not to teach their sons lessons?'

Fullarton thought about leaving, walking out. He would not stay to be mocked. But he knew Bell was drunk, and as he turned his head he saw Nancy's small white face at the door. Suddenly he remembered their planned meeting that afternoon.

'No,' he said, putting his hand to his mouth.

'Wha . . .' said Bell, whose eyes were beginning to close.

'I was supposed to meet Nancy.'

'Ah, never mind about her,' said Bell. 'She'll have gone home. Have another drink.'

'She's here!' hissed Fullarton. He stood up and walked towards her, holding out his hand.

'My dear,' he said. 'What are you doing here alone?'

'You were supposed to meet me,' she said icily, 'over

half an hour ago, at Le Jardin de L'Hyvreuse! I was alone there, as you know.'

'I'm sorry,' he said. Then he lowered his voice. 'Listen, your brother is here. He's in liquor, he won his cockfight. I don't like to leave him. Come and have a drink for a moment and then we can take him home.'

Reluctantly she followed him, looking around her.

'They're all watching me,' she said.

'They're not used to seeing a lady here.'

'I can see one over there.'

'She works here.'

'I'm sure she does,' said Nancy sourly. She sat down on the edge of a chair.

He knew she resented having to sit there, and it made him sip his drink all the slower.

'Ah, Nancy,' said Bell. 'What do you think, Black Bull the champion again?'

Nancy gave a look of disgust. 'They get those birds worked up into such an unnatural state.'

'It's perfectly natural,' said Fullarton. 'They were born to fight.'

'Hah,' said Nancy, 'you've obviously never seen the cocks in the yard. They have a little scuffle, yes, but the weaker one always backs down. They don't kill each other.'

'Of course they do,' said Fullarton. 'It's their nature.' He thought of the cockerels in the tounmal, but they had only had one. His mother killed all the male chicks, except the one they needed to breed. He had never actually seen a wild cockfight. But he would argue with her anyway, because he had had too much of the cock-ale himself. He looked to Bell for support.

'Ach,' Bell said to Fullarton. 'Don't mind her. What would we do for sport if the women had their way? Kill each other probably!'

'You do that quite successfully already,' said Nancy. The blood was up in her face, too, and she looked back to Fullarton. 'Do you think in the wild they're given strong ale, and kept penned in till they'll attack the first thing they see? They've been imprisoned for so long they're made mad by it. There's nothing natural about that.'

Fullarton pulled out a small silver snuff box and took a pinch, sneezing once. 'Nancy,' he said coolly, 'you don't know what you're talking about.'

Nancy looked at Bell, who had fallen asleep against the chair, and tutted in disgust. Then she turned and looked hard at Fullarton.

'John,' she said, 'do you really want to marry me?'

Fullarton felt a pang of fear. He softened at once, and took her hand. 'Why, my darling, of course I do. Why would you ask a thing like that?'

'I don't know, it's just that you seem awfully distant. You hardly come to see me, or ask about the wedding plans. You don't seem interested. I know nothing about you and you avoid all my questions. Are things going to be different when we marry?'

Fullarton leaned forward. 'Of course they are. I'm just busy, with your brother's business, that's all.'

Nancy leaned forward too, and lowered her voice. 'John, can I ask you something?' she said.

'Of course.'

'Do you think it's really my brother you want to marry, and not me?'

Fullarton looked up sharply. 'What nonsense,' he said with irritation. And then he hesitated a moment. 'It's just that . . . we don't have to be together all the time, do we? I mean, when we're married we'll see enough of each other. You ask me questions all the time, and I've my own affairs to put right, after all, and, damn it, surely a man is entitled to some time alone before he is to be imprisoned for ever!' He knew that he sounded petulant, but he took another gulp of his drink, staring past her.

'Well, if that's how you see it,' she said quietly, 'perhaps we should think about freeing you.' She tilted her head to the side and gave a small, impertinent smile that infuriated him, because he could see she understood him too well.

'Perhaps we should,' he said in retaliation, but then to his surprise she started to cry, loud enough for some of the men at the bar to turn around. He noticed Bell stirring a little.

'Nancy,' he said, a little more softly, aware that she might indeed choose to back out, and that his chances of making his fortune might be lost. 'I am sorry, it's tiring being weeks at sea. And on my own, with only sailors for company. I need a little time to myself, to get used to the normal world again. And time is different too. That's why I forgot to meet you today.'

'Does the motion of the sea change the motion of your watch?' Nancy said, looking up. Her tears had vanished.

He reached out and took her hand. 'Please,' he said, 'let's meet later instead.'

'What about now?' she said, looking him in the eye.

'Well, you know that I could, but I have this to finish' – he held up his drink – 'and some affairs to sort out.'

'You mean debts to pay?'

'Only small ones,' he said. 'From the cockfight.'

'You know when we are married,' she said, her face set, 'this will have to stop. My brother can do what he likes with his money, but I won't see my fortune lost on a few old birds.'

Fullarton hardened again. 'I don't see why a man can't play a game once in a while.'

'Well,' said Nancy, seeming offended again, 'in that case, I'll leave you to your games.'

She stood up abruptly and turned to walk out. But she didn't move with any speed, lingering for him to follow. Fullarton waited until she was in the middle of the tavern before he stood up.

'Nancy,' he said, 'don't go like this.' But he knew that for her to back down then would be to do so in front of all the men, the mixture of merchants and rough-looking seamen who were watching her at that moment.

She saw it too, her face reddened, and she gave him a look of confused disgust, then strode out.

Again, he waited a little before jumping up and going to the door to follow her. She was halfway along the street, and he called her name, but quietly. She glanced back for a moment, saw him watching her, and hesitated, as if expecting him to join her. But he only called her name again, and she continued to walk away.

He studied her figure as she walked. She was pretty, it was true, with small proportions and black hair and dark eyes, but there was something about her he disliked. He could see it in the way she carried herself. She was quick and lively, and, more than anything, sure of herself. Too sure altogether.

Or perhaps it was that she had hit on something when she had said he would rather marry Bell, that it was not only Bell's money, but his approval, that had drawn him to, and kept him in, St Pierre. The idea of needing Bell more than he needed his money filled him with a sense of dread.

He walked along the promenade. The late afternoon air was cool and soft and the boats knocked together with hollow clicks as the water stirred gently. The sky and sea were a pale lilac streaked with red cloud. Men and women took the air and Fullarton again looked at the detail of their dress, the women's delicate lace parasols and the fine fabrics and French cut of the men's clothes. He touched the lace of his own ruffles. Suddenly he took hold of one and ripped it away from his neck, tearing the fine lace to shreds in front of two old men, who smoked their pipes and watched him curiously.

He threw them on the ground and turned back to the tavern, in time to see Bell coming out. Fullarton felt foolish, looking down at the remains of his ruffles, but Bell didn't even notice he was there. He lumbered past, his face determined, set on the act of putting one foot down after another. Fullarton watched him until he disappeared around a corner. Then he entered the bar again.

He was served by the boy who had stood beside him during the cockfight.

'Bad luck earlier,' said the boy.

'Yes,' said Fullarton, 'but I'm about to reverse that. A bottle of claret and a pack of playing cards, please.'

'Good luck again then, monsieur,' said the boy, smiling as he handed him the cards and wine.

Fullarton approached a tall Guernseyman who he had noticed was sitting alone.

'Would you like to share a bottle and a game of cards?' he asked.

The man nodded.

As Fullarton began to deal, the memory of the cock-fight, of Bell and Nancy, began to fade as his mind focused on the details of the game. He held two queens, and he could tell by the expression of the man opposite him that he had nothing to speak of. He laughed quietly to himself, and put down some coins, not stopping to count them. Then he looked at the Guernseyman and smiled slightly. 'What've you got?' he asked.

The man laid down his cards to show three kings. Fullarton looked at them in disbelief. Then he stood slowly, and his hand went towards his pistol. But the Guernseyman was there before him; he drew a short sword and held it towards Fullarton's hand. Fullarton stepped back and began to laugh.

'Put the sword away,' he said. 'And take your money, here.' He pushed it across the table. 'Have it with my blessing. Let's play again.'

By the time the Guernseyman got up to leave neither man knew who had won. Fullarton later remembered seeing the money on the table and the Guernseyman on the floor. From the corner of his eye Fullarton watched as his partner was half carried across the floor by the *cabaretier*. What an idiot, he thought, before he fell asleep, to get so drunk.

~

Fullarton awoke a little later with the blood pounding in his head, and found he was leaning on the shoulder of a boy, maybe eighteen, who was helping him up the stairs. He looked down at his feet, which seemed to be moving independently of him.

'Who in the name of God are you?' he asked, glancing at the boy.

'Don't you remember?'

Fullarton fixed his eyes on him, and realized that it was the same boy who had spoken to him at the cockfight earlier.

'This hasn't been a good day for you, has it, monsieur?'

'What happened?'

'You fell asleep.'

'Did I win?' asked Fullarton.

'Win what?'

'The card game, did I win it?'

'Can't say I was watching, sir.'

They reached the door of his room.

'Here you are, monsieur.'

'Please,' said Fullarton, recovering himself, 'you've been so kind, won't you share a drink with me?'

'I think you've had enough to drink, sir.'

Fullarton looked at the boy, whose hair was black and thick, ragged like hemp, and whose skin was the colour of a smooth, brown hazelnut. He put his hand on the boy's chin and stroked it. The boy looked at him.

'Here,' said Fullarton, 'I'll pay you, look.' He began to rummage in his pockets, but found they were empty.

'You had better save what you have left,' said the boy, 'for the bill.' And he gently pushed Fullarton into his room. Then, to Fullarton's surprise, the boy followed him in, locking the door behind him.

15

It was only when they were back on board the *Isabella* that Mary noticed the change in William's character. He was continually on edge, even more so than usual, as they rowed out to the ship. Once on board, he kept checking his pocket watch and inspecting every last rope, knot and dial on the ship before they set sail. If it wasn't for the fact that he hardly seemed to notice her presence, then she would have suspected that he knew about herself and Robert. Instead she put it down to the threat of privateers, though she had heard there were fewer of them than before, now that they were focusing on the wealthier Spanish prizes to the south.

Mary watched as the port of Amsterdam pulled away from them, but the land continued for a long time, little squares of neatly laid-out fields. She wished her own life could run in such neat lines and crosses. Instead, it was more like the piece of fancy work she had hardly touched since she left Leith, an imitation of neatness at the front, but at the back a tangled mess of knotted threads.

When the strips of land finally came to an end, and they were in the open sea, she saw William even less than before. He spent the evenings playing cards with the other officers, while Mary sat in her cabin and read. When William did appear he was irritable, complaining about every little thing, such as the neatness of her mending or the fact that she had set out the wrong clothes for him. He would leave in a temper and not appear back in the cabins until late at night, when Mary would pretend to be asleep. Very occasionally he would wake her to make love, but those instances were rare, and that silent animal communication was the only thread that remained between them.

Robert came to her room each evening. She waited for his familiar knock, and his visits were the only thing that broke the monotony of her days. They made love, and afterwards Robert lay drowsily beside her, whispering.

'I can think of nothing but you,' he said.

'I'm sure that's not true,' she said with a laugh, quite sure that it was.

'I think of you all day long,' he said. 'I can hardly work for it.'

'It's nice to think of you,' she said, 'thinking of me, while you are treating all manner of bloody wounds and septic diseases.'

'Do you doubt me?' he murmured, kissing the warm, oily skin beneath her breast.

'I doubt the smell of brandy that's on your breath,' she said, but she closed her eyes, because in truth she loved this smell, along with all his others.

She never worried about William appearing. Each night, she asked Robert where he was, and he replied with the same two words: 'Drunk, sleeping.'

But she continued to feel that familiar yearning, as though there were something more about him that she needed. At times she almost wished she could slice him open, like a surgeon, and climb into the warmth of his skin. There was a distance she could not overcome. It grew into a kind of anxiety in her, and she was anxious, too, about practical matters. What if the sponges didn't work? They weren't foolproof, Anneke had told her. What if she did fall pregnant? Would Robert support a child? She couldn't help but remember Anneke's warning, that Robert had no money other than what he earned on this voyage. It preyed on her mind increasingly, until at last she had to say something, one evening, as Robert lay almost asleep beside her. She sat up, and threw off the blankets. She felt irritable somehow.

'Robert,' she said.

'Whaa?' He was half asleep, too lazy even to finish the word.

She reached out and shook him. 'Robert,' she said sharply in his ear. 'Wake up.'

He sat up drowsily, scratching his head. 'What is it, my darling?'

'Are you not even slightly concerned about what might happen if I am made with child by you?'

Robert put his hand on her arm. 'You suppose I can think of such matters, when I am faced with your beauty before me?'

'Oh, be quiet, Robert, you take it too far. Please answer me. Would you support me and a child of yours?'

Robert looked away, then shook his head. 'How can you ask me that? You know I would do anything for you.'

'But would you do that? And would you take me away from him?'

Robert bit his lip. 'If only I knew how,' he said. 'You know as well as I do how difficult it would be. Even if we ran away, the scandal would spread. We would be found out, and things would be far worse for you then.'

'Surely such practicalities are of no consequence when faced with someone of my beauty,' said Mary bitterly.

Robert said nothing.

A few moments later, she began to cry. Robert came close to her and she put her head into the crook of his neck, feeling the wiry scratch of his hair.

'We must only be careful,' said Robert. 'Perhaps, if we wait, a chance will come.'

But Mary's irritability had increased. These vague promises were no longer enough for her. She wanted more from him now.

'Well, you needn't worry, in any event,' she added, 'about my falling with child by you. I've been shown a way to prevent it.'

Robert sat up and turned to face her. 'But why would you want to prevent it?' he asked. 'A young woman like you should want to have children.'

'Should I?' asked Mary. 'Perhaps you're right. Perhaps I am unnatural. But the fact is, I don't want to be ruined any more than you want to be scandalized. So I've taken my own precautions.'

Robert was quiet. 'What kind of precautions?'

'A kind of sponge, soaked in vinegar.'

Robert nodded his head slowly, as if he understood perfectly. 'I see. Who gave you that?' he asked.

'Anneke,' said Mary.

Robert nodded again. 'That's no surprise. That woman knows all the whore's tricks,' he said.

Mary got out of bed quickly and put on her mantua. 'How dare you speak to me like that!' she exclaimed.

He sat up. 'Mary, I didn't mean that you—'

'Yes, you did,' she interrupted. 'You meant exactly that.'

'If it sounded that way then I apologize,' he said, and at this she softened, resting against the wooden walls of the cabin. 'It's only . . .' He appeared to be thinking. 'That woman you stayed with, Anneke. I know you were fond of her, Mary, in your innocence, but you know that she is not a reputable woman. Her profession, well, it used to be something quite different from what it is now.'

'I don't know what you mean.'

'How plain do I have to make it, Mary? Surely you understand me. Surely you know the kind of establishments that exist in such ports.'

'I can't believe it,' said Mary.

'Anneke's establishment, to be sure, was one of the more respectable, if such a thing can be said.'

'I still don't believe it.'

'There's no reason why you should. I know you're the kind of person to see the good in everyone,' said Robert. 'And I wouldn't have told you, only I don't want you to place your faith in all that she says.'

It occurred to Mary that Anneke was one of the few people she had met since marrying William who had spoken the truth. But she said nothing.

'Would it be such a terrible thing, Mary, if you were to have my child?' he said at last.

'But don't you see,' said Mary, 'it's impossible.'

'Nobody need know that it was mine.'

'I would know,' said Mary, 'and so might William.'

'William barely knows himself, at times,' said Robert scornfully. 'But perhaps I could arrange something to help you, that would help us both. Yes, perhaps something can be done,' he said, as if talking to himself.

Mary looked at him, and though her pride would not let her show it, she hoped.

~

It was her custom to slip the sponge inside her in the evening, and she had whispered to Robert in the corridor that day the time he was to come to her. She had finally learned the times of William's watches. He said that he would, as he flicked the tip of her nipple gently through the silk of her clothes, and that he had some good news.

But when the door opened half an hour earlier than they had planned she looked up in horror to see not Robert but William.

'Has something happened?' she asked.

'Has something happened?' he said. 'Well, let's see, let's not ask has something happened, but is something happening? Something happening behind my back. Something that you have chosen to conceal from me!' In his hand he held the cane that he used to start the young boys on deck when they were not working hard enough.

Mary opened her mouth, but managed to compose herself enough to speak. 'I haven't the slightest idea what you're referring to,' she said.

'Oh, perhaps you've forgotten then, how you've tried to trick me.' And to her horror, he strode towards the bed, opened her private drawer, and took out the little veneered box, which contained her sponge.

'You meant to conceal this from me!' he exclaimed.

'No,' she said quickly. 'It was only that there hasn't been the opportunity.'

'You mean to cheat nature,' he went on, ignoring her, 'and deny me of my right to an heir.'

'No, sir,' she said. 'I did not, only that when the time was right—'

'God himself shall decide when the time is right!' he bellowed. 'Not some slip of a girl. God help me, I should beat you to within an inch of your life, to cheat me in this way,' and he lifted his cane.

Mary took a step back. 'I'm sorry to have offended you,' she said. 'It's only that I was frightened.'

'Frightened!' he bellowed again. 'Of what you were made for, what nonsense.' His hand with the cane in it shook. 'Give me your hand.'

She refused to move it, and he grabbed hold of it instead, striking it across the back of the knuckles. She curled her fingers as the pain knifed through to the bone, but he held it fast, and struck it again, then let go. Her hand was numb and tingling, and her fingers would not move.

Then William took out his pistol, and her breath dried in her mouth.

'What . . .' she whispered, but her words became tangled.

'Take your box, and come with me,' he said.

He pushed her on to the deck. She carried the box in her aching fingers, and felt the point of the pistol in her ribs. When he reached the deck he pushed it a little further through the silk of her gown, until the soft flesh gave beneath.

'Now!' he said. 'Cast it overboard.'

Mary looked into William's eyes, and although she gasped at the thought of the pistol in her ribs, she thought she could see a weakness in him. She held on tightly to the box. But another rap on the knuckles, and a jab of the pistol, released it from her hands. She watched it fall. It disappeared into the fog, and she did not see it hit the water.

She turned to face her husband, and the hatred in her eyes was such that even he seemed to recoil from her.

'Now you can have your heir,' she said, and walked past him, back to the cabin. She felt him watching, but he did not follow her.

Mary sat in her cabin. She didn't cry, she was too shocked. She simply went over in her mind what had happened, over and over again. It was only when Robert finally arrived, twenty minutes late, and she began to tell him, that the tears came easily, as they always seemed to when Robert was near.

'We can't go on now,' she said. 'I'm going to speak to William, and ask him if I can go home.'

Robert put his arms round her. He didn't speak. Suddenly she stopped crying. A small poisonous thought had crept into her mind.

'The only person who knew,' she said quietly, looking up at him, 'was you.'

'What are you suggesting?' said Robert, drawing back from her.

'I'm not suggesting anything,' she said, her voice trembling. 'But then, how did he know?' she said.

'If you had given me time,' he said, 'if you had trusted

me, then I would have explained it to you.' He turned away from her now, and he looked as though she had hurt him.

She felt suddenly desperate as he made to leave the room. 'Oh, Robert,' she said. 'I am sorry, I do trust you. Please don't leave.'

He rounded to face her and softened. 'He told me that he suspected it,' he said, 'and asked me if I had supplied you with anything. I told him I was sure he was wrong, but he said he knew you were using something, else you would have been expecting by now. Then I saw it was no use pretending, so I told him that you had approached me, and told me that your grandmother had died in child-birth, and your mother very nearly, and that you were anxious not to fall pregnant until we were within a safe distance of land, and that I had agreed this was a sensible plan, from a medical point of view. But he wouldn't hear of it. He had liquor in him as usual, and said it was perfectly natural and that there was no risk whatever for a healthy young girl like you. There was nothing more I could do.'

He put his arm around her again, and wiped away a little smear of tear on her cheek. He began to kiss her. She responded with fury, pulling at his clothes.

'But, Mary,' he said. 'You just said we mustn't, it isn't safe.'

'I don't care,' she said. 'I'll give him his heir, if it's what he wants, only it won't be his, and he'll find it out too late.' She found the place where his breeches met his shirt, sliding her small fingers beneath, feeling the cool skin respond. 'I hate him,' she whispered.

'I wish he was dead,' she said as he entered her.

She felt a kind of redemptive justice at Robert's final convulsion.

'Robert,' she whispered, as he rolled off her.

'Yes?'

'You said earlier you had good news. What was it?'

He seemed uncertain again. 'I need to work out a couple of things first.'

He looked at her, and she gazed back into his black eyes. They were solid, unmoving, unmoved. She knew she had no choice but to trust them, and she nodded her head.

16

Fullarton woke the next morning to the sickly cries of the gulls outside. He turned and retched over the side of the bed. He rolled back and saw the empty, but ruffled space in the bed beside him. Outside a gull screeched three times, as though laughing.

A couple of glancing memories of the previous night began to return. He checked his purse, and saw that it was empty. He must have lost at the card game after all. Then another thought occurred to him, and he picked up his pillow, reaching well into the stuffing, feeling for the place where he had stored his remaining money, the proceeds from the ship he had sold shortly after starting to work for Bell. It was gone. He sat down on the bed. The sick feeling had returned to his stomach.

He had offered to pay.

The money itself was of little consequence. He would have enough of it after his wedding, but at that thought his blood ran cold. What if the boy had done this deliberately, in order to spread a shocking tale all over the town, and elicit some kind of payment from Bell in order to keep it quiet? Then Nancy might not agree to marry him at all.

But then another fear crept in, one that seemed much more plausible to him at that moment. What if Bell had arranged this, in order to discredit him and get out of the agreement he had made with him? What if he had had second thoughts? Nancy had cooled, it was true, and Bell had accused him of being disloyal. Suddenly it all seemed to fall into place. Bell had never loved him as his own son. He had only seen him as a way of making more money, and making his strange sister seem a more attractive proposition than she was.

He should have felt sick again, but instead he felt a rush of joy. Then that dispersed as he realized that being poor was no kind of freedom. The only way out of this mess was to marry Nancy as quickly as possible, before she discovered.

There was no escape. Yet escape was all he could entertain. His mind brimming with these thoughts, he loaded his possessions into his portmanteau. There were many of them. His silk scarves and waistcoats, his gold pocket watch, his best hat and two wire wigs he had bought in France. The case was full, and he considered what he might leave behind, but he couldn't decide. In the end he knew he could part with nothing. These possessions were who he was. In fact, they were all he was, because without them he was nothing more than the small boy from Orphir who had been on a big adventure and grown a little older. And to be that boy again, Fullarton thought, was to be nothing at all.

On the way downstairs he saw that the bar was empty. Suddenly the *cabaretier* appeared and Fullarton made as if to duck away, but the *cabaretier* had seen him and called out.

'Monsieur Fullarton, how are you this morning? I hope you are not too sore in the head.'

'Thank you, I am fine.'

'I saw my boy had to help you up to bed.' He began to laugh. 'Why don't you come in and take a morning draught? You know there's nothing to cure a hangover so well.'

Fullarton looked at the glass of brandy the *cabaretier* offered. He could see no sign of the boy. As he looked at the drink he began to feel a little more secure. The boy had stolen his money after all, chances were he wouldn't want to run into Fullarton right away. He entered the bar and took the drink.

'And a little extra addition,' said the *cabaretier*. He broke an egg into the brandy, and whisked it around. 'This will help you.'

'I doubt that much can help me this morning,' said Fullarton. 'But thank you. Your health.'

As he sipped the harsh spirit, his hands began to still, and his heart to slow. He looked around. There was no sign of the man he had played cards with. There was no sign of the boy. He felt an anger burn like indigestion in his stomach. They had both taken his money and disappeared. But as the numbness of the brandy took hold the boy came to mind again and his anger faded slightly. He would have liked, he thought for a moment, to have seen him, not to touch, just to look, once more.

'Incidentally, have you seen my bar boy?' asked the *cabaretier*.

Fullarton turned sharply. 'No, why?' he asked.

'Didn't turn up for work this morning.' The man shrugged. 'I saw him leaving in the night, no doubt off to spend his wages at some whorehouse.' He shook his head. 'He's an orphan, you know, had a tough life. I took him in when nobody else would. But he needs a little of the Lord in his soul.'

Fullarton looked at him and smiled bitterly. 'Don't we all,' he said.

'You lost a lot of money last night?' the landlord asked.

Fullarton nodded. 'A fool's game,' he said.

'The problem with that game,' the landlord said, 'is that the stakes are not high enough. You win some, you lose some, you never make enough to stop. I'm not against gambling; don't we gamble every day in our lives. But in that game, the risks outweigh the benefits. The trick is not to play the game, but to run it.'

He sat back on his chair and lit a pipe; he was enjoying the company, and Fullarton sat in a kind of dazed trance, listening.

'When you run the game, you get all the money, and none of the risk,' said the *cabaretier*. 'Once this war ends, things will be easier. It's not easy for the traders when they can't get access to the ports. The only people who are winning right now are the privateers. That's where the money's to be made now.'

Fullarton looked up.

'Bunch of murderers and thieves most of them,' said the landlord. 'But there's money to be made, to be sure.' He winked as he finished.

Fullarton said nothing, but the landlord seemed to read his mind.

'Monsieur Guillaume Henri, the silversmith, organizes such things,' said the *cabaretier*. 'Do you know him?'

Fullarton swallowed. 'I believe the silver for my wedding has been purchased from him.'

'Of course, Monsieur Bell spares no expense to see his sister married to such a gallant gentleman,' said the *cabaretier*, and Fullarton wondered if there was a note of sarcasm in his voice. Perhaps he, too, was an ally of Bell's. Perhaps Bell had arranged the whole deception through him.

'But the other business that Monsieur Henri is involved in is most profitable, I believe,' the *cabaretier* went on. 'He is the best *négociant* in the town, and can obtain a letter-of-marque in no time at all. You see, he runs the game, but he is not fool enough to play.'

Fullarton got up to go. 'Thanks for the drink,' he said.

'That's all right Monsieur Fullarton,' said the *cabaretier*. 'And Monsieur Fullarton,' he said as Fullarton was almost out of the door.

'Yes?'

'I notice you are carrying your portmanteau. If you intend to leave, you will remember to pay your bill, won't you?'

'Of course,' said Fullarton. 'I'm not sure if I'm leaving today or not, but in any case, Monsieur Bell will be paying the bill for me. You may send the account to his house.'

'Ah!' The *cabaretier* immediately put up his hand. Perhaps he wasn't in league with Bell after all. 'Have a good day, monsieur.'

~

Monsieur Henri was a small man, with tight, weaselly eyes, a prominent nose and an almost continuous smile. His teeth were completely eaten out, and it was clear by that and by his swollen belly that he enjoyed his share of the good things in life. When Fullarton asked how quickly he could obtain a letter-of-marque, he smiled.

'For the right price,' he said, 'I have one here,' and he held up a piece of paper.

'But,' said Fullarton, 'how can that be?'

'My hand bears a striking resemblance to the hand that signed the original of this,' he said, holding up another piece of paper, and Fullarton nodded, comprehending. He looked at the piece of paper in the old man's hand.

'What happened to the original vessel?' he asked.

'She's not been seen these last three years,' said Monsieur Henri, smiling. 'The authorities suppose her lost in action, but they have no proof, so there'll be no surprise should she turn up again with some story of capture and escape. I'm sure you can think of something.'

'But I have no money,' he said, 'except this,' and he took out his gold watch.

Monsieur Henri examined it. 'I'm afraid this won't pay it,' he said, giving it back to Fullarton. Then he saw the desperate look on Fullarton's face.

'There is another way,' he went on. 'I am willing to invest in such a venture, for a reasonable return, of course. I will give you a contract. But you must be able to invest a little yourself. Remember,' he said, with a sly smile, 'I will lose yet more money if the silver plate for your wedding must be returned.'

'Oh, the wedding will happen,' said Fullarton quickly.

'Just a little delay, that's all. But don't worry, I'll find your money.' He backed out of the shop. An idea had just occurred to him.

He found Margot at home, not yet dressed, and it was thirty minutes before she could receive him. When at last she came in he fell to his knees.

'Whatever's the matter?' she asked.

'Margot,' he said, 'I'm so sorry to break in on you like this.'

'It's all right, but whatever is it? You are a mess!' She put her hand on his head and he stood up.

'Is Thomas in?' Fullarton asked.

'No, he's out on business.'

'That's good. I mean, it's better that he doesn't know. I lost money last night, Margot, gambling.'

'I know,' she said, smiling. 'You bet on the wrong bird.'

'No, not then, afterwards, at cards. I know I shouldn't have. I'm ashamed of my behaviour. But I owe a great deal, and Margot, I don't have the money to pay. I fear that if I don't appear with the winnings then the man I gambled with will demand a duel.'

Margot put her hand up to her mouth. 'Just tell me, then, how much you owe, and we shall pay it.'

'Margot, you are too kind,' he said. 'But I can't take your money without endeavouring to pay it back. I've decided,' he continued, looking down, 'that I will have to postpone my wedding to Nancy until I've paid you your money. I'm going to take a commission on a privateer.'

Margot stared at him. She opened her mouth a little,

and the edges of her eyes appeared wet. 'But the plans have been made!' she exclaimed.

'You are good at organizing, Margot. I am sure that you'll be able to settle things for me.' He took a step towards her, and put one hand on her arm. With the other, he lifted her chin, so that she looked into his eyes. 'You must understand. I want to be worthy of Miss Bell's hand,' he said. 'I want to bring as much to the match as your husband brings on her account. It's a matter of honour,' he finished, straightening.

Margot nodded, and blinked.

'I want to thank you,' he said, 'for everything you have done.'

She looked as though she might cry then. 'I only wanted to see you settled here,' she said. 'You're like one of our family now.'

Fullarton stroked the side of her cheek, and for a moment he felt the strength leave his legs. Out of all Bell's connections, he decided then, he had liked Margot the best, perhaps because he knew how she needed him. 'I will make all good on my return, madam,' he said stiffly. Then he leaned forward and kissed her, once, on the lips.

'Thomas will be furious,' she whispered.

'I am sure if you explain my reasons,' said Fullarton, 'and that he will be recompensed fully for any losses . . .'

~

Twenty minutes later, his purse full of Margot's money, Fullarton lifted his portmanteau and walked briskly away. He turned back once, to see Margot's small, pale face watching him. He looked at it for a moment, and then walked on. A cool breeze filtered up the street from the harbour and on it he could smell the fermented growth of the sea.

17

Mary felt it as a gnawing desire to chew, to draw nourishment from whatever came her way. She sucked at pieces of salt beef until they were dry and pale. But she felt no nausea, and no fear. To her surprise, she felt less frightened of the child growing in her womb than she had of anyone, or anything else in her life.

She knew it was Robert's. William had come to her bed only twice since the incident, and he had been so drunk she doubted anything could have resulted from it. She didn't tell Robert at first. She knew that as soon as she told him, there would be a bond between them, something more than the warmth of his breath and the salt taste of his skin. Something real that he would be forced to acknowledge, and act on. She didn't expect him to do so right away, and she was astonished when she finally told him that he seemed to quiver with excitement.

'Mary,' he said, 'this is wonderful news. What more could I want than for you to bear my child, my boy!'

They were the words she had been waiting for. But somehow, she didn't feel the joy she should have felt. What good was it, bringing another man's child into the world? If William acknowledged it as his own, he would control its upbringing. He would send her home to school it. She might never see Robert again. If William didn't acknowledge it, if he guessed it wasn't his, he might cast her out, and she might have nothing. Robert had made no promises to her.

'You don't know it's a boy,' she said.

'I feel sure it is.'

'There's no certainty. And in any case,' she said coldly, 'why should you care? He will be raised as William's child.'

Robert was quiet for a moment. His expression was dark. 'Perhaps that doesn't have to be the case.'

Mary stood and threw up her hands. 'Robert, how can it be otherwise? This is the predicament we are in. A child can't live on thin air. No more can its mother.'

'No more can its father,' said Robert, laughing a little. Mary looked at him, unsmiling, and Robert stood up, taking her hands.

'We'll think of something,' he said. 'Don't worry.' He held her close, and for a moment she buried her face in his familiar scent, his cinnamon, brandy, fire and opium sweetness. Then she pulled away.

'I'll have to tell William,' she said.

'Tomorrow,' said Robert, pulling her close again.

~

It took longer than that to tell William. His behaviour had become so erratic that she avoided him whenever she thought him near. Whenever he saw her he would find fault with something she had done. The sailors got even worse treatment, and she frequently heard him cursing at them. Once she heard plates smashing in the galley and saw William leaving. When she came to the door she saw the cook picking up fragments of plate. When he saw her he tried to conceal them, almost as if he were ashamed of his captain's behaviour. William now slept in the gunroom rather than in his own cabin, and Robert said he was suffering some unknown pain in the gut for which he received medicine each evening.

When she decided that she could wait no longer she found him lying asleep on his back in the gunroom, though it was nearly nine o'clock in the morning, with a desolate expression on his face. She wondered whether he had missed his watch, and who had taken his place. She woke him and told him the news flatly, expecting either fury or indifference. But to her amazement, he sat up and stared at her. Then he started to cry.

'William!' she said with impatience, as though to a child. 'Why are you crying? Isn't it good news?'

'The best news!' he said. 'The best,' and the tears continued to roll unchecked down his cheeks.

She put her hand on his arm, as much to steady herself as to comfort him.

He took hold of it, and held it tight. 'You must be careful,' he said. 'You must take care of yourself.' He stopped and looked at her.

For a moment she thought she understood him perfectly. The loss of his first child must still be strong in his memory. But then he lay down again, and began to moan.

'Are you ill?' she asked.

'Ill?' he repeated, as if he were unsure what the word meant. 'Well, yes, I suppose I am.'

'Can I help you?' she asked. 'Can I bring you something?'

'Help me?' he said, looking at her in surprise. 'You want to help me?'

'Well,' said Mary, 'if I can.'

He laughed scornfully. 'You can't help me!' he said. 'What interest have you ever shown in me?'

Mary was taken aback. 'As much as you have shown in me,' she said.

William looked at her, a vague smile on his face, and then it suddenly disappeared. 'Oh, well, after all, you are right. Nobody can help me,' he said, turning away. 'Not even God himself.'

'For goodness' sake, William,' said Mary. 'What on earth is wrong with you?'

But he didn't answer. Robert had said that his depressions had grown more intense, and sometimes lasted like this for days at a time. He was concerned for his mental condition, he said. Mary was disturbed by his behaviour, not only for his own sake, but because she saw that, without Robert, this would be her burden. She left the room with a new sense of weight on her shoulders.

~

The months wore on, and the little brig continued to ply her trade between Amsterdam, Leith and London. Mary let the routine of ship life numb her senses, and lived only for Robert's visits. She told herself to be patient, and waited, either for some promise of a future with Robert, or for some change in William, whose melancholia seemed to grow deeper as time passed. One day he would seem intensely interested in her progress and welfare. He would send Robert to make sure she was in good health, and order him to make special herbal tinctures for her. He would tell the cook to keep back the best food for her plate. This behaviour would last for a couple of days, and then for a week or more he would pay her no attention at all, often walking past her in the corridor, or worse, ordering her to run some pointless errand, or blaming her for some mistake in the serving of the meals he never ate.

The cook noticed it too, and for the first time he had a few kind words for her. He began to save the choicest food for her even when he had not been ordered to. One evening, he noticed her lean on a beam for support. Her pregnancy was advanced, and her ankles felt heavy and swollen, and the heat of the galley was making her light-headed.

'Can't be far away from your confinement now, ma'am,' he said.

'Long enough,' said Mary, smiling wearily. 'Eight weeks at least.'

The cook shook his head, and began to stir the pot he was standing over vigorously.

'When my wife was expecting,' he said, 'I had her back at home after just a month of pregnancy. A ship's no place for a lady in your condition.'

Mary looked at him. 'I didn't know you were married,' she said. For the first time, instead of a toughened, ill-tempered old jack, she saw only an old man.

He put the spoon down and went to cut the bread.

'A long time ago,' he said. 'She's with him above now.' He kept his back turned to her.

'Oh,' she said. 'I'm sorry to hear that.'

It was obvious that he didn't want to discuss it, as he was now clattering the dishes around him. Then he turned around.

'You go on now, ma'am,' he said roughly. 'I'll finish this.'

'I can't leave you with it all.'

'Go now,' he persisted. 'For the good of your health, go and rest.'

She left the galley. In truth she was glad of it. Her legs ached and for the first time since she had set sail the motion of the ship, mingled with the smell of animal fat and salt, was starting to nauseate her. She picked her way carefully along the dark corridors. Usually there was enough light from above to see by, but now the nights were getting dark and she had not thought to bring a lamp. Perhaps it was because of this that the light and noise from the gunroom attracted her. She heard a voice she recognized as Robert's. Then she heard William's voice, a quick laugh, and what sounded like a song. She paused outside the door and was surprised to see Robert and William, sitting side by side, singing together:

If fortune then fail not, and our next voyage prove,
We will return merrily and make good cheer,
And hold all together as friends linked in love,
The cans shall be filled with wine, ale and beer.

William's head then slipped to the side, and she saw Robert rise. His own gait was a little unsteady.

'Come on then, boy,' he said. 'Time for bed,' and he put out his arm to support William, who linked his own in this. Mary watched as Robert laid William down on a bunk at the side of the room and gently covered him over with an old coat. William lifted up his hand to Robert's

247

face, and then dropped it by his side. Robert seemed to be taking something out of a leather satchel, but she couldn't see properly what he was doing. She could only hear as he spoke in a low voice. 'That's it, William, sleep.'

Robert moved towards the door, and Mary shrank back. She walked quickly to her cabin, wondering what she was hiding from. Once there, she sat on the bed. Something about the scene had disturbed her deeply. Why? Nobody had done anything wrong. But it was the way they had looked. And more particularly, how Robert had looked, how he had spoken to William. She tried to reason it in her head. How could he be so affectionate to a man he was betraying? But then couldn't she do the same, at times? She could be a good enough actress when she chose.

Yet for some reason, when Robert appeared in her room later that evening, she didn't mention what she had seen. She had given up asking what he would do once the baby was born. They made love, and afterwards she begged him for a draught to help her sleep. Now that the baby was large it kept her awake most of the night, and there was too much noise to sleep during the day. He gave her a dose, and after he had gone she fell asleep almost immediately. But in a dream she woke again, and climbed out of bed. She put on her mantua and drifted to the door; strange how footsteps make no sound in sleep. She knew there was something outside, something beyond the door. Opening it noiselessly, she stepped out, and there they were, the shadows of two men, moving beyond the strip of moonlight that filled the narrow hall. She called out to them, but they appeared to be joined in a deep breath. It was the cook and the cook's boy. They were arguing, fighting. The cook was beating the boy. When she got closer, though, she saw that it was the boy who was beating the cook. She called out to them, and took a step forward, as the ship heaved suddenly and the strip of moonlight illuminated their faces. Then she saw that it wasn't the cook and his boy after all, but the faces of William and Robert. And they weren't fighting. Their heads were together, and she heard their strangled, urgent whispers.

She looked down and saw that there was a child beside her, a silent young girl, who looked up at her, questioning.

'I'm sorry,' she said to the child, 'I can't explain it to you. I don't know the answer.'

At this the child took hold of her arm and clung on affectionately.

But the figures were dark again and coming towards them both, with threatening looks and raised fists. She grabbed the child and flew along the tiny hallway. She found the cabin and closed the door, locking it tight behind her. But all she could hear was their fists, banging and banging at the door, until she put her hands over her head to drown out the noise.

She opened her eyes, and the banging continued. She was in her own cabin, and someone was hammering at the door. At last the door burst open, and she saw the silhouette of Robert standing in the doorway, blocking it. Then pushing past him she saw the unmistakable frame of William. Even in the dim light she could see that his face was tight and purplish, and looked pumped full of black bile.

18

Mary looked at the clock. It was just after midnight. Robert stepped forward. He looked awkward. 'Apologies for disturbing you like this, Mary,' he said.

Mary only nodded.

'William wanted a report on your progress.'

'In the middle of the night?' she said, but she couldn't hide the tremor in her voice.

'A man can have a report on the progress of his child whenever he likes,' said William, and his voice was challenging, 'can he not?'

'Why, yes, of course, William, but surely during daylight hours is a more appropriate time, and I spoke to you earlier today and assured you of your wife's good health,' Robert said.

'Oh, so you've examined her already,' said William, turning on him.

'Well,' said Robert, catching Mary's eye. 'Anyone can see . . .'

'Not anyone, perhaps,' said William. He gave a small, high laugh. 'Unless of course you are a surgeon, and have special powers in that regard.'

'Don't be ridiculous, William,' said Mary.

'And why should I take your word for it?' said William, ignoring her and turning to Robert. 'Didn't you say it once before, with Elizabeth, I remember? In perfect health, you said—'

'William, this is hardly the time,' Robert interrupted.

'But then she wasn't, was she!' William's voice was beginning to rise. 'Not at all in her right spirits, was she?'

'That was different,' said Robert, and his voice took on its own dangerous edge, as he glared at William. 'I would warn you against going too far, sir.'

'Too far! Too far! It is you who has gone too far,' William said. Then he turned suddenly and flew at Robert, gripping his neck with his hands.

Mary could hear a choking, gurgling noise coming from Robert's throat. She climbed out of bed and took hold of William's shoulders, gently at first, but then firmly, trying to pull him away. But he was locked tight, and she could see the veins expanding in Robert's neck, so she rolled up the sleeve of William's jacket and dug her nails deep into the side of his arm.

She doubted it had hurt him, but it seemed to release something in him, and she felt herself knocked away as he removed his hands from Robert and flung them backwards.

Robert clutched his neck and looked at William. William sank to his knees and began to cry. Mary watched them, mesmerized. The two men seemed almost unaware of her now. She stood up, as though to intervene, but Robert put up his hand to stop her. Then he reached out and gently touched William's shoulder.

'Come with me,' he said. 'You just need to rest.'

To Mary's surprise, William went with him obediently. But she heard his voice again, quiet and tearful.

'Am I to blame for everything?' he was saying. 'Do you play no part?' He seemed to have deflated now.

She heard Robert speak under his breath as he walked the drunken man down the corridor. 'It's just the liquor, William, you need to sleep it off.' And then Robert said something that puzzled Mary. 'I don't understand you, William,' he said, and there was passion in his voice. 'How can you mourn what was never yours?'

Mary followed them. She watched as Robert settled William down, just as he had earlier, but then she saw what she had not seen before: a small bottle that Robert drew from his waistcoat. She stared as he tipped it into a glass, and then held it to William's lips.

'Drink this,' he said. 'It will make you sleep.'

She observed her husband's body begin to relax. As before, he raised an arm, and then let it fall below him.

Robert looked up to see her standing at the door. 'He was beginning to say too much,' he said.

'He knows?' asked Mary.

Robert met her eye. 'I fear so.'

'What did you give him?' she asked.

'Something to help him sleep.'

'It's certainly worked,' she said.

'It's powerful stuff,' said Robert. 'Could kill an elephant, in the right dosage.'

Mary looked at her husband, then at Robert, then at the medicine chest by his side. She saw in Robert's eyes that the same thought was running through his head as was running through hers, and she immediately looked away and coloured, ashamed.

Robert followed her back to her room. He took hold

of her arms, which were trembling, and she buried her face in his sickly sweet scent.

'I knew something like this would happen,' she said. 'He's been behaving so strangely.'

Robert sat back on the bed a little. He appeared thoughtful.

'Mary,' he said, 'I want you to come away with me, as soon as the child is born.'

Mary looked at him. She had gone through this so often in her head, where they would go, how they would change their names, how they would make a living. She had indulged herself with dreams of their future together. But now that the cold reality of it was presented to her in this way, the idea seemed insane.

'Robert,' said Mary, resting her head on the pillow, 'if it were only me, I would go with you without a penny in the world, without a thought. But things are different now. It's not only myself I have to think of.'

Robert smiled at her, and it was a smile of wonder, as if an idea had occurred to him. 'You think I intend to be poor?'

'You have a living?' Mary sat up a little.

'Not quite.'

'You'll have to forgive me asking,' Mary said quietly. 'But I have to know, Robert, if I'm seriously to consider what you say, exactly what your fortune is.'

Robert smiled. 'Ah,' he said, 'but that's the whole beauty of it. You won't need my fortune, because you'll have one of your own.'

'One of my own?' Mary looked at him, confused.

'But you'll have to wait until the child is born,' he said, 'before we can benefit from it.'

Mary grew impatient. 'Please just tell me what you mean.'

'I don't know why I didn't think of it before,' he said. He was trembling and seemed excited. He jumped up, and walked the few feet from one end of the cabin to the other.

'William,' he said at last, 'has been promised a fortune, which will be paid to him on the birth of his first son.'

Mary opened her mouth. 'Why did he never tell me?' she asked.

'Perhaps,' said Robert, looking almost ashamed himself, 'because he never intended for you to see any of it.'

Mary looked away, turning it over. 'For all his faults,' she said, 'I can hardly believe that of William.'

Robert only shrugged. 'Men are corrupted by wealth.'

'But what if the child is a daughter?' she said.

'It won't be,' said Robert firmly.

'But what if it is?'

'If it is, then you must have another.'

Mary looked despondent. 'I can't survive like this for that long.'

'Mary,' said Robert, taking hold of her arm, 'you have to. We must remain calm, and patient, because if we do, the rewards will be handsome.'

Mary thought this out a little. 'But even if what you say is true,' she said, 'how would I gain from the fortune, if I leave him? He'll only cut me off.'

'I'll deal with that,' said Robert. 'William trusts me. I can find a way to have him give us the money, to take care of it for him. I have influence.'

'What kind of influence?'

'Never mind. All that matters is we will soon be together,

with our own child. We'll have a new life,' and he touched a strand of her hair. 'All you have to do,' he said, as if it were as easy as making supper, 'is bear the child.'

'He knows,' she said, the terrible realization coming to her again. 'What will he do when he wakes?'

Robert shook his head. 'I don't believe he knows everything. He only suspects. We need to make sure he doesn't remember.'

Mary looked at him. 'With what you gave him earlier?'

'Yes, which is easy enough, while he's under my care. Then we must target the lady. Yes, that's how it must be done. There's no use in speaking to his uncle. We must convince her, and she will persuade her husband that William is incapable. But while we are there, you'll need to maintain his dose.'

Mary shook her head. 'How can I?'

'Mary,' said Robert, drawing her near, 'we need to keep him quiet. It's the only way, or his tongue will undo all of us.'

Mary nodded. All of us. Robert, Mary and the unborn child. That was who he meant, Mary thought. It was only afterwards that she began to doubt.

Part Three

19

Fullarton stood on deck as his privateer *Promise* was piloted into the port of Plymouth, her only Spanish prize in tow. The town had grown since he had seen it last. Building was going on all along its edges. Through his glass he could see figures carrying the wrecked bodies of naval men from the launches of warships up the waterside steps to the new hospital. There were numerous large men-of-war in the port, and Fullarton noticed this at first without thinking anything strange in it. But as they came closer to the quayside, he noted crowds of people lining the water's edge. Little launches were rowing back and forth with yet more people on board. He began to feel uneasy.

'I don't like the look of this,' he said to his first mate. 'Something's happened.'

The first mate only grunted. He and the rest of the crew were unhappy that their prize had not been returned to Guernsey, as promised. They did not know that Fullarton had never intended to return to Guernsey. He was convinced, now, or at least he had convinced himself, that his engagement to Nancy and Bell's patronage of him had been nothing more than an elaborate joke at his expense. He had responded to the crew's complaints by retreating to his cabin and drinking the ship's supplies of strong rum and gin, which he sweetened with a little treacle. Only the eventual capture of their prize had prevented the men's discontent from being expressed in open mutiny and even now there were grumblings about their eventual share. But Fullarton ignored them. He had made up his mind to dispose of them and find another crew as soon as he had received his prize money.

Once they had landed he sought out the harbourmaster.

'I've a fine Spanish man-of-war,' he told him, 'with some live prisoners on board.'

The harbourmaster shook his head, a small smile on his face. 'I'm afraid they're not much good to us now,' he said.

Fullarton looked at him, confused.

'The war's over, man,' said the old man, laughing. 'Didn't you hear?'

'But . . .' said Fullarton, stuttering over his words. 'What about our reward?'

'Well, she'll go through the prize court, as usual,' said the man casually. 'Go see Mr Fanning at Pinham's coffee house. She'll go by the candle there. No doubt you'll receive some recompense.'

'I should think so – there's two hundred tons in her, not to mention guns, twenty-four pounders and all, with plenty of grapeshot and powder.' Fullarton's voice was growing desperate, and the man put his hand on his shoulder.

'She sounds a fine prize,' he said. 'But look. They've signed a treaty. At Paris. We're at peace. Can't you see them all celebrating?'

~

Fullarton almost ran across the cobbles to find Fanning. Everywhere he went people were rejoicing, laughing. He fought an urge to push each man he passed into the harbour.

'I'll do you a favourable commission,' Fanning said. 'But items of war won't be so much in demand as they were before, see. Last month there warn't a ship in this port that warn't a privateer. But next month it'll be a different picture. Price of peace.' He smiled to show the space where his teeth had been.

Fullarton left his fate in Fanning's hands. He could do nothing else. He walked through the narrow streets, pushing against the celebrating crowds. The end of the war meant the end of all his hopes of making a swift fortune. The idea of going back to the tedious regularity of merchant trading filled him with a slow dread. He had begun to expect more. But even worse was the prospect of going back to St Pierre and letting Bell see his failure, pleading with him for the hand of a woman he could not force himself to love.

And Bell might be after him already. He might have agents in all the major ports. For all Margot's skills, he would have been furious at being humiliated in this way. The joke had been turned against him, thought Fullarton with some satisfaction. But the people at the prize court might already doubt the legality of his own letter-of-marque. And even if he got the money, would it be enough? By the time he shared it out between the crew, Monsieur Henri, and paid the balance of the victualling and fitting out of the ship, he might be left with nothing.

The thoughts swam in his head, with no sign of a solution, so he looked around desperately for something to take them away. He walked in the direction of the nearest Barbican bar. It was the wildest he had seen, and he chose it deliberately because it suited his mood. It was full of sailors, their low-class wives and a few whores. All were drunk and lusty, the men guffawed and the women sat on the men's knees and squawked like parrots. At least by spending his time with people more wrecked and degenerate than himself, he could find some comfort in the midst of his misfortune. He was, at the very least, better than them.

He watched them with a seething hatred as he slowly worked his way through a bottle of gin and lime. The more he drank, the more he found the idea of getting back on a merchant ship impossible. It was as though his tongue had touched the sweet edge of something, and he must find out where the source of the sweetness lay. Somewhere, out in the blue, floated rafts of sugar candy, waiting to be taken by those strong enough to try. Why shouldn't he be one of those people? He was different from the people around him, different from Bell and all the so-called gentlemen he had met in St Pierre. He had always believed it, and he believed it even more now.

A flash of blue caught the corner of his eye. He turned his head involuntarily and was struck by the bright gleam of buttons on a naval uniform. An officer's uniform. He noticed it mainly because it was so out of place in this bar, full of people of low birth and little promise. The man who wore it looked directly at Fullarton. He was young, with the dark pink glow of health not yet made ruddy and purpled with age, and his wig was well powdered and neat. He sat upright on his backless stool as he drank. He could only be here, Fullarton thought, for the same reasons as himself.

The man smiled, as if he recognized him, and stood up. He walked over to where Fullarton was sitting, and extended his hand.

'I know you from somewhere, don't I?' he said.

Fullarton looked at him, shaking his head.

'I'm sure I do,' the man said again.

'I'm sorry, sir,' said Fullarton, 'but I don't recall.'

'Not to worry,' said the man. 'It will come to me. May I?' he said, pointing to the empty seat beside Fullarton.

'Of course.'

The stranger sat down and motioned to the barman. 'A quart of rum punch,' he said, 'and two glasses.'

The barman appeared presently and placed the jug and glasses on the table. Fullarton noted the unusual painting on the side of the jug, a beach scene, with two almost naked Negroes pulling a longboat on to a pale shore.

'I thought your glass was needing filled,' said the man. He poured a liberal measure into Fullarton's glass.

'Thank you,' said Fullarton. 'That's very generous.'

'The name's Keppel,' said the man, extending his hand. 'And I can always spot a man in need of a drink.'

Fullarton took hold of Keppel's hand and was startled by his eyes. He thought how strangely green they were, a translucent green, the colour of the distant ocean painted on to the side of the porcelain jug. His hand was cool and smooth. Fullarton felt as though someone had poured ice-cold water on his burning skin, and some kind of burden began to lift from his shoulders.

'Like the commodore?' he said. He had seen an image of the aristocrat while in St Pierre and recognized the aquiline nose in the man before him.

'A distant cousin,' he said.

Fullarton nodded. He congratulated himself on knowing a gentleman when he saw one.

Over the hours they drank and talked together, Fullarton told Keppel about his predicament, the failure of his privateering enterprise, his reluctance to go back to coastal trading, and Keppel nodded as though he understood perfectly everything that Fullarton said.

'There was a time when the privateers were bringing in good money,' Keppel said. 'I saw them, and I envied what the most successful gained from it. More than I did as a naval captain, though I took the same risk.'

Fullarton nodded. 'But what can be done?' he said desperately, draining the last of his glass.

Keppel sat forward and his eyes grew narrow. 'Let me speak plainly, Fullarton,' he said. 'I like you. I'm a good judge of character, and I know a ruthless man when I see one.'

Fullarton wasn't sure whether this was a compliment or not, but he waited for Keppel to continue.

'Now that the war's over I'll be put on half pay or discharged,' he said. 'But I won't wait to be discarded in that way. There are plenty of ways for good seamen to make a fortune outside war, as well as during it.'

'I know them well,' said Fullarton, thinking of the money he had made smuggling wine and tobacco in the past.

'No, no, no,' said Keppel, shaking his head, 'I don't mean free trade, that's small beer compared to what I'm talking about. I mean prizes, Fullarton, big prizes, big gains. Listen, I know Fanning well, and I can make sure you get a good settlement. I can secure a ship, and have her made ready. We can use the money to find a crew, perhaps some who have served on privateers already.'

'I have a crew.' Fullarton had suddenly realized what Keppel meant. 'But they were poor enough privateers, they'd be hopeless pirates.'

'Don't use that word,' Keppel hissed, glancing behind him. 'We are not pirates. We are privateers, only our wars are our own.'

Fullarton nodded and smiled. He liked this idea.

'And we'll find a new crew,' said Keppel. 'The best and most skilled seamen in Plymouth.'

Fullarton didn't know whether it was Keppel's strange, calm confidence, or the flicker in his pale eyes, but as he took hold of his cool hand to shake it once more, he felt that in some way this man held the power to shape his future.

20

It was early in the morning when they pulled into the bay of Plymouth. Mary stood on deck, looking at the pretty policies that surrounded the town, laid out neatly, and the gardens kept by the lords of Edgecumbe that ran down to the water's edge, lined with trees and carpeted with snowdrops. She wished she could be there, walking in those quiet woods, away from everyone: William, Robert or the creature that had burrowed inside her, without her permission, and decided to grow.

Then she felt her skin prickle and Robert's breath at her shoulder. He slid his hand beneath her cloak, and she felt the touch of cold glass.

'Is that it?' she whispered.

'That's the phial,' he said. 'It's sealed, but be careful with it, and hide it. I'll only see you tonight at the Blatchfords'. I can't be with you at any other time, and you must maintain the dosage. Not too much. Just enough to make him sleepy, but not incapable. Here,' he said, nudging it against her. She sensed the pressure of his hand upon the curve of her hip, but it didn't make her skin bristle the way it had done several months ago. Her eyes were still on the fringe of trees, and her mind was far away.

'Mary,' he said sharply, bringing her back to reality. 'Did you hear me?'

'Yes,' she whispered. 'But won't people wonder at his behaviour?'

'He's a sick man,' said Robert, with a little relish. 'Suffering from a rare condition.'

'What kind of condition?'

'One that I have just diagnosed,' he said.

She put her own hands beneath the cloak and took the phial, slipping it into the pockets above her gown, whose seams she had had to let out to allow for her swollen womb.

Mary's silk shoes slipped on the wet rope ladder as she climbed off the *Isabella*. Operations such as these were now becoming difficult. William ignored her, seeming not to notice, and she felt Robert's hand on her, lifting her into the little launch boat. She turned to thank him and caught William's eyes. He watched her, and it seemed there was a flicker of a question there, but then the sense was gone from them. It made her feel cold, and she looked away, into the rainbow swirls of oil that coated the surface of the dark harbour.

~

As Mary and William dressed for supper in their small apartment, she took out the phial, preparing to dose his drink with a few drops. It would settle him for the night. But then she watched him trying to dress, fumbling with the buttons on his waistcoat like a confused child, and put the phial back into her clothing. It felt too premeditated, not like an act of love for Robert, but just a simple act of cruelty. In any case, she told herself, any more and he might not be able to make it to the supper party at all.

For a moment she considered taking some herself, as she tried to ignore the raucous din of the people in the streets celebrating the new treaty with France, and the end of the war. She would have loved to sink into that familiar watery sleep, to forget all she had to do. But she had to remain alert. She dressed her hair with shaking fingers, finishing with pins decorated with gilt and tiny rubies, and clipped on her small gold earrings. Despite months of the ship's diet of lobscouse and salt herring, her young face had not yet taken on the grey-green pallor that it generally induced. She was still pretty, she thought, yet that was no consolation. William took her plump, pink hand in his own yellowed one, and didn't appear to see her at all.

~

The evening at Lord and Lady Blatchford's had been arranged by Robert, who had discussed the details with her, and Mary had spent the short walk there rehearsing what they might say. When they arrived, William's condition was not much improved. He walked as normal, but all his movements were mechanical, and he had to be guided wherever he went. He managed to make a greeting to his aunt and uncle, and then Robert appeared and helped Mary to seat him.

'You must excuse your nephew, he is recovering from a long and most serious illness,' explained Robert.

'How terrible,' said Lady Blatchford. 'I wish you a rapid recovery, William.'

William murmured something incomprehensible.

'He is getting better at last, thank you, Lady Blatchford,'

said Mary. 'Our surgeon Mr Cole has been most attentive. Had it not been for his medical skill, I feel sure my husband would have struggled to get over it.'

'I did what I could,' said Robert, looking at Mary approvingly. 'But, Lady Blatchford,' and here he took the lady's arm and led her away, lowering his voice. She looked surprised but also flattered, and Mary watched them, though it was part of their plan, with a hint of jealousy. She found a place near them so she could hear what Robert was saying.

'I fear,' she heard him say, 'that though he is fit in body, he will never be quite fully restored in . . . in his senses.'

'How dreadful,' said Lady Blatchford. 'And his wife in her condition too.'

'Of course the child is well provided for, as part of his settlement, but I am concerned that in his present condition Mrs Jones may not see the money employed for its intended use, the raising of a worthy heir to your fine estate.'

'Well, I see what you mean. That is quite a predicament.'

'Do you think there is anything that you, Lady Blatchford, as such an influential woman with Lord Blatchford, may be able to do, to ensure that the money is transferred to someone with the good sense to use it wisely? I think you can see, Lady Blatchford, that Mrs Jones is a worthy and sensible woman, who has worked tirelessly to protect her husband's interests in this delicate matter. She is more or less running his affairs single-handedly at the moment. I have no doubt that she will make an excellent mother to Captain Jones's son.'

'Well, we need to ensure that he fulfils his obligations, certainly,' she said hesitantly.

'But,' Robert went on, 'I'm afraid that, in his present condition, that too is unlikely. He has even spoken in his fits, Lady Blatchford, of another woman he loves. I myself saw evidence of it in Amsterdam. He lodges with a lady there whose character is by no means certain, and it is said that they are very close. I have spoken to people who knew her in a former and less respectable situation, and who can testify to her questionable motives in regard of your nephew. I fear that if control of the estate is granted to Captain Jones, some woman less worthy than Mrs Jones may reap the benefits.'

Mary felt angry at Robert for slandering Anneke again. She had, for some reason she couldn't explain, felt some bond with her, some familiarity. She wondered that Robert had not remembered this, that he had not chosen some other woman in Amsterdam or elsewhere whose reputation he considered doubtful. Mary caught his eye, and tried to signal to him her discontent, but he only winked and inclined his head towards Lady Blatchford. By the expression on Lady Blatchford's face Mary could tell that she was shocked at what she heard. It seemed that their plan was working, but instead of feeling delight, Mary only felt a deeper sense of nausea. She looked at William. He sat in his chair, and his eyes began to close, like an old grandfather. But now and then they would flicker open, and he would give a little start, as if dreaming.

'We would have to have a certificate, of course,' Lady Blatchford was saying, 'signed by someone qualified in medical matters.'

'That will be no issue,' said Robert.

'And it will have to stipulate, naturally, that if he regains his senses at a later date the estate is placed back under his control until his son comes of age.'

Robert nodded, and smiled a little towards Mary, but she refused to look at him. Then she saw that William was opening his eyes, and, seized with panic, moved quickly to his side.

'Can I get something for you, sir,' she said, loudly enough for Lady Blatchford to hear.

'Is that you, Lizzie?' he asked, and then, seeing Robert, 'Is she ready? Is my son born?'

'Oh, William,' said Mary, as he closed his eyes again. She felt almost disappointed in him.

Lady Blatchford looked at her with an expression of sorrow and pity. Robert threw Lady Blatchford a knowing glance, and she nodded back solemnly.

~

Mary woke early the following morning. She sat motionless until the dim glow of the dawn increased to daylight. William lay prone beside her. She knew the cause of his lethargy, but it annoyed her still. The longer he lay, his breath deep and settled, the more irritated she became with him. How long would he lie like that, the great whale? How could he put up so little fight? If only he had been different, she would not have been driven to such extreme measures. But now she felt justified in all she and Robert had planned, and touched the phial between her ribs. She looked at the morning draught that she had already poured, ready to pick up when he woke. She pulled out the phial and added the drops. Then she shook him hard and he groaned.

'William,' she said. 'Mrs Truscott has prepared break-fast. You must come.'

William only turned over again. Mary dressed quickly and went downstairs alone.

When she returned, having eaten nothing, she shook him again, and picked up his morning draught. William sat up, and as he saw it a new light came into his eyes. He held out both hands for it and drank it quickly, seeming more alert than he had for days, and motioned for her to pour him another.

'I feel as though I've been asleep for hours,' he said.

'It's late morning.'

'Where were we last night?' he asked.

'At Lady Blatchford's,' she said. 'Don't you remember?'

'Of course,' he said irritably. 'I'm only tired.'

'You've been drinking too much of this,' said Mary.

William gazed straight ahead. 'I know,' he said.

She looked at him, surprised that he had some aware-ness of his condition. She felt a sudden urge to jog his memory. She knew the danger of it, and yet she did it anyway. She wanted to push him, to see how far he had sunk, and whether he might still be able to rise.

'Don't you remember it at all?' she asked. 'Robert was there, too.'

'Robert, yes, I remember that,' he said, nodding slowly. 'He was talking to Lady Blatchford.'

'Yes, he was talking to everyone,' said Mary quickly. 'In fact, he was quite the life and soul.'

'Was he?' said William.

'And you called me Lizzie,' said Mary, and then stopped. She wondered if she had gone too far.

William turned his gaze on her. He seemed frightened, but perfectly lucid. 'Did I?' he said. 'What else did I say?'

'You said, "Is she ready? Is my son born?"' Their eyes met for a moment.

'I'm sorry,' he said, averting his eyes. 'I must have been confused. I must have drunk more than I was aware of.' He paused and examined her again, like a father examining a child. 'But Robert took good care of you, I'm sure.'

'And of you,' said Mary.

'And of me,' said William. 'Yes, Robert always did take good care of me. I wouldn't have had him, otherwise.'

'He is a good surgeon,' said Mary, anxiously.

'The very best,' said William.

While Mary went about her toilet and then tidied up the room, William sat in bed and finished his draught. Finally, with an effort, he heaved himself up and started to dress, his movements slow and clumsy. The drops were beginning to take effect, and Mary had to help him. She pulled on his breeches, and fastened the buttons of his coat. His clothes seemed looser than usual; the fabric hung off him in untidy ripples that would not sit straight, no matter how she pulled and tucked them.

'Keep still,' she said impatiently. 'Stop fidgeting.'

'I seem to be vanishing,' said William, looking at his sagging arms.

'Nonsense, you just need a good meal,' said Mary briskly.

'But you, my dear,' said William, slurring, putting his hand upon her hip and on to the rounded swell of her belly. 'You look in good health. You have what they say all ladies in your condition have, a glow.'

Mary coloured. She couldn't help feeling both surprised and flattered at this attention. 'I am quite well,' she said.

'I'm glad to hear it,' he said. He put his hand on the top of her bump. 'I can't feel it move.'

'He often does,' said Mary.

'Does it? And do you say he?'

Mary blushed violet. 'I don't know,' she said. 'But I feel it will be a boy. I'll tell you, if you like, the next time he moves.'

William regarded her for a moment, his hand still over her belly, his expression almost dreamy. 'I would like that,' he said.

Mary took his hand away and walked quickly to the window. She threw it open and gazed out into the street, where the gulls were circling the small harbour, and the warships lay idle in the bay.

~

Later, when William had dressed, they sat in a local coffee house, and Mary ordered a light meal for him. He ate lazily, untidily. Some of his food leaked from the corners of his mouth and ran on to his chin. Mary looked away, unable to conceal her disgust. Her momentary feelings for him were gone. She poured out some more coffee from the pot.

'Here,' she said, pushing the cup towards William, 'perhaps this will cure you.'

She heard voices just behind her left shoulder. Two men were talking.

'They complain,' one was saying, 'but then what do they expect? The war provided wages, albeit low ones, for many a young lad. Now these lads are just emptied on to the streets. They must look for commissions on other ships.'

'But the merchants too have slowed their activities in certain areas,' said the other. 'It takes time for these things to pick up again.'

'Recruitment will not be a problem,' the first continued. 'And they'll be treated better with us than on any Royal Navy ship, believe me.'

'Not to mention the rewards.'

Mary could hear a smile in the man's voice as he said this, and her curiosity was aroused.

'The ship will need some adjustments. We'll need to find money for that.'

'What about the prize?'

'Once Henri has paid the crew their share, and the balance of the victualling, I don't know what will be left.'

'Don't worry, I'm sure Fanning will come to an arrangement that will be to our benefit.'

Mary tried to turn discreetly, and immediately caught a whiff of strong, slightly stale spirit. She knew the smell too well, not only from her own husband but from most of the crew of the *Isabella*. As far as she knew, it was the smell of men. Then she saw William put down his fork, and his face became grey. She swivelled around towards the two strangers sitting behind her and she also saw, with a jolt, Robert, sitting beside them. He stood up and smiled.

'Captain Jones,' he said, 'and Mrs Jones, of course. What a coincidence. I was just taking coffee with an old friend and his colleague, Mr Fullarton. I believe you know Mr Keppel, Captain.'

William got up unsteadily, and Robert threw an approving glance at Mary.

'I do remember you,' said William, but then he hesitated.

'We served together in the navy, many years ago. I didn't realize you knew each other, too,' Keppel said, speaking directly to Robert.

'The nautical world is a small one,' said Robert. 'Won't you join us?'

Mary looked at the two men Robert had been talking to. There was something about the man facing her, in particular, that aroused her interest. His face seemed oddly familiar. His voice had a Scotch intonation, although it had clearly been diluted by years of absence from wherever he called home. She tried, despite herself, to catch the man's eye. But his own gaze was directed intently towards the man in front of him. It was a strange expression, something she not only recognized but felt suddenly desperate to understand.

The man called Keppel stood up and shook William's hand.

'Captain Jones,' he said. 'How wonderful to see you again. This is my friend, Captain Fullarton.'

Mary stood, and curtsied, and sat down at the men's table. Fullarton nodded towards her, his face a little sour, as though he were irritated at the interruption.

'We were just talking of the labours of making money in these times,' said Keppel to William.

'Yes, yes,' said William. He seemed thoughtful, but Mary knew he was only trying to register what the man had said. At last he gave up, and turned to Robert. 'I thought you were gone to Plympton to see your father,' he said.

Robert's face was tight. 'I decided against it,' he said. 'Nothing to report, yet.'

'What if he finds out you've been here, and not called?'

'What of it?' said Robert. 'I've not seen him these five years. Another can't hurt. And it's back to the ship tomorrow.'

'Where are you headed next?' asked Keppel.

'They say there're barrels of claret been stacking up in France since the war began,' said Robert. 'Now there're so many of them that they'll sell them cheap at the price, so we're making for France.'

'We'll be going out that way as well,' said Keppel. 'Perhaps our paths may cross again.'

They talked on. But Mary wasn't listening. Her gaze rested on the window. She sipped her coffee, though she had never much liked the stuff. Today, however, it had a rich, round flavour and filled her mouth with a memory of their first landing, in Amsterdam, when she had tasted it for the first time. How exciting it had all been then: the motion, the goods being carried back and forth, the unfamiliar people and foreign tongues. And Robert, so new to her, with his smell of herbs and alcohol. She had felt at the beginning of an adventure, as if there were so much in the world she had yet to know. Now she wondered what she had learned. She knew that they drank coffee in this country and tea in another, that this region favoured wine and that one brandy. She knew that the Chinese produced the most delicate silk and the French the best lace. She could recognize a language by its sound, and the nationality of a man by his appearance and dress. She knew the pain and the pleasure of lying with a man, the touch of skin to skin. She had experienced all these sensations, but it was as though she could no longer feel them, not as she once had.

Just as she had once longed to be away from her, she now felt a sudden yearning to be with her mother. Not because her mother knew her any better than anyone else, or because she would have been any comfort to her. She wanted only the familiarity of her, to smell the sourness of her skin, to rub her cheek against her coarse hair. And perhaps, she thought, it was not her mother she wanted at all, but herself, some sense of herself as she once was, as she would have been if the world had not conspired to change her.

Mary's eyes began to sting. She bit her tongue until she thought it might bleed, and the stinging subsided, but only, she realized as she put her hand to her face, because the tears were now flowing noiselessly down her cheeks.

She made a mumbled excuse about air and walked away from the group to stand near the door.

'Mary?' said Robert, suddenly behind her. She turned to face him, and he saw her tears.

'Come outside,' he said, taking her arm. They stood behind the frame of the door, and he took hold of her small hand, enclosing it in his own as she remembered he had done on that first day.

'Mary,' he said, his voice unnaturally soft, 'whatever is the matter?'

'I don't know,' she said. 'I was thinking today about my mother.'

'That's to be expected,' said Robert. 'Especially in your condition. But you must be strong. This will all be over soon, and we'll be together.'

Mary nodded, but the tears still fell. She felt Robert's grip tighten, and she looked at his face, expecting to see anger there. But what she saw was uncertainty, and fear.

'Listen,' he said, 'think of the alternative, if you can't do this. A lifetime with that!' Her eyes followed his pointing finger, to where William's head was sinking into the folds of his neck.

She nodded. 'I'm only tired,' she said. 'He's difficult, like this.'

'Come,' said Robert, 'you need to rest. Let's take him, and you, back. I'll walk with you as far as your lodgings.'

They took leave of the two gentlemen, and the three of them walked together along the narrow street. As they were about to enter the building Robert pulled her back.

'Wait, do you have enough left in the phial?' he whispered.

Mary hesitated. She didn't, but she was reluctant to take more. He pressed another phial into her hands.

When they got up to their rooms and William had fallen asleep on the bed, she lay down beside him, and looked at the small bottle of liquid. How much would it require, she thought, to take her and her child away from this miserable situation for ever?

She must have drifted off, because when she woke William was up. He sat on the bed beside her, his head almost between his knees.

'William,' she said, 'what is it?' She realized she still held the bottle in her hands, and quickly stuffed it between the folds of her clothing.

'I'm remembering a time,' he said, appearing not to

notice, 'when I knew that man Keppel. He was a ruthless man. But I wasn't, Mary. I wasn't always like this.'

'Like what, William, what do you mean?' She looked at him curiously.

'Life used to be so simple, before I met . . .'

'Me?'

'No.'

Mary nodded. He must mean Elizabeth. 'I know. But you must try to put it behind you. It's the future that matters now,' she said, without meaning to, because of course she knew there would be no future for them.

William said nothing, but rolled his head between his hands.

'Lie down,' she said. 'It's only rest you need.'

When he lay down she put her arm around him and stroked the nape of his neck, until he fell asleep. His breath was heavy and pungent, and she moved her head away, but she kept her arm around him. It was the least she could do; after all, she was his wife. She thought that this must be why poor people married, when they had no estate or dowry to recommend them, for nothing more than to feel another person's sleeping breath, the warmth of their body, the proof that both were alive and warm at that moment, no matter what the future held. She wondered if there was a point in their lives where they, too, ceased to feel, when the sheer effort of turning the mechanisms of life took over, when their only purpose became to produce new life, then punish it for what they had lost.

21

It was April before Captain Fullarton and Keppel's large, two-masted, square-sailed brig sailed out of the Plymouth bay. They were later than they would have liked. The prize settlement had been complex, but Keppel had persuaded Fanning, while handing him a gift of one hundred pounds, to have Henri's share sent to him and to give the money for the rest of the crew to Fullarton. Fullarton paid off his crew with a retainer, and told them the rest of the money would be ready at the end of the week. By then, however, they had already sold the *Promise*, bought the much faster *Neptune*, and left the town behind.

After around an hour they began to pass the tree-covered ridge of green land known as Mont Edgcumbe. Beyond were the sheltered coves of Cornwall that Fullarton had used during his smuggling days, to which he was now directing the ship. On her purchase they had been told that the hull would need attention, to remove the thousands of tiny worms that had bored into the wood, leaving a surface as pockmarked as old skin. The ship would have to be turned over and her timbers basted with a mixture of stinking tallow and tar, before she was worthy for a long sea journey.

They anchored out at sea until they received a favourable wind, which took long enough, but finally a good wind turned shorewards and they steered the ship in until her bow ran through the fine sand.

A few men stood along the shore, preparing fishing gear, and some others were working in the fields behind the beach. They paid the ship little notice, except discreetly to move their work further away. The inhabitants of the nearby villages were used to seeing ships come and go, smugglers, press gangs, privateers and pirates, and they had learned that keeping themselves to themselves was the best way to avoid trouble. The day was bright and unusually warm, and Fullarton unbuttoned his shirt. They would have to wait now, until the tide receded. Only then could her great flanks be exposed and raked over and rubbed clean by the men before being sealed up again against the ravages of the ocean beds.

Fullarton made sure the men were occupied and then took off his shoes and stockings and bathed his feet in the sea water. He squeezed his toes into the sand, felt the wind on his face and the first of the spring sunshine seep into his skin. Then he padded back over the sand to where Keppel's pale body was already stretched out flat, his hands behind his head.

'A fine day,' said Keppel, raising his head slightly from where it lay cushioned in his arms. 'And a good light breeze. Let's hope this holds until tomorrow.'

Fullarton lay down beside him and tried to appear as relaxed as Keppel, but his arms didn't fold properly beneath him, and he wriggled to find a comfortable place in the sand. Eventually he rolled on to his front and looked at the man beside him. Keppel gazed back with his crystal-green eyes, and his smile that was both a question and a challenge. Fullarton noticed how his torso was stretched so that it hollowed into the bones of his groin, and wondered how a man who dined almost exclusively on beef and Burgundy could have remained in so narrow a frame. He was younger than Fullarton, around seven and twenty, but he had the authority of an older man. He seemed well made for a naval captain.

'Didn't you like the navy?' Fullarton asked.

Keppel turned over to face him, head resting on his folded arm. His shirt sleeves were rolled up to his elbows. He looked at Fullarton a moment, as if it were he who had asked the question, and was awaiting the answer, and then something happened to Fullarton that had never happened to him with any other man, or woman. He found that he couldn't meet Keppel's eye. Instead he averted his own slightly and studied the soft, blond, downy hair of Keppel's arm, bleached white against his dark skin.

'I didn't like being at the beck and call of masters,' said Keppel. 'I used to look at the ships that went back and forward, thinking of the wealth they carried. Sometimes we captured them, but we had to tow our prizes, and rich prizes they were, back into port, where somebody who had never before set foot on the planks would be benefiting from them. They'd be rewarded for doing nothing, while we'd be sent out to sea again.' He shook his head. 'Months at sea, away from families, homes.'

'Do you have a family, then?' asked Fullarton.

'Me?' Keppel gave his idiosyncratic smile again. 'I don't love to attach myself to women,' he said.

'Nor I,' said Fullarton.

'So I'd heard.'

Fullarton turned his head sharply. 'You know about her?' For some reason he had kept this from Keppel, sensing that he would disapprove.

'You had the look of a man who has been attached to a woman,' said Keppel.

'The look?' asked Fullarton.

'Yes,' Keppel replied. 'There is a look of those attached. And there is another look, a specific one, of those men who have been attached, rather than having attached themselves, and who intend to detach themselves at the earliest possible opportunity. But I know, mainly, because Thomas Bell's agent approached me in Plymouth.'

Fullarton sat up. Keppel smiled.

'I thought I'd wait until we were safely at sea before telling you. You would only have panicked. He said someone had spotted you with me and I said I'd met you in a bar, but you had been heading north and had left the next day.'

'I'm indebted to you,' said Fullarton.

'It's nothing,' said Keppel. 'But I'm surprised at you, Fullarton. She was a rich prize. As rich as any you'll find on the ocean.'

Fullarton clenched his jaw. 'It was nothing more than a trick, by Bell, to mock me and blacken my name.'

Keppel gave Fullarton a quizzical glance. 'Why would he want to do that?' he asked.

'Perhaps he changed his mind about my marrying his sister.'

'Then why would he be so furious at your leaving? In my experience,' said Keppel, 'people only do things when they stand to gain from them. I don't see what a man like Bell could gain from humiliating a man like you.'

Fullarton flushed. Unlike Bell, Keppel had guessed he was not the gentleman he pretended to be. He couldn't reply. Instead, he stood up and walked off across the shore. Eventually he stopped some distance away and sat on the rocks, his legs stretched out in front.

He could hear Keppel's approach behind him, but ignored him. Even in this he felt belittled. To show his emotions would have been to admit defeat, but to be forced to conceal them meant he had been defeated anyway. Then he felt Keppel's hand burn into the bone of his shoulder. He turned to face him, and the emotion melted away.

Keppel grinned. 'I apologize,' he said. 'I didn't mean to offend you. It's your life. You may do as you please with it.' He put out his hand and Fullarton took hold of it. Keppel pulled him up and they walked in silence back to where the overturned hull of the ship lay prone in the cove. The tide had drawn back so that the whole of her flank was exposed.

'She's uncovered,' said Keppel. 'Let's get the men together.'

They spent the rest of the day at it, scraping the surface of the wood free of barnacles and replacing broken planks, then coating it all with tallow and tar. Keppel and Fullarton worked alongside the men. At first the work was hard, and the weather was hot, but as the sun dipped in the sky, and the air cooled, Fullarton began to enjoy the monotony of it. The warm breeze rippled his open shirt.

When the ocean was the colour of blood, Keppel took off his shirt, and then his breeches, and waded into the open water.

'Are you insane?' shouted Fullarton after him. 'It's freezing!'

But Keppel shouted and gasped as he splashed the cold water over his body, wiping off the sweat and soil of their work.

'Try it!' he called. 'It's not cold.'

So Fullarton stripped off too, and waded in. Despite the heat of the day the water was cold, icily so, and it throbbed around his ankles. He plunged in deeper, following Keppel, until the cold became too much and he retreated back into the shallows. But now the shallows felt warm, and he sat there a while, half submerged, until the sun disappeared altogether, and the shallows chilled.

~

They slept on the beach that night, in the open air, covered in their cloaks. The night was mild, and Fullarton listened to the rich breathing of Keppel beside him. It was the breathing of a man in a deep sleep, rested and calm. Fullarton, in contrast, was restless and hot. He lay awake, watching Keppel's silhouette rise and fall in the dark, under a blanket of diamond stars.

22

When the tide came in the next morning, the ship was righted and launched and they watched the gilt ridge of the Cornish coast slip away under a cloudless sky.

Fullarton walked around the ship, watching the men working, their golden earrings flashing in the sunlight, to protect against blindness, and their abdomens tightly trussed, to protect against hernia. As they looked up to watch him pass he saw their expressions, and began to wonder about the set of men that Keppel had picked out for a crew. They were all sun leathered, and bore the typical pock marks of syphilis or some other degenerate disease. Their clothes were a strange assembly of ill-matching colours, rich fabrics and dirty rags, and the lack of care that appeared to have gone into their arrangement filled Fullarton with distaste. Their general appearance was one of degeneracy, sickness, lameness and physical weakness. That much was to be expected; they had been gathered in haste after all, and were competent enough for their task. But there was something about them that made Fullarton uneasy. He felt the same mistrust of them he had felt on board the *Promise*. They each had an expression that seemed to mingle together fear and hatred, and the smiles they flashed at Fullarton went no further than the curl of their lips.

~

That evening Keppel and Fullarton mapped out the route they planned to take, from the English coast to France.

'Why don't we head for Rochefort,' said Fullarton. 'I have contacts there. And if we don't have a prize by then, at least we can pick up some of that French wine Robert Cole mentioned.'

'More likely your liquor stocks are getting low,' said Keppel, staring at the red-tinged whites of Fullarton's eyes. 'You need to practise a little moderation.'

'I moderate myself in other ways,' said Fullarton, defensively. His self control was always something he had been proud of. But since he had come on board with Keppel even he was aware that something had slipped out of place. Perhaps it had even been happening before now, but Keppel's presence seemed to highlight it. An aura of superiority seemed to surround him even when he was paying Fullarton no attention at all.

'But that's a good idea, of yours. We'll make for Rochefort first,' added Keppel, still looking at the map.

Fullarton couldn't conceal a childish satisfaction. 'It's a good plan,' he agreed.

'In fact,' said Keppel, 'I had already mentioned to Cole that we may see him there.'

Fullarton nodded, but bit his lip in irritation. Keppel was still deep in concentration, and Fullarton tried to join him, looking again at the charts, but he had taken too much wine already, and the lines were beginning to swim before him. He sat back, trying to ignore the laughter and music from the fo'c'scle. He began to flick his overgrown nails against his skin, in time to the tick of the clock in the gunroom.

'Do you think this crew will remain loyal?' he asked at last.

Keppel looked up. He smiled and shook his head. 'Of course not. I don't expect loyalty from them, not for a minute,' he said.

'But aren't you worried about mutiny?' The flicking of Fullarton's nails grew faster.

'No. I don't expect them to be loyal, because I don't expect anybody to be loyal,' Keppel said, still smiling. 'It's not in our nature. But I do expect obedience. They've all signed the articles. They know the rules. No fighting, no women on board, no drinking until sundown. And the word of the Captain, or in this case the Captains, is final.' Keppel and Fullarton had from the outset decided that they would each have equal status on the ship.

'They look the kind of men that will turn at the first opportunity,' said Fullarton, shaking his own head. 'Most of them seem barely sane.'

'They have the right kind of madness,' said Keppel, as he leaned forward and poured brandy the colour of molasses from a glass bottle. 'They know the risks, but they'll also know the rewards, when we find our prize.'

'You seem confident of that,' said Fullarton. He had heard, in Plymouth, that there were many pirates operating following the end of the war, and that as a result, many merchant ships had not reduced their supplies of powder and guns. Already weeks had passed by with hardly a ship in sight, except for fishing vessels and men-o-war from which they kept a safe distance. Though he said nothing, Fullarton had begun to worry. He was sure that the crew of the *Promise* had been near to mutiny, and he was convinced this crew would do the same. But there was something infectious about Keppel's confidence, and even now there was something in Keppel's expression that caused the flicking movement of his fingernails to grow still.

'Oh, we'll find what we're looking for, all right,' said Keppel. 'It's only a question of when.' He poured another glass of brandy. Fullarton had watched him drink several already, yet he never seemed to suffer the effects of the liquor, and spoke as slowly and clearly as always.

They finished the bottle, and Keppel continued to point to the routes on the charts. Fullarton followed his finger but couldn't make sense of it. He simply sat and smiled, nodding his head every so often. Somewhere within his blurred consciousness he felt ashamed, and to hide it he refused to open his mouth at all. He had never felt the need to conceal his drunkenness before, never with Bell, or with Hampton, who had always been a good deal more drunk than he was. He remembered the disdain with which he had regarded Hampton, the way his self pity increased with each brandy he took. Looking at Keppel, he felt sure he could see the hint of a similar disdain in Keppel's expression. But there was nothing he could do. The drink had taken its effect and finally his head started nodding of its own accord. The room began to fade around him. But his head jerked up painfully and suddenly as the door crashed open and a young man burst in, brandishing the broken end of a bottle.

In the presence of this sailor, Fullarton felt sober at

once. The man was almost too drunk to stand, and was muttering something about his allowance of salt beef.

Keppel waved his hand at him. 'Don't waste my time with your mumblings, young man. Go back to your quarters and see me in the morning when you are coherent enough to speak.'

'Fuck you,' said the man, which was the only part of his speech Fullarton had found intelligible.

The sailor stood, swaying a little, appearing pleased with the strength of his own outburst. But something had switched in Keppel's eyes and a second later he was on his feet with his cutlass drawn. At the touch of the blade the man shrank back and Keppel grabbed him by the arm. Now fully awake, Fullarton followed them into the cool of the night as Keppel marched him on to the deck. Fullarton helped Keppel to hold the man against the rail, where Keppel replaced his cutlass into its sheath. He took the broken bottle from the sailor and ran his hand along its edge.

'A good choice of weapon,' Keppel said, 'but is it sharp enough, do you think?' He rolled back his sleeve. 'Have you seen my tattoos?' he asked. 'A pretty pattern can't be made without pain.' Then he held the serrated glass edge to the man's face.

Fullarton felt the skin of the man's arm tighten beneath his fingers. He felt the cool wind against the side of his face, diluting the effect of the brandy. He looked at Keppel's face as he held the man. Keppel appeared to show no signs of drunkenness. His speech was crystal clear and his movements were measured. Then Fullarton watched with a slight sickness as Keppel drew the edge of the broken bottle lightly along the man's cheek. At first he thought he had done it only to warn the man, had not applied pressure, but then he saw the blood begin to run in thin black rivulets.

'Let him go,' said Keppel to Fullarton, who was glad to, since his own arms were beginning to shudder from the strain. The man sprang back as his arm was released. He clutched his face where it had been cut and stared at Keppel with wide open eyes. He said nothing, but backed away.

'I told you when we set sail,' Keppel said, 'and I'll tell you again. I will not tolerate foul language on this ship. Now go back and tell the men that the next one of them to speak a foul word in my presence, or in Captain Fullarton's, will face a worse punishment than you have tonight.'

'You're a madman,' said the man.

'I am a gentleman,' said Keppel. 'Now go, and be sure to tell the others how you were decorated.' As the man lurched unsteadily into the darkness, Keppel leaned back against the rail and watched him almost fondly.

'A fine young man, that,' he said, as he faced Fullarton. 'But I won't tolerate foul language. I don't care if the man be a peasant or a gentleman, there's no necessity for it at all.'

It was only then that Fullarton saw any sign of intoxication, a kind of glassy unawareness in his eyes. Keppel stared both towards and past Fullarton at the same time, and suddenly Fullarton had a memory of his father, how easily he could switch from drunkenness to razor-sharp lucidity. He looked down at his hands, which were trembling.

'Perhaps you were right,' Keppel said, as they walked back to the cabin. 'What we need is a prize, something to raise their spirits.'

~

They sat in the gunroom again, and except for a few hands still on deck, the ship was quiet. There was only the creaking of the wood, the white boom of the sea and the crying of an occasional insomniac gull.

'I do feel there is good fortune coming,' said Keppel, as he took another gulp of wine. He leaned back on a bunk and started to unbutton his shirt. 'It's hot,' he said. 'It's like an oven in here.'

Fullarton nodded, still standing up. He was thinking about the look in Keppel's eyes. It had both unsettled and fascinated him. It was like the look he had seen in the eyes of his father, in the eyes of his grandmother, and in the eyes of the Minister at home. A kind of belief, an unshakeable faith, even in the intangible. It was something he had never quite been able to master.

'Why don't you take off yours?' said Keppel, watching him. 'I can see the sweat pouring off you.'

Fullarton looked down. He put his hand to his brow, and found it was wet. He started to unbutton his shirt.

'Come,' said Keppel, 'sit down. Have some wine.'

Fullarton sat, and Keppel poured wine into his mug.

'Are we not like brothers now?' said Keppel.

Fullarton nodded again. Keppel leaned over to look at a scar on Fullarton's back.

'Where did you get these marks?' he asked.

'A flogging,' said Fullarton. 'A long time ago.' The wounds

had gone septic, and they had been so far out to sea they had never been properly treated, so the scars had remained. Fullarton barely remembered the incident, now. Nor what he had done to provoke it. He only remembered how sorry Hampton had been afterwards. He had wept, nursing Fullarton's wounds in his cabin, and Fullarton had despised him for it.

Keppel ran his fingers along the lines of each scar. 'They are beautiful,' he said. 'The marks of heroism. I love a good decoration.'

'Do you have any of your own?' asked Fullarton.

'Only these,' said Keppel, pointing to his tattoos. 'But then I've not yet had the chance to ennoble myself in the way you have.'

Fullarton looked at him. It was the kind of comment he would normally have assumed was mocking. But Keppel seemed in earnest. He had never thought of scars as ennobling, but was happy to admit that they were if Keppel thought it so.

The candle was growing lower and began to pool and flicker as the ship suddenly set herself into a deeper motion. Keppel's fingers were still on Fullarton's spine. Finally the candle sputtered and hissed its last and the room was black. Fullarton's skin froze in the quiet darkness.

'Time for bed, then,' said Keppel's voice, after what seemed like minutes. 'Save the candles.'

Fullarton climbed into his bunk and lay awake until the sound of Keppel's steady breathing filled the void. His back burned in straight lines where Keppel's fingers had been.

Fullarton woke in a patch of damp sheet which he soon realized was the sweat of his own body. He sat up, steadying his vision against the dizzying effect of movement, and looked out of his open cabin door. Through it he could see Keppel, already dressed, taking his morning draught at the table.

'Ah,' he said, brightly, 'you're awake, good. I have an excellent feeling about today.'

Fullarton got out of bed and threw back the blankets to air and dry the sheets. He put on a clean shirt and waistcoat, and splashed his face with some dirty salt water that sat in a bowl beside his bed. He staggered a little as he walked to the table and Keppel watched him.

'You can drink like a man, Fullarton, that's certainly true,' he said, his eyes narrowing.

'I didn't have much.'

'Not that you remember,' said Keppel. 'You should cut back a bit. Intemperance does nobody any good.'

Fullarton was quiet, still thinking about the night before. 'That man,' he said.

'What man?' asked Keppel.

'The one you cut, last night.'

Keppel gave him an odd look, 'It wasn't me who cut him, my boy,' he said. 'It was you.'

Fullarton shook his head. 'No, I remember quite . . .'

'This is what I mean about intemperance,' said Keppel. 'Messes with your senses.'

Fullarton regarded him for a moment. He knew it had been Keppel. He had seen it with his own eyes. But then he had been asleep, and then woken. There was a grain of uncertainty in him. Keppel's eyes were full of that same unshakeable faith he had seen the night before.

'He was bleeding badly,' Fullarton said quietly, deciding not to pursue it further. 'Perhaps he'll raise a riot among the men.'

'Nonsense,' said Keppel. 'He'll get a little respect for trying, and the men will fear us more, and that scar can only do him good, in the long run.' He smiled at Fullarton, his face opening up. 'There's no need to feel regret. I never do. Here, have some biscuit, a hard-boiled egg, and this lemon preserve is delicious.' As he spoke he took large spoonfuls of the lemon preserve and smeared it over his dry biscuit. Then he cut open his egg and smeared the preserve over that as well.

Fullarton looked away. 'I'm not over fond of preserve,' he said.

'You should eat more,' said Keppel, with his mouth full. 'Look at you, you're wasting away.'

Fullarton looked at himself. He was lean, it was true, but then he had always been that way, hadn't he?

'I'm fine,' he said, and poured himself a brandy from the decanter. 'I'll eat later, just my draught.'

'Have some tea.' Keppel poured some from a pot, a pretty Dutch one that he had brought with him. He seemed to drink tea all day long, until evening, when he switched to brandy. 'And there's some sugar, there.'

Fullarton felt as though the table was shimmering in front of him, and his skin prickled with cool sweat. He quickly excused himself and ran upstairs to heave the small drop of brandy he had drunk over the side of the ship.

When he had recovered he leaned on the rail. The day was warm and windless and the ship appeared to drift on the water. His mouth felt baked, full of a burning thirst that he knew was due to the vomiting, and would soon pass. It was not enough to disturb the ship's water supply for. Move slowly, that was the answer, until his body had produced enough saliva to replenish his mouth with moisture.

The sun dimmed as they drifted into a thick cloud of haar. It clung to his skin and blocked his pores. He choked again, and it was as he was looking up after one of his bouts of sickness that he saw what looked like the rising bulk of an enormous whale.

At first he stared at it, locked in a kind of trance. He had always disbelieved tales of strange sea monsters. The lower orders might entertain each other with nonsense of that type, but he had never seen one, and so, as far as he was concerned, they didn't exist. Now for the first time a moment of doubt struck him. But then there came a shout from behind him, and he was startled out of his spell, and looked again to see it for what it really was. Rising close out of the mist was the hull and stern of a large ship, the prize they so desperately needed.

23

I

They gave chase at once, but the ship appeared almost stationary in the water. Fullarton looked through his glass, and then again at the vague shape with his naked eye, and then once more with his glass. He saw several gun holes. The ship was well armed. He ordered the men to fire a couple of warning shots, which plumed into the mist, their sound deadened by it, seeming to echo somewhere further off. They were not returned. Finally they raised the red flag. Still the ship did not respond. They were gaining on her quickly now, and he could see no sign of life on board.

Fullarton felt Keppel breathing behind him. He turned, and Keppel grinned.

'Go on,' he said. 'See if you can talk the nice captain into giving us his ship and everything in her.'

They pulled alongside, and all was quiet. Fullarton climbed on board, touching his ear where Keppel's lips had hovered, but despite Keppel's confidence, he felt uneasy. The capture had been too smooth, the ship had surrendered too soon. He stopped, and looked round for a moment to where Keppel stood watching him. A few of his own crew climbed on board behind him. But he could see nobody. The decks were deserted. He had heard of ghost ships, floating across the ocean devoid of men, with no explanation for where the crew had gone, and for a moment he wondered if this was one of them. His unease began to turn into a very real, creeping fear, and he put his hand on his cutlass.

He sent his crew to search below deck and walked from one end of the vessel to the other, looking into the galley door and the cabins, but all were empty. A couple of sheep bleated from their pen by the side of the deck. He could hear the waves washing around him, the sound of his own feet knocking on the wood, and the occasional shout from his ship.

But then, as he came around the back of the cabins, he saw that a few men were gathered there. They were not enough to make a crew, only five or six. It crossed his mind then that the ship might already have been plundered, with most of her crew taken. They would have left the weakest, most useless men, and as Fullarton swaggered over to them, looking at their poor, tattered clothes, it certainly seemed that these would have been the men to leave behind. They looked no more than deckhands. One held up a piece of old sail, presumably as a sign of surrender. He approached Fullarton now and held out his hand. Fullarton smiled contemptuously, and stepped forward to take hold of it.

'You'll be the captain, I presume?' he asked mockingly, and the man smiled too. But as their fingers touched Fullarton froze. He felt the point of a pistol in the small of his back.

'Won't you be so good as to address yourself to the real captain first?' said a man's voice from behind him.

Fullarton turned around slowly to face the owner of the pistol, a smartly dressed man in a neat black wig. Then a blur of activity emerged around him. At once the ship was full of men. Dozens of them came out of hiding and began to attack the few members of his own crew who had come up the deck to search for him. More men poured on to the decks from his ship, but they had got off to a bad start, and he saw two fall immediately. Fullarton stood still, powerless, while the man who was clearly the captain continued to point his pistol into the flesh of his stomach. A blind panic took hold of him as he realized he was unable to prevent his own men being killed.

He was filled with a sense of disbelief. But then he found himself looking into the cool green of Keppel's eyes. He had come quietly on to the deck and stood directly behind the captain's shoulder. Fullarton pretended not to see, and tried to stop himself from smiling as Keppel withdrew his own pistol and held it to the captain's back.

'No,' he heard Keppel say, 'you address yourself to your new captain.'

The captain looked over his shoulder and saw Keppel. He gave a sudden start, and with a quick movement Fullarton grabbed the pistol that was thrust into his belly, and tried to push it to the side. He felt as though he was moving underwater. His arms were weighed down like lead and the pistol felt as heavy as a cannon. He didn't hear the shot. His senses were deadened. He felt it more as a vibration, which rocked his body, as if he had been punched. Then, several moments later, the searing pain.

He held the man's pistol fast, though it burned his hand, and it fired again, making a small hole in the deck.

'Drop it, or you'll be killed,' said Keppel, and the captain finally let his pistol fall to the deck. Keppel signalled to two of his own crew, who took the man and bound his arms.

The crew of the trader, realizing what had happened to their captain, had stopped fighting, and it now looked as if they had taken the worst of it in any case. Fullarton clutched the place where his stomach had been hit and felt warm blood and soft tissue. He lifted his shirt but couldn't look down.

Keppel peered at the wound. 'It's not deep,' he said.

Fullarton had dropped to the deck, and had screwed up his face tight to prevent the tears which he could feel stab the corners of his eyes. He saw the captain, who looked down at him with an air of triumph, despite his bonds. Fullarton felt a deep flush followed by a rage that rose in him and choked his throat.

'Well,' said Keppel, 'what do you want done with him?'

'Hang him!' said Fullarton in a low growl, but loud enough for all his crew to hear. 'Hang him from the mizzen stay!'

Keppel smiled approval. The crew of the trader now began to bay and shout, accusing Fullarton of barbaric treatment. His own crew hesitated, as if they expected him to change his mind, but then Keppel put up his hand.

'Now,' he said, 'this is no act of revenge. This man has tried to murder your captain, and if we were on land he would receive a punishment on the scale of his crime. Our shipboard justice is no different.' He beckoned two members of his own crew, who grabbed the man by the arms. The captain began immediately to pray for mercy as the crew prepared the ropes. Fullarton watched him, but could not pity him. His own humiliation was too fresh in his mind. He looked at his hand, which was swollen with a large bubble of skin on his palm. He clutched his stomach and grimaced.

Keppel stepped forward. 'You'll needs get something on that,' he said, pointing to Fullarton's bloody shirt. 'You!' He pointed to one of the cowering crew members. 'You look like a well-washed swab. Take off your shirt.'

The man hesitated, but Keppel prodded him with the edge of his cutlass, and he pulled off his white shirt. Keppel handed it to Fullarton. 'Hold it tight against the wound,' he said. He turned now to where his men were still holding the captain. 'Go on,' he said. 'You've been given your orders, get on with it.'

As the captain realized that his pleas were to remain unanswered he began to pray to God instead. He did so rapidly, under his breath, repeating the words of some psalm or other. Fullarton watched him with a sudden interest. The pain had numbed a little, but the numbness seemed also to have extended to his consciousness, and in this floating, dream-like state the sound of the psalm had awakened a distant memory in him. He felt momentarily impressed at the man's ability to remember such passages word for word. The man noticed Fullarton's interest.

'Wash me thoroughly from mine iniquity, and cleanse me from my sin,' said the man, looking directly at Fullarton. And then he said, with emphasis, 'For *I* acknowledge my transgressions.'

Fullarton came to a little, aware he was being mocked, and snorted. But an instant of hesitation came upon him. Perhaps if he spared this man, he could in some way be cleansed.

'I was shapen in iniquity,' said the man and, suddenly sneering, raised his voice: 'And in sin did my mother conceive me.'

Fullarton's hand was beginning to sting, and he caught Keppel's eye. He saw something in Keppel's expression that was similar to the captain's, a kind of complacency, and a disdain. He had seen Fullarton's uncertainty, perhaps, his lack of faith. Fullarton felt ashamed, and knew then that it was too late to save the man.

'Stop his babbling, for God's sake,' he shouted to one of the crew. 'It's most distracting.' Then he turned away and looked out to sea.

When he turned back the man's body had been raised up and the rope put around his neck. Then he was tripped and they listened to the choking and gurgling of his throat. Fullarton watched the life ebb out of the man and thought of how close he had been to it himself. If there was a God in heaven, then he must have been chosen, he thought, over this man. Fullarton had no doubt that there was a God, but now he realized what was meant by God's purpose. Everything that had happened was surely intended. As his father had once said, the day he found the wreck, who was he to question that purpose? Even as the man's eyes closed and his head fell, his legs continued to move. How we fight, thought Fullarton, this thing that comes to us all. At last he swung away, though the captain was not yet dead, and would not be for some time. Keppel had already left. He was at the other end of the ship, where he had ordered their men to bind the legs and arms of the other seventeen crew members. He wondered, though absent-mindedly, at the binding of their legs, since they would presumably be stored in the hold until they could be let off at some remote island, and if they were bound now they would not be able to walk there themselves. He staggered to his feet, but then looked at the shirt Keppel had given him, and saw that it was already saturated with blood. The sight of it made him weak, and he sat down, dizzy. He looked towards Keppel, and saw that his crewmen were lifting a bundle, which they cast into the sea. Then they lifted another, and to his horror he saw that the bundle moved. He continued to watch as with a great effort the men lifted a third bound man high over their heads and tossed him over the rail, into the sea below. It was only as the fourth man was lifted that he understood what was happening.

'What are you doing?' he shouted to Keppel, but Keppel only raised his hand in response.

He noticed for the first time a great noise, like a gaggle of geese. It was the noise of the other men as they cried and prayed from where they lay curled on the decks. Fullarton gazed, mesmerized, as, one by one, Keppel ordered every member of the crew to be thrown overboard.

Afterwards, Fullarton managed to stagger to his feet. He approached the place from where the men had been thrown, and looked at the rings in the water, dark and smooth where the bodies had sunk. He saw, for a moment, those dark rings of soft water off the coast of Stromness where the Dutch bodies had sunk so many years before.

Keppel walked up and stood in front of him, smiling. It was the smile of a stranger.

'Well,' he said, 'there's a little excess cargo out of the way. Let's see what this ship's worth.'

Fullarton nodded, grimacing, clutching his wound, and Keppel placed his hand on his cheek. His touch was soft and gentle.

'You look pale, John,' he said. He touched the wound of his stomach, and Fullarton winced. 'You might be losing too much blood.'

'No,' said Fullarton, 'I'm fine.'

Keppel looked behind him to where a pile of the dead men's clothes lay on the deck. He picked up another shirt and handed it to Fullarton, as a replacement for the blood-sodden one he held. Fullarton took it and held it against him, throwing the other into the sea.

'Here,' said Keppel, and he loosened his own necktie, tying it tightly around the shirt. There was a maternal tenderness in his touch, and Fullarton looked at him thankfully. 'This will help to hold it fast. Perhaps you should go and lie down.'

'No,' said Fullarton firmly. 'I want to see what we've won.'

They went into the hold and found that the ship was full of silk, tea and gin, arranged in vast quantities, hogsheads and firkins and barrels. Keppel whistled. Fullarton laughed.

'This must be worth thousands,' he said softly.

Keppel and Fullarton looked at each other. Keppel grinned and suddenly grabbed Fullarton's cheeks, squeezing them tight, as though he were a schoolboy. Fullarton looked at him, his mouth slightly open, unable to speak.

'Let's go and celebrate,' said Keppel.

'I'll be there in a minute,' whispered Fullarton.

'I'll open a bottle,' said Keppel, and disappeared, closing the door of the hold behind him. Then he looked back, and his face appeared concerned. 'If you haven't joined me in the next ten minutes, I'll be back to look for you,' he said.

'I'll be there,' Fullarton said again.

Fullarton's eyes adjusted to the lack of light. He touched his cheeks, and ran his hands over a bale of silk, like the touch of skin in the dark. Finding a beaker, he dipped it into a hogshead of gin and swallowed it down, savouring its perfumed fruit.

II

The next morning Keppel breakfasted with a broad smile on his face, as Fullarton took his coffee and brandy.

'How you can drink so much of that in the morning I'll never understand,' said Keppel, still smiling.

'It wakes me up,' said Fullarton, 'I didn't sleep well.'

'I slept like a log,' said Keppel.

Fullarton poured another measure of brandy into his cup, and his hand shook. In his mind he saw the squirming bundles of sacking being lifted and cast into the sea.

'Do you think we should have got rid of all her crew?'

'It was unfortunate,' Keppel said, 'but necessary. Their ship would have slowed us down, and we couldn't let them off alive at any populated place. After all, you did murder their captain. They would only have testified against you one day.'

'You said it was justice.'

'Oh, it was, but not legal, I'm afraid. We may be hanged for it yet,' he said lightly, pouring out tea for both of them, although Fullarton had shaken his head in refusal.

Fullarton was thinking about the man and his psalm. 'Don't you ever wonder,' he said quietly, 'about the sinning?'

Keppel's face clouded, but then he laughed lightly. 'What,' he said, his smile becoming a mild sneer, 'the day of judgement, that kind of thing? I dare say I'll be able to defend myself well enough. After all, I've only done what was necessary to get by. Who are we to question God's will? Believe me,' he added, 'if it hadn't been them, it would have been us. They wouldn't have hesitated.'

'So you believe, then, in a day of judgement,' asked Fullarton.

Keppel looked up. 'Well, of course,' he said. 'I'm no heathen.'

Fullarton winced as his hand shook again and drops of brandy fell on to his scarred skin. 'But,' he said, after raising the cup to his lips once more, 'if everything is God's will, then what can there be to judge?'

Keppel looked up from the charts he was busy with again. 'You ought to cut back on that brandy,' he said. 'It's making you confused. You know I had to carry you to bed last night.'

Fullarton was quiet then. He couldn't remember past the first bottle of claret. He had eaten nothing that day and had drunk even faster to numb the pain of his wound.

'Let's see the damage, then,' said Keppel, as though he had read his mind. He untied the necktie and took off the shirt, which was saturated. But the blood of the wound was congealing. He pressed Fullarton's stomach gently and placed another hand on his back.

'The bullet's gone right through,' he said. 'Lucky for you he got so close.'

Fullarton sat against a chair as Keppel anointed the edges of the wound with brandy. He winced, though it wasn't the pain that bothered him most, but the way he felt weakened every time Keppel touched him.

'I can see a surgeon in Rochefort,' he said through gritted teeth.

'You'll do no such thing,' said Keppel, taking his hands away and sitting up. 'We'll be discovered at once. And in any case, I've seen more men die from having surgeons' filthy fingers thrust into their wounds than from the injuries themselves. No. You must let nature take its course.'

Fullarton slumped in his chair, too weak to argue.

'At Rochefort,' said Keppel with a smile, his voice softer as he ran his fingers over the broken skin, 'after we've picked up that wine, why don't we return to St Pierre and offload it there?'

Fullarton looked up. 'You know I can't go back there!'

Keppel dipped his fingers in the brandy again. 'Come on, we can't let your personal matters stand in the way of a good profit, can we? In any case,' he went on, still smiling, 'surely you intend to fulfil your obligations one day? You know Bell will hunt you down eventually.'

Despite the pain, Fullarton pulled himself up a little.

'I have no obligations,' he said quietly. Keppel met his eye and sat back, serious. 'The thing is, John,' he said, 'we can't carry on this life for ever. We'll grow old, and this is a dangerous occupation. Look at the old dogs you see on board ships. They've barely a tooth between them. No chance of winning the hand of a prosperous merchant's sister there, no matter how much wealth they have to their name. And not much energy for climbing up masts and furling sails either.'

'Is that why you're doing this?' asked Fullarton. 'To marry a wealthy merchant's sister?'

Keppel shrugged. 'We've all got to settle down eventually. It seems like a good offer to me,' he said. 'A life of parties, eating and drinking. After all, it's not as though you'd have to see her much, if you didn't want to. I know plenty of married men who spend most of their time in London, and pretty much lead bachelor lives, while their wives look after the country estate. It's a good arrangement if you ask me.'

'Well,' said Fullarton, unable to prevent the tide of emotion rising in him, 'why don't you marry her then. If you want her, you are welcome to her.'

'I don't want her!' snorted Keppel. 'I told you, I don't love to attach myself to women. But you,' he said, reaching out suddenly and taking Fullarton's hand, 'you are different.'

Fullarton pulled his hand away and stood up. 'I don't love Nancy Bell!' he hissed. 'And I've no intention of marrying her. If it had been only money I wanted, I'd have done it when I had the chance.'

'But if you don't want money,' asked Keppel, curiously, 'why are you here?'

Fullarton wondered if Keppel was trying to elicit a confession from him. Later, he was to wish he had made one. But now, the pain from the alcohol on his wound and the effect of the brandy hit him all at once, and he felt his legs slide away beneath him. Then he felt another surge of pain as his body was heaved back on to the bunk.

'That's it,' said Keppel's voice. 'And here you must stay, until we reach Rochefort.'

Fullarton nodded and reached out his hand to the place where the voice seemed to come from. But he only clutched at the air. When he opened his eyes, the room was empty.

He lay there for some days, slipping in and out of consciousness. He seemed to have the gunroom to himself: Keppel must have returned to his cabin. One of the crew brought his meals, and helped him to eat them, because the swelling of the wound made it difficult to sit up.

They arrived in Rochefort late at night. Fullarton knew this because the regular pattering of feet running over the deck had reduced to just a few men, indicating that the night watch was up. He was lying in bed, attempting to read, but his eyes just skimmed the page. Too many thoughts raced through his head. He thought of their prize, the money they would make from the sale, how much more they could do together, he and Keppel. Then the door opened and Keppel came in. He walked towards the bunk, and Fullarton could see from his unsteady gait that he was drunk, though when he spoke his words were clear as water.

'How is the patient faring?' he said. He peeled back the covers of the bed and slowly lifted Fullarton's nightshirt. Fullarton winced, every muscle in his body tightening. He felt Keppel's fingers touch the rim of the scar, but only through the vibrations, because a hard crust was forming that was tough and insensitive.

'It's much improved,' Keppel said.

Fullarton nodded. 'I feel the difference, these last few days.'

'You've been in and out of consciousness. You said some strange things,' said Keppel, smiling, 'in your fever.'

'What kind of things?'

Keppel said nothing. He only leaned forward and kissed Fullarton hard on the mouth. Then he withdrew, and Fullarton tried to sit up, but the muscles of his stomach no longer seemed to work. He raised his head a little, and let it fall back again, as Keppel made a strange kind of salute, and left the room.

~

They rowed towards the harbour of Rochefort the following day, towing their prizes. It was the first time Fullarton had risen for breakfast, but Keppel was not there. One of the cabin boys served him and when the time came to leave, assisted him into the launch. Keppel was already sitting in the boat. He looked briefly at Fullarton, and then away, towards the port.

'A fine day,' he said.

'Indeed.'

The cabin boy took up the oars and they drifted silently across the blinding reflection of sunlight on the water, making glossy black shadows as they went. When the cabin boy had lifted the rope to throw to shore, Keppel turned to Fullarton.

'I've been thinking, John,' he said.

'Yes?' Fullarton had tried hard to make the note of his voice flat, to express nothing, but in the end he could not disguise the hope.

'Once we've done our business here, I think we should divide our profits, and separate.'

Keppel stood up and began to climb the rope ladder. Fullarton made to follow him, but stood up too abruptly, and clutched his stomach in pain. The cabin boy rose to help him.

'Leave me,' he said, pushing the boy away. But when he reached the top of the ladder, Keppel had already disappeared. He turned to the boy behind him.

'Where is he?' he asked.

'Mr Keppel told me to tell you, sir, that he's gone to negotiate the disposal of the ships. He said you needed to rest.'

Fullarton stood where he was for a moment, astounded. They had agreed to do this together. They had agreed to do everything together. Did Keppel mean to rob him of money that was rightfully his? And after all that had happened, could Keppel really just leave?

He walked blindly through the crowds of the busy town. He was well known there from his merchant trading days, and several men stopped to raise their hats or nod to him. But he stared through each one of them as though he had never seen them in his life.

24

Mary felt it as a great internal kick that stung down to the tip of her urethra. It sent such a sharp jolt of pain through her abdomen that she jumped out of her seat. She had no doubt that she was in labour.

She began to walk around in circles. The top of her stomach was curled in tight like a clenched fist, tighter and tighter it wrung, and the pain burrowed deeper until she thought she could bear it no more, then subsided.

She walked with some difficulty out into the corridor, where the first person she saw, to her surprise, was William.

'What are you doing up?' she said.

'Are you ill, madam?' he asked.

He seemed unsteady, but more lucid than before. After leaving Plymouth, Robert had been increasing the dose, with the aim of reporting him incapable by the time they reached Rochefort, and William had been confined to his bed most of the time. Now their supplies of medicine were running low, and for the last while Robert had been decreasing it slightly, and increasing the amount of alcohol he mixed it with instead. Still, Mary had not thought it sufficiently reduced to allow him to get on his feet.

'I'm in labour,' she said.

She saw the glaze had returned to his eyes. For a moment she wondered if he was sleepwalking.

'My dear,' he said, 'that's wonderful.'

'Yes,' she said, 'but you need to get help, William.'

'Of course,' said William, wandering past.

Mary realized that she couldn't wait for him to find the right person, so she hammered on the nearest door, which was the cupboard that passed for the cook's cabin. The cook opened the door and looked at her briefly.

'I'll fetch Mr Cole,' he said before she had spoken. 'Go and rest, lass. Go at once.'

Mary returned to her cabin and Robert came hurrying in a few moments later. The cook asked if he needed anything.

'Just fetch me a boy for a helper,' he said, anxious. 'She's not due for at least two weeks.'

The cook stood where he was.

Robert turned impatiently. 'What are you waiting for?'

'Don't you need my help, sir?'

'Why should I need your help?'

'You'll mind, sir, that I've delivered a child before.'

Robert turned and looked at him. 'Have you indeed?' he said, almost sarcastically. 'Well, in that case you should stay.'

~

Seven hours later Mary's contractions were only minutes apart. Whenever Robert tried to leave she held on to his arm.

'Don't leave me,' she cried, 'don't leave me.'

'I won't leave you, Mary, I won't,' Robert replied.

Mary was terrified of the power of her own body. She could not hold back the life force that was bursting from it, whether or not it killed her in the process. She could feel the immensity of the pressure building within her body. She glanced at Robert's face, and was surprised to recognize the panic that was clearly displayed there. Robert looked towards the cook, who was busy wringing out cloths and placing them over her belly.

'She's bleeding,' said Robert, turning away.

Then Mary felt something pushing inside her again. She heard the terrible scream that came from deep within her but sounded like somebody else.

'Where are you going?' she heard the cook say.

'I need some air.'

She looked up and saw Robert standing at the door.

'But the child is coming now,' said the cook. He then addressed himself to Mary. 'Ma'am, you need to push the baby out.'

The baby seemed to be pushing itself, and Mary had little control over it. Yet nothing was happening. She met Robert's eye, and saw the fear in it, which convinced her that something was wrong. The baby was stuck, she decided, and she was going to die. Well, at least then the pain would be gone. It was so intense at that moment, that even death seemed inviting.

She shut her eyes, waiting for it, and heard the door close. But when she opened her eyes again she was still alive, and Robert was gone. The searing pain remained, and she heard once more the distant scream that had apparently come from her body.

The cook looked at her, and then at the door. He shook his head, and she heard him murmur under his breath. 'The second time,' he said.

'What?' said Mary, breathless, only aware that he was angry about something. 'What's wrong? Why did he leave? Am I going to die?' Her voice sounded high and childlike. And somewhere within she felt a dark, seething anger, at Robert, at William, even at her mother. They had all known how close the act of bringing life into the world was to the act of dying. Yet her mother had married her off, William and Robert had congratulated her on her pregnancy, as though *this* was something to celebrate. They were all ignorant, or evil, or both.

'No, lass, you're not going to die,' said the cook.

She saw him smile, and wished she were strong enough to hit him. But when he picked up a glass of wine he had poured earlier and held it to her lips, she gulped it greedily.

'Don't worry, lass,' he said. 'Drink this, and then give me one last push, all your strength now. That's it, lass, I can see the head now.'

Mary felt the baby's head beginning to burn, to tear the fragile skin, and as she sat up a little to push she caught sight of the blood that covered the cook's arms and the sheets beneath her.

'Is it all right?' she called. 'Is everything all right?'

The cook was busy with blood-soaked towels, but suddenly she heard a strange, gull-like cry.

'It's all right, ma'am,' said the cook. 'It's a right bonny girl.'

'A girl,' called Mary, half delirious. 'I can't believe it, a girl.'

The cook smiled at this, but it was not maternal delight that had made Mary cry out. When she said she couldn't believe it, she had meant just that. She couldn't believe that a live child had emerged from her body. She didn't feel the ownership of it she had expected. It was quite independent of her. She had only been its temporary mode of transport. The cook had wrapped it tenderly and placed it on her, still attached by the cord of the placenta. But she could do little more than look at the creature that chewed at her breast, then later lay in its cot staring at her with insolent, wide-open eyes, as some kind of parasite, that had taken the life from her and made it its own. Weakened, then, as she lay in her own cot, being rocked by the motion of the waves, she knew she would never be the same person again.

When the placenta was delivered the cook washed his bloodstained arms down with an old towel and warm water. He worked quickly, his face set. When he had finished, he put his hand on her head.

'No fever,' he said to Robert.

She hadn't noticed Robert come in, and saw him now for the first time. Maybe she had only imagined him leaving, she thought. He sat in the corner of the room, his head in his hands.

'Wait a while, and then come to the kitchen. I'll make her some chicken, and she should have a little more wine,' said the cook.

Mary was suddenly aware how much she owed this old man, and realized, looking at him, that the sneering expression she had always detested was actually carved into the lines in his face, and was probably something he could not prevent. 'Thank you,' she said to him.

'You did well, lass,' he answered roughly.

'I didn't know you could deliver babies.'

'Delivered my own,' he murmured. 'The midwife got stuck in snow and couldn't get to her on time. She died a few hours later, and the child lived a few days,' he went on. 'It was a bad winter that one. Didn't give them a chance.'

Mary said nothing. She remembered the cook saying before that his wife had died, but she hadn't known how. She saw how hard it must have been for him to deliver her baby, and she looked disdainfully at Robert.

'Who'd have thought a surgeon could be so squeamish,' said the cook, a little more brightly. He put his hand on Robert's shoulder. 'Only usually see that with the fathers,' he added slyly.

Mary looked at him in surprise, wondering what he knew, but then it all faded into insignificance again as her womb began to contract painfully.

'Why won't it stop?' she moaned.

'Takes a while, even afterwards,' said the cook. He turned to Robert. 'Better give her a potion,' he said. 'That's more your style, isn't it?'

Robert made her drink something, and she quickly fell asleep. When she woke she was alone. Then came another knock on the door, which she supposed would be Robert. She didn't care, now. What she had been through was so great that their little scheme seemed hardly to matter, and her anger still had not faded. She could barely think beyond the next time the baby woke. But in fact when the door opened it was Captain Jones who came in. He seemed more alert than before. He kissed Mary and picked up the little girl, holding her gently under her head.

'Isn't she beautiful?' he said.

'Yes,' said Mary flatly, and without feeling.

'What shall we call her?'

'I don't know,' she said weakly. 'Why don't you choose a name?'

He took her to the light. 'She has your eyes,' he said. But this only cut Mary deeply, for it meant that her eyes were no longer her own, and as if to prove it, her sight began to grow dim with tears.

William turned and saw them. 'You're not disappointed,' he said, 'that it's a girl?'

She shook her head. 'It's better that way,' she said.

'Let's call her Margaret, after your mother,' said William.

Mary looked at the child at last, and then at William. She shook her head again. 'No,' she said. 'I'll call her Lucy, after the light. Perhaps then she'll see things more clearly than her mother.'

She could feel William watching her.

'You must be tired,' he said at last.

She didn't reply. She was wondering when Robert would come. William waited for a moment, and then left her.

~

Robert did come, but not until two days later.

'I wanted to let you rest,' he said.

'I told you it would be a girl,' said Mary.

'It only means we have to wait a little longer,' said Robert. But he seemed impatient. He sat on the bed, and his knee jolted up and down. He didn't ask for the child's name.

'She's called Lucy,' Mary told him.

'Yes,' said Robert, 'that's lovely.' He chewed on his nails. Mary wondered if he had the strength to wait at all.

~

The ship drew closer to Rochefort. The baby cried and fed alternately. Mary responded mechanically, hating each moment of it. The baby's feeding hurt, her nipples were raw and bleeding, but after a while they began to grow hard. And it seemed that the harder they grew, the softer Mary became. Where at first she had dosed the baby with brandy to make her sleep for longer, as they drew closer to Rochefort she found herself desperate for her to feed. If the baby slept for too long her breasts would ache and the watery milk would leak from her. When she lifted the child and opened her tiny gaping mouth until it locked tight, she would lie back, and once the parching thirst had subsided, a kind of blissful calm would take its place. It was then that she finally understood she needed this child, far more than it needed her. For the baby, any old wet nurse would do, and she would forget her eventually. But Mary saw that she could not live without the little crinkled face, its mouth opening to draw out the life force she now needed to give. It was mutual dependency rather than love, but it would bind them together until a time when she recognized that emotion again.

~

Robert came to see her once more, the night before they anchored at Rochefort. He picked up the child.

'She has your eyes,' he said.

'I know,' she said. 'But what will she have of yours?'

Robert looked at her for a moment. She knew he under-stood her meaning.

'She will have everything I have,' he said briskly.

'Then she will have nothing,' said Mary. She looked at the child lying in her cradle. The baby made a short, snuf-fling noise.

'I would still go with you,' he said, 'if you want me to.'

'That's gracious of you,' she said, laughing. 'Surely with your medical training you could make a good living anywhere,' she said, with a note of scorn in her voice.

'What do you mean?' he asked, though not with his usual sharpness.

'I suspected some time ago that you weren't a doctor,' she said. Then she laughed. 'Jesuit drops are for wounds, not parasites. My aunt used them for everything. But the birth confirmed it. Never seen a medical man so fright-ened of blood.'

Robert looked at his feet. 'I did train, for a time,' he said. 'But I didn't complete it. When I met William again, I was in a tight spot. I knew he trusted me, so I took my chances. Bought a case of medicines, and a book. I would have learned,' he went on, 'in time.'

The baby had begun to cry again, and Mary spent some time trying to encourage her to feed, but she didn't seem interested. Eventually she latched on, and the silence was broken only by the small, wet, sucking sounds of the child.

'So,' Mary said at last, 'you would take me, and the child and feed us and clothe us, on nothing?' She looked directly into his eyes, but he lowered his swiftly.

'If that's what you want,' he said.

'You know it isn't,' she said, 'or else you would not promise it.'

'What do you know of what I want?' he barked suddenly.

Mary shrank back, surprised at this sudden display of emotion. It reminded her of how she had felt during their first days together, and for a moment she thought she might cry. But then she looked down at Lucy's suckling face. Lucy was hers, of that she could be certain. But of Robert, even of William, she would never be sure again. It was clear there was no future for them together. He must know this as well as she did. From the corner of her eye she saw that his hand was trembling. It occurred to her that this should have moved her, that several months ago she would have done anything for this kind of show of emotion from Robert, always so self-assured, with that flicker of vulnerability that made him attractive. Now, however, it only unsettled her. She refused to meet his eye, her gaze resting on Lucy, stroking her small pink head with its silk threadwork of hair. It seemed that they sat like this for some time, and she found herself relieved when at last she heard him stumble to the door, slamming it behind him.

~

They arrived in Rochefort at night, and anchored a little way out. Mary had a restless night. The baby woke her several times, and she heard voices above her head and the sound of men stepping over the boards. The sound of goods and boats being lowered. She thought nothing of it. They were preparing to disembark the following day. She fell asleep again at last, but when the sudden jolt of another launch being lowered wakened her, she picked up the book beside her, and from it dropped a note, in Robert's hand.

She opened it at once and read quickly, darting over the words, scanning up and down. When she understood its meaning she sat upright and covered her mouth.

It told her that Robert had left the ship already, and rowed himself over to the port of Rochefort. He would find a commission on a ship travelling home. That didn't surprise her. What surprised her was what she read next.

She looked at the paper again, her hand still across her mouth. Then she took a deep breath, rolled the note into a narrow tube, and held it over the candle until it shrivelled and burned into black confetti. She dropped it into the candle tray where it flaked into ashes on the melted wax. Then she sat back, sucked her burned fingers and tried hard to swallow her fear.

25

*W*illiam knows about us.

That was the first thing Robert's letter said. It came as little surprise, as she had suspected it for some time. But to see it there, written down, was different. She had never quite believed that he knew it all, because he seemed to care so little.

She read on. And what she read caused her to pick up her sleeping child and squeeze her until she began to cry. Mary put her to the breast to keep her quiet, but the child didn't want to feed, and writhed and squirmed. When at last she latched her on, she was sure that the baby bit down harder than usual.

What I am about to tell you may shock you, but you must know that it was William's idea, and I merely promised to help, because I knew how much he needed it. He is not able to have children. He has known this for many years, and when I met him again for the first time in so many years he told me he was resigned to Bachelorhood. He said he was content, but that his uncle, his mother's brother, who as you know has been his guardian since he was a child, told him that unless he was able to produce an heir his inheritance would pass to the children of her younger sister.

It was only because of my regard and esteem for William that I suggested the scheme which we then put into practice, to regain what was rightfully his. Through Anneke, whose past you are already acquainted with, I introduced William to Elizabeth, a woman of great beauty, and experienced in the ways of the world. She was made to understand that if she played her part, and produced a male heir, she would then be given a handsome settlement, and some way found either to dissolve the marriage or settle her anonymously in some other place. Anneke, whose honour I know you esteem so much, was aware of this arrangement, and would benefit from it.

Elizabeth then made the silly mistake of falling in love with William, which complicated things greatly, but in the end I fathered Elizabeth's child. This unluckily turned out to be a girl, whose sad fate, followed by that of Elizabeth, you already know.

William was devastated, of course, but not so devastated not to want to try again. I agreed, though reluctantly, to try an introduction. This time, however, I vowed it would be with someone different, someone young and innocent who could not possibly think to manipulate the situation for her own ends. I knew your uncle through a family friend, and heard about you. I arranged the marriage before I saw you for the first time, and how was I to know, my darling Mary, that you would capture my heart? Capture it you did, however, and so I contemplated turning William's little scheme on its head. But it seems your love for me was not strong enough to cause you to leave without a fortune.

At this Mary put the paper down for a moment and gave a hard laugh. But she noticed the handwriting from this point on was jagged and untidy.

But there is something else I need to tell you, before you make any grave errors of judgement. You have a child to protect now, and as I will be gone when you receive this letter, you will have to consider how best to do that yourself. What I have to tell you will shock you greatly, and indeed my hand shakes as I write these words. You must know that the husband you stand by so faithfully is a murderer.

It was not Elizabeth but he who was responsible for Alice's death. When he found out that Elizabeth's child was a girl, he drank himself into a fit of rage. He took the child from her cot one night, and gave her a dose of laudanum so powerful as to cause her to die in her sleep. When Elizabeth discovered what had happened she threw herself into the sea to join her child.

Mary swallowed and read on.

You can easily imagine the horror and reprehension I felt at so unnatural a crime, especially since the child was mine, in nature if not in law. I threatened to have him hanged for murder as soon as we reached port, but then he was so penitent, not remembering what he had done, and seemed to feel the loss as though it were his own, that I agreed to give him a second chance. However, you see how his character is changed by it. Increasingly he shows his instability, and he is not one person but two.

I found myself having to subdue him with a draught more and more often, even before you were aware of it. But laudanum is an expensive habit. His income, and yours, cannot sustain it. Now he will not be subdued, and you will see his true character.

Now do you see the nature of the choice you have made? I do understand, my darling Mary, that your youth contributes to your weakness, and they say many women become unreasonable after giving birth. I will therefore do you the honour of supposing that this is what has happened to you. Perhaps in time you may come to know the love I feel for you, and contemplate putting your faith in me again.

As always, your humble and faithful servant
Robert

While the words were curling into ash, Mary remembered something she had overheard Robert say to William: 'How can you mourn what was never yours?' She realized now he was talking about Alice. She felt her grip tighten around Lucy's back.

When the knock came on the door, hard and sharp, Mary had her trunk packed and ready. She was already dressed and wearing her cloak, and Lucy was well swaddled and wrapped. William entered and reached out for the child, but Mary held her fast.

'She's almost asleep,' she said.

'Please let me hold her,' said William softly. Mary released her with a trembling hand. He held her for a moment, and it was hard to believe, watching them together, that what Robert had said could be true. But then Lucy looked up into William's face and started to cry.

'Give her to me,' said Mary, a little more sharply than she would have liked. 'I think she's tired,' she added.

The baby quietened in her arms. Mary glanced at William, his eyes lined with dark rings. At that moment, he looked incapable of anger or malice. But he had persuaded Robert to seduce her, to tell her he loved her, to give her some kind of hope. A sickness rose in her throat, and she almost hissed the words.

'Robert is gone,' she said.

'What do you mean?' asked William.

'He's left the ship,' she said. 'He left behind a note.'

'A note,' said William. His dull eyes had come to life. 'Where is it?'

'I burned it,' said Mary, looking at him coolly.

William stared at her for an instant and she saw an awakening in him.

'Why would you do that?' he asked quietly.

Mary stood at the entrance to the small cabin, with William blocking the doorway.

'It was full of lies,' she said quickly. Then she pushed past him with the child.

~

Once on deck she felt better. All the men were assembled there, and even when William came up behind her, taking her arm a little too firmly, she knew there was nothing he could do in front of his men.

Once they had found their lodgings, in a respectable-looking house, run by a well-dressed mistress, Mary asked her at once if she had a woman they could employ as a nurse for the evening. She sat in the hallway waiting on her small chest. Only when the nurse arrived did she climb the stairs to join William in their room. With the nurse tucking Lucy into her cot, Mary unpacked carefully, taking out her Bible, a bottle of perfume, reading spectacles and writing paper, a bag of jewellery and some powder. This mundane action brought her some comfort, prevented her from thinking about the time when she and William would have to be alone, but the last thing she took out, quite by accident, was the remaining phial that Robert had given her, with only a few drops left inside. She looked at William. His back was turned, and the nurse was bending over Lucy. She poured the contents of the phial into William's drink, wishing there had been enough to poison him. Then she began to dress for dinner.

In lodgings she took far more time over her toilet than she did when on board the ship, and like the unpacking, the slow precision of the business of dressing had a calming effect upon her. She put on a powdering gown and powdered her hair. She rouged her cheeks. She took the time to pull on her red silk gown with a double muslin handkerchief around her breast, lammer beads, an apron of fine Dutch lawn, a new mob cap, her scarlet cloak and high-heeled shoes. She dressed her hair with ruffles. She carried out these actions in a careful, matter of fact way, and each action seemed to draw her further away from the terrible reality that surrounded her, that Robert was gone, and that her own husband had tried to cheat her. But then they were called for dinner, and she took his arm and smiled at him as any ordinary wife would do. William looked back at her. He didn't smile, but he didn't look angry either. If he looked anything at all, it was confused.

As they descended the stairs, he stopped.

'But why did he leave?' he asked, as if they had only just finished a conversation.

Mary opened her mouth to speak, but then they were spotted by their hostess, who came forward and smiled at them, leading them to the table.

When Mary saw that there were other guests, she breathed in relief, knowing she would not have to answer his question, not yet. Then she recognized them.

'My goodness,' she heard one of them exclaim. 'Look who it is!'

At the table sat the two mariners they had met in Plymouth, the old naval captain William had known from his days in the navy, Keppel was his name, whom William had called ruthless, and Captain Fullarton, the tall man with the unusual accent. They looked quite different from their appearance in Plymouth, less dishevelled, and smartly and expensively dressed. Captain Keppel greeted Mary and her husband politely as they sat down together, and didn't look at all ruthless to Mary, but rather charming. Captain Fullarton nodded but said nothing, his face pained and sullen like a small boy in trouble.

'What a coincidence,' said Captain Keppel. 'And where is your friend, Mr Cole?'

Mary looked at William's grey face, saw the lines around his eyes twitch.

'Mr Cole is no longer with the ship, Captain Keppel,' she said coolly.

'Where is that damned hostess with the wine,' William said, agitated.

Mary stood abruptly and picked up the water pitcher. 'Let me pour you some water,' she said, but William pushed her hand away.

'You know I do not love water,' he said fiercely.

'Water feeds the blood,' said Keppel, holding out his own glass for Mary to fill. 'And flushes impurities from the body. If Mr Cole was here, he would tell you that. Won't you have some, Captain Fullarton?'

But Captain Fullarton only glared at him, as did William. Then the hostess appeared with the wine and William seemed to relax a little. Mary surveyed the food spread out on the table before her, dressed and roasted capons, pommes dauphinoise, long beans cooked in a tangy lemon butter, apricot tart and a kind of sweet yellow cream. But she could not find an appetite. She drank her claret, gulping it like water. Then she turned her head as a third couple came to sit at the table: a tall man, dressed in the French style, and a slim, pretty, dark-haired woman.

'*Je suis desolé, nous sommes en retard*,' he said.

The party looked at them blankly, until Fullarton stood up. 'That's all right, *asseyez-vous, s'il vous plaît*,' he said.

'You're most welcome,' said Keppel.

'Captain Keppel refuses to speak French,' said Captain Fullarton, with a hint of venom. 'Even when in France, he assumes his character will be enough to make him understood.'

'And so it always has been,' said Keppel, smiling at Fullarton and refusing to return his sarcasm.

'It is no great issue,' said the Frenchman, with a bored tone. 'I speak English. Are you on business here?'

'We are,' said Keppel, smiling at the young woman, who glanced back shyly.

'Thank goodness the war is over,' said the man, 'so that respectable French and English merchants can trade freely again.'

'Indeed,' said Keppel. 'You must have been hit hard by recent events.'

'Most certainly.' The Frenchman reached into the middle of the table and poured wine into everyone's glasses. 'To free trade,' he said, raising his glass.

'To free trade,' they echoed.

'My name is Michel Chardin,' he said.

'And your beautiful wife,' said Keppel, 'does she have a name?'

'She is called Madame Chardin,' said Monsieur Chardin, sharply. 'She doesn't speak English.' He took out a small tortoiseshell snuff box and passed it around the table.

If the young woman didn't speak English, she seemed at least to understand it, and flashed a look at her husband.

'Claudette,' she said gently, smiling at Mary first, and then, shyly, at the rest of the company, finishing with Keppel, after which she quickly looked down.

The Frenchman fixed his eye on Keppel as he lifted a large capon on to his own plate and then a smaller piece of another on to his wife's. But Keppel ignored him, continuing to stare openly at Claudette.

They ate for a while in silence. After a time, Captain Keppel started talking about the lowering of the duty on tea.

'It is certainly a boost to legitimate trade,' he said. 'But in England it has brought the drink within the range of people of all backgrounds and classes. Even the tradesman of the lowest class, the miner or the fisherman will take tea with his breakfast. It seems that the appetite for it is incurable, and it has the most pernicious levelling effect.'

'In France,' said the Frenchman, 'the peasants do not waste their time with such luxuries. They eat good, simple food, and are some of the hardest-working peasants in the world.'

'They seem to be very poor,' said Mary, who had been shocked at the sight of ragged children in the streets, come in from the countryside to sell apricots. They wore no shoes, and were so painfully thin that their heads seemed barely to balance on their tiny bodies. Mary had glanced at them, and had turned away.

'They are not so poor as they believe themselves to be,' said the Frenchman, smiling with the confidence of one who knows a subject better than anyone else. 'Or as they would have respectable travellers believe.'

'They cannot miss what they don't have,' said Fullarton, who seemed irritated, though by what Mary couldn't tell. 'No doubt if they had tea, they would drink tea.'

'Yes, and they would become as corrupt as our English peasants,' broke in Keppel, 'who believe that all it takes to become a gentleman is a pot of tea and a pair of silk breeches.' As he said this he smiled at Fullarton, whose expression blackened.

'I cannot help but think,' Fullarton said, 'that in the main, tea is a drink for ladies.'

He looked at Keppel angrily then, Mary thought, as if expecting a reaction, but Keppel only leaned towards Claudette, and addressed many of his comments to her directly. She sat with her hands folded on her lap, and glanced at him now and again, sideways, from the corner of her eye. In time she began to flush a little, and smile. Mary turned to Captain Fullarton. He was also watching the couple, and seemed anxious.

'Where are you from, Captain?' she said, to distract him. 'You have a most unusual accent.'

'Orkney,' he said abruptly.

'Really,' she said, smiling brightly. Her nervousness and the wine she had taken had made her feel light headed and talkative, and his sullen manner no longer seemed to matter. 'My father was from Orkney.'

At this he looked round at last. 'Was he?' he said, sighing a little, as if at her persistence. 'Which part?'

'I don't know,' said Mary. 'I never knew him. He was pressed into service before I was born. But I've often thought it would be lovely to go there, just to see what it's like. I always imagined it would be very beautiful, in a lonely kind of way.'

'It's a poor place, and the winter is long and dark,' Fullarton said.

'Is it?' said Mary. 'But then it isn't winter all the time, surely?'

'No,' said Fullarton. 'There's the springtime.'

'That must be beautiful,' said Mary hopefully.

Fullarton took a sip of brandy and glanced towards Keppel again. Then he faced her for the first time. 'There's no beauty in the world like that which springs from darkness,' he said, and his voice sounded rough and broken.

Mary examined the dark skin of the back of his hand,

which was hard and very lined for his age, and trembled continuously. But his face was quite different. It was also carved with deep lines around the mouth and eyes, but his eyes were quick and active, always moving, youthful in comparison to his skin.

'Do you miss it?' she asked.

'Miss what?'

'Home,' she said. 'Orkney.'

'Orkney isn't home,' Fullarton said, laughing a little. 'Not now.' But then he softened a little. 'I've considered returning. I've been looking at buying an estate,' he said with a sense of pride that he couldn't disguise. 'For my mother.'

'That's very generous of you,' said Mary. 'Your business must be most profitable, or else Orkney estates are easy to come by.'

But Fullarton's attention had wandered again. He gazed at her for a moment, and then past her, as if he were trying to remember what she had said.

~

After a while they retired to the drawing room and the hostess brought out the brandy and port. William sat on a chair beside the fire and appeared to fall asleep. Monsieur Chardin said that he had some business to attend to, and would be back shortly. Keppel, Fullarton, Mary and Madame Chardin sat to play cards, but once they were seated Keppel ignored everyone but Madame Chardin, staring at her face intently. She held her cards high so that they covered part of her face, glancing shyly back. After a time she grew less timid. Mary noticed that she looked at Keppel more often

335

than before, and that their eyes met several times. Their behaviour was making her angry. How dare this man act in such a forward manner with this woman, and, as for her, well, she was clearly encouraging him. Mary began to deal the cards more and more furiously, until she was almost throwing them at the other guests.

'Mrs Jones, a little more slowly, please,' said Keppel, smiling at Claudette. 'You could take a man out throwing cards at him like that.' But he seemed to adjust his manner a little, and was not quite so direct in his addresses to the Frenchwoman.

Fullarton, who had sat quietly with a black expression for most of this time, turned suddenly and picked up Mary's hand.

'What a fine dealing hand,' he said. 'You are obviously an accomplished player.' He held it close to his face, as if examining it, and she felt his breath brush the small hairs of her skin. Then he looked at Keppel. 'Don't you think?'

'Of course,' said Keppel, smiling at Claudette.

'Thank you,' said Mary, hesitantly, removing her hand.

Keppel threw down his cards. 'Well, I'm out,' he said. 'Dash it, there's no air in here, won't you join me for a walk, Madame?' he said to the Frenchwoman.

'But Captain Keppel,' said Fullarton, 'the game is not yet finished. Madame Chardin still has a hand.'

'You can play it for her,' said Keppel. 'It will be a welcome addition to the rules.'

Keppel and Claudette got up to leave, and Fullarton fidgeted with his cards. He seemed suddenly lost for words.

Mary turned anxiously to where William still slept.

336

Fullarton was staring at the door, at the place where Keppel and the woman had vanished.

'Perhaps you would like some air, too, Mrs Jones,' said Fullarton to Mary, suddenly. 'This game doesn't really work with two.'

Mary stood up and took his hand. Outside, they stood on the balcony for a while, Mary shivering a little, though the night was warm.

'A pleasant evening,' said Mary.

But Fullarton was distracted. He could hear the faint voices of Keppel and the Frenchwoman, somewhere in the shadows of the garden.

'Captain Fullarton,' said Mary softly, 'are you quite all right?'

Fullarton focused on Mary for the first time.

'You seem familiar,' he said. 'Did you say you were from Leith?'

'Yes,' said Mary.

'I knew a girl there, once . . .' said Fullarton, and his words tailed off. He paled a little, and clutched at his abdomen.

'Are you sure you're all right?' Mary asked again.

'I'm fine,' he said sharply. Then he turned as a woman's voice came out of the shadows. Keppel and Claudette stepped on to the little balcony.

'A fine evening,' said Keppel, as he opened the door that led back into the lodgings. 'I hope you're enjoying it as much as we are.' He smiled slyly at Fullarton, who stared back without expression.

Fullarton looked at the door for a moment, then followed them, without a further word to Mary.

Mary stood alone on the porch. The night was still,

and she could hear the soft whirr of crickets in the lawn, like an orchestra tuning up, not quite at the full crescendo of summer. The sudden absence of distraction brought the reality of her own situation crashing down around her. In the strange events of the evening she had almost forgotten that, sooner or later, William's drops would wear off. She thought of Robert's letter, how he had said that William's true character would become apparent. But she already knew William's character, far better than Robert had done. What terrified her more was that from now on, she would have to manage him alone.

She shuddered as the door was thrown open. It clattered against the wooden frame, and she saw the tall silhouette of the Frenchman.

'Where is my wife?' he demanded.

The shock had knocked the breath from Mary, and she could only look at him.

'Is she out here?' he snapped.

Mary shook her head.

The Frenchman disappeared back into the house, and Mary followed him. When she entered the little parlour Keppel and Claudette were nowhere to be seen. The fire was high, though the night was warm, and William still dozed before it. Fullarton stood alone, staring at the flames.

'What's happening?' asked Mary.

'Oh nothing,' said Fullarton airily, looking up. 'It seems we've been deserted.'

'Where is Madame Chardin?' she asked. 'Monsieur Chardin is looking for her.'

'Yes,' said Fullarton quietly. 'I met him in the hall, and

338

told him where he could find them both. Come, drink with me,' he went on, before she had time to speak. Mary opened her mouth. She thought of the Frenchwoman, what her husband would do when he found her. Something had to be done. But Fullarton thrust a cup of punch into her hands and lifted it to her lips.

'Drink,' he said, 'to love.' She took a small sip, still trying to think of what could be done for Madame Chardin. Her previous anger had melted away, and she realized that it had not been anger at all, but envy.

She felt nauseous. The wine she had drunk over dinner was the most she had had since that night on board the ship, the night Robert had found her, and already she felt herself losing control, the tears gathering, tight in her throat. If she released them, she knew they would come faster and thicker than ever before.

Then, without warning, Fullarton grabbed Mary clumsily around the waist, attempting to kiss her, making her drink splash out over her hand and on to her sleeve. His cold lips grazed her cheek as she twisted her head away.

'What are you doing?' she hissed, her voice high.

'Come, you're a married woman, surely you know,' said Fullarton.

'William!' called Mary. But William didn't answer. She cursed herself for having put the drops in his drink.

Fullarton put his hand beneath her jaw, attempting to turn her head, and she dropped her glass. It smashed on the tiled hearth. Then she felt the cold edge of William's knife between her throat and Fullarton's.

'Leave my wife alone,' she heard him say.

Fullarton let go, and Mary stepped back.

'I've been trying to wake you,' she said reproachfully.

'I wasn't asleep,' said William, putting his knife away. He stepped forward and hissed in her ear. 'Don't think I don't know how you spend your time in private. And don't flatter yourself that I care. But when we are in public, you will behave like my wife.'

Then he moved away from her.

'Go to our room, madam,' he said. 'I would like to have a word with Captain Fullarton.'

Mary turned immediately, glad to make her escape. But as she opened the door, a long and tortuous scream came from the corridor outside.

Fullarton's face turned grey. He drew his sword and ran past her, into the corridor, and up the stairs.

'William, the Frenchman – he's murdering his wife!' said Mary urgently. 'Can't you do something?'

'Don't we have business enough of our own to deal with,' he said coldly, 'without getting involved in other people's?'

'But William, he's going to kill her!'

William looked at her. 'Well, of course, you must sympathize with the lady's case,' he said, his voice soft and mocking. But he did as she said, leaving Mary standing alone at the door.

~

Mary set off weakly back to her room. Once in the hall she stopped to catch her breath. She could hear noises in one of the rooms above her, a scuffle and two clear thuds. Cautiously, she crept up the dark stairs. A light shone from an open door at the end of the narrow hallway, and

340

she caught sight of a shape that she recognized at once, her husband's frame, bent forward slightly. At first she thought he was wrestling another man, and quickened her pace, but as she drew closer she saw that they were not wrestling, but embracing, and that the other man was Captain Fullarton. Fullarton had stuffed the cloth of her husband's waistcoat into his mouth, trying to stifle his sobs.

Then, at their feet, she saw the dark stain on the already dark carpet, and as Fullarton raised his body up for a moment, she had a clear view of the dead Captain Keppel beneath him. His eyes were open, and he lay on the sheets of the bed, which had fallen on to the floor. His blood had turned them the colour of claret.

26

Mary's first thought was for Lucy's safety, and she turned around and stumbled through the dark corridors until she came to the door of her own room. She threw it open and ran towards the nurse, who looked at her as though she was insane.

'Hush, madam,' she said. 'The child is only just asleep.'

'Oh,' said Mary.

'Madam, what's happened!' asked the nurse, seeing the terror in Mary's face.

Mary hesitated. For some unknown reason, she couldn't tell the nurse what had happened. It was as though she felt somehow responsible, as though she had to conceal the facts of the murder for her own sake.

'It's nothing,' she said. 'Just an unfortunate incident.' Her voice shook as she spoke, and she could only think of being alone with Lucy. 'It'll be dealt with. Just leave, won't you? That is, thank you, that will be all.'

The nurse backed away. She collected her things and moved to the door. Mary picked up the child from her cradle and held her tight, as though she could obtain some comfort from the little living bundle, but the baby began to cry. She bounced her up and down, walked around the room, patted her back. The crying only got louder.

'Hush, hush,' she said at first.

Then she became angry. 'Why won't you stop?' she said sharply. 'I'm here. It's Mama. Oh Lucy, why won't you stop?'

She held the infant away from her, looking into its screwed-up face. The child looked back, and Mary was sure she saw hatred in her black eyes. She threw her roughly back into the cradle.

'Be alone then, if that's what you want,' she said. But this only made the volume of Lucy's cries increase. It was a different kind of cry now, less angry, more anguished, and it made Mary cry too. She picked her out of the cradle.

'I'm so sorry,' she whispered, holding her tight. 'My precious, I'm so sorry.'

The nurse, who had not left but had been standing at the door all this time, now came forward.

'Let me,' she said, holding out her arms. 'You are tired.'

Mary would not give up the child.

'It was only that she had been settled,' said the nurse, reproachfully, 'and you woke her.' She held out her arms, and Mary handed Lucy to her at last.

At once Lucy quietened. The nurse whispered some French words, and laid her down in the cradle, rocking it a little. She tucked the covers around her, and then looked at Mary.

'You'll be all right?' she asked, though to Mary it sounded more like a statement than a question. She felt a sudden need to embrace the small, neat woman, to hold on to her stout firmness, her ordinary surety. But instead she simply nodded.

~

It was in the early hours of the morning that the door opened. Mary was still awake. She had listened to the sounds in the corridors all through the night, the conversations between William and the landlady, then other conversations, between unknown men, in French. She supposed they were constables. Then finally silence, and William stood before her. His wig was in his hand and his few natural hairs stood up on end. He took a step towards her.

'Mary . . .' he began.

'Don't come near me,' she said, her voice trembling. She held Lucy, whom she had been feeding, and who now lay quietly in her arms. 'I don't want her upset,' she said.

'Why would I hurt my own child?' said William.

'You know she's not your child.'

'What do you mean?' said William. 'Of course she is.'

'She's Robert's, and you know it as well as I do. It's what you always intended, is it not?'

William's mouth opened, and then closed, but he said nothing.

'She was supposed to be a boy, wasn't she, William? But now it turns out it's another girl, and Robert's gone,' she said. William's face seemed to whiten. 'So who will you have seduce me next?'

'You need little seduction,' said William.

'And what about you?' said Mary. 'Did he have to work hard, to seduce you, to persuade you to agree to his plan?' The child was sleeping now, and Mary looked at her, rocking her a little. A strange kind of peace came over her. Whatever the consequences, there would be no more secrets now.

William looked at the ground and his voice was barely a murmur. 'I didn't think I was hurting anybody,' he said. 'It was clear you had no desire for me, from the start. I thought that once the child was born, you could go home to your mother, and with the money I would start up a company of ships. Then I thought we would both be happy, you at home, raising a child, and myself at sea.'

'With Robert?' asked Mary.

William looked at her, and she saw that he understood more than he said.

'Yes,' he said. He was quiet for a moment, then he spoke again. 'I was afraid you . . . and he . . . were becoming attached.'

Mary was quiet. She stroked the down of Lucy's head and put her into the cradle.

'Did Elizabeth become attached?' she asked.

William shook his head. 'Yes, but not to Robert,' he said. 'She loved me, you see, though I didn't deserve it at the time. She wouldn't yield at first. Said she didn't want the money any more. But Robert was persistent, and in the end he succeeded. When she became pregnant she said she would not leave, she would claim full rights as my wife. She even threatened to expose Robert if he disagreed. She made such a fuss that he had to subdue her in Amsterdam. Anneke begged Elizabeth to stay with her after that, not to get back on the ship. She'd never trusted Robert. But Elizabeth refused. Then of course the child was born, and it was a girl, so there would be no settlement anyway. Soon afterwards Alice was taken ill. Her

345

fever ran higher and higher, nothing would settle her. It was the first time Elizabeth had spoken to Robert after the birth. She begged him to treat the child, and eventually he relented, gave it a tincture of something or other. But whatever was in it was poisonous to the poor creature, and she was found dead the next morning.'

Mary sat perfectly still, her hands in front of her mouth. She glanced towards Lucy and closed her eyes.

'You mean Robert killed the child?'

'No, I don't mean that,' said William. 'It was an accident. Robert had no interest in making an enemy of Elizabeth. After all, she could still have borne a son. But he didn't want anyone to know, because it would destroy his reputation, and he told her it had not been the medicine, that she was dying anyway. I don't think Elizabeth believed him, but it didn't matter to her by then. When she jumped into the sea the following night, she was holding Alice's body.'

Mary felt a sudden urge to cry. To prevent it she stood up abruptly and tucked Lucy firmly into her cradle in a swift, businesslike manner, then draped a lace shawl over the cradle to shade it. She noticed that for the first time Lucy had not cried on being laid down.

When she turned back to William she saw that he had his hands over his mouth and she thought for a moment he was choking. But in fact he was sobbing intermittently. He had begun to shake, and his eyes were watery pink. Mary reached out for his hand and held it.

'Why did he leave, Mary?' he asked.

'I don't know,' she said. She breathed in through her teeth. She didn't tell him what Robert had said in his note, that William, and not Robert, had poisoned the child. She had known, when she watched William hold Lucy, that it couldn't have been him. She glanced at the table beside the bed, and saw that the drink she had dosed earlier was still there, untouched. She picked it up and handed it to him.

'Drink this,' she said. 'It will help.'

William looked at it for a moment. Then he took the glass and gulped at it. When he'd finished he buried his face in her chest and she put her arms around him. She felt the bones of his shoulders, his elbows. He had the frame of a boy. She smelled the brandy as it seeped from his pores. She swallowed a feeling akin to disgust. But she sat where she was, holding him tight, until his breathing became rhythmic and she lowered his body gently on to the bed.

27

The hostess was so distraught that William paid the dead man's bill as well as their own. Mary noticed his hands shake as he handed over the money. His face was ashen and his eyes were dark. Though he had fallen asleep in Mary's arms, he had barely spoken to her that morning. She knew that he had drunk a great deal, and wondered how much of their conversation he remembered. She felt she could barely recall it herself and so many questions remained unanswered. The one memory that was clear in her mind from that evening was the one she most wanted to forget, the touch of Captain Fullarton's lips, cold against her skin. It made her think of the first time Robert had kissed her, how warm it had felt, how every hair on her body had seemed to rise with it, and how every kiss she gave or received from now on would be cold like Fullarton's, cold like the kiss of a dead man.

Before they left the hostess caught them at the door. Her mood had changed and Mary noticed she had brightened since she'd been paid.

'I've been speaking to a few of the agents around the port,' she said. 'And it seems that your English friends were not quite what they seemed.' She smiled complacently, as if she were reaffirming a truth that they had disagreed with.

'What do you mean?' asked Mary.

'They were both known pirates. Very bad men,' she said. 'Wanted for killings and robberies.'

Mary put her hand to her lips.

'I think it is that man Keppel who is to blame,' the woman prattled on. 'Captain Fullarton has been coming to my residence for many years, and he has always behaved like a gentleman.'

'Gentlemen,' said William, 'are not always as they seem.'

'And nor are ladies, for that matter,' said the woman. 'Which was the cause of it all, it seems.' She looked meaningfully at Mary, as though Mary were to share in her conjecturing. Mary turned away in disgust.

~

As soon as they were on board the ship Mary disappeared to her cabin. A little later William knocked on the door.

'Just take me home, William. I only want to go home,' she said.

'I know, and I can't blame you.' He took a step towards her, and she took a step back. 'But you're still my wife, Mary.'

Mary shook her head. 'Only in name,' she said.

William looked down at the child in her arms. He held out his hand and stroked underneath the baby's chin. Lucy gazed at him, and a deep smile spread over her face, creasing into her plump cheeks.

'Can't you forgive me?' he said.

'Forgive!' Mary said, her voice high-pitched and incredulous. 'I think we're beyond forgiveness, don't you?' The baby grew restless in her arms and began a small, snuffling cry. She shoogled her back and forth and paced around the room.

William sat down. 'I forgive you,' he said.

Mary swung around. 'Do you think you would have cared if it had been anybody else?' she said.

'I cared when I saw you with that man Fullarton,' William said.

'That was your own pride, not love for me. You said it yourself.'

'I was angry,' he said. 'But not with you.'

At this, Mary was quiet. 'He's made fools of us both, hasn't he?' she said, smiling ironically at Lucy, who only sneezed in reply.

William spoke again, more desperate. 'Mary, you're all I have left.'

Mary nodded. Her anger had subsided. 'I know,' she said. 'That's why I have to go home.' She knew she wasn't strong enough to bear the burden of a man who needed her this much.

She heard him get up, and approach the door. But before he left, he turned round.

'All right,' he said, and she could tell he was making an effort to control his voice. 'But will you agree to one thing? You can go back to Leith with Lucy. I will return in a year. If by then you haven't changed your mind, then I'll seek a divorce.'

Mary laughed mockingly. 'You . . . that is, we . . . can't afford a divorce. No,' she said, 'listen to me. If nothing has changed when the year is out, you must disappear. Change your name. You can find another wife in some foreign port, or whatever it is you want.' Her voice was now strangled and bitter. The door slammed, and only then did she start to cry.

William left her alone after that. She spent much of her time on deck, where, despite the cold, the air felt pure. She stood there for hours at a time, looking out at the vast expanse of sea around her, this strange prison where all the doors were open.

28

Fullarton looked up from the body of his friend and into the face of Captain Jones. He had stopped crying, but every so often a convulsion ran through him, a shudder of pain. Jones now stood back from him, and his own face seemed contorted.

'What can I do to help you?' said Captain Jones.

Fullarton shook his head. 'Nothing.'

'We'll have to inform the landlady,' said Jones.

Fullarton looked up. Of course, the body would have to be dealt with. The realization made Fullarton snap into action, but it also gave him a sudden lucidity, and all at once he saw how desperate his position was. That he would be accused of Keppel's murder, there was no doubt.

He asked Jones to go and fetch the landlady, and as soon as he was gone, he climbed out of the little window and jumped into the Rochefort night. A drunken man whom he landed beside jeered. He ignored him and made his way to the harbour. Although it was after three in the morning, there were still people about, mostly drunk, but some just standing round and talking. He tried to walk normally, as though on some kind of business, but every so often a weird, animal sound issued from him that he was neither in control of nor aware of.

Miraculously, he found one of their launches, a small

rowing boat, and climbed unsteadily on to it. With his hands shaking it took some time to untie the boat from its moorings, but finally he was rowing weakly across the water to his own ship. He managed to climb on board and fall on to the deck just before the world went black around him.

~

When he woke there was a faint band of blue light in the east. His head pounded and his body was freezing. The port around him was quiet and still, and the all-night revellers seemed to have disappeared. He stood up, and his memory suddenly returned. He fell to his knees on the deck of the ship, and was startled by a voice.

'Captain?' it said. 'Is something wrong?'

He turned to see one of the apprentices, a boy called Jude. He was young, around the same age as Fullarton had been when he had first set sail. The sight of him brought Fullarton to his senses a little.

'Captain Keppel has been murdered,' he said flatly.

'Oh,' said the boy. There was a silence, in which they could hear the port of Rochefort beginning to stir behind them, the clash of metal and the echo of men's voices shouting across the docks. 'I'm sorry,' said the boy at last.

Fullarton looked up. 'Are you?' he said, almost pleading with the boy to be genuine.

'Who killed him?' asked the boy.

'A jealous lover.'

'Oh,' said the boy again, and he looked frightened.

'A Frenchman,' said Fullarton. 'Keppel had made advances on his wife.'

The boy stepped forward. 'You must be cold, Captain. Can't I fetch you a blanket?'

Fullarton looked down at his shaking hand. 'He was a great friend to me,' he said.

'He was a good master,' said the boy, taking Fullarton's arm gently and leading him across the deck.

Fullarton stopped and put his head in his hands. 'I loved him,' he said, 'like a brother.'

'Sir,' said the boy, 'does this mean that we won't be leaving tomorrow?'

'On the contrary,' said Fullarton, suddenly snapping awake. 'We must leave immediately.' He shook off the boy's arm. 'Wake all the men. Tell them to come up on deck for orders.'

'But, sir . . .'

'What?' Fullarton snapped.

'What about the others?'

'What others?' he asked.

'The women,' said the boy.

Fullarton remembered. The women. It had been Keppel's idea to keep the crew on board the ship. They were not in a pirate haven, but in a respectable port and the ambiguous nature of some of the crew was only too obvious. However, he also knew that if they were to be kept on board they would need entertainment. So, Keppel said, if they needed whores, they would have to take them on board the ship, the way the navy sailors did. He had arranged personally for a boatful of women to be rowed over.

'What will you do?' asked Jude, who had followed close on his tail, a look of panic on his face.

'Send them off the ship,' said Fullarton.

'But who will row them to shore?'

'They'll row themselves,' said Fullarton. 'They have arms as well as cunts, don't they?' He started to walk towards the fo'c'scle, but Jude pushed in front of him.

'I'll go, sir,' he said. 'I'll tell the men they have to go. You get warm, sir.'

But Fullarton only found an oiled cloak and wrapped himself in it, remaining on deck. A little later, he watched as the women, bemused, half dressed and half asleep, emerged from the fo'c'scle and climbed down the little ladder into the boat. Once they were all in they sat for a while, as if waiting for a pilot, until one of the women picked up an oar, and motioned to another to do the same.

When the ship was clear of the harbour and moving away from the fortifications of the town, Fullarton went below deck. He went into the gunroom. The maps and charts were still on the table, alongside Keppel's teapot and teacup, and a bottle of brandy. Fullarton poured the brandy into the teacup and drank it down. Then he picked up the teapot and threw it against the wall.

He looked at the charts, to the strips of land in France, Guernsey and Plymouth where he knew it would no longer be safe for him to land. They all merged into one. He had no idea where they were going. They would head back into the Channel, he supposed, and see what they came across there. Maybe, if he found a big enough ship, he would sail west, across the Atlantic. But not with this crew; he would have to find himself another, he thought, as he poured out another teacup of brandy. This crew didn't like him, he knew it, except perhaps the boy Jude.

He watched them murmuring among themselves whenever he grew close. Now Keppel was dead, they would turn against him. The thought of it made him bristle with anger. Why had Keppel commanded their respect where he seemed to command none?

But after a third teacup of brandy he realized he knew the answer, but it was too painful to admit. They knew Keppel was stronger than him. Keppel had no attachments, not even, he grasped, to Fullarton. He put his head in his hands. All he had ever wanted was to make his own way, to be dependent on nobody, to show that he was as good as the men who had sneered at him in his poverty and his illegitimacy. The world had been against him at every turn, but he had beaten them all. And then, after all that, he had destroyed the thing he had loved the most.

And then it came again, the understanding. It returned like clockwork every few minutes, and every time it did it took the strength from his limbs. The knowledge that Keppel was dead.

He would show the crew that he was just as good as Keppel, he thought, and then perhaps Keppel's ghost would forgive him.

He sat through days and nights in the gunroom, emerging only to refill his bottle with brandy or rum. The crew left him alone. Meals were brought to him, usually by Jude, but he left them untouched. The navigator came down to ask them where he was to steer for, but he only waved his hand at him and said, 'West.'

Then, on the fourth day, he suddenly awoke with a ravenous appetite. He started to eat his breakfast of boiled eggs greedily, and was immediately sick, but afterwards he began to eat again, and managed to keep some of it down. He drank a draught of small beer laced with only a little brandy. Then he heard a shout from the deck, and rose quickly, almost losing his balance. He supported himself against the wooden wall, and then made his way to the door, stepping on the remains of the broken teapot. He climbed on to the deck. And there it was, a vague shape in the distance becoming a beautifully sculpted outline, a large ship, laid out in full sail, steering directly into his path.

29

The ship was a large three-masted barque, a rich prize, and she surrendered easily, knowing Fullarton's ship was fast and light, and perhaps expecting merciful treatment for not having resisted. Fullarton watched as his men captured the ship, and once she was theirs, he drew his pistol and climbed on board. His head felt light and airy. His feet seemed to barely touch the deck. He ordered the crew to be bound and approached the captain, a tall Guernseyman who seemed somehow familiar.

'I know you,' he said, looking him up and down. 'But I can't remember your name.'

'But I know yours, Fullarton,' said the captain. 'Is this what you've come to?'

'What I've come to! Look at this,' Fullarton said to the captured captain. He pointed to his own clothes. 'See, Dutch linen, Spanish leather, finest oriental silk. I wouldn't have got that as a run-of-the-mill trader like you now, would I? Well, what do you say?' he asked.

The man said nothing.

Fullarton placed his hand on the man's arm and ran it up and down the length of it. 'Come to think of it,' he said, 'your cloth is not so poor either; that is a fine velvet jacket. I can't imagine you've come by all that through honest means. Come,' he said, aiming the tip of his pistol at it, 'take it off.'

The captain looked at him for a moment, but Fullarton held up his pistol, and the captain took off his jacket. Fullarton removed his own and pulled on the velvet one. He did a small turn in front of his own men.

'Does it look handsome on me?' he asked. The crew sniggered, and Fullarton felt the blood rush to his head. He was beginning to enjoy himself.

'And the breeches, too,' said Fullarton.

'You are nothing but a common thief,' said the captain, taking off his breeches.

Fullarton picked them up, running his hands over the fabric. 'Very nice,' he said. 'I shall have my tailor work on them as soon as we are in port. Now,' he went on, 'stockings!'

'This is too much,' Fullarton's bos'n said, though he was trying to suppress his laughter. But Fullarton carried on until the man was completely naked.

'This is a fine suit of clothes,' Fullarton said, smiling at his crew. 'I think they suit me better than they did him, don't you agree?' He took the man's hat at last, and threw it towards his crew, who grappled for it. Then he picked up his own jacket and waistcoat and handed them to Jude.

'They'll be a little big, at first,' he said, 'but you'll grow into them.'

'Thank you, sir,' said Jude. 'You look like a real gent, sir.'

'That's because I am a real gent,' said Fullarton, with mock offence. He felt a strange, wild kind of joy.

'You look like what you are, a macaroni and a poor excuse for a man,' said the captain, 'who leaves poor Guernsey maids to whom he has betrothed himself waiting indefinitely for his return. You know her brother is after your head!'

Fullarton snorted with laughter.

'And where is this partner of yours?' the captain went on, his teeth beginning to chatter. 'The famed Captain Keppel. Everyone thinks he must have been suffering from a bout of insanity to have set up with a smatchett like yourself.'

Fullarton heard laughter from behind him, and his own smile dropped. He couldn't tell whether the laughter came from his own crew or the captured one. Without turning to find out, he drew his pistol and shot the naked man.

He swung round and saw expressions of shock on the faces of the captured crew. The smiles had frozen to the faces of his own crew, and he caught the eye of the young boy Jude, who watched him with an expression that was neither disapproving nor admiring, but rather concerned.

'I don't tolerate insults,' he said. 'Any better than Captain Keppel tolerated foul language.' He walked over to the remaining crew of the captured ship, and his gaze fell upon a young man with a pretty face. He noticed something flashing in the sunlight. He took out his pocket knife, watching the fear spread on the young man's face. He put the knife to the man's throat, held it there, and then cut through a gold chain hanging around the man's neck. On the chain was a cameo of a young woman.

'Give it back,' said the man. 'It's of no value to you.'

'What are you upset about?' said Fullarton. 'It's only an object. It's not as though I'm taking her.' He pocketed the cameo and sat down beside the man. He took a sip of brandy from his hip flask, feeling suddenly tired.

'This is the thing,' he said to the man, 'that nobody realizes. All these material belongings are of no worth, in the end, when we enter the world of the spirits, as we all will. Some of us earlier than others,' he added, looking at the dead captain's pale, crumpled skin. 'We'll not be able to take them with us.' He took out the cameo again and looked at the woman's silhouette. Then he raised his hand and cast it into the sea.

'You see. There's nothing to be upset about,' he said. 'They're only objects. Everything else, everything outside here' – and he put his hand on his chest – 'are only objects. Here,' he offered, 'have some of this.' He put his hip flask to the young man's mouth, but the man turned his head away and the liquor trickled down his neck.

'Now, stop that nonsense,' said Fullarton, knocking him over the head gently with the side of his pistol. 'That's good brandy, not to be wasted. French, you know.'

He stuck the edge of the blade of his knife into the deck where the man was bound and began to cut a line in the wooden planks.

He looked towards his own crew and picked out Jude, who he felt sure would do as he was told. 'Bring me the kindling from the stove,' he said.

Jude looked confused, but did as he had been asked. When he returned Fullarton broke the sticks into varying lengths and held them out to the man whose cameo he had taken.

'You can choose first,' he said.

Then he held the kindling out before each member of the crew in turn, encouraging them with the point of his pistol. When all the men had pulled out a stick he ordered them to compare.

'Whatever you may think,' he said, addressing his own crew as well as the captive one, 'I'm not unnecessarily cruel. I have room for ten new crew members,' he said, tapping his chin. 'And I must leave ten of my own crew on board this trader, so I will need twenty more. That means that ten of you . . .' He counted on his fingers and looked thoughtful. 'Yes, ten,' he said, 'are not required.'

He inspected the sticks. 'You, you, you, and you . . .' he said, 'have drawn the shortest sticks. That means that you are no longer needed. You are sentenced to die by hanging.'

The men began to cry and plead. One or two fell to their knees. Fullarton watched them with a combination of anger and disgust.

'Sir,' said his carpenter, stepping forward, 'is this necessary?'

Fullarton swung round. He bit his lip. He put his hand to his pistol, but then stopped.

'What is necessary?' he said. 'I consider these men unnecessary, and, if you cross me again, perhaps I may consider you unnecessary also.'

The carpenter backed off at this.

'I'm damn hot,' said Fullarton. He felt a flush of heat prickling beneath his clothes, and he removed the velvet jacket he was wearing. 'Sorry, Keppel,' he shouted, realizing that he had cursed. He removed his shirt, and his shoes and stockings, cursing several more times as they got stuck in the bends of his body, until at last he was wearing only his breeches. His crew watched him, bemused, as he walked the decks almost naked, his wound exposed and raw, leaving a trail of clothing behind him. He walked unsteadily around the condemned crew, knocking each one across the head and neck with the flat part of his knife in a kind of bizarre silent ceremony. His own crew looked on, quiet and sullen. Then he began the hangings.

30

Fullarton woke in his own bunk, with a vague memory of the preceding day. A small pile of fine clothes lay crumpled on the floor, and this sparked further recollection. Somebody must have brought them from the decks. He sat up slowly, and began to dress. His body felt as though it had been severely beaten, and his lips were stuck together with white salt paste.

He drank a draught of brandy water, to moisten his lips, and emerged on to the deck. There he saw the ship they had captured a short distance behind them. He realized he had not even bothered to check the cargo.

A little later he found Jude and ordered him to row him over to the ship. He found himself calling on Jude more and more often, because for some reason the boy was the only crew member he still trusted. Jude was not a skilled sailor, just a shy, fumbling boy, always being started by the bos'n, but he seemed to want to please Fullarton, as though Fullarton's welfare were in some way important to him.

When Fullarton climbed on board the captured vessel he walked around it, nodding to the members of his own crew and a few of the existing crew who had escaped the hangings and been kept on as helpers. From the sullen looks they gave him it was impossible to guess which was which.

Then he halted as he heard a familiar intonation. A sailor was speaking to another, with an Orkney lilt. As he became aware of Fullarton's presence he turned to face him and Fullarton saw a boy's terrified eyes staring at him from a man's face. A boy he had last seen smirking at him from the stern of his father's fishing smack.

'Hello, John,' the man said.

Fullarton looked in astonishment at the fair hair and browned complexion of his brother, Sandy Fullarton.

'Sandy,' he said, and he at once embraced him, then stood back stiffly, aware of his unwashed and dishevelled appearance. Sandy recoiled, and Fullarton remembered that he must have been there, yesterday. He must have watched as his captain was murdered, as his crewmates were hanged. And he had said nothing.

'Still as much of a coward as ever,' he said under his breath. But then he spoke more loudly. 'Come, take a glass of brandy with me, we have some years to catch up on.'

'I think I may know some of your news already,' said Sandy.

Fullarton looked at Thomas sharply. 'Don't believe everything you hear,' he said.

'I hear that Bell's agents are after your head, that's all,' said Sandy. 'You'd better be careful.' Fullarton said nothing.

They rowed back to his own ship. Below deck, Fullarton ordered the boy Jude to bring down some breakfast, biscuit and eggs, along with the brandy.

'A fine boy,' he said to Sandy, when Jude had left the room. 'Reminds me of myself when I started out. He doesn't know it yet, but I'm going to make him my personal servant. I've marked him out for first mate, soon as he's old enough.'

'He seems keen, anyway,' said Sandy. His voice trembled as he spoke, and Fullarton smiled.

'How are things at home?' Fullarton asked.

'Well, it's been some time since I was there myself,' said Sandy. 'But much the same. My mother died.'

'I'm sorry to hear that,' said Fullarton.

Sandy looked at him for a moment, then nodded. 'I know your mother and she wouldn't speak, and your mother had some cause to be offended,' he said, 'but my mother endured a lot with him. Yours was lucky, in the end.'

Fullarton said nothing.

'Aren't you going to ask how our father is?' said Sandy.

'I wasn't,' said Fullarton. 'But tell me.'

'Much the same. Still chasing the lasses, only they run away when they see him coming now. I don't know if the hand of God is at play in these things or not, but he's not in his right senses now, John. It's sad to see.' Sandy's voice was under control, as Jude brought in the breakfast.

'Some things have changed,' he went on, 'and some have stayed the same. But once you've left, you can never go back. I mean in time. You can go back to the same place, but it's no longer the same. I've moved on now, on and away. It's the darkness in the winter. It seems to swallow you whole, like entering the jaws of a whale.'

'But then,' said Fullarton, who had eaten half a boiled egg and drunk another draught while Sandy was talking and was beginning to feel better, 'there's no beauty in the world like that which springs from darkness.' For a second he saw the face of the girl Mary Jones as she had looked in the darkness that night. She had been beautiful, in a way, though he had not seen it at the time.

'That's true enough. But what about you, John?' said Sandy, looking at him strangely. 'What has happened to you? Is it true you abandoned this woman in Guernsey?'

Fullarton sat back, and the egg began to burn inside him. 'Sometimes,' he said, 'I don't know myself what is true or not. Who am I to say whether I did, or whether I didn't? Who am I to question God's will?' He lifted his hand to pour Sandy a drink, but Sandy stopped him.

'Thank you,' he said, 'I've had enough.'

At this Fullarton put the drink down. There was a pause, while he waited to ask about the only person he had not mentioned, and the only person he cared to hear about.

'And how is my mother?' he said at last.

'As far as I know, she is in good health,' said Sandy. 'Your grandmother died last year.'

'About time, the old bitch,' said Fullarton. 'Has my mother heard any of the rumours about me?'

'She may have,' said Sandy, 'but I doubt she believes them.'

'Do you believe them?' said Fullarton.

'I make a point of only believing what I can see with my own eyes,' said Sandy.

Fullarton nodded. 'I haven't forgotten my duty,' he said, 'but I've never yet made enough money to be able to make any real difference.'

They were both silent for a moment. Fullarton knew the money he had made would have bought his mother's house fifty times over, but that didn't matter. What mattered was what he had just said. Why should he care what Sandy thought of him? But he did, all the same.

'You know my father never thought I could make a success of anything,' he said, refilling their glasses.

'How wrong he was,' said Sandy, though Fullarton wondered if he was being ironic.

'He thought I'd just be another poor seaman, dying of ill health at sea before the age of thirty.' Fullarton looked at the roof of the little wooden room.

'It's my birthday this month,' he continued after a pause.

Sandy's head was nodding, but he looked nervous again.

'Perhaps I'll go home for it this year.' He didn't really mean it until he saw the doubtful expression on Sandy's face.

'Your mother would like that,' he said.

Fullarton nodded. 'Perhaps she'll have bought me a present,' he said with a hard laugh.

~

An hour later Fullarton watched as Jude rowed Sandy over to his ship, with orders to set her free, along with the crew.

He thought of his mother, how she had been when he left. What would she say when she saw his scarlet gilded coat, his fine new wig, all the way from Paris, picked up in Rochefort? He had had moments of glory, had he not, those moments when he had not been shooting or hanging men from the mainstay. And these things were necessary, after all, as Keppel had said, part of the business of war. There was so much he could tell her about: the strange sights, sounds and smells of other lands. He ran through them in his mind, and each moment became more spectacular, more heroic. He pictured his mother's face: surprised, adoring, enthralled.

31

The *Isabella* continued to ply her scheduled route for the following weeks, although William had all but ceased to command the vessel. They stopped at the port of St Pierre, with the aim of disposing of a large quantity of claret, the remainder of which would be taken to Leith. But in the two weeks since they had left Rochefort, William had deteriorated badly. He had made up for the absence of Robert's phials by drinking the ship's supplies of brandy. Mary rarely saw him. When they did pass each other on deck or in the corridors, he was pale and thinner than ever. He clutched his own trembling body and his eyes were wet and glossy like the glass eyes of a china doll. He looked towards, but beyond her, as though seeing something she couldn't see, and his expression was one of fear. Other times he would be consumed with anger, shouting at the air, reaching out for some invisible enemy.

But what hurt her most now was not William's abuse of her, but the way the men laughed at him, throwing her sympathetic looks; the way his ruin was so publicly on display, so that she felt somehow responsible for not having been able to prevent it. His body, which had been so robust, became bony and hunched. His legs were no more than thin sticks on which he seemed to balance precariously. She watched him climb the rope ladder from their launch to the promenade of St Pierre, and she was more terrified of his falling than she was of her own safety as she climbed the ladder clutching Lucy, tightly wrapped into the folds of her clothing.

She was glad when they were finally sitting in one of the bars of the port, and the wine trader Thomas Bell came over to their table with a bottle of claret, setting it down. They drank the King's health, and Bell watched William as he sank his glass of claret in one go.

'Your husband drinks like a Scotsman,' he said.

'Yes,' said Mary, looking at her husband. 'But he isn't one. Only married to one.'

'And which part do you come from, madam?' asked Bell.

'I was born in Leith,' she said.

'Ah, and so was I!' he bellowed. 'Do you hear this, William, your wife and I are as good as neighbours.'

A slight nod was the only acknowledgement William gave.

'Is he ill?' asked Bell, refilling William's empty glass.

Mary put her hand over her own. She adjusted Lucy in her arms. 'You must excuse my husband,' she said, colouring. 'He's not quite himself. We had a run-in with some pirates in Rochefort and my husband found one of them murdered.'

Bell raised his eyebrows. 'That's a nasty business. Were they English?'

'Not the murderer, I believe. He was a Frenchman. Of the other two, one, the one who was murdered, was an Englishman and the other was from Orkney.'

Bell looked up. 'An Orcadian?'

Mary nodded. Bell's face had turned a darker shade of red, as though someone had inflated it.

'And what was the name of these pirates?' he asked.

'Captains Keppel and Fullarton.'

'Fullarton,' Bell whispered under his breath.

'Do you know the men, sir?' asked Mary.

Bell seemed lost in his own thoughts, and ignored the question. 'And do you know the whereabouts of this Fullarton, madam?'

Mary shook her head. 'He escaped on the night of the murder. No doubt he thought he would be accused. His behaviour was very odd. He seemed to be jealous on account of a Frenchwoman, and it was her husband who committed the murder.'

Bell smiled a little. 'Jealous, was he? So the man is capable of some feeling, after all. Well, so much the better, as he will feel me more when I find him.'

Mary became curious at the fury in the man's face. She looked at William, who was listening to the conversation with an awareness unusual for his present condition.

'Do you have a quarrel with the man, sir?' she asked Bell.

'I apologize, madam,' he replied. 'I have made my passion too apparent. It is a personal matter. This pirate is known to me, you see. He is responsible for deserting my own sister, to whom he was engaged. The wedding plans were made, the silver was ordered, and he left the islands quite suddenly with a good deal of my wife's money, saying he would return when he had made enough to pay the foolish woman back. Eight months have passed now, without a word.'

'Oh,' said Mary, 'the poor girl.' Her eyes prickled with

tears of anger, not for this girl she didn't know, but because the girl's story had made her suddenly aware of her own personal tragedy. She had been deserted by the man she had believed loved her. And the man who was supposed to love her, her husband, was now only a fragment of a man. Miss Bell was fortunate, she thought. At least she could claim the sympathy of those around her, while Mary could only suffer in silence. She had not allowed herself the luxury of thinking of her position in these terms before, but somehow this girl's story had given her the permission she needed.

'Oh,' said Bell, lighting a pipe and coughing slightly over it, 'she was distraught for a week or two, as women are. There was no comforting her. But a ridotto or two at the assembly halls and she was soon recovered. My wife was another matter; it took her some time, and I am not so quick to forgive. To my friends,' he said, 'I am a loyal servant for life. But I will not be made a fool of. Those who injure me, I never forget.'

'Nor do I,' said Mary. She was still thinking of Robert, the opium cinnamon smell of him. Lucy began to wriggle in her arms.

Then William leaned forward and spoke for the first time. 'Sometimes,' he said, 'it is better to forget.'

Bell and Mary both looked at him. Bell reddened.

Mary shook her head. 'Not in this case, William,' she said. 'Surely you can see that Mr Bell's anger is well founded.'

William sat back again. His eyes had clouded over, and he took a sip of his drink. 'Well,' he said, 'I suppose it is.'

'At least when he's found,' said Mary, turning to Bell, 'he'll be hanged.'

'Yes,' said Bell, 'but I plan to find him first.'

Mary seemed thoughtful. 'Mr Bell, there's something I've remembered, that may be useful to you. At dinner, in Rochefort, Captain Fullarton mentioned something about going home, to Orkney. He was going to buy his mother an estate there. If you want to find him, I'd start there.'

'I sent my agents there already,' he said, 'and they found nothing.'

'I think he said it had been a long time since he'd returned home,' said Mary. 'Perhaps you were too early.'

'Thank you for your help, madam,' said Bell. He took her hand and kissed it, and Mary felt a kind of righteous satisfaction. She had only told the truth, and if the pirate suffered by it, he had only himself to blame. But as she turned to William she saw that his expression was dark and serious.

'Mary,' he said, 'I am not well, I must return to the lodgings.'

Mary looked surprised. 'But we are not concluded,' she said.

But William had already risen, unsteadily, and was heading for what he thought was the door. He gave it a sharp tug, to reveal a small closet and a man sitting upon a chamberpot. Then he closed it again, mumbling some apology. Several men in the corner roared with laughter, and the *cabaretier* emerged wearily from behind the counter and steered William to the outside door.

Mary watched him in despair, no longer even capable of embarrassment. She turned to Bell, who must have seen her expression.

'I'll send a man over to conclude in the morning,' he said.

'Thank you,' said Mary, feeling grateful but ashamed that Bell had known this was necessary.

'Your husband needs a doctor, Mrs Jones,' he said.

'I believe you're right,' she replied. 'But I think a doctor is the last person he would see.'

'Well, I don't blame him. I'm not too keen on medical men myself,' said Bell, standing up. 'A generous dose of kindness and a good broth always does the trick for me. Perhaps it will work for your husband too. It was nice meeting you, Mrs Jones.'

~

Outside, William leaned against a wall. His complexion was grey, but there was more sense in his eyes than she had seen since Rochefort.

'Let's go back to the lodgings,' she said briskly. She altered the swaddling so that she carried Lucy against one arm, and she took William's with the other.

'Why did you tell him about Captain Fullarton?' asked William.

Mary felt uncomfortable under his gaze. 'Why not?'

'You know if he ever finds him, he'll kill him.'

'It was only the truth. I simply wanted to tell the truth.'

'That's never interested you before.'

Mary looked at him sharply. 'Nor you,' she said. 'But things are different now.'

They walked in silence. But halfway along the road William stopped. He ran his fingers along the fine hair of Lucy's temple.

'Is it worth it?' he asked.

'What?' she snapped. 'I don't know what you're talking about.'

'Revenge, is it worth it?'

Mary said nothing, only steered him along the road towards their lodgings.

~

Mary watched William as he slept most of that afternoon. She wondered whether he was right, whether sometimes it was better to forget. Perhaps in time she would, if only William could recover. She pondered what Bell had said. Perhaps a little kindness was all he needed now. Despite everything, she could not hate him.

When they climbed back on to the ship and sailed away from the little port, she even began to harbour some hope that, given a year or two, they might live out their lives together in some degree of contentment.

So she began to try, in secret, pouring away part of the decanter that he kept in his room, hoping that he wouldn't notice and would be too drunk to refill it. She tried to make him eat, in the hope that the food would line his stomach and prevent the drink from taking effect. At first she seemed to be making progress. He spoke about the future. He went into the gunroom and consulted the charts. He discussed navigation with the bos'n. But then she would find the decanter refilled, the food left untouched.

On the night before they sailed into the Firth of Forth, she served the last of the salt beef, diced finely into a stew with gherkins and potatoes. As she put down the plate,

William's body slumped forward, landing with a thump on the table. His elbow fell into his plate.

The crew looked at Mary with what seemed like a mixture of pity and reproach. None of the men spoke, or moved. Then the cook, who had been watching from the door, came forward and, with Mary's help, managed to get him back to the cabin.

'I don't need it,' William grunted, 'I don't need your help.'

'No, of course you don't,' said Mary, as he leaned heavily on her shoulder.

He fell into a deep sleep as soon as he was laid down. Mary felt a sudden need for air. She rose abruptly and climbed on to the deck. The ship had begun to roll. They were entering a part of the sea that she always remembered. The bad weather seemed to linger over that area, and you could see it from a distance. The sea was filled with coloured cross-currents and whirlpools, a gyrating mass of pattern and depth, blue and grey, pewter and charcoal all converging, as if they were fighting for prominence. But it was an enduring fight, in which none ever succeeded, or even seemed to exhaust themselves in the process.

32

Fullarton stood on deck as a dry wind stripped the oil from his face. The low-lying land looked as though it had been dipped in dark ink and the ink was just beginning to wash away with the rain. The sea was a slow-moving syrup of turkois. The red cliffs of Hoy that he had passed were smaller than he remembered. When he had sailed away from Stromness nineteen years before they had seemed enormous. But that was when he had believed the world to be much larger and full of promise.

Once in town he discharged his crew and took some time to explore the streets of Stromness. They were brighter than he remembered, less dirty. There were a few newly built houses, more shops. The streets were busy with traders and fishermen bringing in their catches. He hired a little horse, a native that seemed to have been crossed with some more elegant breed, and set out for Orphir.

He had worn his best coat, the blue velvet military-style one with gold brocade and brass buttons, and a hat with a large feather in it. As he approached the village he saw some people in the fields, who looked up briefly and then seemed to disappear. No doubt they thought he was the exciseman, and were running to tell their families to hide all their contraband. He laughed out loud.

The sunshine disappeared behind pewter clouds, and as he rode he thought he heard the hooves of his horse echo across the moors. Even when he rode on softer ground, however, the echo continued, and at length he turned to see another rider some distance behind him. The rider was too far away to tell his identity, but at once Fullarton began to feel apprehensive. He remembered Sandy's warning about Bell. He cursed his horse for its stumbling lethargy, and drove it on as fast as its country legs would carry it.

He was being followed by one of Bell's men, he was convinced, but he was also convinced that it wasn't Bell himself, and he felt fairly sure that Bell's agents would not have been ordered to harm him. Bell would want to do that in person. But he rode on. Even if he had to escape, he must see his mother first. Somehow, he thought, she would know what to do. The very sight of him, returned after all these years, would inspire that kind of youthful initiative in her. Spurred on by the thought of her, he put some more distance between himself and the rider who pursued him.

He reached his mother's house and dismounted some distance away. He wanted to surprise her, but also it gave him time to retrieve his breath, which had become a little shorter as the wind seemed to rip all the air from his lungs.

Then he saw her. She was outside, busy with a brush in the yard. It was the way he had pictured her all these years. She had always spent so much of her time brushing and sweeping. Moving dust from one place to another. Sweeping dirt into dirt, he thought, and never removing it. It looked as though she were wearing the same dress as she had worn the day he had left, with the same apron. Her hair was tied back in the same fashion, and was only just streaked through with grey. He saw her eyes, as she looked up towards him, and a shudder went through him. They were not what he had expected. He had imagined them full of sorrow, dull and lifeless. But now, before she recognized him, he saw that they were bright and sparkling, and only clouded with pain when she saw at last who the well-dressed stranger was.

She gave a small scream. He watched as she turned and ran into the house. John could hear her shouting inside.

Then she came out again, followed by a man he didn't know, covered in mud and wiping his hands on a cloth. She ran up to John and embraced him. She held his face and looked closely at it.

'Oh, John, I'm sorry. I just canna believe it's you. You were like a ghoul just standing there. You should've sent word you were coming. I havna even made a bed for you.'

John didn't answer. He had his eye fixed on the old man behind her. Who was this man to look so comfortable with his mother? And he did know him somehow – behind the lined and gnarled face, the eyes were familiar.

'Aye aye, John,' said the man. 'It's been a long while.'

His mother appeared to calm a little, and looked him over.

'This is Tam,' she said, 'Tam Loutit, you might remember? Oh, Tam, look at the boy, he's done well for himself, has he no?'

'It seems so,' said Tam, smiling briefly, reaching for John's hand.

John took the hand and held it for a moment, before dropping it. 'Of course,' he said, 'I remember Tam.' Tam was Katherine Loutit's brother. No more than an onca was Tam, a poor cottar, tied to the landlord and with nothing but a couple of hens to his name.

'Tam is my husband now, John,' said his mother quietly.

Then they turned as the sound of hooves approached the little dirt yard. As the rider grew nearer, Fullarton saw that it was not one of Bell's agents at all, however, but the boy Jude from his own ship.

'Sorry for following you like this, sir,' the boy said as he dismounted.

Fullarton glanced from his mother, to the hovel she called her home, back to Jude. 'Wait for me at the top of the hill,' he said. He would not let the boy see that this poor woman sweeping dirt from dirt was his own mother.

'But I have to warn you, sir. Thomas Bell is in Stromness.'

Fullarton had not expected to encounter Bell himself, not yet. He looked at his mother. She stood a little apart from him, holding on to Tam Loutit's arm. He had planned to tell her about the house he was going to build for her, a grand mansion outside Stromness with a gable end chimney and much more besides, fine leam plates, a marble hearth, a mirrored hallway, with tiles shipped from Holland. Now, with Jude there, he could say nothing of his plans.

'I have to go,' he said.

'Already!' she said, laughing. 'You've just arrived.'

'I have to. But I'll be back.'

'Is that a promise?' she asked, and he wondered if she was mocking him.

'Yes,' he murmured, 'it is.'

His mother looked at Tam. Tam returned her gaze and shook his head slightly.

'Well, John,' she said quietly, 'I wish you luck.' She didn't step forward to embrace him. Instead, she took a step back.

Fullarton mounted his horse. Jude began to guide his own animal up the hill. He seemed to sense that he should not be there. Fullarton looked at his mother once more, and then turned his horse away to follow Jude.

At the top of the hill, he spoke to the boy without looking at him. 'We'll leave the harbour at nightfall,' he said, 'and anchor round the other side of the bay. Then we'll set off early for Leith, before Bell sees we're gone.'

'I'm sorry, sir,' said the boy, 'but I won't be coming.'

Fullarton swung round sharply, to see Jude pulling a girl on to the back of his horse. She had been waiting at the top of the hill while he spoke to his mother.

'What's the meaning of this?' demanded Fullarton.

'I'm sorry, Captain Fullarton,' said the boy, 'but this is my wife, Julienne.'

'Your wife!' Fullarton's laugh was almost hysterical. 'Where in the name of God did you find time to get yourself a wife?'

'I found her in Rochefort, and stowed her away, after you sent the women off the ship. We married today, in Stromness, and now we've joined up with another ship, a Hudson's Bay trader. But in Stromness I found out about Bell, and I had to come and tell you.'

'But you are contracted to me.'

'Not a legal contract, sir, if you please.' Jude looked

away, suddenly awkward, and Fullarton felt that if he was to threaten him now, he would probably leave the girl and go with him. But he didn't want him now. He fought a desire to pull out his pistol and shoot them both, there and then. But the boy had come all this way to warn him, when he could have just made his escape.

So instead of withdrawing his pistol, he watched as the boy and girl rode away together in the direction of Stromness. Then he made his way to the shore, the same beach he had run along with his mother as a child. He sat down and picked up a pebble, wound through with silver and gold threads. Putting his hand into his pocket, he pulled out an almost identical one, taken from this same beach many years before. He threw them both into the sea. Then he sat down on the damp shingle, letting the tiny jewels of stones run through his hands, waiting for the darkness to come.

33

August 1763

Mary watched as the *Isabella* sailed into the Firth of Forth. She carried Lucy, and she lifted her up so that she could see the familiar landmarks: the little Isle of May, now so peaceful-looking; the white guano-spattered Bass Rock, with its grim old prison now black-windowed and empty; the ruined castles, the little villages. To Mary these places meant a return to something of what she was, or at least what she might have been. She wanted Lucy to feel this too. But Lucy only felt the cold air on her cheeks and began to cry.

As they passed the island the haar began to gather around the coasts, obscuring them from view, and Mary noticed the sail of a brig that seemed to be gaining on them faster than was usual. She paid it little mind at first. She was thinking of her mother, and the streets she knew so well in Leith, and how in returning to them she might in some way start to free herself from the nightmarish collection of memories that plagued her daily, as well as the increasing burden of William. She thought of her daughter growing up, then, into a small child, and how she might walk with her on Leith sands. She thought of how they would both take off their shoes and stockings and turn their toes in the sand, and how she would not even care if somebody stole them; they would walk home barefoot like the schoolboys from the parish school.

Half an hour later, however, the brig was closer, and she grew uneasy.

'What do you think of that?' she asked the bos'n, who was also watching the ship. William was still below deck. He had not yet risen.

'I don't like the look of it,' he said. 'I don't like it at all. I'll order the men to their stations.'

Mary ran downstairs to their cabins. She put the child in her cradle and shook William violently.

'William,' she said loudly, 'William, wake up. There's a ship chasing us.'

William came to a little and looked at her. When he saw her, he seemed disappointed. He turned over again and began to snore.

She picked up the decanter at the side of the bed, poured out a measure of brandy, and emptied it over his head.

Immediately he jumped out of bed and grabbed hold of her arm, before realizing where he was.

'It's a ship,' she urged, 'giving chase.'

But then he appeared to go limp. He walked around the room, tottering slightly, as though looking for something.

'I'll see to it,' he said, his voice slurred. 'You stay here, and don't come on deck.' He reached out for some invisible object but lost his balance, sliding on to the floor.

'William, for God's sake.' Mary's voice was high pitched as he picked himself up unsteadily. 'With you in this state, what chance can we possibly stand?'

'I'm sorry,' he said.

She took out his clothes, flinging them at him one at a time. He put them on slowly, sitting on the bed. Then he put out his arm impatiently.

'What is it?' she asked.

'My hat, come on, come on.'

'William, surely it doesn't matter.' But she opened the closet, where clothes and hats were piled untidily on top of one another. She pulled one out and tossed it at him.

'Not that one!' he barked, throwing it back. 'The Kevenhuller.'

'Is this really necessary?'

'Do you think I will meet my enemy without a hat?' he snapped.

She found the Kevenhuller, and handed it to him. She looked him up and down. His waistcoat, coat and breeches were neatly fastened, but beneath them his legs and feet were bare.

'William,' she whispered, 'your shoes and stockings.'

William looked down at his feet, and started to laugh. Mary suddenly felt that she had lost all strength, and she sat on the bed.

'It doesn't matter,' she said. 'You need to go now. Go!'

William had dropped his hat, and then found it again, and was busy replacing it in the correct position beneath his arm. But the action was troubling him, as however he rotated it, it never seemed to sit quite as comfortably as it should.

'Go!' she shouted. 'Before we are all murdered!'

William looked at her and seemed to be sobered by her

fear. He put a hand on her shoulder. 'Don't worry,' he said. 'We're well armed. I've fought off privateers before.'

'Yes,' she said, 'I know, but that was when you were still at least an eighth of a man. Not the pitiful creature you are now. I'd be better up there myself.'

William opened his mouth to speak, but said nothing, and his eyes were wounded.

'I'm sorry,' said Mary. 'I'm just frightened, that's all.' She looked at him, and felt suddenly ashamed of his ridiculous appearance. 'Come here. You can't go up like that.'

She bent down, pulled on his stockings and laced up his shoes. When she had finished she stood, facing him.

'You look handsome,' she lied. 'Go now.'

At the door, William caught hold of her arm. 'Did you love him?' he asked.

Mary stopped. She thought for a moment. 'No,' she said. 'I don't know. It depends.'

'On what?'

'On what you mean by love.'

She tucked a hip flask of brandy into the pocket of his breeches, and opened the door.

'Did you?' she asked.

William took the hip flask out and swallowed some. He nodded once. Then she watched his stick legs disappear up the ladder to the deck above.

34

Fullarton had escaped Bell for the time being, though half his crew had been left in Stromness. And he knew that he would remain at risk as long as he stayed in Britain. He had kept his money in his account in Leith, with the intention of taking it out and using it to build his mother's estate. But now he decided that she would see none of it. He would take it out himself, every penny, and use it to fund a new voyage, somewhere far afield, perhaps the Americas, where he could live the life he had heard of so often, with native servants to attend to him, where he could be master of his own small kingdom. Perhaps he would see Jude there, settled with his new wife in some home-built hovel, burdened with children, and he could show the boy what he might have been if he had chosen to walk in Fullarton's shoes.

He was full of these thoughts as his ship drifted into the Firth of Forth on a grey, slightly foggy day. As they rounded the Isle of May, he saw a great shape emerge. He took out his glass, and saw that it was a ship, and that she was heavily laden. It reawakened his spirit. One more prize, especially a rich one, would make a great difference to what he could do in America. Perhaps one day, he thought, he might even invite his mother to join him there, so that she could see what she had thrown away by letting him down. He imagined showing her round the rooms of his mansion, the lush gardens of his estate. In his imaginings, Tam Loutit was always absent.

He ordered the men to manoeuvre nearer to the ship. She was well armed, but so was he, having adapted his brig to make more space for cannon. As she came near to the rocks, he saw his chance. He would drive her nearer, back her up against the Isle of May, then threaten her with superior cannon. She would have no choice but to let him board. He did not expect much of a fight.

So confident was he of his likely success that he was stunned, even offended, when his grapeshot was met with a volley of the trader's own guns. The orange fire exploded into the smoky air, illuminating the skeleton of his prize.

He ordered the men to fire again with their carbines, and they peppered the ship with a hailstorm of bullets. But yet again the big ship returned fire, and then began to take advantage of a stiff westerly wind to slip out of his grasp towards the north side of the isle.

Fullarton felt his power over the ship slipping away, and grew angry. He shouted at his men to give all the firepower they had.

'And there'll be a reward for the man who brings me that captain,' he shouted.

They fired another volley of grapeshot at the ship's mast. He saw some men fall, but the ship was still moving fast.

'Get closer,' he shouted to the navigator, and to the sailors on the mast, 'unfurl the studding sails.'

Half an hour later they had drawn close enough to

the trader for Fullarton to see clearly the figures on board. Then he reloaded the cannon himself, aimed carefully, and fired.

He stood back, and watched with pleasure as he saw the great ship's mast fall with a deafening crash. Their own vessel began to rock with the motion of it, and the trader pitched desperately. Fullarton watched carefully, in fear of losing the cargo he had fought so hard for, and that was, as he now saw it, rightfully his.

Now that the ship was unable to draw wind they quickly moved alongside her. Immediately his men withdrew their cutlasses and pistols and climbed aboard, swiftly rounding up as many of the crew as they could find.

Fullarton climbed on board, looking for the captain. He felt a seething anger at the insolence of the man to resist him in this way, risking not only his prize, but his own ship. What he saw now, however, walking somewhat weakly and unevenly towards him, was a small, frail man, brown, wrinkled and shrunken like a raisin, his face a map of thread veins. He appeared to be unarmed. Fullarton walked towards him. Finally they stood, face to face, before the debris of the *Isabella*'s broken mast.

'How do you do, Captain Fullarton?' asked Captain Jones.

How different he looked, his face thin and pale. But the voice was unchanged. Then Fullarton saw it all before him, in a flash of horror, the events of that night in Rochefort: Keppel's cruelty to him, his harsh, sneering face; his bloodied body on the floor, the life seeping from the face of the man he had loved, but who, after all, had not loved him. Suddenly all his dreams seemed meaningless, and fell away around him.

Fullarton put his pistol to Captain Jones's brow. Captain Jones began to whimper.

35

Mary had listened to the cracking of the small cannon. Lucy began to cry in her cradle. Mary picked her up, walked up and down, but nothing could soothe the child, and Mary grew irritated. She tried to feed, but no milk flowed, she was too terrified herself, and it only made the baby cry more. Then she felt a sudden crash and lurch of the ship, which made the walls and the furniture around her tremble.

She knew there was no longer any safety in staying where she was. She had to go on deck and find out what was happening. She swaddled the child well in a blanket and mixed a little sweetened brandy with the remainder of the laudanum, which she had kept for emergencies. She held it to Lucy's lips, and the child put out her tongue and lapped it greedily, like a little cat. Then she put Lucy into her cradle and kissed her, turning away before she could change her mind.

She opened her husband's drawer where he kept a small flintlock pistol, the one he had threatened her with months before. It was highly decorative, with silver cherubs emblazoned on the handle, and in the midst of the turmoil that was taking place above her head she couldn't help but take a moment to admire it. As she left the cabin she wondered why it was that human beings sought to make destructive things so beautiful. It was like the intricate lace of a newborn baby's shawl, made to mimic the wonder of life and death itself.

Slowly, she climbed up the stairs and looked from behind the mizzen-mast at the air filled with the smoke of gunpowder. Men ran back and forward with what seemed to be no clear purpose. Some already lay moaning on the decks. Then, looking towards the starboard side of the ship, which had dipped over with the weight of the fallen main mast, she saw around thirty strange men climbing over the barrier, the blades of their knives flashing in the weak sunlight.

She clung to the mast. Her breath grew uneven and she struggled to regulate it. She clutched the pistol close. Would she kill herself, she wondered, if they came near her, as she had heard some women did. They had become martyrs, those women, heroines after their death. They would rather turn to the mercy of God than submit themselves to the shame of humanity. But Mary had seen too much of life, had too much of life to give, to understand this. She thought of Lucy, so small and brittle, lying in her cradle. Misfortune, ill treatment, humiliation: all these can be endured, she thought. Pain can be overcome, but death is final.

Suddenly she held her breath as she saw that she was standing near to the back of one of the pirates. He was handsomely dressed in a velvet jacket and pure white silk breeches. Facing her and the pirate, unsteady and dishevelled, stood William. He appeared not to see her at all.

It crossed her mind, a glimmer of a thought, uninvited,

as she fingered the decorative silver of her pistol, that from where she stood, one bullet would be enough to end the misery of William's existence. She could shoot her husband dead, and it would look as if it had been the pirate. Nobody would ever know.

But at that moment the pirate moved, walking towards William, partly obscuring him from her view. William appeared to be unarmed. What was he doing? She saw him extend his arm to the man. Was he surrendering so easily? Did he value their lives and safety so little? But it was the way they looked at one another, her husband and the pirate. They appeared to be conversing. Almost as if they knew one another already.

The pirate moved again, and William saw her. He looked directly at her, and she realized her error in thinking she could ever have killed him. She tried to mouth a signal to him. But the muscles of her face were tight and immobile. His eyes did not flinch, did not give her away. Then they focused on the pirate. She heard his voice, saw him extend a hand. Then she heard the crack, saw the smoke from the pistol's end.

Before William slid to the floor, his eyes met hers.

She put her hand to her mouth to stop a scream, but she had lost her voice. The pirate kicked the body of her husband so that he turned over, empty face to the heavens. Then he stepped over it and called to his men to haul down the ship's colours.

Mary tried to control her shaking. Her teeth were so tightly pressed together it was as though somebody had run a knife into the back of her skull. It was as a ghost of herself that she stepped out openly across the wooden boards of the deck, with the knives of many men drawn around her, and found herself at the side of the man whom William had known, who she now herself recognized, the pirate named Captain John Fullarton.

'I know who you are,' she said.

As Fullarton turned his head a smile began on his face, a gentle, half-forgetful smile, a smile of recognition. Then the smile froze as he became aware of the touch of lead and silver at his brow. He opened his mouth to speak.

'No,' she heard him say. 'You can't, I—'

Mary pulled the trigger. She watched him as he fell on to the planks of the deck and died before her.

36

The moment Fullarton fell the crew of the pirate ship surrendered. The *Isabella*'s crew worked around her, clearing up the last remaining skirmishes, tying up the prisoners. Mary kneeled down over the bodies of the two men. She examined their wounds, took their pulses. She did not yet believe they were dead. She ripped clothes from their bodies and used them to bind the wounds. She did Fullarton's last, wrapping the cloth gently around his skull. Her hands were warm and wet with seeping blood and fluid, but still she felt sure that he had the pulse of life within him.

But the bos'n came, and without examining the body, told her she was wrong. She watched as he and another of the crew lifted the pirate and dropped him over the side of the ship. The *Isabella* headed for Leith with her broken mast, while Captain Jones was carried down into his cabin and laid on his own bed. Mary sat with the body as they made their way down the Forth towards the port of Leith.

She had waited for this moment, sailing into her home port to meet her family and her mother, complete with all the treasure of her voyage, her fine clothes, her jewellery, her chests full of presents and trinkets to decorate the home she would live in with Lucy.

She looked at the shape on the bed. She put a ha
it. How quickly it had cooled. She could not bring he
to pray over her husband's body.

~

It seemed like hours later when the *Isabella* finally sailed
into the port of Leith. When it did Mary didn't want to
leave the ship. She sat in the room, as still as stone, looking
at the cold, covered body, until there was a knock at the
door, and she opened it to the cook.

'It's time to go home, lass,' he said.

Mary nodded, and draped a black shawl over her face,
not so much to display her mourning as to hide her shame.

She turned to the cook. 'Did they pay you,' she said,
'to keep quiet about Alice?'

He looked surprised, and almost angry, so that she felt
sorry she'd said anything.

'I've never been one to talk about other people's business,'
he said.

Then Mary picked up Lucy, who hardly seemed to
breathe, and the cook took her arm to help her on to the
deck.

Word of the events in the firth had got around quickly,
and a small crowd had already gathered to see the strange
sight, the large merchant vessel still flying the half-raised
flag, with the pirate vessel in tow. Mary stayed on deck
while they brought a makeshift coffin to take out William's
body. They draped a cloth over it and she walked out behind,
cradling Lucy. There was an awed silence, followed by a
murmur that stirred throughout the crowds assembled
on the quay.

'Who is it?' she heard one ask.

'It's Mary Jones,' said another, 'the pirate slayer.'

'Three cheers for the pirate slayer.'

The crowd cheered around her. But Mary felt only the shortness, the cheapness, and, as the tiny child moved in her arms, the merciless persistence of life.

The body was washed up a week later. Mary and her mother heard about it and rushed down to the shore. The assembled crowd recognized her and parted to let her walk through. She saw the man without emotion, and confirmed that it was him. A gold pocket watch hung out of his waistcoat, and she wondered that nobody had yet taken it. She looked briefly at the face, now bloated and made green by the sea water that had pumped through it, and she turned away. She wondered why she had come.

Now Lucy grew restless in her arms and began to cry, and Mary walked away to find a place to feed her, leaving her mother standing beside the body.

She had just sat down when she heard it, and leapt to her feet. The baby's hungry cries almost drowned out the screams of Margaret, who had fallen to her knees in the sand before the body of Mary's dead father, the pirate John Fullarton.

The streets were eerily quiet compared with the throngs of the previous day. The little girl had watched the people from her window, returning from the execution, on their way back to the city. She had wanted to go too, but her grandmother had refused. She didn't argue. She had known from a young age the story of her great-grandfather's death, and that her grandmother was known as the pirate slayer. It was for that reason that she had been desperate to go, to see how a pirate looked in the flesh.

The following day she had asked to go down to the sands, but in truth she only wanted to see the bodies, hanging at the high tide mark.

'It's too cold for walking out today,' her mother had said, and her grandmother's head had turned sharply.

'Nonsense,' she had said. 'You have the lass wrapped up like a doll. Look at her, she's pale as china.'

So they all went, and it was cold. But they walked quickly, and generated their own heat. The girl held on tightly with one hand to that of her mother's. With the other hand she held her grandmother's long bony fingers. The girl loved her grandmother and her mother. She depended on them and they on her.

The little girl noticed a piece of paper, abandoned,

skitting across the frozen ground. Her mother bent down and picked it up.

She read out loud: 'A full, authentic, and particular account of the execution of Peter Haeman and Francois Gautiez, who were hanged on Wednesday the 9th January, 1822, for the piratical seizure of the schooner *Jane of Gibraltar* . . . and for the barbarous murder of Thomas Johnson, master, and James Paterson, seaman.'

'In my day,' said the grandmother, 'you didn't need an account, you just went and watched it.' She drew in her lips and stuck out her chin, which had become more pronounced with the loss of her teeth.

'Yes, Granny,' said the girl, both patiently and politely. She knew that her grandmother was sometimes irritable. Her mother had told her it was because of the pain. The girl understood this. She had once fallen and grazed her knee very badly, and had not been able to speak for some time afterwards.

The girl's mother agreed. 'It's good for her,' she said, 'to see what happens to criminals.'

'Like in this book,' said the little girl excitedly, pulling a bundle from her school satchel, which she had insisted on bringing. Her grandmother picked up the book.

'What rubbish are they giving you now?' she said. *The Newgate Calendar*, the title read. She opened the book and spotted a name that seemed familiar.

'Norman Ross,' she said. 'I was at that execution. When was that, now?' Seventeen fifty-one, said the book. In 1751 she would have been seven. And then the memory became clear. She could almost smell it, the rough frost of the January air as she walked down the old Leith road with her mother. She had held her mother's hand, and she had looked into the eyes of her father, staring at her from a coach.

'I remember it now,' she said. 'My mother took me. She had a notion it would help me grow.'

'You see,' said her daughter. 'It worked for you. You became a heroine.'

'I'm not sure that that means it worked,' said the grandmother. She was silent for a moment. 'My mother said I asked too many questions.'

'You don't need to ask questions, Granny,' said the granddaughter, squeezing the old woman's hand. 'You know everything already.'

The grandmother broke into one of her rare smiles. 'Well, that's not true. The older you get,' she said, 'the less you know.'

'They say that's the surest sign of wisdom,' said the mother.

'No,' said the ageing lady sardonically, 'it's the surest sign of senility.'

They had reached the shore now, and the little girl looked to see the bodies hanging at the flood mark, but the glasshouses hid them from view, and now they were walking in the opposite direction.

When they were upon the sand the girl dropped to her knees, despite the cold, and began to mould it into little shapes. Her grandmother unfolded a little wooden stool that her mother had carried there, and sat down on it. She took out her knitting, and concentrated on the click of the needles.

Suddenly the little girl began to shout in excitement. 'Look, there they are! Look Granny, there they are!'

Her mother hushed her, but in the distance they could see the black figures, the bodies of the dead pirates, emerging from the water as the tide retreated. And then, for the first time in years, Mary remembered the letter she had received from Robert, a decade after William's death. It said that he had gone home, and got married to a lady of his father's suggestion. But that she had died in childbirth, along with his child. It had set him thinking about the other child that he had, and the only woman he said he had ever loved, Mary. He said that he was older now, and wiser, and would not make the same mistakes again, if only she would have faith.

Mary put down her needles, and reached for the hip flask of brandy that she kept perpetually by her side, to numb the pain of the chronic arthritis that had overtaken her at the age of forty. At first she had resisted its use. She had no desire to follow poor William's example; but now she was an old woman, one of the oldest she knew. She was on borrowed time, and though she would not tell her granddaughter, she had no faith. She knew that when the end came there would be nobody to answer to.

She had never replied to Robert's letter. He had never written again, and his memory had been misplaced, somewhere in the muddle of day-to-day life, of shopping lists, piles of mending, pensions to be drawn, accounts to be settled. But for a second, when her granddaughter had spoken, she had felt as though a pin had pricked somewhere into her skin, awakening a pain that she had forgotten. A part of her wanted to find the pin, to prick other parts of herself, until her whole body felt alive with the intensity of it, the pure and youthful knowledge of pain and pleasure.

She took out the gold pocket watch that her mother had given her, the one that had been her father's. For a moment, she almost hoped it would be broken. It was too big, and for some time she had wanted a new one, but she refused to replace anything that was still working. She shook it a little. The hand moved.

Then suddenly she threw down her hip flask and needles, and grabbed her granddaughter's hand.

'What are you doing, Granny?' the little girl gasped.

'Come on,' cried Mary. 'Take off your shoes.'

'Why?'

'We're going for a paddle.'

The girl squealed with delight, ignoring the protests of her mother. Mary kicked off her shoes, and together they ran into the waves. The water was cold, and the shells were sharp. She felt the little rivulets of pain travelling up through her body, until her teeth were chattering together uncontrollably.

'Granny,' said the girl. 'You're freezing, I think we should get out.'

'I'm fine.' Mary almost snapped, but then she looked down at the girl's worried face, and squeezed her hand.

'Come on then,' she said.

'Mother, you'll have caught your death,' said her daughter, when they reached her again.

Mary glanced at her gold watch. It still kept time. She sat down, leaving her shoes off, and dug her toes into the sand. Then she raised her flask, swallowed deeply and watched the movement of her fingers at her knitting, as if they were detached from her body. In this way she ignored the cold, the aching of her feet, the way she ignored the painful swelling of her joints. She knew that the body could be made to believe whatever the mind wanted it to, and soon enough her body felt numb again and the pain washed away.

Acknowledgements

With thanks to Hi Arts for commenting on early drafts of this book through their Works in Progress scheme.

Read more . . .

Kirsten McKenzie

THE CHAPEL AT THE EDGE OF THE WORLD

A wartime love story richly told

There is a chapel built by Italian prisoners of war on a barren Orkney island. There is a hilltop village in Northern Italy swept by war. There is a couple in love.

The story of the chapel at the edge of the world is enthralling, moving and extraordinary.

'A fine debut inspired by a wartime act of optimism . . . I can't imagine a finer tribute than this lovely book' *Independent on Sunday*

'Unusual, fluently written . . . [an] unshowy, absorbing read' *Guardian*

Order your copy now by calling Bookpoint on 01235 827716 or visit your local bookshop quoting ISBN 978-1-84854-150-4
www.johnmurray.co.uk

Read more . . .

Amitav Ghosh

SEA OF POPPIES

An epic seafaring adventure set against the backdrop of the Opium Wars

Deeti is a widow to opium, saved from her husband's funeral pyre by the low-caste Kalua, who has been waiting for her. Paulette is the orphaned daughter of a French botanist and Jodu, the son of her wet nurse, is the only link to her past. A bankrupt raja is chased from his estates which fall into the hands of an avaricious opium dealer. Fate throws these characters, and a host of others, together as a motley crew on an old slaving ship, the *Ibis*.

Set against the backdrop of the Opium Wars, this unlikely dynasty is what makes *Sea of Poppies* so breathtakingly alive — an absorbing masterpiece from one of the world's finest storytellers.

'Profoundly moving' *The Times*

'A remarkably rich saga' *Guardian*

'It is the sheer energy and verve of Amitav Ghosh's storytelling that binds this ambitious medley' *Daily Mail*

Order your copy now by calling Bookpoint on 01235 827716 or visit your local bookshop quoting ISBN 978-0-7195-6897-8 www.johnmurray.co.uk